# We Owr

## By

## Ian Fiddes

To Dorothy e David
Hope you enjoy the book.
Best wishes
Ian Fiddes
Sept 2018

Dedicated to all those who protect, support and care for those subjected to sexual exploitation.

I am especially grateful to the following for their advice and encouragement; Tracy, Stuart, Vicky, Roz, Mick, Tom, Laura and Richard.

Special mention to the Staff of Women's Services, Changing Lives (changing-lives.org.uk). They give people the strength and belief to belong to themselves.

www.ianfiddes.com

# Chapter One

# Success, then Austerity

It can take months to put a good enquiry together, but the few moments before a strike team moves in are perhaps the most important.

The prospects of success or failure are so close together the suspense can be unbearable. Will there be a recovery of drugs or stolen property? Will the main offenders get caught, hopefully red-handed? Will the investment in time, resources and technology finally come together? Has someone or something given the game away at the last minute?

In truth no one really knows until they hear those key words 'Strike-Strike-Strike' over the radio and the doors go crashing in.

The fifteen strong group of Detectives who made up the North Eastern Constabulary Crime Team was having a good time of it, even by its standards. Two successful drugs raids inside two weeks had grabbed the headlines and had made the Chief Constable happy. The month of July had been busy and successful for the Force Crime Team, or FCT as they were known.

They say you make your own good luck, so when an unexpected tip-off from a tried and tested source set the wheels in motion for a hat-trick of successful raids. The expectation of another large recovery was tempered only by the lack of background information on the address upon which they were about to converge. There was no intelligence or associated 'bad lads' tied to the house. It was not in the worst of areas and the current occupant was not really known - he had one minor conviction and he had long since succumbed to a life dominated by alcohol.

Two members of the FCT, Detective Sergeant Albert Bennison and Detective Constable Derek Baty, had rushed to Newcastle Magistrates before the afternoon session of Thursday 26th July was over, to apply for a warrant to enter and search the house at 2 Holly Gardens in the West End of the city. They had struggled to fill in enough detail on the paperwork, but their persuasive skills had convinced the Magistrates to grant the all-important document. The house was believed to be a temporary storage place for a large importation of class 'A' drugs, most likely heroin or cocaine. The informant was confident the drugs would be there by early afternoon, but would only be there for no longer than a day, at the most. The information had arrived too late to cover the delivery to the house.

Once the court hurdle was over, it was just a case of mustering enough staff to do the job. Of the fifteen DCs on the FCT, three were on annual leave. Twelve DCs and a DS were enough, so the team assembled for a quick briefing at the office.

Albert Bennison took centre stage; "Okay, we are off to 2 Holly Gardens. We expect one occupant who will most likely be a bit merry. It is little more than a two-up two-down terrace and thankfully no dogs or guns. Derek and Jimmy - you are on the ram - please try the door first though, remember Wallsend?"

He was referring to a similar job a few months earlier when Derek and Jimmy demolished an entire door and the frame, only to find that it had been unlocked. The occupant later complained and was compensated when the warrant was negative - nothing had been found on that occasion.

"That was a one off Albert. Anyway it was one of those flimsy plastic doors, we'll be gentle this time". DC Jimmy Richards tried his best at defending his enthusiastic entry skills.

Albert continued "No messing on this one, we have no idea where the drugs are stored. The snout says there are multi-kilos and this is just a staging post. So get in your cars, make sure we have all the paperwork and a search kit. We will leave in five minutes."

Albert had been on the Crime Team for five years. He had been a detective for most of his career and he was known to be a good operator, but not a good diplomat. Senior Officers, colleagues, witnesses and those in the legal profession had all been subject to his forthright views. Albert did not always have an effective filter mechanism between his thoughts and his mouth.

DC Hugh Murray, another experienced detective, was in need of more information "Albert, do we know about the neighbours, the address history and the layout of the house?"

"No" said Albert. He was used to Hughie's methodical and careful approach to every job.

"Hughie, this is one of those times when your arse will have to move faster than your brain. We just need to get there quickly and secure the house. Got it?"

A nod from Hughie indicated an acceptance that on this occasion his love of detail was not going to be fulfilled. He knew Albert was on a mission.

A few moments later the team assembled in the car park, ready to move in their unmarked vehicles. Albert and Hughie took the lead, followed by Derek and Jimmy. The other members of the team crammed in to the two remaining cars. DCs Craig, Couley, Tempest, and McGuinness were followed by DCs McAllister, Morton, Noone and Gallagher.

The route to the house was a direct one. For once, the convoy stayed together and reached the junction of Holly Gardens in very little time. The area was quiet; the street had just a few cars parked on the road. Perhaps the occupants were busy preparing the evening meal or not in from work. Whatever the circumstances, it was not a bad time to go unnoticed. Albert tried his best to look down the street for number two, without making it obvious. They had to be quick as four cars full of strangers would soon stand out after a while.

"It will be the first house on the right, the evens always start there" crackled Hughie over the radio in his best informative tone for the benefit of all. "I don't know what I would do without you" said Albert "When you retire you can be a walking, talking encyclopaedia".

Albert took charge of the radio. "Confirmed. It is the blue door, first house on the right. Strike-Strike-Strike."

Derek and Jimmy were first to the door and with no hesitation took it off its hinges. So much for trying the door first.

Through the hole where the door had been went DC Dave McGuinness, a young officer who was always keen to be involved. He wasted no time in grabbing the poor occupant.

"Police" said Dave McGuinness, "We have a warrant to search the premises for drugs".

The occupant, a man in his 60s, struggled to speak. He was rooted to his armchair due to a mixture of alcohol and shock. He continued to watch as the rest of the team entered the house.

Albert surveyed the scene "I take it the door was no problem?"

"Not likely" said Jimmy, "one hit and it was away."

"That's because it was open and one of the hinges was broken" said the dazed occupant, who had composed himself enough to utter a few words.

Albert shook his head and had visions of more paperwork and compensation. "We had better start searching for evidence then - that would be a good idea Jimmy, would it not?"

Jimmy nodded and thought better of trying to make a wise crack.

With the house secured, there was no need for every officer to be in the house. Two search teams would suffice, with Albert supervising and Hughie completing the relevant documents.

Jimmy and Derek were assigned upstairs. Dave and his partner, DC Alison Morton, started with the living room.

The house was in a state; plastic cider bottles, newspapers and magazines littered the floor and the sofa. One lamp lit the far corner of the room, the main ceiling light was missing its bulb. The walls and woodwork had not seen a paintbrush in years and the light from the windows could hardly filter through the saggy net curtains. On top of the TV was an old framed photograph of a young couple on their wedding day. The TV was a large bulky set, not a modern flat screen. There were no obvious signs of the wealth that drug dealing brings to those who trade in large quantities. The house was neglected, tired and had probably been that way for a decade or more.

Albert introduced himself and asked the occupant for his name.

"Frank Drysdale, 21st December 1949" came the reply. He was obviously getting over his immediate panic and pulling himself together.

Albert did not see an experienced criminal sitting in front of him. Frank Drysdale looked drawn and unhealthy, the empty cider bottles clear evidence of his struggle with alcohol. His clothes hung off him, like hand-me-downs.

There was no need to give Frank a hard time; if he was providing a safe house he was probably being paid a pittance. He had clearly hit hard times and became a target for criminal gangs who saw a weakness in him and exploited it.

"Frank, we need to search the house. Is there anything in here that there should not be"

Albert waited for a reply from Frank, who leant forward in his chair and stared at the floor. He then looked up at Albert, as if he wanted to speak, but hesitated at the last moment. He looked around, assessing who was in earshot. He glanced across towards the doorway where the other members of the team had been before Albert sent them back to their cars. It was obvious he was under pressure and Albert tried to put him at ease.

"Listen Frank, we can see you are not the main man, far from it. If there is anything in this house we will find it and you will get every opportunity to explain your side of things. I take it you live alone?"

Frank nodded. "I've lived in this house all my life. My parents got it just after the war when it was built and I took it on when they moved out in 1972. Me and the wife lived here from then on."

DC Alison Morton was still behind Frank looking through a pile of letters on the sideboard, but listening to the conversation. She glanced at Albert and then Frank, pausing the search as she did so. She had an instinct for those who were genuine and Albert recognised her reaction towards Frank. Albert asked him again if there was anything in the house.

Frank lifted his hand and began pointing upwards, just as Jimmy shouted down the stairs for a search lamp.

"There is your answer" said Frank. "I've touched nowt, they just come and go and I get a few quid for drink. Do what you need to do, I've got nothing else to say". Frank looked like a man admitting defeat, long before the final whistle had been blown.

Jimmy shone the search lamp into the loft to reveal a number of large plastic bags, cocooned in brown tape. Twelve in total, sitting on makeshift boards across the top of the insulation. The bags were not hidden and this indicated that they were not going to be there long.

Should they have sat and waited for the real criminals? Albert was already fielding the questions he fully expected from the HQ experts and their hindsight.

"This is another big recovery. Looks like they have been chucked up there in a hurry." Jimmy left the bags alone until they could be assessed.

The bags were photographed by Hughie and a small incision was made in two random packages for a field test. They both indicated cocaine. The best estimate was 45 kilos in total. Not bad for a last minute tip-off, so the informant was in for a big pay day.

The Scenes of Crime Officer arrived and examined the loft area for prints. As usual it would be difficult; "It is too dusty up there, but I will try my best." "What a martyr" thought Albert, hoping that one day they would turn up and declare the conditions perfect and there was a guaranteed chance of success. And cows might fly.

Jimmy had found the drugs and Albert congratulated him on avoiding another 'door report'.

Frank was arrested and taken to the Area Command police station, where he would stay until he could be interviewed. As the search was almost done, Albert took another look at the photo on the TV and realised it was Frank and his wife on their wedding day. Dressed in their 1970s suits, Frank and his Best Man looked happy and relaxed. His wife smiled for the camera, linking arms with Frank and holding on to her veil with the other. Albert could not help but wonder why Frank had ended up the way he had.

As the team packed up the evidence and left the house, one of the neighbours asked about Frank. "He is okay" Dave informed the lady from next door.

"Mary will be spinning in her grave, the state of the house and the way Frank has got it. She would be disgusted." The neighbour seemed to have no sympathy for Frank.

Dave told the neighbour that the door was about to be boarded and if there was a problem overnight, she could ring the police straightaway to let them know and someone would respond.

She said she would and she then seemed to soften her attitude to Frank "He used to work hard you know, doing plumbing and a bit of building. Mary and him had the house lovely and the garden was always full of flowers in the Summer. Frank liked a drink and when Mary died about 12 years ago he just went downhill. He hardly goes out now and they had no family, so Frank just has a brother who he sees at Christmas. Who are you lot anyway? You are not the usual police we see around here."

Dave left some details and the neighbour began to take things in. She told Dave that she had lived in the street for 25 years and had been a school dinner lady until she was made redundant and now she had a pension. She did the odd cleaning job when she could but nothing regular. Her name was Mrs Baker and she knew everyone in the street. Dave asked her about the area and about Frank.

"This is a quiet street and when you lot broke the door down I got a fright. Nothing much happens here, the last bit of excitement was when the brothel across the road was closed down. Must have been about April. The two lasses in there were no bother and I thought they were students because they were always having a bit of a party or lots of visitors. Frank sometimes spoke to them and he fixed a leaking tap. He could still do a job but all he wanted to do was sit and drink. Then again, he is not the only one who does that around here."

Dave was beginning to realise that Mrs Baker could have talked all night, so he thanked her and made good his retreat.

Frank had only been known to the team for about an hour, but it was becoming clear he had been targeted by the main drug traffickers as a lonely alcoholic who they could easily manipulate. At least he had some sympathy from the police, if not from his closest neighbour.

Back at the office, the members of the team who had not taken part in the search were allowed home. The rest updated the records and prepared their statements. The search took a while, but the paperwork takes forever.

Albert found a quiet side office and phoned Detective Inspector Bill Reynolds to update him as he had overall responsibility for the FCT. They had worked together many years before and Albert had been pleased to see Bill when he arrived on promotion four years earlier. He apologised for ringing so late (it was just after 10pm) but Bill had been waiting for the call, grateful for the brief outline Albert gave him. The pair of them were on the same wavelength when it came to practical police work and long conversations were not necessary.

Bill asked Albert to congratulate the team for another good job and told Albert not to worry about any criticism regarding the warrant being executed too early.

"What would the experts have done Albert? Called out another load of officers and sat on the house for a day or two? No chance, money is too tight. The budget is all over the place. The Superintendent is in a state of frenzy trying to make savings."

Albert sensed a level of despondency in Bill's voice. "What's up Bill, is there something the matter, surely Sunderland can't be relegated already; the season is just about to start." Football had always been a source of humour and rivalry between the two.

"Very funny, it will not be long before the black and white shite are singing to sack the board" said Bill.

He then paused and his voice slowed; he was emphasising something to Albert without actually saying it. "Listen Albert, I need to see you first thing tomorrow. Keep it quiet, but I have to make a decision pretty soon about how things can keep going. I need to run it past you. I will let you know everything I can, but don't worry you are safe."

"Safe from what Bill? Are we that skint? Look at the success we have had recently, surely that counts for something?"

"In days gone by it would have. But the financial pressures are too much now. I will see you tomorrow, well done on tonight. Cheers." Bill rang off as he obviously did not want to say anything more.

Albert returned to the main office. The drugs had been locked away in a disused cell downstairs. The Police Station from where the FCT worked had not been operational for three years, so there was plenty of space. The uniform staff had been sent to one large station closer to the city centre, all in the name of efficiency. Every team member had a desk to themselves, a filing cabinet, a locker and a

8

choice of chairs. The building that was once a hive of activity was now occupied by a team of specialists who operated out of sight.

Albert passed on the message of thanks from DI Reynolds. "The Boss was impressed, as usual. He will be in tomorrow for a full update, so let's get away home if all the paperwork is done and we will sort an interview team first thing. I take it Frank is getting his head down for the night?"

Alison Morton nodded. "He is out for the count according to the Custody Officer. Perhaps this is a weight off his mind. Can I interview him with Dave?" Alison was a good interviewer and Albert had noticed that she wanted to give Frank a chance.

"Sure, I think you might get on better with him than the pair who demolished his door."

Albert smiled and looked at his watch, "That's a shame, it is too late for the pub and I was just thinking I would buy everyone a pint. Time for home unfortunately."

"Well at least you were *thinking* about buying a round, which is a step in the right direction" replied Hughie, in one of his rare attempts at humour.

The next morning the team were in at 8am. The officers who were not involved to any real extent the previous evening, resumed another job which involved static observations. Boring they could be, but always useful in the end.

Albert caught up with Alison and Dave and went through their interview plan. It was relatively straightforward; Frank was the occupant and he needed to account for 45 kilos of cocaine in his loft. His nominated Solicitor was Mr Daniel Brannigan whom Albert had encountered many times before.

"He is no problem as long as he has full disclosure. If he thinks there is something being held back he will instruct his client to 'no reply' throughout. Give him everything about the warrant and the drugs then see how the first interview goes. Watch him though; if you ask a difficult question he taps his client on the foot under the table."

"We will sit them as far apart as possible then" laughed Alison "I think we can get started soon, so we will let you know how we get on".

Bill Reynolds walked in just as the discussion was ending. He again thanked everyone for their efforts and told them he would be preparing a press release for the Superintendent to use. Unless there were any developments, the papers and the local TV would have the details by around midday.

Bill and Albert then went to one of the many sparse offices attached to the main floor as they both knew there was a conversation to be finished from the night before. Bill Reynolds wasted no time with what he had to say.

"Well Albert, my time is up. I have 32 years in the job and the Chief wants rid of everyone who is over their service length and can retire. It is cheaper to employ a brand new snotty than someone like me. They will probably be able to afford two probationers on basic pay when I go. I had hoped to stay on for a couple of years to see the kids through university, but it is not going to happen."

Albert was not entirely surprised as it was common knowledge that the budget was under pressure from all sides. "Can they make you go? What does the Federation say about this? Can they make some noises in the right places?"

"I could try to stay and we both know what would happen. I would find myself back in uniform, on shifts, dealing with things we both left behind years ago. They would set out to make things as uncomfortable as possible. I am 55 and the thought of rolling around the floor with drunks on a Friday night is not a good one. You have a couple of years to go and I am sure the FCT will see you out. That is what I really need to talk about."

Albert sensed a degree of concern. Bill continued.

"We lost five officers to the cuts a few of months ago, which was not brilliant but at least we got rid of some dead wood."

Albert agreed "Dead wood? That is an understatement; there were the two happy shoppers and the other three would not sleep in the same room as a pair of work boots. We have not missed them!"

"I thought you would say something like that, but this time you are going to lose another five DCs. The Superintendent has not made the case for any more. The team will be down to ten and you. I'm not sure I will be replaced, so you will only have the duty Inspector to refer to."

10

"So that could be someone who has never set foot in the CID?" asked Albert.

"Could well be. Of course you will have the hierarchy at HQ to fall back on . . . . but some of them are not exactly experienced detectives. It is just the way it is Albert; you are going to have to bite your tongue. The Super is on his way over so not a word unless he tells you and then look surprised. He wants his photo taken next to the drugs you recovered last night for the press release. The press should not be long behind, but they don't know why they are coming just yet. Someone from the Press Office will be babysitting them all."

Albert was disappointed but knew that Bill had thought things through and had there been an alternative, he would have tried it.

"Are you going to let the team know soon, about your retirement?"

"Yes, today or Monday. The form has already gone in to HR and my last day is next Friday given all of the annual leave I have left. Perhaps it is better that way, I don't want to hang around now that the decision has been made".

Albert understood entirely. He was about to reflect on some good memories to try to lift the mood, when Superintendent Miles Ashley walked in.

"Morning Sir, the press are gathering as we speak. I've told them to get your best side on the photos".

"Thank you Albert. I am always extremely grateful for your suggestions. Others probably would not be. Plus the fact you have just made that up."

Miles Ashley was not from the same school of policing as Bill and Albert. They shared a commitment to do the right thing, but their methods were poles apart. While Albert acted on his instinct and experience, Miles preferred procedure and a careful, less eventful approach. He still had a long career ahead of him and he wanted to climb the promotion ladder as far as he could. Bill was more thoughtful than Albert, but he struggled being a buffer between the practical demands of officers on the ground and the strategic demands of those who had ditched their biros in favour of writing with fountain pens.

Miles was officially a CID resource, but he had to wear a uniform. He had confided in Bill that this was not his choice and he would prefer to wear a suit as Bill did. Albert was a traditionalist; he also wore a suit, unless there was a search warrant to do and he would 'dress down' to a pair of chinos and a polo shirt. Alison often threatened to buy Albert a pair of jeans, despite his opinion that blokes in their 50s should dress 'properly'.

Miles Ashley supervised both Bill and Albert, but he knew from his first day with the FCT that their experience and knowledge far surpassed his. He also realised that his predecessor had found themselves in the same position. Miles knew he had to work with the pair of them no matter what; he tolerated their gentle mickey-taking about the days when police officers 'had to be tall to join'. Miles was only 5'7" so both Bill and Albert towered over him.

It was expected that as soon as a new boss arrived, he or she would immediately re-arrange their office by moving the desk and the cabinets to distinguish themselves from the previous occupant. Because of the way HQ ran the upper ranks, a boss might last 18 months or so before the next position in their career development cropped up.

Miles Ashley had been involved with the FCT for just over a year, so he was unlikely to be there much longer. He had also re-arranged his office within a week of arriving. After three months it was back to the way it was when he moved in, as he realised he could not see his computer when the sun shone through from the corridor. Neither could he have more than four people in at one time as he had placed the spare table up against the window wall. Bill, Albert and the team had all enjoyed the running joke, taking it in turns to predict the day the furniture would be moved back to the original layout simply because that was the way it worked.

Miles turned the conversation to the warrant at Frank's house. "That was a good recovery of drugs last night. The Chief passes on her thanks. She would like to hear about the main culprits once they are brought in. I'm sure Albert has considered the next move. We can cover all of that later, but I need to talk about the future of the FCT and staffing. I take it DI Reynolds has given you an update on the budget?"

12

Miles Ashley knew fine well that the two old mates would have spoken about the matters in hand and he also knew they would not admit it.

"No, not yet Sir" replied Albert, enjoying the pretence. "Not a word."

"Really? Well in that case, the news is not too good. We need to lose another five DCs; I would prefer volunteers but if they are not forthcoming I want names out of a hat."

"Is that fair, names out of a hat?" enquired Albert.

"Well, it is less problematic than the five who went last year. I spent two months batting off grievances from the officers you decided had to go. They had the Federation backing them and it was only when they got the jobs they wanted, that things settled down." Miles appeared slightly agitated at the prospect of further HR problems.

"Can we just keep it simple and let the team know that anyone who volunteers to go will get a job within the CID, unless they want a complete change. There are enough vacancies due to retirements. That should help and I need the names before Bill rides off into the sunset. I'm sure that has been discussed between the pair of you."

Albert and Bill conceded it had and were still taking in the news.

With little else to say and a reluctance to engage in small talk with Miles, Bill and Albert pointed him in the direction to where the drugs were stored and left him to the press.

By 11am Alison and Dave had spoken to Frank. He had admitted allowing a number of men to use his house for unknown 'storage' activities and had produced a prepared statement during the taped interview. Mr Brannigan made representations to the Custody Officer that unless the drugs could be linked to his client, then he should be released or bailed. Mr Brannigan knew that it would take time to examine all the packaging for fingerprints and DNA.

Albert wanted to know how Frank was reacting to Alison and Dave and it appeared that he was cooperative, to an extent. Mr Brannigan was unusually keen to have long consultations with Frank and he accompanied him to and from his cell.

Albert and the interview team came to the conclusion that it was of no benefit to interview Frank for a second time until all the

13

scientific evidence was available, so a long bail date was set for him to return. The press could have the story, so Albert sent a text to Bill and Miles Ashley to let them know.

"Make sure you take him home and leave him with contact details" asked Albert when he phoned Alison.

"We will. I have a feeling he will come around eventually. I just hope he does not get blamed for the job, the informant must be very close to dealers."

Albert had no time for informants, who were just a necessary evil in his eyes. Once in a while a good one would surface, but the average 'snout' could not be trusted. They were either after information for themselves or just wanted to dispose of the competition by using the police to do it for them.

"We'll leave the informant to his HQ handler. The last thing we want to do is get involved and we will only act on anything which is given to us in writing. Make sure Frank knows who his real friends are."

"No problem" replied Alison. "Dave spoke to Brannigan just before he left and he has arranged to see Frank in a couple of days. He seemed very keen to help him; I thought he went a bit over the top to be honest. It was a big recovery but Frank is just a small cog in the wheel".

"Female intuition clicking in Alison?" Albert was hopeful.

"Maybes, maybes. Frank knows who the real players are, but he would be in big trouble if he said anything. Is Brannigan above board?"

"As far as in know he is, yes. He has defended some high profile gangster types in the past, but so have a lot of others. He is a man of habit and he does not seem to have much to do with his colleagues. Junior Solicitors dismiss him as old fashioned and a bit of a creep. I'm not so sure, he just keeps himself to himself. There was another Solicitor at his practice who used to take notes from one co-accused to another, but the CPS decided there was insufficient evidence to proceed against him. He has gone off on his own now, doing house conveyancing, so he is probably making more money than Brannigan."

Albert knew the value of a professional relationship with a defendant's solicitor. They were not the enemy and they were just doing a job, so it was not in anyone's interest to cause unnecessary friction. Just like police officers, there were good ones, bad ones and a whole lot in between. Brannigan had been around for about 25 years and made a good living until the legal aid fees were reduced. He was always friendly, almost to the point of being patronising at times, something which got under the skin of many. Perhaps Brannigan saw Frank as a bit of an 'earner', so he wanted to keep him happy.

Albert found a quiet corner in the office and updated his notes for the Holly Gardens warrant. Paperwork took up about three quarters of his time and the latest news about the budget meant a whole host of HR forms to fill in for those who would have to leave. Albert was far more at home barking out his orders or opinions than being stuck with paperwork. At least there would be a bit of a party before they left. Bill's retirement function would also be a decent night; he deserved a good send off after all the work he had got through over the years.

By 3pm all the team had returned to the office. The weekend would begin at 4pm, so Albert decided against telling everyone about the staff cuts and Bill was not around to tell them about his retirement. There were three others on annual leave so he reasoned it was not fair on them to be kept in the dark. Monday was the best day to catch everyone, go through the options and set a 48 hour deadline for volunteers. He told everyone to get a flyer and enjoy their time off. He did not have to say it twice and soon the office was deserted. Albert could often be abrupt, sometimes downright rude, but he still wanted the best for his team. If they worked hard he would make sure they got a little bit in return.

Albert began to think about his own retirement. He quickly calculated that he had two years and four months to go. He had not given it much thought up until that moment; the catalyst was probably Bill's announcement earlier in the day. The police force he joined was completely different from the way things were being done in the present day. Had it not been for the introduction of personal radios and the panda system, nothing much had changed from the

1950s to when he first put on his uniform and set about making the world a better place. The huge advances in technology since Albert and Bill joined had changed the way criminals worked and the way the police tried to catch them.

Albert went around the office, closing down any live computers and generally surveying the scene. Hughie's desk was so neat and tidy anyone would have thought it was vacant, or spare. In contrast, Jimmy and Derek's adjoining desks looked like the council tip, with tea cups containing what looked like a mini mushroom farm at the bottom. The rest of the desks had box files, half written statements and lunch boxes piled high. Albert promised himself that a tidy office was needed and he would mention it to the team. He switched off the lights and set the alarm. The following week was going to be tricky, so the weekend had to be enjoyed.

Bill Reynolds had also decided to call it a day after a meeting at HQ about the budget and rang home to tell his wife he was on his way. She was well aware of his impending retirement and the thought of having him around the house had caused a strange feeling. She had often said he was married to his job and not her.

"Should we go out for something to eat, I won't be long" Bill asked Audrey.

"Well, will you actually turn up? I have heard that a hundred times before. If you do manage to make it home and not get way-laid by your job or the pub, I would love to go out." Audrey, along with many other police spouses, enjoyed a bit of pay-back every now and again. Bill accepted the gentle teasing, as it had often ended up a lot more strained in the past.

"Yes, yes, I will be home in half an hour. Can you start getting ready now so I am not sitting waiting in the car for ages?"

"Careful Bill, I can always add more to the list of jobs I want you to do when you retire". Audrey reminded Bill who was in charge, now that he was about to become a pensioner.

Bill drove a short distance and noticed he needed some petrol, so he decided to get it on the way home, rather than later. He called at the supermarket about half way, filled up and at the cash desk he noticed the afternoon edition of the Tyne & Wear Gazette. On the front page was a photograph of Miles Ashley, surrounded by the

16

Holly Gardens drugs haul. He had his 'efficient yet satisfied' look on his face. Bill read the headline "Drugs Cartel Smashed."

Drugs cartel? Where did that come from? There was only one arrest and he was not even sober. The article went on to detail the street value and how the police had acted quickly following an intelligence-led investigation.

Bill stood in the petrol station engrossed in the paper, muttering under his breath about Albert's reaction to the article. He looked up and saw the cashier looking at him.

"I'm pleased it is Friday" he said to her.

"That's £25 please. Want your points?" Bill handed over his card and the money.

"Do you want that paper? We are not running a library you know." Bill snapped out of his far away thoughts and bought the paper as the cashier had suggested in her own unique way.

Bill half expected a phone call from Albert and as he arrived home. He remained pre-occupied with his friend's potential reaction to the headlines.

Audrey was ready and waiting. Bill gave her the paper as he walked in and indicated that there would be an explosion a few miles north of their house if Albert caught sight of it.

"Bill, just get changed and we are going out. You can't do much now. You have a week to go at work and then that is it. Albert will have to survive without you".

Bill could not really argue with her, it was no use weighing up the options over and over again, it was time to switch off and get used to doing other things. He quickly ditched his suit and tie; Bill had never worn casual clothes to work.

Audrey continued "I have worked out that you owe me at least a dozen holidays and the outfits to go with them. Your retirement is going to be catch up time for me and you Bill Reynolds!"

Again, Bill was hardly in a position to disagree. He did not look at the paper again that weekend.

Albert was not likely to see the headlines as he was already at home preparing to cut the grass. This was his 'thinking time', when he was able to walk up and down, ear protectors on and lost in his own thoughts. He lived far enough out of the city for his house to be on the fringes of the countryside and an area he had known all his life. Albert remained pre-occupied when his wife, Polly, arrived home in her battered old car. Albert had refused to buy her a new one as she had a habit of dunching into static objects every few months.

They say that opposites attract. Polly and Albert were living proof that this was more than likely true. He was always practical, liked to get things done immediately and made decisions to suit. Occasionally he would be short with others when they did not see his point of view or if they did not follow the rules. Polly, on the other hand, did what she wanted, when she wanted and how she wanted, but she had the charm and personality that rarely offended anyone. She often joked with her friends that she had married the modern day Jesus; Albert had lived at home until he was 30 and had the same 12 mates all his life. His Dad was called Albert and so was his Grandfather. Polly was outgoing, often jumping from one project to another with great enthusiasm. She had been an art teacher for 28 years before semi-retiring to concentrate on her own art and to teach on a more individual basis.

Polly and Albert shared interests such as their garden and their holidays, but she had no understanding of his love for Newcastle United and he had no time for her constant re-arranging of their home.

Polly had at one time convinced Albert to accompany her to a dancing class, only to be scuppered at a family wedding when a nephew of theirs described the couple as a "Walrus dancing with a penguin" when they took to the floor. Polly had to accept defeat on the basis of that description, but she still made Albert dance in their living room every time her favourite movie appeared on TV – 'Mama Mia'. Albert lived in fear of this activity becoming common knowledge and knew that his colleagues would have a field day if they found out.

Polly and Albert did not have a family. The plan was to have children, but it never happened.

## Monday 30th July
The working week began well for those who did not know about the cuts and Bill's retirement news. For once the entire team was

present at the office and Albert asked everyone to make themselves available for a briefing, once they had checked the computer for any urgent issues relating to current work. The three members of the team who had been on leave were keen to hear about the Holly Gardens recovery and there was a lot of talk regarding informants and who the main men behind the job could be.

Bill and Albert decided to have a short discussion in private before the briefing. Bill was waiting for Albert to have a rant about the newspaper headlines, but Albert had not seen them.

"We will just have to say it as it is Albert. Five have to go and volunteers would be best, but names out of the hat could well be a disaster. There are quite a few I would hate to lose."

Albert had pondered all week end "Definitely. There are three who nearly went the last time and they know who they are. Pat Noone, John Green and Jill Crawford all came close, but were saved by the simple fact that there were five ahead of them when we did all the assessments. They are not bad detectives, it is just they do not take on as much responsibility as the rest. Pat needs to do a bit more work; he tends to hang back a lot."

Bill then asked about Tommy Douglas and Sam Brown and what their thoughts were likely to be.

"You must be telepathic Bill. I don't really want them to go but both of them have been on the FCT for years. It is time someone else had a chance, neither of them has that long to go so regular hours at a command unit might suit them. Sam has just bought himself a cottage in Northumberland to renovate so fixed hours and less call-outs might appeal. Tommy has threatened to go on a number of occasions, especially when he keeps missing rounds of golf with his mates."

"Why don't we see how it goes and then take the likely candidates to one side and explain as best we can? We've got until Wednesday afternoon to supply the names to Ashley and HR." Bill then added that he would announce his retirement to the team once they had been given a chance to ask questions about the budget cuts.

"Right, let's get the show on the road". Albert was keen to get it over with and rounded up the team.

"Okay everyone, phones on silent, computers and any other little gizmos that you lot possess switched off please. There are a couple of important issues to cover before we go in to current workloads. DI Reynolds has some news from HQ."

Bill paused. He wanted to make sure everyone was listening as there was only one thing worse than delivering bad news and that was delivering bad news twice.

"It is not good unfortunately. You all know we lost five colleagues to the cuts not so long ago and now we must lose another five. This is out of our control; the force budget has been reduced again, so every department and command unit is losing staff. This is either by a recruitment freeze or retirements. The only thing I can say is that anyone who leaves the FCT will stay within the CID, unless anyone wants to try anything else."

No one responded to the news, other than to look disappointed and to glance at each other in anticipation of a reaction.

Bill continued "The FCT has been very successful to say the least, especially in the last few months or so. If I were a DI at a command unit being offered one of you I would snap their hands off. We need volunteers by Wednesday afternoon so don't think you have to make your intentions known here and now. Sleep on it and both Albert and I are available all day to talk things through. If no volunteers are forthcoming, names will have to come out of a hat. This is not ideal, but that is what we have been told to do."

This revelation did get a reaction. DC Neil McAllister was first to comment "Surely they can come up with something better than that? We are not picking a school football team."

Albert agreed, but on this occasion the timetable was short and the budget would not allow anything else.

DC Jody Gallagher got straight to the point "If no one volunteers, then surely those who do the least should go first." Jody rarely left anything open to interpretation and Albert was pleased she produced a sentence without a swear word, but his relief was short lived.

"This is a right pile of crap to come back to after my fucking holidays. Sometimes I think they can shove their fucking job up their fucking ...."

20

"Thanks Jody" said Albert, cutting her off before she started using words with swear words in the middle of them, such as her favourite "Fan- fucking-tastic."

Bill then decided to share his own news.

"There is something else to tell you all. I have decided to retire and I have submitted the forms to HR. It will all happen quickly and my last working day is Friday. All I can say is that I have enjoyed every minute of working with you and I hope you all join me for a few pints when I get something arranged".

After a short pause everyone stood up and took it in turns to shake Bill's hand and wish him well. It was not an easy few minutes for Bill; the realisation of his retirement was becoming all too close. Jody and Alison grabbed him in a double bear-hug and all three seemed lost for words. This was a first, as none of them was vocally challenged to say the least.

DC Alan Tempest, the largest member of the FCT and resident body-beautiful, moved towards Bill and said "Don't worry Boss, I won't hug you" and grasped Bill's hand.

Bill winced at the strength of the handshake. "Well don't crush my hand instead you muscle bound galloot!" The relief on Bill's face as Alan released his vice-like grip made everyone laugh and not for the first time Alan had to apologise for inflicting pain on people he admired.

Scott Craig, one of the youngest members of the team, thanked Bill for all his guidance and advice since he joined the FCT. Bill saw a lot of promise in Scott, who had started to show his potential with his leading role in a number of recent successes. Bill asked him if he would be around later in the week so he could make sure all the paperwork Bill was involved in was done and dusted. Scott said he would make sure he was available. Scott seemed a bit withdrawn and pre-occupied to Bill but it was not the time to ask why.

Tommy Douglas and Sam Brown expressed their plans to retire as soon as they could. Both had less than two years to go and asked Bill if he would like to join their 'Grumpy Old Detective Club' when they set it up.

"Thought you already had" reflected Jody.

Before everyone went their separate ways, Albert reminded everyone of the Wednesday deadline and that he was around all day.

It was not long until the office was more or less deserted, only Hughie remaining at his desk. The rest had understandably gone to find a place to ponder the news, discuss things with their closest colleagues and no doubt work out what to do.

About thirty minutes passed by and Albert's phone rang. It was call from Alison Morton.

Albert answered with a declaration "Alison, you are not going anywhere so do not even think about volunteering."

"I'm not. I have not managed to get my head around it yet. It is not that . . . I'm ringing because Frank Drysdale has sent a text and wants to see me and Dave. He says it must be today, outside his Doctor's Surgery at 2pm. Should I say yes?"

Albert had hoped that Frank would come to his senses, but this was quite quick.

"Try ringing him and get a flavour of what he wants. We cannot talk about his circumstances, but if he wants to give us a clue as to who was behind all the drugs, then it will remain confidential."

"Okay, give me five minutes."

Albert wandered down the corridor to catch Bill and told him that Frank had been on the phone to Alison. They then discussed the options - perhaps he was not prepared to take all the blame and wanted to help himself or was he being set up by the others to find out a bit more from the police? Whatever the case, it had to be recorded correctly and kept close.

Alison soon rang back. "There is no answer on the phone, but I have had second thoughts about ringing again or leaving a message. We have his phone in the property cupboard ready to be examined, so the number he has texted me from is possibly someone else's. Should we just go back to the original plan and meet him at 2 o'clock?"

Albert was in agreement "Yes, do that. I will come down and watch to make sure no one follows you when you pick him up. Text me the address for the surgery and I will see you at about half one."

Albert turned to Bill "I have a strange feeling about this. I am just not sure about the whole job. One minute we get a first class tip off and recover a load of cocaine, then the next minute we get a phone call from the one and only suspect who wants to meet up. It all seems too good to be true."

"Well we don't know what he has to say, but I agree it is a bit fortunate to say the least. Sometimes things come together and sometimes they don't. I'll tell you what - I will come out with you to cover the meeting. It will be my last bit of practical police work before I clear the decks of all the paperwork."

Albert then made his way back to his desk, passing DC Brian Couley as he did so.

"Ah, Brian, the very man. Could you have a look at the phone we recovered from Holly Gardens as soon as possible? Alison has bagged it up and the paperwork has been done for continuity. It would be a great help if there was anything on it of interest."

Brian was the team 'techno wizard' and everyone relied on him for his ability to retrieve information from phones, computers and tablets. He had a reputation for obtaining technical evidence that was beyond the understanding of his more mature colleagues. He was always prepared, thanks to the 'utility belt' he wore. It consisted of various pouches containing tools, keys, his phone and the kit he had for examining electronic devices.

"No worries, I will do it as soon as I can. Erm, by the way Albert, I don't want to go so I won't be volunteering. I want to stay for a few years yet." Said Brian.

"That is good to hear Brian. I don't know what we would do without you when it comes to technical stuff. I don't want anyone to go, but there is no money."

Albert knew he could not give assurances, but at the same time he did not want his best staff to go. If only he could find a way around drawing names out of a hat.

By one o'clock, Albert and Bill were in the car park wandering around pressing the alarm button on some car keys Albert had found in the office.

"Do you not know what vehicle the keys belong to?" asked Bill.

"No idea. The tag with the registration number is missing. At least we know it is a Ford".

At that point the oldest car in the fleet bleeped at them from the corner of the car park.

"Should have known, it is the Mondeo we use when there is a chance of a bit of bother. It has more dents in it than an old tin bucket". Albert unlocked the car and they set off on Bill's last adventure.

"Do they use this car as a bin?" asked Bill as he picked through the cartons, paper cups and crisp packets in the foot well.

As they drove out, Jody and Alan were coming in the other direction. "I wonder where the two old codgers are going" asked Jody.

"For an important appointment in a pub somewhere . . . you know what those old detectives are like" explained Alan. "Wish I was going with them."

The surgery was about a mile from Frank's house, so Albert rang Alison and asked to see her and Dave in the car park of the main shopping centre on the West Road.

Alison and Dave were surprised to see Bill in the car with Albert. "It's his last run out before he retires" explained Albert "I hope something happens before he nods off."

Alison had not heard anything more from Frank, so it was decided that they should run past the surgery at two o'clock to see if he turned up. If there was no sign of him, Bill would walk through the waiting room (as he had not met him) and would hopefully recognise him from his description.

"I will text you if he is there and let you know we have picked him up. We'll drive out of the surgery and on to the West Road, so you can watch for followers." Dave was getting organised as two o'clock approached.

"Sounds good, off you go. Make sure you make a note of everything he says and above all do not let him think he will be getting any favours. Let him do the talking."

Albert and Bill made their way to a convenient spot and waited for the call. The conversation naturally turned to the cuts and Bill wondered if anyone had approached Albert.

"Brian and Alison are the only ones so far, not that much detail was discussed but I don't want either of them to go."

Just as the pair got around to discussing suitable venues for Bill's retirement function, Albert received a text from Dave. "Frank in car, with you in one minute".

As promised, Alison and Dave appeared at the junction of the West Road and turned left, away from the city centre. Albert sent a message back telling Dave to let them know where they ended up so they could be close by. Albert and Bill stayed and watched the junction for a few minutes and, as soon as they were happy, they followed in the general direction of their colleagues.

Another text from Dave came through "In Ambassador Hotel car park. Frank only has 10 mins." Albert replied confirming they were not far away.

Alison and Dave thanked Frank for being on time and explained that they were there to hear what he had to say. Frank moved to the middle of the rear seat and sat as low down as he could. He was nervous, looked pale and told them he had not been able to concentrate on anything else all weekend.

Alison asked him what he wanted to tell them.

"It is not what you expect, I bet. I am not going to tell you anything about the drugs. I will just have to take what is coming. All I can say is that you were okay with me at the police station and there is something on my mind I have to tell you. If you have done your checks you will know there was a brothel across the road from my house up until the back end of April."

Dave confirmed he had heard about it.

"Well, the two young lasses in there asked me to fix a few things in the house for them and I did, but I did not know it was a brothel when I first went over. I did a few other bits and pieces for them and they began to tell me about their pimps. They are cruel bastards, they got most of the money and the lasses had just enough to cover their food. The pimps turned up every day, sometimes more than once to check on them. An older woman was also at the place, not every day but often. They had to take customers at any time night or day. They hardly slept and if they did not do as they were told they got a hiding. I mean they were just kids, about 20 and these big fat arseholes used to turn up and push them about. I have seen the marks on their legs and the cuts on the back of their heads where the pimps bashed them with their mobile phones. Whatever money they did make they had to use to buy their drugs off them so they were trapped. They told me they had nowhere to go. Here is the number of one of the cars the pimps used".

Frank handed over a scrap of paper with a registration number on it.

"The lasses used to give me some of the money they got for the extras they used to do for men, over and above the usual charge. The pimps would have gone mad if they had found out. But what is really bad is that the lasses told me that their pimps had a copper looking after them so they would never get caught. When the brothel got closed down there was no one in the place. They knew the police were coming the day before, so the lasses collected all their belongings and took their money from me and I have not seen them again. It became common knowledge around the doors that it had been a brothel, but the police just got the landlord to change the locks and that was that."

Alison wanted to know more about the copper who was involved.

"I was in the brothel one lunchtime fixing the sink for them as the water was leaking all over. One of the lasses called Becky was in the kitchen with me as Lexi was busy with a client in the bedroom. I was trying to be as quiet as I could as I did not want anyone to know I was there. Just as I was packing up to leave, the bedroom door opened and the bloke Lexi had been with came out. I only saw him for a couple of seconds, but I recognised him straight away when you burst in to my house."

"You mean he was one of the officers who came to search your house" stuttered Alison.

"Who, which one?" asked Dave; the need for more information made him anxious.

"The lad with fair hair, about 35 and he had a blue T-shirt on. He sort of stood at the back and then left when that older copper decided there was enough to search the house".

Alison and Dave stared at each other momentarily and the realisation of who the officer was came to them simultaneously. They knew exactly who Frank meant.

"How can we be sure about this Frank? This is serious to say the least." Alison sensed that Frank was genuine but they would needed a lot more information out of him whilst they had the chance.

"Lexi had been with him and said he was a freebie. I heard her tell Becky that she had to give him a blow job for nothing as he was a friend of the pimps and he was useful to them. It all makes sense now that I know he is a copper. I know I am in a bit of a state with the drink and you probably think I'm making it up, but I don't think the police should be covering for those bastards."

"Who are those bastards Frank, you must know?" asked Dave.

"Check the car number and you will see for sure, so you know I am not lying. It is the Doyle Family."

Frank looked at his watch. "I must get going, I don't want to be seen. Can you drop me off back near the Doctors?"

Alison and Dave had many more questions but they were also keen to ensure Frank was not put in any danger.

"Can we meet again Frank? How do we contact you?" Dave tried to make some sort of plan as they set off on the return journey.

"I will text Alison when I have a chance. Don't try to ring me for Christ's sake. I don't know what else I can tell you, just get those lot sorted. Those young lasses will end up dead one of these days."

It was only a few minutes before Frank was dropped off and on the way Dave sent a text to Albert asking him to meet up urgently and before they went back to the office.

"Blimey, they must have got something good. Should we all meet at the Terrace Café?" suggested Albert to Bill.

"Good idea, tell them 10 minutes."

All four of them descended on the café at more or less the same time and found a quiet corner at the rear. Albert insisted on buying, so Bill asked Dave and Alison how it went.

"It is a bit delicate to say the least." Alison was still trying to weigh things up and Bill could see that she had something important on her mind.

Bill looked around for Albert, "Here he comes. I get the feeling you have something you would rather tell us both at once?" Albert placed the tray on the table.

Both Dave and Alison nodded enthusiastically.

"What are you going to tell us" asked Albert "Is he Mr Big after all?"

Alison looked at Dave and he urged her to pass on what they had heard.

"If only. Frank has told us that he thinks Pat Noone is corrupt. To cut a long story short the Doyle Family were running the brothel opposite Frank's house. Frank saw Pat with one of the prostitutes at the premises and he recognised him on Friday when we did the warrant. The prostitutes had told him that there was a copper on the payroll and that they could find things out. Pat did not have to pay and got 'freebies' from the young lasses. Frank says the prostitutes are treated very badly and had gone when the brothel was raided because they had been tipped off the day before".

"Bloody hell" sighed Bill, shaking his head. "I despair. What does he think he is doing the stupid idiot. Can we confirm this any other way?"

"He seems to be sure of what he was saying and he gave us a registration number to check for the Doyles". Dave produced the scrap of paper Frank had given him.

Albert sat staring at his tea. "Right, we need to keep this as tight as we possibly can. Not a word to anyone, not your best mate, your partner and definitely no one at FCT. Just Bill and me for now."

"I take it no one else knows you have met Frank" asked Bill.

"No, no one" confirmed Alison.

"Right, I want you to go somewhere and write up everything word for word. Do not put it on to the data base until you are told to. I do not want anyone reading it and passing it on. Keep everything in a sealed folder and locked away. We will meet again tomorrow morning at nine. I will have to inform Complaints and Discipline and they might want to see you at some point tomorrow. Don't run a check on that registration number either, let Complaints do that on their secure terminal."

Bill then turned to Albert "Can you think of anything else we need to do?"

"We just need to account for everything, so the notes have to be thorough. Complaints will want to check everything. If anyone asks where you have been tell them you went to the lab with some

28

exhibits from the Wallsend job. That should keep everyone happy. But apart from that, well done for getting Frank on board the pair of you. Part of me wants him to be wrong but I don't think he is."

"Neither do we" said Alison. "He would not make this up, especially as he is in a lot of trouble to start with. If he is trying to divert attention away from himself he has chosen an odd way to do it."

Bill had more or less finished his tea by then. He looked at his colleagues and said "Thirty two years' service and this job never fails to surprise you. Just when you think you have heard it all, something comes along which knocks you for six. Come on Albert, we'll go back to the office and get things sorted. I am pleased I only have four days left."

Albert and Bill went back to the office and tried to look as relaxed as possible. Jody was first to bump in to them.

"Nice run out for the pair of you. Just like old times was it?"

"It was, Jody. But in days gone by we had a better car, not that mobile skip. Who is supposed to look after it?"

"Have a guess - who in this office would be best at home in a skip?"

"Ah, righto. Tell Jimmy and Derek to get the blasted thing cleaned out would you?"

"With the greatest of fucking pleasure"

"Jody, did you come out of the womb swearing? I think we'll have to bring the swear box back."

"Fuck that, the last time all my wages went in to it. Bollocks to that idea." Albert recognised a lost cause when he heard one.

Both Bill and Albert quietly went about making their notes of the events surrounding Frank's meeting with Dave and Alison.

"I can see it all getting much worse. I can't understand why people take such stupid risks. Can you remember that entire shift that helped themselves whenever they went to a burglary? They managed to get televisions, microwaves, clothes and god knows what else. They only got caught when the probationer told someone else on a different shift. By that time the shopkeepers on their patch must have lost a fortune. I often thought they probably staged the burglaries in the first place."

Albert was also feeling dismayed about the behaviour of a few colleagues over the years.

"My mate Joe worked in Complaints for a while before he retired and he reckoned that out of 3,000 officers, 2,990 would most likely be perfectly honest and trustworthy, but there was always the potential for any one of them to drop an almighty clanger and ruin their career. A further five he described as 'tosspots' who sailed very close to the wind. The other five would be essentially corrupt. They might not be corrupt all of the time, but they would certainly do something if they had the chance to make a few bob, or in this case a free session with a prostitute".

"But why would they risk everything for short-term gain Albert? This is what I can never understand".

"It is because they don't think like everyone else. It is the same when we all sit around and discuss what the next move is for a criminal when we are running a job. Sometimes we might guess right, but it is only a guess because we work within the rules. Career criminals don't abide by rules, the law is an inconvenience to them; not a legal boundary which would stop most people from doing the things they do. They want money and power so they go and get it and it does not matter who or what is in their way. They are motivated by greed and by their egos, so I don't think it is any more complicated than that. The only exception are those who are addicted to drugs or alcohol; they just need to get through the day by whatever means. They also get caught a lot more and the cells are always full of them."

"If the story about Pat turns out to be true, don't give him an inch will you Albert?"

"I won't." Albert then had a sudden thought "Hang on Bill, shall we tell Miles Ashley? He has been at HQ all day and he won't be best pleased if he is the last to know."

"I forgot all about him. I will text him to ring me and at least he can't say we did not try. To be honest I can't be bothered with a load of questions from him this late in the day. Let's head home. I have also left a message at Complaints."

Albert checked in with Alison who confirmed she had all her notes written up and she would keep them until the next day.

# Chapter Two

# A Hidden World

**Tuesday 30th July**

Albert and Dave McGuinness were first to arrive at the office, both of them keen to get the day started. Albert took the chance to have a quick word with Dave about how they would make everything look as normal as possible.

"Dave, just to let you know we sent a message to both the Superintendent and Complaints last night. Hopefully we will be able to update them with everything without any fuss. Can you and Alison continue to look busy with the file for the Wallsend job and do not get roped in to helping with the surveillance on the new job Jody and Alan are running. If anything is said refer them to me."

"Will do. I spoke to Alison last night and we are both a bit concerned about Frank. He seems to be a loner and we are not sure how good he is at covering his tracks. The phone he used to contact us could be anyone's. He seemed to be pretty upset at what had happened to the two young lasses, Lexi and Becky, and I just can't see why he would not tell us the truth about the police involvement."

Albert nodded in agreement "There are things we can do to help him, but the rules are pretty strict. It will be up to Complaints and the hierarchy to decide."

"They are called Counter-Corruption now Albert, not Complaints."

"Oh yes, old habits die hard. Counter Corruption sounds more important. They must have a new gaffer with a big ego; they are probably 'agents' and not detectives like the rest of us. I just hope we get someone sensible to get to grips with it and it would not surprise me to find out they already have an idea from somewhere down the line."

By eight o'clock everyone was in and Jody briefed those who would be covering the latest drugs job of which she and Alan had been put in charge. There were enough resources to cover all the observation posts without Alison and Dave. Only Hughie would be left in the office, monitoring the radio for the rest of the team and doing background checks for them as things developed.

Albert asked the team to think about a retirement present for Bill and he also mentioned that the deadline for volunteers was edging closer. There was not a lot of response apart from a few moans and groans and some mumbled suggestions for Bill's gift. Understandable, thought Albert. He also felt a bit deflated about the future loss of staff and Bill's retirement, but most of all by the prospect of a traitor in the camp.

Bill rang Albert and explained he had been summoned to see Miles Ashley and then they had a meeting with Counter Corruption at 10am. He wanted Albert, Alison and Dave to be free all day in case they were needed.

Before long Jody's job was up and running, which meant that Hughie chirped away on the radio supplying vehicle and address checks for the rest of the team. He was in his element as he loved facts, procedures and record keeping.

Albert tried to keep busy with emails, but in the end he was little more than clock-watching. He could not concentrate on routine tasks so he decided to take his mind off things and chat to Hughie about his plans for the future.

"I don't want to go back to a command unit, Albert. This job is far better for me to be honest, I like to get involved in the detail of every job and I am not sure I would like to be dashing from one thing to another, without finishing anything properly. Karen (his wife) has always said that I've got OCD".

"Never!" said Albert in mock surprise "I would never have guessed. Is that why she cut all the tassels off the new rug she bought when she got sick of you diving on the floor every five minutes to straighten them out?" Albert gave Hughie a friendly shove on his shoulder.

"Hughie, the place would not be the same without you. I hope we can keep everyone happy. Have you seen Alison and Dave?"

"They were supposed to be making a cup of tea about ten minutes ago. Try the kitchen."

Albert walked down the corridor and found the pair of them in deep conversation, without any sign of a cup of tea for Hughie.

"Hughie is waiting for his tea you know. It is past his usual time and you know how tetchy he can get if his schedule is disrupted."

"Oops, my fault" said Alison, who immediately began the task in hand. "We were just talking about Frank and the information about Pat. It is still a bit hard to believe."

"We were also thinking about the two young women, Lexi and Becky. What will we do about finding them; they must know everything" commented Dave.

Albert explained that he was also preoccupied and was just killing time until Bill rang with some direction from HQ. "I take it neither of you wants to volunteer?" They did not. Dave saw his long term future at FCT and Alison said she enjoyed the job too much to give it up at the moment. Albert was relieved and asked them to bide their time until the deadline was past.

Miles Ashley and Bill Reynolds had been delayed from starting their meeting with Counter Corruption at HQ. Miles had predictably asked Bill a hundred questions about the information Bill had passed on. Most of the answers had been along the lines of "we do not know yet" or "we cannot do anything until we are sure it is the best thing to do." Miles and Bill were eventually summoned to a small meeting room in the Counter Corruption 'wing' at HQ.

Detective Inspector Susan Fenwick introduced herself and apologised for the delay. DI Fenwick had transferred to the force from East Midlands on promotion which meant she had not met many of her new colleagues. She was accompanied by DC Steve Taylor, who knew both Bill and Miles from previous roles in the CID.

DI Fenwick continued "Again, I am sorry for the delay, Steve was tied up with another job that has just come through this morning. Can I ask you both to sign this confidentiality form which will cover this meeting and every other contact we have from now on."

The form was signed and DI Fenwick explained that both she and Steve would take notes for their benefit.

"I must also apologise for my lack of knowledge of the area and some of the characters you might talk about. I was brought up in the North East and left to go to uni. After that I worked elsewhere for fifteen years. I'm pleased to be here though and my Geordie accent is just about back."

Miles thanked her for arranging the meeting and then asked Bill to go through the information Frank had passed on to Alison and Dave.

Bill did not take long to outline the allegations of corruption on the part of Pat Noone and his suspected arrangements with some well-known pimps.

As Bill finished, Miles added that they needed to take action about this at FCT as there were a number of sensitive jobs ongoing and it would be a disaster if those jobs were compromised.

There was a short pause whilst Susan Fenwick scribbled a few last notes. She then sat back and looked deep in thought. Steve caught the eye of Bill and nodded towards him. Bill's immediate thought was that this information was not a bolt from the blue.

Susan sat forward again and said "Steve can you run through what we know for the benefit of everyone; this is all in line with what we have heard from another source."

Steve was clearly ready to divulge his knowledge to Bill and Miles.

"On 20<sup>th</sup> July we received a call to our confidential staff hotline from someone who did not give his name. We strongly suspect that he is a cop, as the language he used and references to the intelligence system gave the game away. It is unlikely to have been a civilian employee as far as we can tell. The essence of the call was that at least two, if not three, male officers regularly use prostitutes then pass on their experiences to each other via a secure social media site or 'app' to which they have access to. They are supposed to detail basic things such as the appearance of the sex workers, the willingness of the sex workers to do certain things and so on. It is all a bit pathetic. The most worrying thing is that the caller suspects that the brothels they visit are mostly run by the Doyle family."

Steve then opened another file with some of the corroboration he had been able to find.

"I have been able to confirm some of what was said from historical intelligence. The Doyles seem to have moved away from drugs to prostitution. They know there is less risk as the police are not particularly interested and they can make similar money. We have checked all the addresses we know of in the force area and whenever there is a danger of the police taking an interest in a brothel, they move out before anything gets done. We had a look at the Holly Gardens brothel amongst others and a complaint came in about the amount of men calling at the address. The caller got sick of them ringing her door bell instead of the brothel door. The call came in on 27$^{th}$ April and by the time the police called on 28$^{th}$ April, the place was deserted."

Miles was listening to every word and hardly moved while Steve went through his information. Bill was on the point of checking that he was still breathing when he spoke with his reaction.

"I know we probably have a lot more questions than answers at this stage, but I am very concerned that we have a serious problem to sort out. I think we will have to work together on this and we at FCT are going to have to do something pretty quick with DC Noone."

Bill was already thinking ahead. "We have to lose five DCs due to the cuts and he could be one of them, but wherever he goes he can still access information regardless. Is there any way we can identify who else is involved from what we have so far?"

Susan and Steve both shook their heads. Susan continued; "If we could find out who the whistle blower is, then we may have a chance. We can also look at DC Noone's phone billing and his computer activity, but that will take time. We have also lost staff, including an analyst, and that means we are hardly keeping up with the work load."

Miles had made his mind up, despite the obvious logistical problems they faced. "Bill, I know you are in your last few days at work but can you and Albert get together and draw up a list of all potential lines of enquiry. If Susan and her team can start the billing and the computer logs, we will make some time available to do some other enquiries, starting with Frank."

Susan agreed to start as soon as they could and that Steve would be the main contact for now.

Miles also had responsibility for Force Intelligence and he decided to make some enquiries as to what was known from a force-wide perspective. A further meeting was arranged for Friday 3$^{rd}$ August unless anything urgent cropped up.

All four then made their way back through to the general office and Steve asked Bill about his retirement. Bill explained that he had just made his mind up and was beginning to feel relieved that he was going. "This could turn out to be a major investigation as you probably know. Perhaps the Doyles will end up on a charge sheet but there will be a lot of collateral damage. What do you think?"

"The press and media are generally all over a corruption case and the public always take an interest. At the end of the day there are those who think we are all bent bastards and their opinion will not change. The rest, who think we do a decent job, will be encouraged by the fact that we have locked up one of our own and thrown the book at them. We just have to get it right from the start before it festers away and gets worse. I have no doubt that there will be a load of characters coming forward after the event to say that they knew there was something dodgy about Pat Noone, but the same people did fuck all about it when they had the chance."

"Yes, yes, it happens all the time . . . . . the phone call you received, can I listen to it?" asked Bill.

"Sure, I will get it for you. I should have thought of that first." Steve disappeared into another office.

Bill had a nagging thought developing. What happens if the two or three mentioned in the call were all at FCT? Who could they be?

In the meantime Miles and Susan had exchanged mobile numbers and agreed that a joint budget application should be made to Finance if the job required it.

Miles joined Bill and he explained that Steve was fishing out the tape.

"This is potentially disastrous for us Bill. We have other trials coming up in the next few months and they are bound to say we are all corrupt. We need to find out who might be involved and get them sorted as soon as possible."

"Too right, best of luck. I will think of you all when I am on a beach somewhere."

36

Steve reappeared with the recording of the call. "It is not the best of quality. There is some wind noise and traffic in the background. It is a mobile call as opposed to a land line . . . here we go."

The call began with the date and time.

A male voice is then heard. *"I would like to pass on a concern about DC Noone of FCT. He is seeing prostitutes and passing on his reviews to other officers who are also seeing the same women. There are two or three of them and they have an app on their personal phones. . . "*

"Stop there" said Bill. I think I have heard enough and I want Albert Bennison to hear this.

"Do you know who it is Bill." Miles demanded to know.

"I think so. It is young Scott Craig but I still want Albert to confirm it."

"But you are pretty sure"

"I am but it is better to be safe. Can you play some more please Steve?"

The recording continued.

*". .. . . and they talk about sex acts and the size of their breasts and so on. DC Noone discussed the Doyle family in a phone call to one of his associates last week. They run brothels all over Tyneside and down to the Teesside area. Do some billing and log checks and there will be evidence there. I have decided to call this number because I do not know who else is involved. I have to go"*

"That is just about it; the call ends and we have not had another one as yet." Explained Steve.

Bill repeated his wish to have Albert listen to the tape. He suggested that no one mentioned Scott's name so Albert did not have a pre-determined idea in his head. Bill vouched for Scott Craig, as he saw him as a promising detective. The only disappointment was that he had not approached him or Albert with his concerns. It would be interesting to hear why he had not.

Before he phoned Albert, Bill told Miles that Alison Morton and Dave Gallagher were the two who he trusted to continue to work on the initial enquiries. He had gauged their reactions to the information Frank had provided and he could see how difficult it was for them to come to terms with the thought of potential corruption in the office.

He expected that any difficulty they had would soon turn into a determination to put things right. He also hoped that Scott Craig would be the next one to get involved.

Bill then made his way back to his car and he began to realise that, amongst all the talk of corruption, collateral damage and resources, there had been no proper discussion about the two young women that Frank was so concerned about. Frank had put more thought and effort in to their welfare than any police officer had so far. Bill immediately felt guilty at this omission and struggled to work out why no one had prioritised them. Was it because the police were so used to hearing about one sort of abuse or another, or was it because prostitution was so far down the list of priorities that their plight was written off as a self-made predicament?

Bill rang Albert and gave him a summary of the meeting with Counter Corruption. He also told him that he felt guilty about not thinking or doing enough about the two sex workers that Frank wanted to help.

Albert immediately saw where Bill was coming from.

"We will have to put that right Bill. We just don't think of prostitutes as victims. They are always left alone to get on with it, because our attitude is that they do no harm and there is no point in prosecuting them. Perhaps we should change that around completely and look at the harm that is done to them. I think Alison and Dave have already started to think like that and we need them to get on with some basic enquiries."

"Exactly. Can you bring them both over to HQ straight away and lets' get some work done. Ring me when you are close." Bill might have had just three days to go, but he knew he had to ensure the enquiry got off to the best possible start.

Within the hour, Bill met Albert, Dave and Alison at Counter Corruption and introduced them to Steve Taylor. The obligatory confidentiality form was signed and Bill explained that the three of them would not be involved if he did not trust them one hundred per cent.

"Albert, can you go with Steve as he has something for you to listen to. I want to draw up a list of priorities with Alison and Dave."

38

Albert and Steve retreated to a small office used by Counter Corruption for all their technical gear. Steve already had the tape ready to go and explained that it was not the best quality, but he would be grateful if Albert could try his best. Despite not having been given any pre-warning Albert suspected that the voice he was about to hear belonged to someone he knew. There was obviously a good reason why Bill wanted him to listen to the tape before doing anything else.

Steve pressed the button and the call began after the date and time.

Albert listened, using every ounce of concentration he could muster. The voice was indeed familiar to Albert and after no more than three sentences he turned to Steve.

"That is Scott Craig."

He listened to the rest of the tape and confirmed his initial identification.

"It is Scott without a doubt. He sounds a bit nervous but that is no surprise. He works with Pat Noone a lot; they have been in obs points together recently and he must have overheard something he does not like. What a mess this is turning out to be."

Steve confirmed that Bill had recognised Scott's voice when it was played to him earlier on. They then went back to the main office and Bill asked Albert what he thought.

"Same as you. No doubt in my mind."

"Good. We will discuss what to do with the Super as soon as we finish here. Dave and Alison have a list of jobs to get on with and I'm hoping they will be able to find a bit of space here. Is that possible Steve?"

"Yes no problem. I can share all the information I have got at the same time."

Bill then ran through the enquiries that needed immediate attention. Top of the list was Frank, Lexi and Becky.

"We are going to try to contact Frank somehow and give him a new phone so we can keep in touch. He needs to be seen as soon as possible so that every bit of detail we can get is looked at. We need descriptions and phone numbers for the two young lasses and we need to locate them as a matter of urgency. Anything could have happened since Frank last saw them in April. The premises identified by Steve as potential brothels also need to be progressed and the computer logs and billing will no doubt throw up a load of information. Hopefully we will get some progress there too."

Steve Taylor confirmed he was available full time and he needed an operational name for all the paperwork.

"We will think of one" said Albert, "Give me a couple of hours. I keep a list of likely names on my desk."

"And they are all to do with Newcastle United, he is so predictable" said Bill having a dig.

"How about Operation Third Division, or Operation McMenemy?" responded Albert, swiftly countering with Sunderland FC's drop to the old third division in the 80s' when they were coached by a Newcastle-born manager.

Alison and Dave, who were too young to know what the references to 80s' football meant and had no interest in finding out, went with Steve to find a desk and a computer to start their research.

Bill and Albert decided to track Miles Ashley down at Force Intelligence (FI), walking the short distance from one end of HQ to the other.

They took the chance to discuss how to approach Scott. Neither of them suspected that he was involved in any way, shape or form, as he had taken the first step to report his suspicions through the correct channel. Both agreed that Scott was a bright lad, generally quiet and thoughtful so he would have already worked out that his call would spark an enquiry.

Miles Ashley was just finishing one of the many meetings he attended during the working day and he was pleased to see Bill and Albert. He was about to summon them to reveal the result of the discreet enquiries he had made at FI. They gathered in the small office he used when at HQ.

"I was worried that we would be starting from scratch on this as we had no central collection for intelligence in relation to prostitution, which in hindsight is a major failing on our part. But I was wrong; one of the lads here at FI has kept an unofficial list of all the brothels in the force area, plus a general run-down of the escort agencies and who he thinks runs them. He only keeps the information updated now and then, as he is usually dealing with other jobs at the assessment stage. The only reason he did this was because he was involved in a Home Office initiative a few years ago which concentrated on trafficking. It was centrally-funded in the days before the cuts but it looks like it turned out to be just a big intelligence gathering exercise for us. There were no arrests apart from a couple of sex workers who came to the attention of the Borders Agency."

"So can we have all his information?" asked Albert.

"Of course we can. He is unaware of the current problem, as I am wary of mentioning anything until we have identified the others we know are out there."

Bill was keen to discuss the rest of the staff at FCT and the balancing act they would have to come to terms with; who could they trust and who was to remain on the team. The easiest way was to go through the list and make some initial decisions.

Albert mentioned John Green, Jill Crawford and Pat Noone as the three who were next on the list to go, based on their overall performance since the previous five left FCT. None of them had made known their intentions this time around and all three had been very quiet since the news broke about further staff cuts.

Albert gave his thoughts on the rest.

"We need to keep Alison and Dave at all costs, they are always first in the queue to get involved. Alison is through her exam and she can act up and Dave is both practical and he knows his stuff. Hughie and Brian Couley have specific skills which would leave us short so they must stay. Jody does my head in but her ability to connect with victims and witnesses means she also has to stay. She also works hard and she takes no nonsense from the lads. Scott is a good detective and he may end up integral to the corruption issues, so he should stay. He is still young in service, but he picks things up quickly. Jimmy and Derek are joined at the hip, but they get things done and you can always trust them to do what they are told. I want them to stay, even though they live like a couple of swamp rats. Alan Tempest and Neil McAllister are also good detectives. They would be a lot better if Alan spent less time in front of a mirror and Neil was less of a barrack room lawyer. Having said that, they are useful

41

in many ways. That leaves Tommy and Sam whom I have a lot of time for, but we were thinking they may go on the basis that they both have about 18 months left before they retire."

Bill nodded throughout in agreement.

Miles knew that a lot of thought had been applied by Albert as to who he wanted to keep. It still hinged on the right people volunteering to go. He then realised that his plan to draw names out of the hat was likely to backfire. All they could do was to approach everyone and see what could be achieved.

"Try and have informal chats with everyone before they go home today and remind them we have to know by tomorrow. Hopefully the hat will stay on the peg and we won't need it. You were right Albert; it is a bit unfair and I have made a rod for my own back."

"I have a plan" replied Albert.

Miles pretended not to hear, but he was not entirely surprised. He collected his files for his next meeting and told Albert that everything should be done fair and square.

Bill and Albert made their way back to FCT and Bill explained that he had opened a policy book with all his main decisions documented. He would hand it over to Albert on Friday when the next meeting with CC was scheduled. Bill knew Albert was the best person to run the job, especially as the alternative was a temporary appointment from HQ. Miles Ashley had made no other suggestions.

Alison and Dave had been busy working out how to contact Frank and a subscriber check on the number he had used the previous week revealed that he had borrowed Mrs Baker's mobile. They had decided to leave that phone to one side and purchased a pay-as-you-go mobile with credit on it for Frank. Steve Taylor was going to deliver it, using one of the unmarked vans from CC, whilst trying his best to look like a delivery driver. Alison contacted Albert and he appreciated the progress. He was more than happy for them to get on with it and make contact with Frank without any delay.

Bill and Albert arrived back at FCT to find the team had returned earlier than expected. One of the obs points they were using had to be abandoned when a team of builders arrived to start work on the roof.

"Sod's law," commented DC John Green. He explained he had noticed the van turning up at the front to the building, giving him and Jill just enough time to get out the rear. The landlord had told John that the work was to take place the following week, so things had obviously changed.

Albert took his chance.

"Right, rattle through the de-brief and we want to see everyone individually before we go off-duty. I don't care what order, just no one disappear until you have been seen."

Within 15 minutes the first of the team came to see Albert and Bill. They had chosen the office overlooking the main car park which was far enough away from the main office so no one could be overheard. They could also keep watch for anyone trying to escape their turn to have a chat.

"Come in Jody . . . all we want to know is what you think about the cuts."

"Load of fucking bollocks" she replied to Albert.

"That is 10 pence for the swear box"

"Fuck off"

"That is 20 pence for the swear box"

"I'm not taking part in your poxy, fucking swear box"

"30 pence"

Jody saw the joke when Albert could not keep a straight face any longer. Jody then told Bill and Albert that she wanted to stay. It suited both her working life and personal life as she still had two teenagers at home. She was not keen to work night shifts back at a command unit. Jody was always to the point and Albert appreciated that.

Next in was Derek Baty. He also wanted to stay as he relied on the overtime he earned to keep up with his complicated private life. Derek had been married and divorced three times in 12 years, spanning a period between his late twenties and his recent fortieth birthday.

Albert turned to Bill and said "He has eaten more wedding cake than my local vicar. As long as I have known him he has been engaged to be married, then married, then separated, then divorced in a never ending cycle. Must have cost a fortune."

Derek reflected for a moment, as if he was trying to calculate the thousands he has spent on ex-wives. "It's true, but two exes have got re-married and they don't contact me much anymore. They will still want a share of my pension though."

Bill had been married for 33 years and was pleased he had not experienced anything like Derek's problems.

Bill reminisced "When I was an apprentice sparky in the shipyards, in the mid 70s, one of the older blokes used to come to work in a foul mood if he had been arguing with his wife. One day he was sitting having his bait and he turned to me and said - *do you know what it is son, men and women should live separate lives, then meet up on a Saturday night to copulate. Life would be much easier.* Shame you never met him Derek."

Derek was used to getting advice from relatives and colleagues so he just shrugged his shoulders and thanked them both for their wisdom.

Next was Neil McAllister and he wanted to challenge the 'names out of the hat' policy straight away. Albert shut him down.

"Forget it Neil. We need to move on, do you want to stay or go?"

"Stay" came the sheepish reply.

"Good, I hope you do. Anything else?" Albert could see people were waiting and time was passing by. Neil was happy to leave the discussion and Albert followed him out in to the office.

"Okay everyone, time is marching on. I just need to see Alan, Tommy, Sam, Pat, Jill, John, Jimmy and Scott. I've spoken to Alison, Dave, Hughie and Brian earlier. I don't want to keep anyone hanging about too long."

Alan asked if he could be next as he wanted to be home before 6pm. He was very brief and asked to stay. His mind was clearly elsewhere and it did not take long to work out that he had his latest girlfriend waiting for him.

"On a promise Alan?" enquired Bill.

"How could she resist?"

In unison both Bill and Albert told him to clear off.

Jill and John then came in together. Jill spoke first "We both realise that we were close to going the last time, so if the situation is still the same, then I will go back to the CID in Newcastle if there is a place".

John added that he had considered things carefully and he would like a post nearer home in Sunderland. Bill assured them that there were vacancies and they would have first choice. He thanked them for their past efforts and for volunteering.

Pat Noone appeared at the doorway and asked if he could be next. "Of course" said Albert.

This encounter was going to be difficult as Albert had not spoken to Pat at length since the revelations of his misconduct had come to light. "Have you had a chance to think about the options?"

Pat wanted know where he stood in the pecking order within the team. Albert reminded him of the conversation they had after the last staff cuts. Pat was left in no doubt that he was not in the top ten.

"So the choice is not mine is it? Looks like I have to go."

Albert was careful not to push the issue too much, even though it would be a relief if Pat went quietly.

"Well, you are a competent detective Pat. The problem is there are a lot of outstanding individuals in the office. You do have a choice at the end of the day and there are vacancies within the CID as promised."

There was a long pause as Pat pondered what to do. Bill sat up in his seat and edged closer to Pat to get his attention.

"Things could change in the future Pat; there will be opportunities to return if the budget improves and with your experience you would be first in line".

Brilliant, thought Albert, Bill was building him up but trying to get rid of him at the same time.

"Okay, okay I think it would be best if I went; I've had a good couple of years. I just wanted to hear what you had to say."

Albert thanked Pat and Tommy arrived almost immediately, as if he had been listening outside the door. Albert was taken by surprise and he had no time to appreciate his overwhelming sense of relief at Pat's decision. He offered Tommy a seat.

Albert then quietly asked "Were you listening Tommy?"

"No of course not. As if I would do such a thing. But I don't mind going either. I know Sam and I are a bit long in the tooth and I would like to make way."

"So you were listening" deduced Albert.

"Well, just the last bit. Pat should have went the last time and I just wanted to make sure he did the right thing."

Bill and Albert expected little else from Tommy who had always been a good operator and covered his options well. They thanked him and confirmed he would go somewhere he wanted. They both noted his choice of words, but they would have to wait for another opportunity to ask Tommy to explain.

Sam did not waste any time when it was his turn. He said he wanted to stay as it had always been his intention to see his time out at FCT. He looked determined and did not sit down for a chat. Albert sensed that he needed to arrange a further conversation with Sam, who at times could be stubborn.

Jimmy Richards had been busy with some exhibits and he strolled in expecting to be last in the queue. He also wanted to stay but he said that he would accept it if he had to go. He also added that he was convinced his name would come out of the hat as he had dreamt about it the night before.

"Perhaps you could have a dream about tidying your desk as well Jimmy" quipped Albert.

Jimmy promised to have a spring clean if he "survived the night of the long knives."

That left Scott. Albert looked out in to the corridor but there was no sign of him. He walked the short distance to the main office and found Scott staring out of the window overlooking the rooftops of the nearby housing estate.

"Penny for your thoughts" said Albert to get his attention.

"Sorry Albert I was miles away. I think I am last to be seen and if you have five minutes I need to talk to you about something else."

Scott looked dejected, his usual positive attitude was missing.

"Come on then, I think the DI is waiting for us both."

Albert and Scott returned to the office where Bill had remained, using the time to check his emails. As Albert walked in he raised his eyebrows and nodded to Bill in an effort to communicate with him that Scott was ready to talk.

"Scott is last in and we probably have something we need to talk about at length. Is that okay with you both?" Albert wanted the conversation to progress beyond the cuts to Pat Noone as quickly as possible.

Scott sat down, his nerves affecting his voice. "Ye-Yes, no problem."

Bill could see that Scott needed to be put at ease and he told him that he wanted him to stay as he a good future at FCT. Albert told Scott that anything he had to say would not influence future decisions and he also wanted him to stay.

"I do want to stay. I love being involved in long term jobs and locking up the real bad lads at the top. This is the type of thing I joined for in the first place."

"That's settled then, but there is obviously something else we need to go through . . . is that fair to say?" Albert again wanted to come to the point, his impatience shining through.

Bill was used to Albert's blunt enthusiasm and told Scott to take his time.

Scott paused and gathered his thoughts. He had probably ran the words he was about to say through his head over and over again for weeks.

"I have to tell you about an officer who I think has gone over the line. I don't know how else to put it."

Scott was waiting for any sign of recognition or a shared concern from either Bill or Albert. Bill decided to make things easier for Scott as his anxiety was obvious and it was unnecessary to let him continue in such a state.

"If it is about another member of FCT, brothels and sex workers, then we have some idea of what you are going to say."

Scott's head rolled back and he gave a huge sigh of relief. His entire body relaxed in an instant and he regained his composure.

"I'm sorry I have not said something to you both earlier but I have been in turmoil; I have not been able to concentrate for weeks. How did you know I was going to tell you about brothels?" Scott was quickly coming to terms with the conversation.

Albert then explained that the some similar information had been passed to them from a source, which was separately confirmed by CC.

"My phone call to the confidential hot line?" said Scott.

Albert nodded and asked Scott to go over what he knew. He also told him that he had done exactly what anyone else would have in the circumstances.

"Pat Noone uses brothels, I have no idea why as he has had a couple of nice girlfriends since I have known him. One was a police woman and the other worked for the post office in Newcastle somewhere. I did not know what he was up to at the start, but since about January he changed from being quite hard working to just being along for the ride."

"Literally" remarked Albert.

Scott wanted to continue without hesitating and missed Albert's sarcastic comment.

"He spends forever on his personal mobile, texting and taking calls from his friends or going on the internet. When we were on obs, he would disappear to take calls and a couple of times he was away for 15 minutes or more when we were on surveillance. I was in the car with him and if there had been a contact and we had to move, I was stuck without him. I asked him a couple of times what was wrong but he just said he was having problems at home. I had hoped things would get better, but at the end of June I saw a message on his phone about an escort agency called Superior Escorts and a review. From then on I tried my best to see what he was doing on his phone when we were parked up or on standby. It was the same every time; escorts, reviews, texts from others who were looking at the same women. In the end I did something that I perhaps should not have and I searched the database for brothels but there is hardly anything recorded. The one thing that did make me worried was the mention of the Doyle Family moving in to prostitution. He has asked me a couple of times what I knew about them, but apart from a case six years ago when the oldest Doyle was done for fraud and blackmail, I have had little to do with them."

Bill recalled the same case and commented that Graeme Doyle had got six or seven years imprisonment, serving about four.

"I'm sure that is right. Anyway, Pat uses an app called 'punterdate' to contact his associates who use the same escorts. A couple of times he has received a phone call and you know there is someone on the other end talking about whatever they do. He uses abbreviations such as OWO and GFE and a lot of others as they are sex acts or services. He thinks I don't know what BJ stands for. He has become more and more arrogant and I am sure the others must have noticed something."

Albert asked Scott if the addresses of the brothels had been mentioned.

"No. He has been very careful to keep most things to himself, but I am pretty sure a couple of the others he sends messages to are also cops. I can just tell the way he talks to them, he once mentioned *address history* and then in another call an *incident log*. Members of the public would not know what he meant. I have kept notes of what has been going on since the end of June. A couple of weeks ago I got completely fed up with him disappearing to make calls and not pulling his weight so I phoned the hot line. We had been out on surveillance all day and we lost the subject just as things were getting interesting. Pat could not give a fuck and he asked me to go to the nearest cashpoint as he needed some money. I thought to myself that it was to pay an escort. I knew as soon as I phoned the hot line that something would happen sooner or later, so it is a massive relief to know that I am not wrong."

Albert asked if he had heard the names Lexi or Becky mentioned in any of the conversations by Pat.

"No . . . come to think of it I don't think I have heard him mention any names other than Graeme Doyle and his girlfriend's name. He almost speaks in code with a lot of smug comments thrown in."

Bill had listened carefully to Scott and was entirely happy that he had told the truth. Scott had been in a very difficult position but Pat had pushed him to the limit. Because Scott was quiet and unassuming, Pat had most likely been a bit more relaxed in his company than with some of the others. Jody or Neil would have confronted him or been more vocal in the office had they known. Or at least that is what Bill hoped.

"Has anyone else known what has been going on? You said others could have noticed" asked Bill outright.

"I am not sure, I thought Tommy was getting a bit sick of him as he has been out with him on obs, but not as much as me. There has been the odd comment about his attitude but I just did not know how to approach it, I wish I had spoken to you earlier. I don't think anyone from FCT is involved with Pat, he is not on good terms with anyone really. Not like Derek and Jimmy or Tommy and Sam who are great mates."

Bill reassured Scott that things would work out fine and he should not worry, after all he had made the phone call to the hot line two weeks ago. Scott left the room with a weight off his shoulders.

Albert's mobile then rang. Alison wanted him to know that they had delivered a phone to Frank with a note saying that they would ring him at 5.30pm on the dot. The delivery had been easy; Frank had been on his own and after a bit of confusion, Steve had got the message over that we needed to speak to him urgently.

Albert looked at his watch and saw that it was 5.20pm. Another day gone without identifying or locating the two young lasses, Lexi and Becky. Albert asked Alison to get as much information from Frank as she could over the phone and if necessary to make arrangements to see him as soon as he was available. If that meant staying on for a few hours to get it done, so be it as overtime was available.

Bill caught Scott as he was leaving for home and told him that his notes would be crucial to the investigation. Scott explained that he had kept them at home because he was very wary of Pat finding them as their desks were next to each other.

Scott was far more relaxed and Albert told him to go home and get a good night's sleep as he looked like he needed one. There was also a lot of work to get through in the coming days and weeks and Scott was going to be involved.

"I will and thanks for listening. I won't take so long next time. See you tomorrow."

Bill and Albert remained in the office to go over all the information and to discuss what should be done next. Bill read an email from Miles Ashley to Albert about a meeting at FI the next day at 9.30am.

"Looks like we are going to have access to all the intelligence they have. Hopefully Frank will be forthcoming tonight so we will have a bit more to go on. We need to speed up a bit."

Bill then had to leave as Audrey was waiting for him at home to finalise a last minute holiday she had planned for the following week. She was wasting no time and had a shortlist for Bill to look at on the internet.

"Expensive evening Bill?"

"Looks like it, but to be honest I am ready for a holiday. It is one thing to be chasing gangsters, but bent cops are entirely different. I still can't believe anyone would be so stupid and for once I don't really want to know all the sordid details."

Albert decided to stay a while until he heard from Alison and Dave. Hopefully, they would get to see Frank.

By 6.15pm there was no word, so Albert rang Dave. No answer.

He rang Alison's mobile. No answer.

He waited five minutes and tried Dave again, but the phone went straight through to answer machine. Perhaps they were with Frank and did not want to be disturbed.

Albert sent a text to Alison asking her to ring. She normally replied in an instant, but not this time.

Albert was worried; had he paid enough attention to the plan to get hold of Frank and allowed Alison and Dave to walk in to danger? Another ten minutes went by and Albert was at the point of driving down to Frank's house to see if there was any activity when a call came in from Dave.

"Dave, I have been trying to get in touch . . . what is going on?" Albert was being blunt, but at least he was also showing some concern.

"Sorry Albert, but Frank wanted to meet well away from his house and there was no signal where we ended up, next to the river. He has given us more to go on though."

Albert calmed down immediately and he knew he had sounded overbearing. "Ah, okay Dave I was just a bit on edge about what was happening. Are you on your way back?"

"Yes, five minutes".

Albert decided to make amends and put the kettle on, which was his way of apologising for his sharp words. He had put the kettle on a lot over the years.

Dave and Alison seemed to think nothing of Albert's phone call and they settled down to go through the notes Alison had made of the meeting.

"According to Frank, Lexi and Becky were at Holly Gardens for almost six months. He saw them once or twice a week and it seems like he gained their trust quite soon after they moved in. Frank knows the Doyles from their reputation and he says he does not have anything to do with them. Lexi was 20 and Becky 21 when he met them. Lexi is about 5 foot tall, long dark hair and always wears loads of make-up. Frank remembers that she was always worrying about her false eyelashes for some reason. Becky has blonde hair cut short and is a bit taller. Both of them were skinny according to Frank. He has not seen or heard from them since they left and he has no way of contacting them apart from one number on his mobile. He says it ends in 6677 but we should be able to find that no problem. He says there might be a text from them saying they had to go and they hope he will be okay, or words to that affect. The most money he hid for them was about £120 each, but the usual amount was around £50. The pimps took £80 out of every £100 they earned and they usually got the rest by selling heroin to them both. Frank has no idea of their surnames . . . he is sure Lexi mentioned her family name once but he cannot remember it. He feels bad that he cannot do more, he told us that he had tried to persuade them to leave the brothel when they had the chance and get out of sex work. They said it was no use trying as they would be found and forced back after a good hiding. There were lots of stories about other girls getting the same treatment according to Lexi and Becky."

"Brian has the phone so we will see what he has managed to get off it" confirmed Albert.

Dave then added "Frank thinks that they do not use their real names when meeting punters. They would think up a new name every few weeks or so. He has no idea how they got punters either. I don't think Frank has ever owned a computer or been on the internet.

He did see a laptop in the flat and the mobiles were always ringing or bleeping. Lexi told him that there were at least 10 other brothels controlled by the Doyles and their hangers-on."

"How is all this going on right under our noses?" queried Albert out loud.

"If the Doyles are earning about £400 per day from both Lexi and Becky and there are another 10 brothels it means they are potentially making in excess of eight grand per day, less costs. No wonder they moved in to prostitution" observed Alison.

"And we just let it happen because we think they do no harm."

"It is a completely hidden world Albert, or at least it is on our patch. Frank had asked Lexi and Becky to go to the police after they had got a hiding around Easter time but they said that was impossible; they were convinced the police would lock them up for being prostitutes and the Doyles would get away with it regardless." Alison sounded dejected.

"And we have Pat Noone and his mates to thank for that" added Albert, his determination increasing.

Albert asked Alison to keep her notes safe and told them both to be at FI for a meeting at 9.30am the next day.

**Wednesday 31st July**

Bill Reynolds had not slept well. His mind had not been on his forthcoming holiday but he had, at least, gone through the internet booking process with Audrey, who was determined that they should start Bill's retirement with a holiday. They were off to Scotland for a short break, followed by ten days in Cyprus. Audrey wanted to go for longer but Bill insisted that he should be at work on his very last day which was Friday 30th August, even if he just popped in to hand over his warrant card.

Bill arranged to meet Albert at HQ before the meeting and he was relieved to hear that contact had been made with Frank. They also decided that Scott, Brian and Hughie were brought on to the enquiry. They needed Scott to help with the basics, Brian to do the technical stuff and Hughie to be disclosure officer.

"This enquiry has the chance to run away with itself if you are not careful Albert. It is bound to open up a whole new world as far as this force is concerned. I had a look on the internet last night and there are hundreds of escorts between here and North Yorkshire. Gone are the days of business cards in telephone boxes and the back room of the barbers. There is not much left to the imagination either, some of the photos . . . good grief!" Bill shook his head.

Can you remember that scene in Auf Weidersen Pet when Oz came out of the brothel in Dusseldorf and said "Denis, sex is in it's infancy in Gateshead."

Albert nodded and smiled.

"Well not any more, sex in the North East has grown up fast since then."

On an entirely different subject, Albert wanted to know if Bill had arranged a retirement function. Bill had booked the East End Club for the first Thursday in September as that was the most convenient date and people were back from leave by then, after the holiday month of August was out of the way.

The meeting at FI started on time, with everyone sensing that the operation had to start gathering pace. Miles Ashley was keen to obtain as much evidence as possible against Pat Noone and his associates, so they could be taken away from police work before any further damage was done. There was no reason why extra staff could not be deployed. DI Susan Fenwick confirmed that Steve Taylor was allocated full time from now on and she would free up an analyst within the week.

Alison ran through the meeting with Frank. She concluded that it was beneficial to have made contact, but he had not been able to give them the whereabouts of Lexi and Becky.

Miles then suggested that DC Mick Miller should join the meeting. He was the officer who had kept an informal database on prostitution.

Mick Miller had been told by Miles to keep himself handy and it was not long before he entered the room. He clearly had no idea what was expected of him and as soon as he saw members of staff from CC and FCT he appeared uncomfortable.

"Don't worry Mick, we just need to pick your brains but can you sign this confidentiality form first?" asked Miles.

A relieved DC Miller signed the form and sat down.

"Mick, we have a potential problem with escorts and an inappropriate relationship with a serving officer. I know you have kept tabs on escort agencies since the Home Office gave us some money a while back to look at trafficking. Anything you have will be useful I'm sure so can you give us a summary of your information?" Miles also asked him to introduce himself to anyone he did not know, which turned out to be Susan Fenwick and Dave McGuinness.

Mick Miller began to gather his thoughts and asked if they wanted to know about locations, pimps, madams or the numbers involved. Bill urged him to tell them whatever he thought was relevant.

"There are 10 to 15 escort agencies operating in the North East. Some have less than ten escorts and some have as many as 50. There are independents who work for themselves, perhaps 20 or 30 in total; it is hard to be exact. Prices range from £50 per half hour to about £600 for an overnight stay. Prostitution is a natural home for organised crime as it carries less risk of investigation than drugs or other criminality and this fact has been raised many times before. Unfortunately, prostitution has not been made a performance indicator so unless there is another reason to get involved, the whole issue is left to its' own devices. At best we just close brothels down when there is a complaint and since 2004 there have only been eight arrests for prostitution force-wide. We don't have a red light district in our area, which would partly explain why there is little notice taken of what goes on. I have got everything on my computer and you are welcome to have it all."

Susan Fenwick wanted to know why Mick had kept his database going.

"When we did a series of warrants on known brothels a few years ago, the overall reaction from the escorts was that they wanted to cooperate with the police . . . they wanted us to know what was going on. They were sick of pimps and madams taking a chunk of their money and clients abusing them. It is not a glamorous job at all; some made good money but they were all paying for protection somewhere along the line. Two of the escorts we met had to pay £80 per day just be allowed to operate. On some days that was all they made after rent and bills. I felt particularly sorry for a young Kenyan girl who we found working on her own. She was not committing any offence at all, so we were not interested in pursuing her. We just made sure she had a phone number to ring if she needed help. Unfortunately for her we had Borders Agency Staff with us and they identified her as an over-stayer; her student visa had expired. She was eventually deported. We had seized a few documents from the house and I found a letter from a relative in Kenya, thanking her for the money she had sent over. Basically she was paying for food, for clothes and for her younger siblings to go to school. This sort of thing must happen all the time. Since then we have seen a big rise in the amount of Eastern Europeans arriving to work in brothels."

"If things progress on this job, do you think it is likely that the escorts will still want to cooperate?" Albert could see an opportunity.

"I can only hope they will. Most of them think they are breaking the law regardless of where they are working or who with. Once you get to explain things they are generally okay. Proving prostitution is easy; all the evidence is on their website. You then phone up and get a menu of services, make an appointment and send a test purchase operative (TPO) in to confirm the brothel. Once the offer of sex is made for a price, the evidence is complete. The TPO then makes a tactical retreat before anything happens."

"But surely we are not interested in prosecuting escorts . . . it is the pimps we should be after?" said a forthright Alison.

"Exactly. That is how we set about it when did with the Home Office initiatives. I have suggested scoping exercises, intelligence reviews and a central database but it remains a low priority. If you can't catch them importing drugs, why not go after them in different ways? The Doyles seem to be the main players at the moment, but there are one or two others who still make good money. The Doyles have forced quite a few out of business." Mick must have had his fair share of set-backs, but he had stuck to his task.

He continued. "The last excuse was that the risk assessment required for a visit to a brothel by a TPO was too unpredictable. In reality it is more dangerous to visit a drugs den with any amount of people in the premises, than a brothel with one or two women inside. Plus the fact the houses or flats they use are much easier to watch."

Miles could see that the discussion was rapidly becoming a review of recent failings, so he moved the meeting on.

"I know we have a meeting planned for Friday morning at CC. In the meantime we need a cover story for the staff who will be working on this and the two young women are a priority. I also think there will be few more once we get going. Albert will be running the job for FCT, Susan for CC. I suggest all the documents are stored at CC for the time being and we make a start on Noone's phone billing and computer activity sooner rather than later. There is an overtime allocation for this, but do not go mad."

Steve Taylor had reviewed the intelligence belonging to Graeme and Colin Doyle. There were a number of pages with general information, sightings and vehicles they used. None of the females associated with them had the names Lexi or Becky. He then asked if there was an operational name.

"Blimey, my fault" said Albert. "It slipped my mind yesterday, but I have a suggestion – how about *Neon* as it is time we shone a light on this whole issue."

"I'm impressed" remarked Bill "I was expecting something like Gallowgate, or Gazza or Shearer".

"Neon it is. Thank you Albert; I see where you are coming from." Miles was running out of time. "Make sure we have some progress to discuss on Friday. Bill, Albert, I will be over to FCT later today to discuss the cuts. I've got Bill's email with the latest update so it sounds like we are almost there."

The meeting broke up and Albert told Dave and Alison to meet him at the Terrace Café before going back to the office.

Bill had to go for his retirement interview at HR. "What on earth do they want to know? I have never been asked my opinion about the organisation before and now they want to see me with two days to go."

"Better late than never Bill. See you at FCT later on. We'll have to use Plan B for the names out of the hat but I will explain everything then." Albert's plan required an assistant.

"Plan B? What happened to Plan A? The last time I got involved in one of your plans we ended up in front of the Chief."

"Yes, but I saved his backside years ago so we were never in any danger, plus the fact he was almost retired too and he was in a good mood."

Albert swiftly left FI and made his way across to the Terrace Café. All he wanted was to arrange a cover story and let Dave and Alison know they would soon be joined by Scott, Brian, Hughie and as many others as possible. Alison was ready with a credible and perfectly timed cover story.

"We have just received a twat of an email from the CPS about the Wallsend file. They want about 20 issues clarified and a load of documents copied for disclosure. It has gone to Jody too, so there will be no suspicions. We'll have to spend some time on it, but the deadline for a reply is not until next Friday so we can do other things. For once the CPS have done us a favour."

"Our luck must be in. Just to let you know you will have some help soon. Pat Noone has decided to go so that will be a priority for the Super once today is over and we have the five names to give him. If anyone asks where we have been, tell them FI had another development job but we have knocked it back for the time being. Jody and Alan's operation is enough for now."

The rest of the team were out and about working on Jody and Alan's drugs job, with only Hughie in the office acting as the command centre for communications and computer checks.

Albert wondered how things were going.

"It is a bit quiet to be honest . . . looks like there is no activity at either address. They must have run out of gear." Hughie sounded bored.

"Anyway Hughie, I have been thinking about your welfare. I'm not sure you are getting enough vitamin D, after all you have not left that desk for days. When is the last time you saw the sun?"

"Ha ha" said Hughie in a less than interested response. "I look forward to your jokes, I really do" Hughie pretended to yawn.

"Can you get everyone back for 3pm please Dracula? We will have to do the draw for the staff cuts. If it is not busy they can come back before that if Jody and Alan are happy."

Hughie rang Jody and put Albert's request to her.

"Fan-fucking-tastic" came the reply, "We will be back soon."

Albert retreated to an office and rang Mick Miller as he had thought of a few more questions since their earlier meeting. Albert was to the point.

"Are there any informants we can use and how easy is it to locate the brothels?"

Mick explained that it would be easy to get the addresses. All that was needed was an authorised TPO, then a phone call to get the details. Sometimes the address is given in the first call and sometimes they will instruct the 'punter' to go to a nearby street and then give him the actual address when he makes another call.

Mick was not aware of any other likely sources of information.

Albert began to feel frustrated at the pace of the investigation. The lack of knowledge he had in relation to prostitution offences was not helping and he was beginning to wonder why most of the issues talked about since the start of Operation Neon seemed so unfamiliar. In 28 years of service, he had not even met an escort or raided a brothel. He had watched a couple of documentaries about prostitution in Holland and the USA, but there was little he could transfer from that to the problems facing FCT.

The rest of the team began to arrive back at the office, relieved to be away from the boredom of watching nothing happen. Albert asked everyone to be in the office at 3pm for the draw, as one person was still needed to make up the five who had to go. He assumed everyone knew who had volunteered and Jill Crawford confirmed that it was common knowledge.

Neil and Jimmy were still grumbling about the draw being unfair, but Albert responded by telling them it was the way it had to be done and the sooner the better. There were vacancies up for grabs and it would suit those who were leaving to be first in the queue.

"If we dilly-dally talking about it and repeating things over and over again, chances will be lost. The DI and the Super have arranged with HR to give the volunteers the first option on the current vacancies, so we are going to get on with it. Is that understood?"

Albert needed the staff cuts resolved and it was obvious to everyone that he would not be swayed. His frustration with Operation Neon was surfacing in other ways and he wanted to clear the decks and make progress.

Bill Reynolds arrived and took Albert to one side. "The Super is beginning to panic now about the draw. He knows we can't lose anyone crucial to Neon, so he is worried about losing a key member of staff. I told him you had a plan so what is it? Please keep it simple Albert."

"It's easy, there are four volunteers so you write the eleven remaining sets of initials on this bit of paper, with this pen. Before you do that, write SB on this bit of paper."

Bill did as he was told.

"I will keep this separate piece in my pocket and when I do the draw I will remarkably pull out SB because it will already be in my hand. All we have to do then is get rid of the other pieces before anyone checks them."

Bill ran through the pitfalls in his mind, but reluctantly agreed as it was getting too late to come up with a plan C. He did suggest using a carrier bag instead of a hat as this would hide Albert's hand.

"Good thinking" agreed Albert "You are as devious as I am."

"Bollocks. How did you think this one up?"

"We used it 20-odd years ago. We were all drinking on duty one day after a job which had gone wrong and we decided to do the debrief in the Crown, instead of the office. There was a pain-in-the arse uniform Inspector who was always after us and someone must have tipped him off. Old Harry Williams saw him through the window as he pulled up outside and he saw Harry, so he told us all to get out the back door while he delayed him. Harry knew he was caught and was eventually fined three day's pay for drinking on duty. He was skint at the time so we ran a raffle and made sure Harry won first prize using the same plan, just with duplicate raffle tickets."

Bill wanted to know what the prize was.

"A bottle of whisky. Harry was grateful for the raffle money which covered his wages and we all drank the whisky. Happy days."

"So you celebrated getting caught drinking on duty, by drinking on duty again?"

"In a nutshell, but that was a long time ago. Don't tell the Super about the plan, as he will probably pass out."

Bill had little else he could add and Albert's story reminded him of how much the police service had changed. The days of parade rooms filled with smoke, misogyny and a drinking culture had long gone.

Miles Ashley was indeed worried about the draw and he came back to FCT earlier than expected. Both Albert and Bill tried to reassure him but he started to quote the odds on Sam's name coming out of the hat. Bill suggested a last minute call to HR to allow them to pick a name, but Miles had already made that enquiry and had drawn a blank.

Albert tried to ease the tension. "If Sam does not come out of the hat, then I suppose we will have to do the best we can. He might still elect to go . . . who knows?"

Miles was beginning to sense the complacency of the other two. But before he had a chance to process his thoughts a while longer, he threw a massive spanner in the works.

"I will do the draw. It was my idea so it is right that I carry it through. This is Bill's last week and it is not fair on Albert. So I will pull the name out of the hat."

Albert and Bill's plan had crashed before they had even put the names in the carrier bag.

"It will be out of this bag. Bill has it ready to go." Albert was resigned to the inevitable.

Miles then said he would like to meet the team for five minutes before the draw and explain how the budget cuts had forced the loss of staff. He also had to leave promptly afterwards.

"I think they would appreciate a few words. I will follow you both along to the main office in two minutes; I must phone HR to make sure they have held all the vacancies until we tell them who is going." Bill began to look for the correct number on his mobile.

Miles and Albert gathered the team and Miles ran through the financial facts and figures behind the most recent cuts. Neil and Alan were the only ones who asked what the Force was doing to ensure there were no more. Miles was unable to answer as it was way beyond his sphere of influence.

Bill appeared with the bag and Miles told everyone he was going to do the draw, apologising again for the way they had to do everything so quickly.

Albert could not bring himself to look as Miles put his hand in the bag. He stared at the map on the wall of the Force area and wished he was miles away. Berwick upon Tweed would be good, he thought.

Miles shuffled the bag and Bill said "I have included the initials of all eleven who want to stay. We are very grateful to the volunteers. Is everyone happy to go ahead?"

There were a few mumbled replies and nods.

"Okay then it is over to Superintendent Ashley to do the honours."

"It's going to be me, I'm sure" said Jimmy. "My dream will come true this time."

"Big tart" said Jody in her usual diplomatic way.

Albert was frozen to the spot, impersonating an Easter Island statue. He could not afford to lose Alison, or Dave, or Brian, Hughie, Scott . . . .

Miles pulled a folded piece of paper out of the bag.

"Okay, the initials are . . . . SB."

Sam looked around at his colleagues and smiled. If it had been a fix, it had been a good one, but as he had not objected to the draw, he stood up and shook hands with Bill and then Miles. Sam told them to give him five minutes and he would think about where he wanted to go.

Albert was still on Easter Island. It took a shove by Bill to bring him back to reality.

Bill and Albert retreated to the side office after a few minutes of general chat with the team.

"How lucky was that?" exclaimed Albert. "I thought we were knackered."

Bill did not reply and quickly emptied the bag of the remaining ten bits of paper. He began to put them in his back pocket.

"Hang on, hang on, let me have a look." Albert made a grab for them and the three he managed to wrestle from Bill's grasp all had the initials SB.

"So there was no chance anyone else would come out, you old so and so" said Albert as he realised Bill had replaced the eleven bits of paper.

"Needs must" replied Bill "I did not have time to tell you and it was worth it because your face was a picture when the Super read the initials out."

Both Bill and Albert felt sorry for Sam, as he had been a good team member and his experience would be missed. Sam quickly made it known that anywhere in the City Centre would be okay by him; if not, further north would be his second choice.

Bill rang HR and secured all the first choice vacancies for the volunteers. A confirmation email landed in Bill's queue twenty minutes later, so he forwarded it to all concerned asking them to choose a date for their official transfer.

### Thursday 1st August

With the HR problems now out of the way, Miles, Bill and Albert had a collective sense of relief. Their mood was made even better when Pat, Sam and John asked for some leave before joining their new departments, meaning they would all effectively leave FCT the next day. Tommy and Jill would leave the following Friday.

Miles called to see Bill and Albert at FCT and they reflected on an eventful few days. Miles could not hide his delight at Pat Noone leaving so soon. It meant that all the available resources could be put in to Operation Neon. He went on to explain.

"Can we scrap all the ongoing operational and development jobs as soon as Noone has left? We will the brief the team and allocate jobs. The Chief wants Operation Neon actioned and cleared up in a few weeks. She wants to have regular updates starting on Monday. CC have been told to offer as much assistance as they can, but FCT will be doing most of the work. We must make sure there is no one else involved at FCT, so I have asked CC to check all FCT mobile billing and computer activity before Monday to make sure there is no connection to the Doyles or the brothels we know about."

Bill and Albert confirmed that this would give peace of mind, but neither of them had any suspicions.

"Alan's brains are often in his underpants, but I don't think he is dishonest and Derek would fall in love every time he went to see an escort and want to marry them" added Albert.

"And another thing," continued Miles "as from Monday Albert will be Temporary Detective Inspector and one of the team will get some acting-up experience in his job. Albert will work with Susan Fenwick on all the details and make sure there is coordination between the two departments. I hope this makes sense to you both."

Albert was surprised to hear that Miles had put so much faith in him, but he was more than happy to see the job through.

Miles Ashley was certainly getting involved and he seemed as agitated as Bill and Albert about Pat Noone's activities.

"One last thing before I go; Mick Miller has been told to work with you on this job. He has more knowledge about sex work in our area than anyone, as you know. I think he will be keen to see things getting done and CC will do some checks on him too, but I know there won't be anything to worry about. I am out of Force for the rest of today at a meeting in Durham, but text if you need me. Otherwise I will see you tomorrow at CC. That will be your last ever meeting Bill? I bet you are relieved."

Miles was in a hurry as usual and he left Bill and Albert to get on with the job in hand.

Albert needed to continue with some basic enquiries, but with Pat Noone still in the office for one more day, there had to be some secret manoeuvrings. He texted Dave, Alison and Scott to meet him away from the office. The Terrace café was always a favourite, but other members of the team used it so Albert chose the canteen at the local hospital. It was busy enough to allow them to blend in and they made good sandwiches.

All four arrived at almost the same time. Dave and Alison had no idea Scott was also invited and for one moment they thought the venue change had been a disaster. Albert soon put them at ease.

"Scott has been aware of Pat's activities for a while and he reported his suspicions through the proper channels. I just want you all to know as much, so we can get some progress made. We need to review what we have got so far and allocate some enquiries. I would like to have as much as possible for the meeting tomorrow."

Albert went on to explain that the rest of the team would soon be joining them and Operation Neon would be their only job until further notice. Scott was updated with the contact that had been made with Frank Drysdale at Holly Gardens. The conversation then turned to Lexi and Becky. There were no clues from the intelligence system and Mick Miller was not aware of either woman. The best chance they had was to trawl through the escort web sites and hope they could match a name with the description Frank had provided. Alison pointed out that this could mean viewing the profiles of several hundred escorts and Frank indicated that they had numerous working names.

"Tattoos" said Albert. "Can he recall what they were and who had what?"

"We can try. I'll contact Frank as soon as we finish. He is expecting a call today as we told him we would be in touch to make sure he was okay" said Alison.

Albert then went through some of the other information that was likely to be useful. Dave explained that the vehicle registration supplied by Frank was not one of the Doyle's cars, but one used by one of their associates called Barry Fawcus. He was 33 years old and had convictions for burglary, assault and criminal damage. He had last been arrested two years previously for a domestic assault which went nowhere, as his partner at the time refused to provide any details following the initial complaint. There was a suspicion that she had been under duress, but without proof the CPS could not proceed. She appeared to have gone off with someone else. Fawcus had not been in trouble since, apart from a fixed penalty ticket.

Fawcus matched the description given by Frank and it would be easy to see how he would be mistaken for one of the Doyles. He was overweight, bald and in the same age range.

Alison had asked Brian about the phone seized at Holly Gardens. There was not a lot of information as the phone was seldom used. There were only six numbers stored on it; Frank's brother called Malcolm, Mrs Baker, his Doctor, Chemist, Benefits and a number for his electric supplier. There were some texts from a number ending 6677 which was most likely to be Lexi and Becky. Frank had outlined how he had received a message after they had left, so there was little doubt he had told the truth.

"We need the subscriber for the number attached to that text. Can you ask CC to put it through at their end as soon as possible as it is the best chance we have to get more on Lexi and Becky?" Albert was pleased there was one positive enquiry.

Albert was interested to know if Pat Noone had discussed the cuts with anyone and what his thoughts were on leaving. Dave and Alison had not had any contact with him, but Scott had been observing every move Pat made.

"He was pretty relaxed about it as far as I can tell. He did say that he knew he was not one of the best thought of in the office and that he had a feeling he would have to go sooner rather than later. It was Tommy who said to him that he could not expect anything different, as he had not worked hard enough. Tommy gets annoyed when people spend all day on their mobiles instead of doing what he calls proper police work."

Albert asked if Pat had any idea whatsoever that they were on to him.

"I doubt it" replied Scott. "Straight after the meeting yesterday when Sam's name was pulled out of the bag, he made a cup of tea for himself and sat looking at his personal phone. I think his mind is always elsewhere. The way we work at FCT means that we are generally with someone else all the time. Perhaps he will have more freedom to do what he wants when he leaves."

All of them knew there were others involved with Pat via 'punterdate' so Albert asked Scott to work with Steve Taylor at CC to research how it works. Access to the 'punterdate' database was going to be crucial.

Albert turned his attention to the following week. Unless there was an unexpected breakthrough with the search for Lexi and Becky, the team would have to identify all the brothel locations controlled by the Doyles.

Albert suggested that they all do some quick studying of the prostitution laws as it was a subject he had rarely looked at since training school. He assumed everyone was the same.

Alison was perhaps the most up to date with the legislation, as she explained that it had been part of her studies to pass the sergeant's exam.

"You are our expert then" concluded Albert. "Saves me a bit of time for me."

Albert wanted Alison to act up in his place as he knew she was entirely capable, but felt that he had to ask Hughie first. He had acted up on a few occasions previously. Hughie passed his sergeant's exam straight after he completed his probation, but had never applied for promotion. He was blessed with a fantastic memory which meant that passing the exam was a mere formality, but he was not comfortable in a leadership role. Albert decided to approach Hughie later and ask him to be the disclosure officer on Operation Neon, hopefully appealing to his methodical, structured outlook.

Albert finished the meeting by going over the drugs warrant at Frank's house. There was little to be done until the forensic examinations of the wrappings were completed. The lab had estimated six weeks before they would even start the task. There were no other lines of enquiry as the drug traffickers had covered their tracks well.

"We will have to extend Frank's bail at some stage. I suppose Brannigan had already advised him that would be the case?" asked Albert.

Alison was on the same wave length "No worries . . . we will sort that out closer to the time. He did say that he had received a letter from him, arranging a consultation before the bail date early next month, after Brannigan's annual leave. Apparently he has a place in Spain he goes to."

Albert looked surprised "I'm not sure how a ginger, pale-faced Englishman like Brannigan will cope with the Spanish sun in August. He must stay indoors most of the time."

Albert returned to the office and sat down to catch up with his emails. Amongst the normal circulars, requests for annual leave, demands from the CPS and other routine updates, Miles Ashley had forwarded an email from Susan Fenwick at CC.

She outlined how they had decided to short-cut the checks on all the staff by looking directly at the logs relating to any known brothels. There was only one member of the team who had looked at the more than one of them and that was of no surprise. Pat Noone had viewed the logs relating to three brothels identified by complaints to the police from members of the public. He may well have looked at others, but as those locations were yet to be identified, it was impossible to progress. Holly Gardens had been checked by Hughie and Brian, but this was in relation to the drugs warrant. Surprisingly, Pat Noone had not checked that address.

Pat Noone had also looked at the records for Colin and Graeme Doyle on many occasions. Only one other team member had accessed the record of Colin Doyle and that was Scott Craig who had updated some intelligence in February.

She had also tasked an analyst to run a search for Superior Escorts through all the phone billing attached to FCT for the past six months. This had proved negative, including Pat Noone, who presumably was not that stupid to use his work phone to contact escorts.

Susan Fenwick concluded that it was unlikely that anyone at FCT was involved with Pat Noone's corrupt activities and the Doyles. She did emphasise that these were just initial findings and further work could be carried out, when, and if, more specific requests were made.

Miles was clearly relieved and satisfied at these findings, as his comments on the email reflected those thoughts. Albert was more or less happy, but further corroboration of Pat's criminality made him both angry and disappointed at the same time. On top of that, they were still no closer to finding Lexi and Becky, or any other young woman caught up in the same circumstances.

### Friday 2nd August

Bill Richards' last operational day and his last meeting. He accompanied Albert to CC for a 9am start.

"Shame my last shift has to be about corruption" reflected Bill as they approached the CC wing. "If anyone had told me that 32 years ago I would have thought they were mad. If I don't get a chance later on Albert, I hope things go well. This all leaves a bad taste and I'm sure that you and the rest of the team will get it sorted out."

Bill offered one piece of advice before they entered the building.

"Do what we always do on a job - assume nothing and check everything. I think that will be even more relevant this time. There will be some twists, turns and surprises before you get to the end of it. I have a strange feeling about all of this."

"Why is that Bill?" Albert wanted to tap into Bill's thoughts in case there was not another chance during the day.

"Call it what you like, instinct, intuition . . . I don't know. I could be wrong but we have not paid enough attention to what goes on in the world of prostitution. It has always been there for us to find, but we simply chose not to look. We have hidden it from ourselves and that could prove to be a disaster. I can't think of another kind of criminality which is so obvious, yet left alone by everyone. All I can say is good luck and . . ."

Bill's phone rang at that point "It is Miles Ashley. Hang on a second Albert".

Bill answered "Morning Sir, we are just outside the building."

"Morning Bill. Can you apologise to the meeting for me? I have been summoned by the Chief to give her an update. I will be over as soon as I can."

Bill and Albert then went straight into the meeting, passing on Miles Ashley's apologies.

DI Susan Fenwick thought it best to go through all the established facts and the ongoing work for the benefit of everyone. Mick Miller had been able to update his information, concluding that the Doyles were currently running about nine brothels, with approximately 45 to 50 escorts. Not all escorts worked in the brothels and some were outcalls only, going to hotels or punter's homes. They would require drivers or taxis so the amount of people involved was likely to be higher than initially thought. The list of associates he had produced included Barry Fawcus. Bill thanked CC for doing all the background checks, explaining that as from Monday Albert was Temporary DI and would be overseeing Operation Neon for FCT. The entire team was to be allocated to the operation.

Alison, Dave and Scott updated the meeting with their enquiries so far. Frank was still being cooperative, but he was struggling to recall the tattoos that Lexi and Becky had so they could be identified from the web photos. He was reasonably sure that one of them had a name tattooed on the inside of their left arm, possibly a boy's name. Alison was in touch with Frank via the mobile she had given him.

Scott outlined how he and Steve had looked at 'punterdate' but to get anywhere with it they would have to join. This would need authorisation and a secure internet connection. The general theme of the website and the App was to allow punters to exchange comments and recommendations via a secure network, without identifying themselves. They would only be known by nicknames or numbers. There was a monthly fee, so a financial investigation would reveal if Pat Noone subscribed. The site boasted that they have over ten thousand members in the UK and the registered office was possibly in Manchester.

Miles arrived just as the problem of appointing an analyst to the job was being discussed.

He was slightly out of breath and was grateful for the tea laid on by CC. He took a seat and began to explain where he had been.

"As you know I have been to see the Chief to give her an update. She has decided that arrests have to be made by next Friday at the latest. She originally said she would review the operation next week, but that has changed."

Miles held up his hands in defensive appreciation of the surprised responses from around the table.

"I know, I know. I asked for more time but she was adamant we move things on. Her opinion is that we will not be able to keep the operation quiet and the other corrupt officers will cover their tracks, making them harder to find and even harder to convict. She keeps referring to a similar problem in her previous force. She does have a point but at the same time we don't have any statements or evidence to rely on as yet, never mind a plan to arrest and interview."

Bill's break in Scotland looked more attractive by the minute. Albert joked that he might join him. Miles continued.

"There is some good news. She has authorised a reasonable overtime budget and she has also indicated that any applications for phone billing, surveillance and technical assistance will be prioritised."

Albert was first to react "Can I go ahead and call staff in for the weekend. We cannot afford to leave things for two days when we have such little time."

"Do it." Miles left no doubt that the operation had to be fast-tracked.

70

Susan Fenwick suggested that everyone should work out of HQ, as there was less chance of compromise over the weekend. This was agreed and all available staff were to be at CC by 8am the following day.

Miles followed Albert out of the meeting as he needed to talk over the Chief's decision with him.

"She would not listen to a word I said Albert, so I appreciate the difficulties we now have. I emphasised the need to make sure we have as much evidence as possible to secure a conviction and that one week was not enough. She acknowledged that but still wanted the job done by next Friday. It is difficult to negotiate with her, as one minute she agrees with you, then she has second thoughts and ends up disagreeing with you on points that were all agreed at the beginning. I end up discussing the same things over and over again. No wonder her staff officer is on the sick with stress."

"So will she change her mind and give us more time?" asked Albert.

"Who knows? Let's see where we are on Monday."

Miles then wondered about Bill.

"Are we having a little gathering today for Bill? I have kept things as clear as possible."

"Yes. Can you make it for around 2pm? We have something small to give him as he is planning a proper function in September."

"See you then" responded Miles.

With a clear mandate and little time, Albert organised his team. He approached Hughie about a possible disclosure officer's role and his thoughts on acting up. He chose the former as his preference. That cleared the way for Alison to be Acting Sergeant. Alison, Dave and Scott had already been warned to work the weekend, so Albert had to concoct a plan to get as many of the others involved, without alerting Pat Noone or the volunteers who were about to go on annual leave.

Albert decided that he had an opportunity after the team had met to see Bill at 2pm in recognition of his last day. He could let those who were off the following week to go early and keep the rest back to discuss future work. It had to sound as informal as possible.

Just as Albert was pondering the details of his plan, Pat Noone appeared and said he was just about to tidy his desk and submit any outstanding paperwork.

"Will you need a statement from me about Holly Gardens?" asked Pat.

Albert was tempted to make comment about his free sex arrangement, but told him that the job was dependent on forensics and should they need a statement he would get an email.

"The same goes for the recent obs; everything will be in the surveillance log so don't worry about statements until the time comes." Albert was already sub-consciously removing Pat from the chain of evidence. He was not one of them anymore; he was corrupt.

Albert took the conversation away from police work.

"Are you going anywhere next week on annual leave?"

"No, I will be at home most of the time. I need to tidy the place up a bit as I am thinking of putting it on the market." Replied Pat. "I have split up with my girlfriend and she has moved out, so it has been a rough week on the home front I can tell you."

"I thought you were a bit pre-occupied. Hopefully things will sort themselves out. Are you around at 2pm for Bill?"

Albert could not help thinking the girlfriend had made a timely escape. Perhaps she knew what he was doing behind her back.

"Definitely. Jody has a card and a bottle for him. We owe her a few quid each." Pat soon became engrossed in his personal phone, so Albert took his chance.

"If we need to contact you, what is the best number? I will need your job phone from you."

"Er, this one I suppose. I will write the number down and give it to you before I leave."

Albert returned to his emails and his plans. He did not want to push things with Pat.

The office soon filled up and the usual Friday afternoon feel-good factor was apparent. Jody made sure everyone signed the card for Bill, including Miles Ashley who wanted to know if he should make a speech or leave it until the function in September. Albert knew Bill did not like a fuss, so a few brief words would be best. There was plenty of time to work on a speech; stories such as the time Bill hit a

72

horse and ended up with his patrol car in a river; his first promotion board when he could not answer the first six questions so he stood up and announced that he would save time and come back the following year, could all be included.

Bill arrived and Miles presented him with the card and his favourite single malt. He stuck to the script and kept things brief, thanking Bill for all his hard work and how the team had prospered under his leadership.

Bill also kept it short, mainly because he was struggling with the emotion of it all. He had not benefitted from a long lead up to his retirement and it was all a bit raw. He now had only a couple of hours to go before he was classed as a pensioner. He told everyone how proud he was of the team and their achievements. He mentioned the East End Club function he had arranged and in conclusion he said:

"This job is like no other. The day you start is the day you promise to look after the vulnerable and the underdog. There are times when you witness human behaviour at its worst and other times when it is at its best. Our job is to make sure those who offend are dealt with. We don't decide guilt, we simply provide the material for others to do that. In doing so we ensure that victims and witnesses have the confidence to allow us to do the job we love doing. I am sure that you all agree with me. I wish you all the best for the future."

Bill struggled with his last sentence and he was soon engulfed by those colleagues standing closest to him who all wanted to express their thanks. Pat Noone was not part of that immediate group and Albert noticed how he stood apart, red in the face and looking dejected. Perhaps Bill's words had struck a chord; he may be feeling guilty or he could just be feeling sorry for himself. Whatever the case, he was going to have a chance to explain everything in seven days' time.

Albert was conscious that there were others who would be leaving and he took the chance to highlight the contributions they had made. He then took those same ones to one side and told them that they could go as soon as they were ready.

Albert asked everyone else to stay for a short time so he could allocate jobs for the following week.

Bill informed Miles that he intended to come in on 30$^{st}$ August to hand over his warrant card and within a few moments he was gone. Albert, Jody and Alison watched from the window as Bill appeared in the car park below and drove off.

"Audrey has plans" said Albert. "In a few weeks he will wonder how he had the time to come to work in the first place."

By 3pm only the members of the team who were staying remained in the office. Albert checked that he could speak openly by taking a route around the office, ensuring the office was secure.

"Right. Phones off. Can you all sign this confidentiality form that I am about to send around. You may think that is unusual and you would be right. I am about to tell you about Operation Neon and nothing will be discussed outside this office. I cannot stress that enough. I think once you have read the caption at the top of the confidentiality form you will know it is extremely sensitive."

Albert waited until every member had signed the form.

Jody's patience was normally non-existent and Albert was fearing a 'swear-a-thon' if he waited any longer before starting the briefing.

"Operation Neon concerns corruption. One officer has been identified and we have perhaps two or more to find. There is a suspicion that those officers have been protecting pimps and been given escorts as rewards. We also know that some of the escorts are under duress and they need to be identified and safeguarded. That should be foremost in our thoughts. You will all be allocated roles in the operation and we have seven days to arrest those involved."

No one had the time to think of a question. Those who had no inkling of Operation Neon were hanging on every word.

"Alison, Dave and Scott are already aware of the intelligence we have and we will be assisted by CC and FI. The reason why I have asked you to stay behind today is that we need to start work on this immediately and there is overtime this weekend to make progress. We need to identify the brothels controlled by the Doyle Family as a matter of urgency. Work starts tomorrow at the CC offices, 8am prompt."

Derek was the one to ask the obvious.

"So who is the officer identified so far? Are we allowed to know?"

"Yes you are" Albert had somehow found it difficult to say his name at the start of the briefing.

"Pat Noone".

"What! Eh? Pat?" exclaimed Derek. "Who does he think he is?"

Jody jumped in with her thoughts "The fucking tosspot . . . that is probably why he keeps having domestics with his girlfriend. She has left him again you know."

Alan, Neil and Brian looked in a state of shock. Hughie wanted to know if this was the disclosure job Albert wanted him to take on.

"Yes it is."

"With pleasure" replied Hughie.

Jimmy was still processing the information from Albert.

"So let me get this straight . . . Pat has been shagging escorts provided by the Doyles for information. Is he for real? How does he think he could get away with that?"

"That is exactly it and we need to find the evidence to prove it. So can I expect a full turn out tomorrow?" asked Albert of his shell-shocked and stunned team.

Only Jody and Hughie were unsure as they had to make phone calls to sort out child care and sporting activities respectively. The rest confirmed they would be available.

Albert then realised that he should have told Polly that the week end was a write-off. He thought about phoning, but decided against it as he would be home sooner than planned.

Jody and Hughie confirmed that they would be at CC for 8am the next day, so Albert asked everyone to pack up and go home. The team members were unlikely to see much of their families over the next two weeks so they had to make the most of it.

As the briefing came to an end, Albert appreciated that there would be many more questions from the team. He asked them to wait until the next day when there would be more time to go through the detail. Until then, no one was to discuss what they had just heard.

Before leaving, Albert tidied his desk. Bill had left the policy book for him, signing it over at exactly 2pm. He had also left a note for Albert, suggesting they went out for a drink in between his break in Scotland and his holiday in Cyprus.

Albert took a few moments to reflect on the work ahead. It was going to take a huge effort to get things arranged in seven days and they would need all the help they could get. Albert decided to contact Tommy and Jill, in the hope they would also be available.

With messages left, it was time to go home and explain how absent he was going to be to Polly.

# Chapter Three

# Assume Nothing,
# Check Everything

**Saturday 3<sup>rd</sup> August**

After a quiet night at home with Polly, mainly because she decided not to talk to him after learning of his weekend at work, Albert arrived at CC to be met by Steve Taylor and Mick Miller. The others were not far behind.

Tommy also turned in after confirming with Albert via texts. He was looking slightly bemused, so he was updated by Jody. Jill had not been in contact with Albert.

"What an arse hole" began Tommy. "So he was looking at escorts, not porn all the time? I saw him on his phone a few times and I just thought he was looking at women on porn sites. His phone is that big it was like a telly, you could not miss it. That internet has a lot to answer to."

"Not like the good old days of pen and paper, eh Tommy?" said Alison, pulling his leg.

"Well, just have a think. All the porn and paedophiles on various web sites. Then there is all the fraud. It is all down to the internet. I preferred it when you used to cut out a coupon from the newspaper, get a postal order and send for what you wanted. There was no problem then. Was there Albert?"

"Actually, there was not. But lets' not get started with all that. I take it you had some suspicions Tommy?" Albert wanted to know more.

"I just thought he was lazy. He started okay when he first arrived, but lately he has shown no interest. I was stuck on obs with him a few times and all he did was mess about on his phone all day. I could see he was looking at women with nowt on, or in their frillies, so in the end I told him to switch his phone off or I would refuse to work with him in the future and questions would be asked. After that he always avoided me and worked with Scott."

"Did he try to explain what he was doing on his phone?" asked Jimmy.

"No, he acted like there was no problem. He just dismissed everything anybody said. He was arrogant at times." Tommy summed up what he thought of Pat Noone.

Albert and Susan Fenwick had drawn up a list of priorities. Brian Couley, Mick Miller, Steve Taylor and Neil McAllister were tasked with searching the internet for escort agencies connected to the Doyles and any other addresses they were linked to. Everyone else, apart from Hughie who already had a mountain of documents to sort out, was allocated to enquiries away from the office.

Alison and Dave were told to meet up with Frank as soon as possible to try to get every last bit of information they could. Derek and Jimmy would be partners as would Jody and Alan. Albert wanted Scott to work with him until there was someone else free.

"Last few things before we start." Albert called everything to order. "As from Monday, Alison will be acting up in my place as I will be Temporary DI. The Superintendent has decided that continuity is best until this operation is sorted out. Alison has a far better knowledge than me with prostitution law, so I will be depending on her in more ways than one. Everyone happy?"

Alison contacted Frank and he was available at 10am. He said he was keen to see them. Scott was assigned as back up whilst Albert got to grips with his paperwork and discussed administration with Susan.

Within a short space of time, four brothels were identified and the enquiry teams were told to go and find them, assess them and return with all the facts they could muster.

Albert also spoke to Hughie, finalising a plan for all the information that was going to be accumulated. Hughie would see every document and he was best placed to make the links between the evidence as it came in. Computer spread sheets and charts were all very good once all the information was to hand, but the human

78

brain was still the best tool for spotting a potential link or breakthrough.

Strategies, meetings, briefings and discussions were also all very good and necessary, but there were times when things had to be *made* to happen. The FCT was good at taking an operation from scratch and developing it in to a full blown investigation. The only problem it had with Operation Neon was that it had to be done in very quick time. Enquiries that should take a few weeks had to be done in days; the sensitivity of the case was an added complexity and this was before anyone had interviewed a victim or a witness.

Susan Fenwick and Albert knew they had a job on their hands. Neither had experience of dealing with sex workers and there was no one in the Force they could call upon, apart from Mick Miller.

"Should we think about contacting another Force who may be able to advise us?" asked Susan.

"Yes I think we should" agreed Albert, "But which one? We can't go to Teesside as yet; the Doyles operate down there too. Perhaps we should go further afield."

"I can always try my counterparts in CC at Teesside. They should be able to recommend someone if there is any doubt."

Susan and Albert decided to make discreet enquiries at the start of the working week.

Alison and Dave wasted no time and collected Frank a couple of streets away from his house, then drove to their meeting place close to the river. Frank was in a good mood.

"I have been looking forward to seeing you since last night." Frank was smiling as he sat up in the back seat to get their attention.

"Why what happened last night?" asked Dave in anticipation.

"Lexi's surname is Morrison. It came to me when I was in bed listening to the radio. The Doors record came on from the sixties and their lead singer was Jim Morrison. It was then that it clicked in my head. Lexi told me a story about her mother going to her school and the teacher calling her Mrs Morrison. Lexi had been in trouble so her Mam was asked to go in to see the headmaster. Lexi began impersonating him as he gave her a ticking off and saying Mrs Morrison you have to do this with Lexi and Mrs Morrison you must take more responsibility."

"Are you sure Frank? This is great for us as we can now have a chance of finding her." Alison could see that Frank was confident, but she still wanted to make sure.

"Absolutely. I was going to text you last night but it was about midnight so I thought best to leave it until Monday. I did not know you worked weekends. I would be so relieved if you found her and Becky. They are just kids, hardly grown up at all. Their lives are not their own."

Dave told Frank to keep his phone handy and they would let him know if there was any news. When they dropped Frank off, he walked away, smiling. He knew he had made a difference.

Alison immediately phoned Albert with the surname, so checks could be made whilst they travelled back to CC.

Hughie quickly found a record that was more than likely Lexi. Her full name was Alexis Ruby Morrison, aged 20 and she had been in trouble for shoplifting and possession of drugs since the age of 16. She had a number of addresses attached to her record, but none of them was current. Some of them were places she was found after going missing from home. The last photo of her dated back two years, when she had been 18. There was no recent intelligence and no mention of the Doyles or Barry Fawcus.

Alison and Dave arrived back and were eager to learn of any developments. They gathered around Hughie's computer and went through every detail. Hughie brought up the latest photo for their benefit.

"That has to be her." Alison was sure they had the correct person. "She has long dark hair and lots of make up on, just as Frank described her. She looks very young."

The lack of a current address was the only disappointment. Her list of associates included her mother, Diane Morrison. Her records included an address that she had been seen at only a few weeks earlier following a report of criminal damage. The crime report attached to the incident described how her windows had been smashed by 'persons unknown'.

"That is where we have to start" directed Albert. "We have little else to go on so I want Alison and Jody to go and talk to her and see

80

how it goes. Make up a story about why you need to speak to her and avoid the real reason. See if she lets you know where Lexi is."

Alison and Jody arranged to meet up and travel to see Diane Morrison at 12 Hawthorn Place without delay.

Jody had worked the area around Hawthorn Place in Newcastle some years before as a uniform PC. She recalled that it was mainly flats, very few houses and a bit neglected. As with many council estates, there were residents who had lived in their street for years and had taken pride in it. Some had even bought their homes when the neighbourhood was in better repair, only to regret it as the lack of maintenance and investment in the other properties led to a sad decline.

12 Hawthorn Place was a second floor flat, built in the 1950s, accessed via a security door leading to a concrete staircase. Jody and Alison decided to use a story about an incident in the city centre, which Lexi had witnessed, but had not left correct details.

Their plan did not get very far as the security door was locked and there was no answer on the buzzer for number 12. They retreated to the car and decided to wait five minutes or so in case there was any activity. Any longer and they would start to get unwanted attention.

They soon had no alternative but to go and park up somewhere a bit quieter, wait 20-30 minutes and go back.

Jody and Alison took the chance to discuss the revelations about Pat Noone.

"I hope he gets a good spell in prison. I cannot imagine what it would be like to be a copper in jail. I wonder if his girlfriend found out he was seeing escorts. What a wanker he must be." Jody clearly had no regard for him.

"If I found out my boyfriend was shagging about I would not even speak to him again. That would be it" replied Alison.

"I'm not sure my Hubby would even think about it. We might only do it once a month, in fact he would rather have a cup of tea and a chocolate biscuit. I could walk about the house starkers and he probably would not notice. He spends more time with his cars than he does with people. Useless twat."

Jody often spoke about her husband Andy in a derogatory way, but they had been married for 18 years and appeared content with each other, despite Jody's criticisms.

"He's good with the kids though and you have a lovely house. You have him well trained Jody."

"Aye, it took a few years to get him the way I wanted. When I married him his bloody Mother interfered all the time telling me what he liked to eat, what he liked to drink and how he needed this and that. Eventually I told her to fuck off as she was never away from the house. It caused a bit of trouble for a month or so, but I told him that he was married to me not his fucking Mother." Jody finished her rant. "Anyway, how is your love life?"

Alison paused and looked out of the window. "My current bloke is a bit clingy. He is not happy about me working the weekend and you have me thinking. . . . his Mother does everything for him, she goes to his flat and does his housework, cleaning, ironing and she even shops for him."

"Mammy's boy, get rid of him, another useless twat" advised Jody.

"He is not entirely useless . . . . " said Alison, smiling to herself.

"Is that right? But it won't be long before he gets on your wick."

Jody continued after a few moments pause.

"None of your blokes last all that long do they? The one before this Mammy's boy ate his food too loudly so you ditched him. Then there was the one who wore sunglasses you did not like, so he went the journey. Then the lad from the Navy who bought you that lovely necklace, he had funny hands according to you, so he only lasted a couple of weeks. You will have to be a bit more tolerant with men you know. Just keep it in your head that they all have their faults, you just need to try and make the best of it."

"I know, I know. They just irritate the life out of me sometimes . . look what Tommy did on his 25$^{th}$ wedding anniversary. Instead of booking a weekend away or a nice meal, he decided to re-arrange the living room furniture as a big surprise. His poor wife threw a wobbler and he could not work out why."

"Bollocks for brains, they are all the same. Having said that I will miss Tommy when he goes" said Jody.

"Yes, I'll miss all his daft phrases – my favourite is nipples like coat hangers."

"What about sharp as a button and eggs are bad for your colostomy. Those were corkers."

They both sat back and chuckled. Jody then recalled another of Tommy's phrases. "What about the time he told Jimmy that he was going to join the *Natural* Trust?"

"Eeeeh, what are we going to do without all our old codgers, Bill, Tommy, Sam . . . . and Albert cannot have that long to do before he retires" said Jody.

"Yes I was just thinking that last night. I prefer working with blokes than an office full of women. When I did a stint on Public Protection there were more dramas in the office than on the streets. The DS spent most of her time going out for a coffee with her favourites, sorting out some sort of private calamity or another. Whoever was out and about got slagged off and then as soon as they came back everything was nicey-nicey. I only lasted a year and that felt like six months too long. I don't think you would have lasted five minutes with those lot, Jody."

"Probably not. It is much easier to deal with a grumpy old man than a drama queen. There are some who spend more time detecting gossip than solving crime."

About 20 minutes had passed and they decided to try 12 Hawthorn Place again. This time the buzzer was answered and they were allowed in. They climbed the two flights of stairs and came to the landing next to number 12. Jody knocked and stood back. The door was scratched and had been damaged near the bottom, as if someone had tried kicking it open.

After a few short moments a female voice asked who was there. Jody held up her warrant card to the spyglass.

"What do you want?" said the female.

"A minute of your time . . . we need some help" replied Jody.

The sound of a security chain and a mortice lock preceded the opening of the door. A woman aged about 40, dark hair and very slight build invited them in. The flat was very neat and tidy. Everything was arranged and in its place; the living room smelled of polish and air freshener. Nothing in the room looked new or expensive; there was a budget for everything and Diane had stuck to her limits.

"Thanks love." Jody wanted to put her at ease as she could see she was nervous.

"We just need to ask a couple of questions about Lexi. Are you her Mam?"

"I am. What has happened?"

"Nothing much, don't worry, she is a witness to an incident in the city centre and we need to trace her."

They quickly introduced themselves and Diane Morrison stated that she had not seen Lexi for weeks. She spoke very rapidly, using one word answers as often as she could. Jody and Alison could tell that Diane did not want the police at her door and she certainly did not want to be seen cooperating. That was her way of dealing with things, like so many in her situation.

Alison asked a few more questions about her relationship with Lexi. Jody noticed the old school photos on the sideboard and asked if she could look closer. Diane agreed, but remained reluctant to keep any conversation going. She lived alone in the flat. Lexi's father had left when she was two. She repeated that she had not seen Lexi for weeks and there was no point in continuing the conversation.

Jody tried another way to get through to Diane.

"Does Lexi work?"

"Work? She went to college and got her certificates, but she has never worked."

"You must have been proud of her when she passed her exams. What did she do at college?"

Diane still did not want to be drawn. "It was a beautician's course" was all she wanted to say.

"She likes her make-up then?" asked Jody.

She did not respond. The conversation was mainly one sided and Diane remained defensive.

Alison then asked about the damage to the door. Diane shook her head. She was not prepared to answer.

"Was it done as the same time as your windows?" Alison was taking a chance.

"What is this all about? Why are you here?" Diane wanted to force an end to the pressure she felt.

"We are here to help you Diane." Jody's tone and choice of words was designed to be a message to open up a little.

"We are also here to help Lexi" added Alison.

"How can you do that? You don't know where she is and neither do I. What are the police going to do, eh? eh?" Diane became agitated.

"Cards on the table Diane. We know she is in with the wrong people and we are here to start the process of trying to do the right thing. We know the police have been useless up to now, but give us a chance" said Jody.

"I did give you a chance. I told the copper when he came here who smashed the windows and why. Nothing happened. Two days later they kicked my door in. What the fuck are you going to do about it now? You are too late."

Alison explained that they were not from the local police and that they dealt with larger enquiries. She emphasised that they were only there because they had heard about Lexi and wanted to help her.

"Is she with Becky?" Alison decided to disclose as much as she could.

"Probably. It was Becky who got her in to all this in the first place." Diane looked straight at Alison. She was challenging her to talk about the real reason they were there.

"I don't want to upset you Diane, but I get the feeling you know as well as I do what Lexi and Becky have been doing. Are they working together in the same place?"

"As slappers, whores, prozzies - is that what you do not want to say? Stupid little tarts who have only themselves to blame? I have tried to get her home loads of times but there is no help from you lot, or social services or the rest of my family. No one is bothered, even the fucking doctor says he cannot do anything and he gave me a leaflet for the clap clinic. Great, thanks a million."

Diane Morrison was at the end of her tether. Her frustration was abundantly clear to both Alison and Jody. There was no alternative but to take Diane into their confidence and offer her the guarantee of positive action at long last.

Alison spoke plainly to her.

"Diane we are going to deal with the people who have Lexi doing what she does. I promise you that. If that does not happen you can tell the whole world that we let you down. The operation has already started, we have an entire team working with us and we need your help. Is there anything else I can say or do which will make you believe us?"

Alison and Jody were taking a huge risk with Diane. Was she likely to take their offer of help and in return tell them what she knew, or would she string them along and put an end to the operation by contacting the Doyles?

Diane did not answer. She stood and stared at Alison and then Jody. Could she trust them? Lexi had told her the police were bent and when her windows were smashed it was strange that nothing had been done about it, even though the name of the offender had been passed over.

"And how can I trust the police?" was Diane's eventual response.

Alison and Jody were now under even more pressure. Diane had asked a question that struck at the very heart of the problem.

Alison retrieved her warrant card from her bag. She took it out and offered it to Diane.

"You take my warrant card. Keep it if you think we won't do as we say. Then go and tell everyone you know, the telly, the papers or just put me on the internet. That would be my career over. All I can say is that we want to get the job done, lock up the bastards who have Lexi and get things turned around. I promise you that we will work as hard and as long as it takes."

Diane looked at the warrant card. She wanted one last piece of information.

"You will lock up everyone, even if they do the same job as you?"

"We will. That is at the top of our list." Alison had no cards left to play.

Diane was assured that the police needed her. They had passed her test.

"Okay. I cannot have you coming back here so I will give you my mobile number and we can meet up in about an hour. All I want is Lexi back, she was doing so well . . . . "

Diane broke down. This was the first time anyone had shown an interest, or discussed a solution to the agony she felt about Lexi. Diane just wanted an end to the sadness, the stress and her overwhelming feeling of helplessness.

Jody hugged her and thanked her for listening to them. They exchanged numbers and arranged to meet in an hour. Diane could not leave any earlier as she had arranged to see a neighbour to borrow a spare kettle. Her kettle had burnt out and she had no money for a replacement.

"We had better go to a good café then . . . you must be in need of good cup of tea" joked Jody.

Diane began to warm to the idea of helping Jody and Alison. She had nothing to lose and at least they gave her some hope.

"I need a good, strong cup of tea." Diane was small and fragile, but she had more than held her own with Jody and Alison.

"You will find her won't you? I can't live with the thought of what she is going through."

"We will and the job starts now. Give us a ring when you are ready" Jody and Alison left the flat, knowing that the next hour or so was going to feel a lot longer.

They drove to a car park about five minutes away and Alison phoned Albert. As usual he wanted to know everything in short space of time. This was always the way he worked, but the limitations on this job made him even more impatient.

"We have found Diane Morrison and spoken to her at length. She has had a terrible time with Lexi and she has not seen her for weeks."

"Go on, go on" urged Albert.

"She has agreed to meet us as soon as she can, probably by around 2 o'clock."

"And?"

"And what?"

"Is she going to tell us what is going on" Albert did not think he had to spell it out.

87

"I hope so. She does not trust the police. Can Hughie have a good look at the crime details for the incident where her windows were smashed? She says she gave a name to the police when she reported it. Nothing has been done according to her so it would be interesting to know before we met up."

"Five minutes" said Albert as he rung off.

Alison and Jody were used to Albert when he was on one of his missions. His outlook was simple; there is a solution to every problem and he wanted to find the solution as soon as possible.

"Could be worse" explained Jody. "We could end up with one of those promotion orientated nobbers who spend their days fretting over risk assessments. Albert just goes ahead regardless."

Alison could find Albert a nuisance sometimes, especially when he was pressuring for progress, but her own decision-making had improved after a few months of working with him.

"He does give you confidence to get on with things. He likes you to make your mind up and if it goes wrong he just tells you to put it right. I've learnt a lot from Albert and Bill."

"Aye, they are good gaffers." Jody knew she wound Albert up now and again with her crude remarks. "And he speaks to your face, not to your tits like Alan and Jimmy do."

"Thanks for that Jody."

They then went through the details they needed from Diane. A way of contacting Lexi would be a massive step forward; mobile numbers and addresses; friends and associates; bank details and benefits; her connections to the Doyles.

Albert then rang back.

"Right. The damage happened on 30th June just before midnight. PC Adrian Blair took the report from Diane Morrison. There are no offenders attached to the crime and it has been referenced off as undetected. PC Blair has logged no other crimes since that date and he has no current duties according to the computer. Bit of a mystery, but we'll get it sorted. Has Diane rang yet?"

"No not yet. She said about an hour so we will just wait." Alison had little doubt Diane would ring when she said.

"How did you get on with her? Will she put pen to paper?" asked Albert. He was already jumping hurdles before he could even see them.

"She needs a lot of support and reassurance before we take a statement Albert, but give us a couple of hours and we will know better."

"Good, see you later." Albert realised Diane was in safe hands.

Another 10 minutes passed by and Diane rang Jody. The conversation was short and to the point. Jody arranged to collect Diane at the bus stop next to the municipal park. By the time they had driven there she would be waiting.

Diane was in the car before there was a chance to decide where they were going to take her. Diane asked them just to keep driving as she was not too keen on a café or somewhere too public. Jody decided to drive north on the A1 and just kept going.

Alison asked Diane if she was happy with what had been said at her flat and she told her again that the police had made a commitment to find Lexi. Diane was still nervous, but she had nothing to lose. Alison asked her to tell them what had happened to Lexi, from as far back as she wanted to go.

Diane paused for moment to gather her thoughts.

"Lexi was a bright kid. She always did well at school until she was about 14, when she just got bored. She began disrupting the class and got into a few arguments with the teacher. I then found out she was drinking cider and alcopops at her friends, but I thought it was a phase. We all did that as youngsters so it was part of growing up. But by 16 she was taking pills and god knows what else. I could not get through to her and we spent most of the time screaming at each other. She would go missing for a few days and then come home as if nothing was wrong. She had a series of Social Workers who would turn up and have a chat with her. Some of them tried hard to get her to cooperate, but she never got to know any of them. I then took her to the college and enrolled her in the beautician's course, much to her disgust. But after a few days she loved it . . . she made friends and the work gave her something else to think about. I was relieved and thought she would make a go of it. She passed her exams like I said and it was then up to her to get a job. She went for a few interviews but did not get taken on. She should have gone back to do another course, but she got fed up and began going out a lot . . . things got worse not long after her 18th birthday."

"Is that when she met Becky, or . . . ? " asked Alison.

"Becky was one of them, yes. She had known her for a while and she saw that Becky had money for clothes and make up, but no proper job. I now know she was working for the Doyles as a prostitute. I think she met another girl, but I cannot remember her name. At the time I had no idea what was going on."

Alison wanted to hear Diane say she was sure that it was the Doyles behind it all.

"It is them and their apprentice Barry Fawcus. I hate him. He goes around dishing out the beatings on their behalf. He thumps young lasses half his size. He is just a big fat coward. If you could get him behind bars Lexi and the other lasses would tell you everything. They run the brothels and make a fortune. I don't know how the police or the tax man is not after them. I got sanctioned on my benefits for making one mistake on a form, while those bastards drive around in cars worth thousands."

"So it was around the time she was 18 that things changed?"

"Yes. She thought she could make some money working as an escort, just like Becky. She had it in her brain that she would meet rich clients and go out for meals, go to posh hotels and get paid hundreds of pounds. They filled her head with shit promises and Becky was the proof. But they were liars. Becky told lies too, because she was told she had to. It was a vicious circle as they used Lexi to recruit a girl called Susanne using the same lies. This goes on every day and no one takes any notice."

"How did you manage to keep in touch?"

"By mobile and I would see her every two weeks or so. They had her working most of the time. She then started using heroin and that was when I knew she was trapped. I never knew where she was unless I found out by chance from someone else. People would tell me she was living at some flat or other. I would go around but she would not let me in. Most of the time I did not get an answer."

Alison began to appreciate the difficulties Diane had faced.

"I more or less lost touch with Lexi after Easter this year until I saw her in the street at the beginning of June. She looked terrible, thin and gaunt. I had tried to look for her before that but she just disappeared. She then told me that she had been working in Middlesborough, because things were too quiet up here. I doubt she was telling the truth. I made sure she had her mobile phone, so I put some credit on it and we spoke a few times after that. In late June I found her at a flat in the Causey Estate. It was a shit hole, it stank. There were needles and old mattresses on the floor, half eaten take-aways in just about every room. I felt sick. Lexi was ill, she had sores on her mouth and she was coughing up blood and mucus. I phoned a taxi and took her to the hospital."

"Did anyone ask how she got in that state?"

"Well, she was kept in as they thought she had breathing problems. They asked a lot of questions and she told them she was a sex worker and heroin addict. One nurse was really kind and wanted Lexi to report everything to the police, but she kept saying she could never do that. She had really bad withdrawal until they got her stabilised after about a week. I also wanted her to go and speak to the police. She then told me that the Doyles had a bent copper looking after them and if she reported them they would find out. I thought that was impossible, until I met Fawcus at the hospital. He had found out where Lexi was and he wanted her to discharge herself and go with him."

"What did the hospital do?"

"He was told to leave when I started shouting at him. I told him I was going to report him for abusing young girls. The senior nurse promised me she would report it to her management and that he was not allowed back. Two days later all my windows went in and Lexi left the hospital the same night. I told the copper who came that I had seen Fawcus's car in the street and that he was the only person who would have reason to smash my windows. I mean they had thrown half bricks, which could have caused someone a bad injury. He said he was on a break the following day, but someone would deal with it. I never heard a thing. I rang up with the reference number and the call taker said she would put a note on the incident. That same night my door got damaged. I think you might realise now why I did not trust you when you called."

"I am not surprised at all. What sort of break did the officer say he was taking?"

"He said it was for two years. Can you do that? Some job you have."

"He must have meant a career break" said Jody.

"Yes, that's it, he said he was going abroad but not to worry someone would be in touch. I did not tell him Fawcus was a pimp because he said he would not be dealing with the crime."

By now they had driven some distance and Jody suggested getting a drink at a drive-through up ahead. All three needed a break. Diane then said she felt a bit safer due to the distance from home, so asked if they could sit-in and it also gave her a chance to use the toilet.

This gave Alison and Jody a few moments to discuss Diane's story.

"This is a catalogue of errors Alison. Lexi and Diane have been in touch with everyone who could have intervened; us, social services, NHS. How many more are there in the brothels? How do we find them all?"

"And in seven days."

Diane reappeared and sat down with the two policewomen. They discussed ways of contacting Lexi, making it as safe as possible for her and Diane.

"The best way is to follow Fawcus. He collects the cash, dishes out the drugs and the hammerings. He takes all the risks whilst the Doyles rake in the money. Fawcus is your best bet; he sometimes takes his Mother about with him. Can you believe that? She must be about 65 and she visits brothels with her pathetic little boy. He thinks it is good cover for him if he gets stopped by the police. She knows she has to hide the cash and drugs as he is sure the police will not search an old granny."

"He's not a Mammy's boy is he? Asked Jody. "We were just going on about that when we were waiting for you."

"He is. She spends his money on jewellery and holidays in Benidorm. If you know where Fawcus is, then it will be safe to see Lexi. I can try to ring her if you want."

Alison asked for the number as it would be useful for them to check it out. Diane handed over her mobile with the number displayed. It ended 6677, so it was the same phone she had used to text Frank.

"That's great. Thanks Diane. I think we need to have a plan before we arrange anything with Lexi. Can you leave it with me? We will probably need some help to cover all options. I will make some phone calls."

Alison left Jody and she updated Albert. He was impressed by the information he heard, giving the team various options to follow. He asked them to return to the office as soon as they could, depending on how much more Diane disclosed.

Albert pondered the next move. They could try and follow Fawcus and locate the brothels, but that would take too long. It would also mean tying up the entire team, so the next best option was technical equipment placed on his car. A quick conversation with Susan Fenwick followed and Brian was tasked with locating Fawcus and his car. Albert wanted the device fitted as soon as possible, preferably in the early hours.

Jody and Diane were getting on well. They shared some interests and found that they had probably rubbed shoulders in the same city centre pubs when they were younger. Diane had Lexi when she was 20 and her husband left her when she was 22. She had been out with a few other boyfriends since then, but she never felt like making a commitment to any of them. She had worked part-time when Lexi was at school, mainly in shops and supermarkets.

"I always tried to stand on my own two feet. I don't want charity from anyone. If I have not got the money, I won't go out and buy anything. Lexi's dad has never given her a penny . . . he sent a couple of Christmas presents when she was just little, but nothing for years. He drives buses somewhere across Hexham and Carlisle but he just walked away from us and that was that. We heard he has a new wife and a couple of kids which made Lexi cry. I know we were too young to start a family all those years ago and we used to argue a lot, but how can anyone just pretend their own flesh and blood does not exist?"

Jody and Alison could now fully appreciate how strong Diane had been, despite the heartbreak of seeing Lexi deteriorate due to addiction and exploitation. Diane had refused to give up on her daughter and she had probably been one of the few who had stood up to the Doyles and their enforcer, Fawcus.

They drove back to Newcastle, talking in general about future plans and just about anything else that came to mind. Diane had been able to offload her fears and anxieties to two people who she thought understood where she was coming from. So many doors had been slammed in her face over the years and finally there was a glimmer of hope. There had been the odd well-meaning social worker or nurse who wanted to help, but they had not come anywhere near a solution to Lexi's predicament.

Alison and Jody dropped Diane off near a local shop, as she needed something before going home.

"Did you manage to get a kettle from the neighbour" asked Jody.

"I did but it is minging. That's why I am going to the shop; I need a pan scrubber to give it a good clean."

Jody promised Diane she would ring her before going off duty and that they would probably meet up again very soon.

"I hope so . . . . I hope so. Thank you so much. I just need some help to find Lexi."

The two detectives drove back to CC, constantly thinking about Diane and Lexi.

Albert and Susan were in the midst of ensuring that all the necessary paperwork and authorities were in place for the tracking device destined for Fawcus's car. Brian had identified it as a black BMW Five Series. Alan and Neil were on their way to his home address to try to locate it.

Albert needed four members of staff to assist Brian, as he was the only one trained in the dark arts of electronic surveillance. Alan, Neil, Derek and Jimmy were the ideal candidates.

Alan was soon on the phone to Albert, confirming that the car was close to where Fawcus lived. His address turned out to be a top floor flat in a newly built complex. An estate agents board at the entrance stated "Last few remaining, prices start at £225,000." The full address was 16 Orchard Mews, South Benton. The vehicle was in a car park to the side of the complex, in amongst a number of other cars.

"That will be another enquiry to do. It will be interesting to know if he has bought it or is renting it. Must have plenty of money either way." Albert asked Scott to make a note and follow up on Monday.

Albert then told those who would be fitting the device to go home and return at midnight. Scott volunteered to stay on, making occasional visits to the address to make sure the BMW did not disappear.

Albert and Susan were keen to hear the full story from Jody and Alison about their contact with Diane. It was immediately apparent that they had taken a big risk leading to the breakthrough with her, especially when they discussed the corruption issue. Albert knew all along that he could trust the pair of them to do a good job.

"It is all down to female intuition. It is an unstoppable cosmic force which runs the universe and everything in it. Us blokes have no chance. You just instinctively knew you could trust her didn't you?" Asked Albert.

"Yup" replied Jody. "She is some woman . . . she will never give up. I will give her a ring tonight just to make sure she is okay."

With the first full day of Operation Neon proving to be very successful, Albert was happy with the progress they had made. He always wanted progress, no matter what.

There was no need for anyone else to stay any longer. Only Scott would remain on duty and keep in touch with Albert, until the device was fitted by the others. Everyone else went home.

Albert made a list of enquiries for the next day. They still needed to link Noone to the Doyle Family and Fawcus with some good evidence. The identity of Noone's partners in corruption was still unknown and top of the list was to find Lexi and Becky.

Albert's phone rang. It was Polly.

"Hello. My name is Polly Bennison. I was married to man called Albert Bennison and I noticed that you have the same name. I was just wondering . . . "

"Very funny" interrupted Albert. "I won't be long, we are just about finished."

"Well if you are the same man it would be lovely to see what you look like after all this time. See you soon!" Polly had made her point.

She also used her female intuition to good effect. If only it could be harnessed thought Albert, we would not need solar panels or wind farms, we could just use the excess energy from women's hyper-active instincts. This was only a thought; he could never share it. Even Albert would not dare repeat this theory out loud. He even promised himself not to think about it again, as Polly often knew what was going through his mind before he did.

Albert stayed in contact with Scott for the rest of the evening and at 12.30am he received a text from Brian declaring "Job done." He slept well after that, encouraged by the achievements so far.

### Sunday 4<sup>th</sup> August

The first task of the day was to go through all the material gathered by the team in the previous 24 hours.

The technical equipment was up and running; Brian and his assistants were due in at about 10am after their late night.

Mick Miller ran through the four premises they had identified as possible brothels controlled by the Doyles. Three of them looked promising, but one flat appeared empty. Dave McGuinness had been to 16 Palace Road, which turned out to be a terraced house. The curtains were drawn at the front and the back and he had taken a walk past the house to have a better look. On the way he had noticed a smartly dressed male go in and about 20 minutes later another male came out and got into a car nearby. The registration check revealed that he was from Sunderland.

Mick added that the other premises also had either curtains drawn or blinds closed and this was in line with what he had found on earlier enquiries. There was not a great deal anyone could do with the brothels until a TPO was sent in. Once that was done the evidence was in the bag as far as Mick was concerned.

Steve Taylor had spent most of his time trying to identify premises from the Superior Escorts website and matching them up with any complaints from the public or any other incident. He too wanted a TPO visit as soon as possible.

Albert, Alison and Susan Fenwick decided to take stock and left everyone to carry on with their paperwork and research. Albert was keen to know what was planned for Diane Morrison. Alison explained.

"Jody rang her last night and she was fine. We have arranged to meet her again today and she is going to show us the different flats where she managed to find Lexi over the past year or so. She also offered to ring her on the number we already have. I think she will eventually make a statement, but we must find Lexi first. The technical on the car should give us the locations of the brothels when Fawcus does his rounds and we can just hope for the best."

"What about Becky? Does Diane know her family and can we do something with them?" asked Albert. Alison confirmed that Jody had that on her list to sort out.

Susan said that she had been impressed with the FCT and had not expected to get so far in such a short time. She suggested contacting a Yorkshire Force to borrow a TPO.

"I know they have a Vice Team in Leeds and Bradford, so they must have a lot more expertise than we do. It is also far enough away so we don't have to worry about the other corrupt officers we think are in contact with Noone. I will ring CC on their patch tomorrow and take it from there. What should we do with Teesside?"

Albert was unsure. "Perhaps we should just contact their CC and take advice. It is a bit close and we will soon know if Fawcus is involved with brothels down there."

Albert then asked Susan if there was any chance of an analyst joining the operation.

"Yes. Tomorrow without fail. I just don't know who as yet." Susan sounded positive.

Albert then went and sat with Hughie to review all the disclosure he had been given. There was a lot of information already, leading to more and more enquiries. Albert knew he did not have enough time and resources to follow up every lead. He asked Hughie to make sure he was made aware of everything linking Noone with the brothels and the pimps.

"Will we be dealing with Pat when he is arrested?" asked Hughie.

"No. That is up to Susan and her team to sort out. We will concentrate on the rest. I can't see us getting everyone in at the same time. We might have to concentrate on the main players and round the rest up as soon as we can. If the Chief had given us another week or two we would be in a much better position."

"Sounds like she gave the Super the run around the other day."

"She did, which reminds me he asked for an update so I will ring him after the lads come in after their late night. Thanks Hughie."

By 10am everyone was in, looking slightly jaded and in need of some caffeine. Albert asked Brian to get his gadget fired up and ready.

"It is still parked up at his home address and has not moved since we put the technical on" declared Brian.

Albert then went through how he wanted the team to react if the car went on the move.

"We will have as many vehicles on the road as we can and Brian will give a running commentary on any movement. If at all possible I want Fawcus linked to the Doyles and to any premises he stops at which may end up being identified as a brothel. Get as much footage as possible but don't take unnecessary risks. We can always have another try later in the week. If there is any sign of Pat Noone, withdraw straight away. He will spot any of you in an instant and that would be a disaster. As from tomorrow I am going to get some hire cars so we at least have a better chance, so just take things easy today."

Albert knew that the technical on the BMW gave them a massive advantage. The team could afford to hang back until the car stopped and then hopefully get in to position to cover any visits to brothels or meetings between the alleged offenders.

Within 15 minutes the team were out and about, covering the BMW. Albert felt confident. Every member of the team seemed to be on top of the job. There were no slackers or whingers and Albert was especially grateful to Tommy who had not hesitated to become involved on his last full week before moving on.

Jody rang Diane and she said she was ready when they were. Alison suggested that they took her around all the places she could identify and if all went well, they could try ringing Lexi after that.

As they were about to leave, Miles Ashley came strolling in. He was dressed in jeans and a t-shirt.

"Morning Sir" said Jody. "You look 10 years younger without your uniform on."

"Thanks Jody. You don't look so bad yourself, despite all these long hours."

Before Miles could start asking loads of questions, Jody explained they were just on their way out to see a key witness and Albert would cover everything.

"Sorry I have not been in touch, but things are moving on very quickly" explained Albert.

Miles appeared relaxed and said he just wanted to call in to pass on his encouragement. He also said he did not want to get in the way and then to everyone's surprise he offered to make the tea and catch up with events when there was time.

There was only a handful left in the office, so Miles was soon up to date after speaking to Albert, Susan, Hughie and Brian.

Miles had not imagined that so much progress could have been made in just over a day. His delight was slightly tempered when he thought of his next meeting with the Chief, who was bound to point out how she was right to set a tight deadline. Albert began to appreciate the hassle he must have been getting from the Command Block, not just about Operation Neon, but also the budget and staffing issues.

Miles was especially keen to see the technical in action. This was an aspect of surveillance of which he had no experience, so he hung on Brian's every word. It became obvious that he had missed out on a lot of exciting investigative work, in favour of the promotion rat race.

At 11.15am the BMW went mobile. Miles was engrossed. Albert had his mobile at the ready, Brian kept up the radio commentary and Hughie started the written log.

The car only travelled about half a mile and stopped.

"He is at the newsagents. Confirmed it is Fawcus on his own."
Scott was not far away.

Within a few minutes Fawcus was mobile again and he started
heading towards the city centre. The BMW went over the Tyne and
past Gateshead, towards South Tyneside.

Albert wanted to know if everyone was in the convoy and
keeping up, so each car checked in with the current position.

The BMW continued on a route towards South Shields, sticking
to the speed limits. There had been no premises identified in South
Shields by the team linked to Fawcus, so there was no chance of
giving them any prior information.

After negotiating a one-way system and a couple of roundabouts,
the car parked up on Deuchar Street, facing the sea at the end of the
road.

Derek and Jimmy were first there and radioed in that the car was
outside number five and number seven. They did not get there
quickly enough to see Fawcus get out.

The team plotted up so they had every route covered. Neil had a
walk past and confirmed that number five was a ground floor flat.
The door to number seven looked like it had not been open for years.

After 15 minutes Fawcus appeared from the door of number five.
Someone closed the door behind him but it was impossible to see
who. Jimmy obtained some good footage of Fawcus as he got in to
the BMW and drove off.

"That's him connected to the car and a possible brothel." Albert
was making note of all the significant progress as they went along.

Miles logged on to the nearest computer and began to do checks
on the address. He was thoroughly enjoying making a contribution.

"Not much on number five" he said "Just a complaint of noisy
neighbours on 27th July and a burglary a year ago. The victim was an
old lady aged 84."

Fawcus continued towards the coastal route and turned north,
back in the general direction of the Tyne Tunnel. Within ten minutes
he was through the Tyne Tunnel and back in North Tyneside.

The BMW then came to a halt again, this time on the approach to
Willington Quay. Brian described the stop as on the junction of
George Street and Queen Street. Dave and Tommy covered this one

and as Fawcus got out of the car, he was talking on his mobile. He walked a short distance and went into a house on George Street, second from the end. The door opened as he approached it and he went straight in; there was no pause to be invited. The house was confirmed as number three and it was another address that had not been previously identified.

"Blimey, what have you lot been doing?" joked Albert.

Jimmy and Derek found a convenient spot to cover the front door of the house. It looked like a two up, two down terrace, with all the blinds closed.

Fawcus reappeared after 20 minutes. He was smoking a cigarette and Jimmy filmed as Fawcus turned around to face a young female in the door way. She had her arms crossed, her hair was tied back and she was also smoking. They were in conversation; Fawcus appeared to be making a strong point to the female. He began shaking his head and she retreated slightly, behind the door. He then pointed his finger at her and began prodding the air in her direction, as if he needed to force his opinion on her. She stood even further back. Fawcus turned and got into the BMW and drove off, his tyres screeching as he did so. The door closed at the house.

Fawcus drove straight back to his home address and parked up in exactly the same place. Scott managed to get footage of him entering the building with a key.

Brilliant, thought Albert. Things were going well.

Albert rang Scott and asked him to return to the office with his footage, so Brian could obtain some stills from it. This would give everyone something to refer to.

Miles was still thoroughly enjoying himself and there was no sign of the man who spent most of his day dashing from one place to another. He sat with Hughie, reviewing all the potential enquiries and the information collected so far. Susan Fenwick asked Miles how he felt about borrowing a TPO from another force.

"If it will help, just do it. I know we are up against it time-wise, so if it ends up costing us then that is the way it will have to be. The Chief has told me to use all the resources we think are necessary, so who am I to argue?"

Scott returned with his footage. Brian down-loaded it and produced a number of stills for the team. Fawcus looked every inch the gangster; he was about six foot two, seventeen or eighteen stone, bald and tanned. He appeared to have a goatee beard and his right arm was covered in tattoos. He was wearing a black V-neck T-shirt and jeans.

"Not the sort of bloke you would invite to tea," remarked Hughie.

With a break in the surveillance, Miles asked to see Albert privately.

"I know it is early days Albert, but what chance have we of rounding up all the main offenders on or before Friday?"

"That is a difficult question. I have no doubt we can link the Doyles and Fawcus to the brothels and cover the prostitution offences. It is Pat Noone I am worried about. We will be able to prove he has looked at some of the brothels and individual records on the Force computer, but that in itself is little more than a disciplinary offence. We still have to prove he is passing information and getting something in return. Alison and Jody have Diane Morrison on board, but all she knows is what Lexi has told her, although she can evidence some of the brothels. Then there are the other corrupt cops that we have no idea about. Diane has given us a possible lead, connected to the damage at her house in June. But it looks like the reporting officer, PC Adrian Blair has gone on a career break. We urgently need to find out who the crime was allocated to when he left. There may have been some doctoring of the crime report."

"In other words we are up against it. Having said that, the team have worked wonders so far Albert. You have some good people working for you."

"I have and I'm sure we will get there in the end. It is just a shame we have such a tight schedule. Are you seeing the Chief tomorrow?"

Miles confirmed he was, at around 9.30am after 'morning prayers'.

"Morning prayers?" queried Albert.

"The Chief decided a couple of months ago that every Monday at 8.15am, all the heads of departments and command units had to gather in the command block and discuss priorities. It started off okay, but then it became a competition to see who knew the most. So now you have people coming in at 6am to study all the incident logs and operations so they can look the best informed. I don't have to bother as FCT and FI operations are not discussed until they are finalised. Operation Neon will not be mentioned at all. I have often envied you and Bill being able to get on with the practical side of things, as oppose to dealing with politics all the time."

"If only the public knew" reflected Albert. "So have you enjoyed your input today?"

"I most certainly have, the time has flown by. The team know their stuff. How do you keep them going?"

"I admire hard workers, whatever they do. I just tell them to go and get on with it and use their own judgement. If something does not go to plan, they invariably put it right. Having said that, it was not always the case. When I first arrived, there were some members of the team who avoided work altogether and it took me a while to see what was going on. They always looked busy, but produced nothing. It was the same people doing the hard jobs, taking a lead whilst the dodgers were almost anonymous. We all have days when we are a bit flaky and not quite with it, or you need to nip out to do a little guvvie job, but those lot obtained their wages by deception. The only good thing about the budget cuts the first time around was that we were able to get rid them."

"Yes, they were a pain. They created a lot of work for HR." Miles was referring to the grievances that were submitted.

"It is all very simple to me; the public pay us to look after them and it is usually pretty obvious what we have to do in terms of investigating wrong-doing and dealing with those responsible. The public soon let us know if they are not happy and the media are quick to jump on the band wagon. This current job has me slightly confused though."

"In what way?" asked Miles.

"Just about every type of offending is reported by the public to the police in reasonably high numbers, whether it be speeding drivers, nuisance youths, domestics, burglary or whatever. They report it to their local police, or sometimes through their local councillor or solicitor if they want to make a bigger impact. But when was the last time a member of the public reported a young woman being exploited in a brothel? I cannot think of one example. I dare say someone has done at one time or another, but it must be rare. Then I realised that those same women are seeing umpteen punters a day . . . perhaps up to ten and not one of those men saw fit to report the obvious. Everyone has heard of Crimestoppers so it is not as if they have to attend a police station. Diane Morrison has told Jody and Alison that Lexi was in a terrible state the last time she saw her, but she must still be getting punters. I just cannot imagine what those men are thinking."

Miles agreed and the only example he could think of was when complaints were received from residents in red light districts.

"I suppose we are different; all of the sex work in the North East is off-street, apart from a couple of small areas in Teesside" observed Albert.

"Out of sight and out of mind" summarised Miles "We are going to get some criticism when this all goes to court."

This was probably the longest conversation Miles and Albert had sat through in over a year. They both had their own agendas and there had not been many opportunities to meet in the middle. Bill had provided a vital link, but with his retirement it was now even more important for them to work as a team.

"Do the team get on together Albert, I very rarely see any friction in the office."

"For most of the time they are too busy to irritate each other. Occasionally there is a squabble, but they are adults and they can sort it out themselves. There is no need for a supervisor to get involved with minor differences, as that is when dramas can often develop. I have worked with other sergeants who made it their business to analyse and counter analyse working relationships and they caused themselves hours of grief. The same happens with people who hide their shortcomings by highlighting those of their colleagues."

"So if you had to sum up your management style Albert, what would it be?"

"It is all about progress and clear direction. Work hard and take your chances. If you don't like it, leave." Albert was back to his blunt self.

Susan Fenwick had been making her own list of urgent enquiries during the pause in activity. She could not get in touch with any of her counterparts in other forces as none of them worked weekends. She also needed to obtain Pat Noone's personnel file without any undue attention. She was confident that PC Adrian Blair was on a career break, as all of his other work was neatly referenced-off prior to 30th June. He had also ensured that all the crimes allocated to him before he left were finalised, or handed over. This would be confirmed by getting access to his emails via CC's normal route to IT. The criminal damage report regarding Diane's windows did not have any comments on by PC Blair, meaning they would need the assistance of IT to go back through the data.

Albert sent a text to Alison and Jody to see how they were getting on with Diane.

"Okay, identified four flats. Will ring soon."

Diane was more than happy to be with Alison and Jody, showing them the brothels she could remember. In between driving around they had chatted about various possibilities and as the day wore on, Diane was talking more and more about rescuing Lexi. It all boiled down to trying her mobile in the hope that she answered, could say where she was and could also be easily found.

In the eyes of Alison and Jody that was a tall order. In Diane's opinion it was all that could be done and without any delay. She had the attention of the police, the police needed her and she knew this was her best chance. Alison decided to ring Albert to discuss all the options, so she sent a short text to him as a pre-warning of what was to come.

"Ring now" came the reply. Albert's texts were invariably brief and on this occasion he excelled himself.

Alison left Diane in the car with Jody whilst she wandered around the car park next to the old sports centre talking to Albert. She explained that Diane had taken them to four flats, one of them being Holly Gardens. That task had taken up most of the day and Diane could not remember any more. That meant that her mind turned to Lexi and nothing else.

"She is desperate to ring her Albert. She wants to find her with our help and take her somewhere safe. Have we got the capacity to look after a vulnerable witness, or even two if Becky is there with her?"

Albert put his phone on loudspeaker so that Susan and Miles could hear.

"The problem is we cannot let them go home to Diane's as that is the first place they would look. So we would have to find some accommodation for them. What are the chances of her answering her phone? We still have Fawcus housed so he is not a problem" said Albert.

"She says she will probably answer if she can. It is not guaranteed though. If Fawcus is out of the way and we already know the Doyles very rarely visit the brothels, I feel a bit more optimistic."

Miles chipped in "Alison it is Miles Ashley here. Can you ask Diane if she is prepared to go to a B&B or a hotel out of the area for a few days? That is our only way around this. I cannot help thinking that we need both her and Lexi to provide us with some first-hand evidence and we need to rescue Lexi. It means a lot of work but she cannot be left any longer."

"Will do. Give me 10 minutes."

Alison went back to the car and as she approached, Diane watched her very step. She was looking for any sign at all that the police were ready to move and find Lexi.

"Diane, I've spoken to the bosses and they want to know if you would be prepared to go somewhere safe and out of the way if we can find Lexi?"

"I will do anything . . . please tell them, please, do it now." There was never going to be any other answer from Diane. Lexi was her little girl.

Alison rang Albert again and he asked to speak to Diane.

"Hello Diane, my name is Albert Bennison. I just want you to know that we want to find Lexi and we are very grateful for all your help. If we find Lexi tonight, we will arrange some accommodation. Depending on what happens, we may be able to go back to your flat so you can collect some belongings, but you will have to bear with us on that. It will be a bit risky as we are doing all this without any prior knowledge of where she is. Are you happy for us to try?"

"Yes, yes, please can we do it? Thank you Alfred."

106

"It's Albert, but you can call me Alfred if you like!"

Diane was shaking so much by this point that she missed Albert's little joke. Alison took the phone back and told him that they would ring Lexi in five minutes.

Miles was keen to point out that a few nights in a B&B would give the police enough time to find out what Lexi knew. It was already suspected that she had met Pat Noone and she may be able to identify the others.

The nature of the operation and the schedule did not allow any second thoughts. Whatever opportunity presented itself, it had to be taken.

Albert asked Brian to recall everyone to the office, apart from one car to remain with Fawcus, in case he moved.

Alison, Jody and Diane remained in the sports centre car park to make the phone call to Lexi. Diane knew she could not tell her that she was with the police and she had to avoid telling her that she was to be rescued and removed to a safer place. The plan was for Diane to engage Lexi in a normal conversation and somehow find out exactly where she was.

Diane rang Lexi's number. Within a few seconds the ringing tone came through, so at least they knew the phone was switched on. The phone continued to ring for what seemed an age. All three huddled around the phone to listen.

"Hello" came the response from a sleepy sounding voice. Diane nodded to Alison and Jody confirming she recognised Lexi's voice.

"Hello Lexi, it's your Mam. Are you alright?"

"Aye. I was just having a lie down. What time is it?"

"It's just after 2 o'clock. Have you been sleeping very much? How do you feel?" Diane was sticking to the script.

"I'm shit as usual. I've been rattling all week and there is no hot water and hardly any food. I am sick of this Mam. I have hardly seen anyone and Becky has gone to another flat in North Shields. What are you doing? Can you spare me a tenner? And I have no tabs left."

Both Jody and Alison nodded their heads frantically. This was the excuse they needed to find out where she was.

"I can give you a tenner, but that is all I have spare. Do you want me to get you something to eat?"

"Yes anything, anything you like ....." Lexi yawned as if she was barely keeping awake. Concentrating on a conversation was almost too much for her.

"Where shall we meet, where are you?" Diane tried to sound as normal as possible, but her heart was thumping like a drum.

"Er, some new place in Wallsend. It is the worst yet Mam. I can meet you wherever you like?"

Alison and Jody shook their heads. It was the address they needed at all costs. Diane took the prompt.

"How about I meet you outside the place . . . what is the address?" Diane was trying to find some middle ground.

It is 39 Waterford Way or something, Water . . . field, no Waterford. When can you come?"

"Lets' have a think, I can be there in . . . . " Diane needed guidance from the police.

Alison mouthed fifteen minutes to her.

". . . Fifteen minutes. Are you on your own? I don't want to see Fawcus" confirmed Diane.

"He won't be out on a Sunday if he can help it. He goes on the drink. If anyone rings it will be his fucking Mother."

"No worries. See you as soon as I can. Love you."

Jody rang through to Albert with the development and he directed the team to the area rather than make their way back to the office. He told Alison to go straight to the address and gain entry without delay.

Hughie carried out some background checks and it appeared that 39 Waterford Way was a collection of bedsits. That meant that the property was spilt into several parts and this caused an immediate problem.

"Get onto Alison and tell her what to expect. She may have to ring her back to see which bedsit she is in."

Jody was following her satnav and they were just six minutes from the property.

"Everyone should be there very soon" explained Hughie. He passed the premises details to Alison who asked Diane to be ready to ring Lexi as soon as they arrived.

Lexi had to be found with the minimum of fuss. The longer the police had her the better before the Doyles and Fawcus discovered she was gone.

On arrival in the street, Jody drove past number 39. It was an old Victorian house with small garden to the front. The main door had a buzzer panel to one side and several post boxes on the other.

Alan and Neil confirmed they were close by, so it was now safe for Diane to ring again.

"Ask her if she could let you in when you get there in a couple of minutes. That will mean we don't disturb anyone else at the house who might know Fawcus. We have to be very careful." Instructed Alison to Diane.

Diane rang Lexi's number. No answer.

"Keep trying" urged Jody. "She was just on the phone not so long ago."

Diane pressed re-dial. No answer.

Back in the office, Albert and Miles were eagerly awaiting any update. Hughie continued to check recent occupants of the address and concluded that it was a sort of last chance saloon, where people who had nowhere else to go or had exhausted every other sort of accommodation would be housed.

Brian's computer then bleeped. "The BMW is on the move. He is just pulling out of the car park." Brian called Steve and Mick who were on standby in case Fawcus went mobile.

"Tell them to stay close, but not too close" said Albert as he phoned Alison.

"Alison, be quick. Fawcus has moved and he is about 10-12 minutes away from you. Has Lexi appeared yet?"

"No, and she is not answering her phone. We will just have to ring the buzzers and hope to get in."

"Okay, go for it. Alan and Neil can deal with Fawcus if he appears. Be careful."

Alison then asked Diane to come with her to the front door, whilst Jody remained with the car ready to leave as soon as they had Lexi.

Derek, Jimmy, Dave and Scott were now just a street away.

"We have plenty of help if we need it. You ring the buzzers and if she answers we go in and bring her out. Hopefully someone answers."

Diane and Alison were at the front door in seconds.

Fawcus was driving on the main A1 travelling south. "If he is going to see Lexi, he is about three miles away" confirmed Brian as he kept up the running commentary. Steve and Mick were not far behind him.

Diane rang the buzzer for flat A and then B. No answer.

"They are probably on the ground floor and look deserted" concluded Alison.

Diane rang flat C and a male answered.

"Oh sorry" said Diane "I was looking for Lexi, can you let me in it's her Mam?"

"Aye, push the door" obliged the male in Flat C.

The BMW was now held at a roundabout where there were some road works. The next manoeuvre he made would be critical.

Diane and Alison dashed up the stairs to Flat D where they hoped Lexi was. The male in Flat C came to his door and said she had gone out about five minutes ago. He had heard her door slam. Alison decided to knock on the door regardless, but there was no response.

"Just wait for her if you like. She'll just be away to the shop or something."

"Okay thanks very much, we'll wait outside" replied Alison.

"Suit yourself . . . everyone that goes in that flat is in hurry" replied the male.

"The BMW has turned towards the coast. He is about five minutes away from Lexi's flat" updated Brian.

Alison got back to the car and informed the team they had not found Lexi. She was possibly on the streets.

Diane was frantic as she was now privy to exactly what was happening. She was so close to finding Lexi with people who were going to help her. It was all going wrong at the last minute.

Scott spoke up on the radio.

"Scott to Alison. There is a young girl walking back in your direction. Green parka, dark hair, short skirt. She looks a bit unsteady. She has a carrier bag in her hand."

110

"Yes, yes. Where is she now?"

"Just turning into Waterford and out of my sight."

Diane and Alison got out of the car and Diane immediately confirmed it was Lexi. They ran up to her and Jody followed in the car. Lexi did not see them coming and the next thing she knew she was in the arms of her Mam.

The BMW was now a matter of a couple of streets away, approaching the first turn off which could take it to Lexi's flat. Brian carefully watched as the vehicle continued.

Diane spoke urgently to Lexi "Don't worry, get in the car, everything is okay. Just get in the car." Diane was not going to let her go this time.

"Alison to the team, Lexi is with us."

"What the fuck, what are you doing, who the fuck are these two." Lexi was dazed and confused.

Diane started to explain and tried her best to calm Lexi.

Brian could see that the BMW was no more than a hundred yards from number 39. "He is almost on top of you . . . . take the north exit from Waterford and immediately turn left. He will not see you if you hurry."

Jody wasted no time and drove away as fast as she could. Albert ordered the rest of the team to pull out as he did not want any risk of compromise. Brian watched his computer screen as the BMW parked up a good distance from Lexi's flat, on the opposite side of the street.

"Leave him for a couple of minutes and if he does not move we will send someone in on foot," said Albert.

Miles and Albert stood next to Brian and they were collectively glued to the screen, waiting for any indication of what Fawcus was up to. They knew that if he went to Lexi's flat and found out from the male in Flat C that she had been visited by her Mam, the operation would have to strike far earlier than they had planned to.

A long three minutes went by and Albert asked Scott to walk past the car. It took Scott a few seconds to get onto the street and get a clear sight of the BMW. As he made his way past Lexi's flat the BMW started to manoeuvre and a few moments later Scott watched as Fawcus drove past him, turning right at the junction.

"He is on his own in the car and he was nowhere near the flat. I don't think he has been at the door," said Scott.

Brian monitored the BMW as it made its way back to the main road, creating a safe distance from Waterford Way. "Looks like he is on his way to the possible brothel he was at this morning in Willington Quay," said Brian as the BMW made rapid progress.

A collective sigh of relief went around the entire team.

"We are riding our luck on this one," declared Albert to Miles and Susan.

Albert sent a text to Alison for her to get in touch as soon as she could.

Jody drove to the sports centre car park so they could speak to Lexi without interruption. They wanted to explain to her as soon as possible, whilst assessing her general state of health. Diane held Lexi's hand as tightly as she could. Alison looked into the bag Lexi had been carrying. It contained a pot noodle and a bag of crisps, which turned out to be all that Lexi could buy with the money she had.

"These two are police officers Lexi. They want to help us. You cannot go on living in places like that." Diane was reassuring Lexi, but also speaking to herself. The strain she had been under was unbearable and this was make or break time. Diane began to cry. As tough as she was, the sight of her daughter in such a bad way was heart breaking.

Lexi was painfully thin, probably only six stone. Her legs were pale, with dirt engrained in her knees. She had small cuts and scrapes to her shins. Her hands looked like they belonged to a 70 year old, not someone who had just turned 20. Her fingernails had the remnants of purple varnish, barely hiding the muck under her nails. She was wearing a green parka, a small grey vest and a short black skirt. She had the smell of someone who had not washed for days, mixed with cigarettes and alcohol.

Lexi sat back in the car seat. Her eyes looked almost opaque in the afternoon sunlight. She tried to speak but nothing came out of her dry mouth. Alison searched for some water and gave it to Diane. Lexi took a small sip and dragged her herself up from the comfort of the head rest.

"No one can help me. I am on my own. I have to go back to the flat, they will look for me. I have loads of missed calls from Fawcus"

Alison tried to explain what was going to happen next.

"We can help you and that is why your Mam is here. We are going to take you somewhere safe tonight and . . . . "

"Safe? Safe? I thought I was safe in hospital until one of yous told Fawcus where I was and he came for me. I have to go back! Let me out of this fucking car!" screamed Lexi.

Jody had put the child locks on so Lexi was unable to escape. Alison continued.

"We know about the police officer and we are going to deal with him too. Please listen to me Lexi."

It took several minutes for Lexi to calm down. In the end she had no energy to carry on and Diane held her tight.

Diane then suggested that they go to her flat and collect what they could, before anyone realised Lexi was missing. They drove the short distance in almost complete silence, Lexi occasionally sniffing and coughing as Alison sent a text to Albert.

Diane did not release her hold on Lexi until they were back at her flat and the door was closed. She sat her down on the settee and began collecting some clothes for them both in a shopping bag. Jody sat next to Lexi, who appeared only half awake.

"Have you had anything today Lexi?"

"One tenner bag, if that is what you mean" replied Lexi, describing the heroin she had managed to obtain that day.

"Okay" began Jody. "We are going to take you somewhere to stay the night. Is there anything we need to get you that you can think of?"

"A tenner bag" suggested Lexi.

"Good try" said Jody, grinning. "I see we have a bit of a comedian here Alison."

Lexi remained on the settee, she did not have the motivation or the strength to do anything else. Diane quickly went through the clothes and toiletries she had hurriedly put together and declared she was ready to go. Alison rang Albert who said he had booked two rooms at a travel hotel near to Hexham. It was far enough away for

113

them to stay for next 24 hours and close enough for the police to respond quickly.

"Why two rooms?" asked Jody as they went down the stairs to the car.

"One for Diane and Lexi and the other for one of us" came the reply.

"That will be you then. I can't trust Andy to get the kids ready for school."

"I thought so" Alison had already worked that out.

Within an hour they were at the hotel, with Alan and Neil nearby. Albert and Susan travelled over and waited until Denise and Lexi were settled.

So, by 5pm on the second day of the operation, the police had at least found one of the young women that Frank had been concerned about and had her in a safe place. Albert was keen to speak to them, but Jody thought Lexi needed an hour or so with Diane.

"She will do the groundwork for us Albert. Give her a bit of time and we will then be able to see how Lexi responds. Her health is a concern though, she is well and truly knackered. She has nothing left in reserve."

"Should we call the emergency doctor out? That is our best chance on a Sunday. I don't want her taken to a nick for the police surgeon, as the records will be on open view. A&E is not an option."

A short discussion followed and Albert asked Alan to arrange the doctor.

By 6pm, Lexi had been washed and changed into the clothes Denise had for her. She seemed to be accepting that things were about to change.

Albert and Susan introduced themselves to both Diane and Lexi. Diane could hardly conceal her joy and her gratitude for the events so far.

"I won't be satisfied until we have everyone locked up Diane, so don't thank us, we need to thank you. We have a doctor on his way and an officer will stay in the hotel with you overnight. We will then have a look at everything tomorrow. I am from the Force Crime Team and Susan is from Counter Corruption. Both our teams are on this operation. Alison and Jody will be with you every inch of the way. Is there anything else you want to know?"

Lexi was not taking much notice of Albert, as she lay on the bed. Diane wanted to know what would happen in the next few days.

"We will see you tomorrow and go through every option. I want you to get some sleep tonight and be ready to tell us everything in your own time. The only question I have for tonight is; where can we find Becky?"

Lexi stirred at the sound of her friend's name. Albert repeated his question.

"She was moved a few days ago by Fawcus. I think she is in North Shields somewhere. Her mobile has been off so I have not spoken to her. She is in a worse state than me. Fawcus raped her a couple of weeks ago. I saw it all, she dared argue with him so he threw her over the back of the chair and did it. She was bleeding."

Susan then asked for Becky's number, explaining that they need to find her more urgently than ever. She also asked Lexi if they could have her phone to look at overnight. She would be get it back the next day. Diane urged Lexi to agree, so she handed it over.

The number Lexi provided for Becky turned out to be unobtainable, despite several attempts to reach her.

Nevertheless, Operation Neon was moving at a fast pace. Miles Ashley was still at the office when Albert and Susan arrived back. Brian was given Lexi's phone to look at. The BMW had returned to Fawcus's home following a brief two minute stop at 3 George Street and a further brief stop on the coast road. Albert stood down as many of the team as he could. He knew there were a number of long days ahead of them.

# Chapter Four

# Keep Looking

**Monday 5<sup>th</sup> August**

Albert, Miles and Susan met in the CC office at 8am. Lexi had eventually been seen by the doctor at around 10pm and had been unsettled most of the night. Jody was going straight back to the hotel to allow Alison some time to get a change of clothes. At least she had managed to get some sleep.

Miles had more than enough to relay to the Chief and he was confident that there would be no more demands put on the team.

Susan had a number of enquiries to get on with; she and Steve were going to concentrate on all the IT log traces they needed to do.

Brian had examined Lexi's phone and he had a print-out of all the calls and texts stored on the sim card.

"The good news is we have a mobile number for Fawcus and both the Doyles. There are also a lot of texts giving Lexi a time for the arrival of various punters. It does not look like she has much choice. The number for Becky ends in 0349 and it is still unobtainable. She also has contact with a girl called Susanne quite a lot and another called Gayle. Once the analyst gets started we will have a better picture of who does what."

It is an inevitable consequence of opening a new enquiry the size of Operation Neon that the amount of work soon outstrips the available resources. Albert was just about to try to track down Jill as an extra pair of hands as he was expecting her to return to work, when Alison rang. She described how the previous night had been interrupted by Lexi's inability to settle. She was suffering withdrawal; feeling sick and she described how every bone in her body was aching. Her heroin habit had reached about five to six 'tenner bags' a day. Alison was not hopeful of being able to interview Lexi anytime soon. She suggested that Jody and Jill try

116

their best to get Lexi an appointment with the local drug treatment service. This would be difficult as she did not have a GP to refer her.

Albert and Alison discussed how to respond if Fawcus tried to contact Lexi by phone or by a call to her bedsit. Alison had managed to establish that Fawcus was only calling to see Lexi once or twice a week. She was no longer seeing punters on a daily basis due to her ill health and her appearance. He had stopped supplying her with heroin as she was not earning any money to pay for it. Neither did she have any money for her rent, so it would not be long before she was homeless. Alison's impression was that Lexi had served her purpose for Fawcus and the Doyles and they were slowly cutting her adrift. Lexi had mentioned several times that Fawcus was bound to come and look for her and she fully expected that he would find out where she was.

Without Lexi's evidence, or at least an account of what had happened, the interviews with the suspects would lack impact and detail. Albert was beginning to realise that for all the progress they had made, there was still too much to do before Friday.

At least the hire cars had arrived and more importantly, the analyst. Ros Stafford had been with CC for over two years and knew exactly what was required of her. She gathered all the material she needed from Brian and Hughie and started work immediately.

Mick and Steve assisted Susan with all the IT checks, so the rest of the team resumed their surveillance on Fawcus. Jody had located Jill and she had been updated on the way to Hexham. She had no idea what Pat Noone had been up to and she sat in shocked silence for long periods in the car.

Miles emailed Albert to tell him that the Chief still expected the arrests to be made before the end of the week.

By lunchtime, further evidence was to hand. Fawcus had travelled to two new brothels and had visited the home of Graeme Doyle. Footage of him at all the appropriate addresses was obtained.

Susan and her team then came back with a pile of paperwork from HR and IT.

"Where would you like to start?" she asked Albert.

"With some good news! Do you know who the other bent cops are?" he said hopefully.

"Well we have one, Sergeant Aidan Dryden. He wrote off the damage to the windows at Diane's flat on 30th June."

Susan then explained that they had asked IT to examine the incident log and the crime report to see who had accessed the data. PC Blair had created the crime report and presumably filled in all the correct details. As he was leaving for a long period, he had left it open for a supervisor to check and allocate to another officer. This had been a stroke of luck for both Dryden and Noone as they needed to cover their tracks and that of Fawcus.

"Dryden took out all of the offender details and changed the MO to persons unknown. He was then able to get rid of the crime straight away, as undetected. Obviously we need to know why he did this and we have looked at his emails. There is one he sent to Noone on the 1st July, with words to the effect that he had sorted out the query their friend had. The email continues with a load of waffle about football."

Susan then went on to explain that Noone and Dryden had joined the police at the same time in 1999 and had worked together briefly in 2008/09 before Noone went to FCT and Dryden was promoted.

"So had we not spoken to Diane, the damage to her windows would have gone completely unnoticed and unrecorded?" asked Albert.

"Exactly. And the only person who could have raised the alarm flew to Thailand on 2nd July to start his career break."

Susan had not found any evidence of a third officer, so there were still questions as to whether he existed or not.

"There are some other items of interest on Noone's personnel file," continued Susan.

"He has had words of advice from his supervision following a complaint from a female witness to a burglary he investigated four years ago. He obviously fancied her, but she was not interested and got tired of his calls. His ex-girlfriend, PC Kelly Sissons, who now works with the training department, submitted a report about his behaviour when they split up. He kept ringing her and contacting her by text. The calls were not abusive, but she was worried enough to report it through her supervision. He was given further words of advice."

"So there has obviously been a few problems in the past?" asked Albert.

"Yes and it goes on. Noone continued to contact his ex-girlfriend via his friends, including Dryden. She again reported it, but the calls stopped and nothing further was done. A month later all her car tyres were slashed outside her home address, but there was nothing to link Noone to the damage. She was convinced at the time he had something to do with it and made representations, but again it was not pursued."

"Sounds like he was continually given the benefit of the doubt and we are left to pick up the pieces. Jody seems to think he has had domestic problems with his latest partner too" reflected Albert.

Susan was not at all surprised. "This happens all the time. If someone is making the same mistake over and over again or continuing with the same bad behaviour, we should be prepared to do something about it. People seem to back off and make excuses. I think we will have to interview PC Sissons and his other ex-partner when we get a chance."

In comparison to Noone, Dryden had led an uneventful career.

"He is Mr Average" said Susan. "He is always punctual, does his bit and by all accounts is very efficient. He has nothing on his file to suggest he has caused a problem for himself or anyone else. He was asked about Noone's contact with PC Sissons and he said he liked them both and thought he could act as a mediator. Perhaps he genuinely thought that, but somewhere along the way he has crossed the line."

Susan had also asked IT to check all the computer activity carried out by Noone and Dryden since the start of the year. This was a massive undertaking, but a quick look back at the previous month on Noone's data log revealed that he was checking addresses and individuals who were linked to the brothels. He also checked Fawcus's record regularly, perhaps twice a week.

"I think he is covering himself" explained Susan. "He is not only watching to see if Fawcus is under investigation, but also ensuring that he has not been linked with him. He must be constantly in fear of being exposed. They must have him over a barrel."

All the material gathered by Susan was given to Ros the analyst and copied to Hughie.

Jody and Jill had managed to get an emergency appointment for Lexi at the drug treatment clinic at 3pm. She was deteriorating due to her withdrawal.

Albert called a de-brief for 6pm and all those who could attend did so. Jody and Jill stayed with Diane and Lexi, who had been assessed and given something to help her by the time of the meeting.

The de-brief was short and to the point. Becky was the main priority, but there was still no clue as to where she was. The second corrupt officer had been identified; he was on rest days but back to work on Wednesday 7th August. Fawcus had revealed more of his daily routine and he was now facing a lot of questions. Lexi could not be interviewed, but a statement from Diane would be obtained. Ros would have her initial charts ready in about two or three days, with all the contacts and links.

Susan had managed to borrow two TPOs from Leeds; they were due to travel up the next day and make their first visits to the identified brothels in the late afternoon.

Unfortunately the communications between the pimps, the cops and the escorts would not be entirely clear until after the arrests were made. The police had to find their phones and laptops at all costs. Noone had not shared his personal phone number with anyone and it was too soon to ask anyone about Dryden's.

### Tuesday 6th August

Preparations for the TPO visits were given priority, with the hope that they would discover Becky in one of the premises. Lexi had endured another uncomfortable night, but at least she was to be seen on a daily basis at the clinic.

Alison accompanied Lexi to the centre and had been able to talk at length with the doctor and the community health worker who were supporting Lexi.

Dr Val Newman was of the opinion that Lexi would take about seven days to improve, or to get over the worst of withdrawal from heroin. Lexi was to have a small amount of methadone every day to stop the cravings and to give her body some relief. Once they had worked out her level of tolerance, a suitable dose could be administered, but there would be risks. Under no account was she to take any street heroin, or any other drug for that matter. She had to be watched all of the time, as failure during the initial stages of withdrawal was often an outcome. She could also die as a result of taking both heroin and methadone at the same time.

Alison could not help feeling that the care of someone so vulnerable and in ill-health, was well beyond her level of expertise and knowledge. This was not a job entirely for the police.

Dr Newman and Nurse Lisa White explained that Lexi's physical health had every chance of improving if she stuck to her methadone programme. There may even come a time when she would be free of addiction completely. It was her mental health that they were more concerned with.

Lisa White explained "With young girls like Lexi, her addiction is one thing, but her dependency is not just the physical need to obtain heroin, she is also dependent on the person supplying it. She says she hates this man called Fawcus, who she keeps mentioning, but she would go back to him in an instant if she thought she could. This happens all the time. He has complete power and control over her and that imbalance will take a long time to overcome. Even though she has suffered at his hands for god knows how long, she will do as he says. This sounds awful, but she will go back to what she is used to until she realises there is a real alternative."

Alison had genuinely believed that Lexi would have been as grateful as Diane for rescuing her from the brothel, so the realisation that there was a risk she would go back to Fawcus was hard to understand.

Dr Newman added "Fawcus was her provider, protector and supplier. He owned her. She needed him for drugs, food, money and somewhere to live. He took away her ability to make decisions for herself the moment she became addicted. He may have shown her a lot of positive attention when they first met, but that would have been replaced by a position of complete control over her. She could not exist without him and she would have been with other girls in the same situation. When it comes to interviewing her she may recall incidents in a matter of fact way, as if she was reading a story to you.

Her emotional well-being has been destroyed. If you could imagine for one minute looking at a brightly patterned piece of luxurious material, which has a vivid colour to it. Then pretend that piece of material represented your healthy emotional response to the world. Lexi's piece of material has been dipped in bleach and rinsed out many times. She has lost her personality, her youthful vibrancy and her ability to deal with her emotions. She is a hollow shell."

Alison was trying to understand issues she had not contemplated before. She had always approached vulnerable witnesses carefully and with empathy, without appreciating how complex it actually was.

"We need to interview her about what has happened over the past two years. How are we going to do it? I don't want to cause any more distress than there already is."

Dr Newman advised that the interviews would have to be short, with as many breaks as required and approached in the order Lexi remembered.

"If you are time-constrained it is perhaps best to deal with any issues the police think are absolutely necessary at this stage and then work through the rest over the coming weeks. Lexi is going to need a lot of patience from us all so that she can come to terms with what has happened and be able to deal with it for the rest of her life."

Alison was beginning to feel inadequate. The discussion had made her realise that an interview was not just a formality to collect facts, figures and points to prove so that the police could get an offender on a charge sheet. Far from it, the interviews with Lexi (and perhaps many more) were the beginning of a process of recovery. Handled correctly, they would assist that process. Handled badly, the process might not even start.

Alison needed to speak to Albert, who was eagerly awaiting the arrival of the TPOs. She asked to see him to go over the care of Lexi. Albert could tell that Alison was deep in thought as she began to recount her discussion with Dr Newman and Nurse Lisa White. Instead of hurrying Alison as he normally did, he knew that he had to listen.

"After talking to the medical staff, I can now see why Lexi is the way she is. The physical effects of withdrawal are obvious . . . we have all seen that with offenders in the cell block who have been in custody for a while. But she seems distant, even to Diane. Her Mam has a natural way of showing her affection towards Lexi; hugging her, holding her hand and encouraging her all the time. Just being with her is a show of genuine love, especially when she is being sick and suffering diarrhoea. Lexi does not look at you when she speaks, she does not hug her Mam back and she says things in such a way that she makes you feel uncomfortable. We are a bit out of our depth Albert."

"Apart from the medics, is there anyone we can get help from? Even some guidance would be better than nothing."

Alison had already searched the internet for projects designed to support sex workers and those who had been sexually exploited.

"There is nothing in our area. No projects, support groups or specialists other than for rape victims. It is as if the problem does not exist north of Yorkshire. We may get some advice from social services, but Lexi has had no contact with them for two years."

Albert began to contemplate problems further down the line.

"This is something that has been happening for as long as I remember. We expect witnesses and victims to be able to remember every detail of traumatic incidents, relate the facts to us, sign a statement and then put it all at the back of their minds until we end up in court months later. They then have to go over it, probably re-living the trauma as if it were happening again. We have far more support for people now, but it must cause a lot of stress no matter what we do. As a young detective I had a rape case at crown court which I will always remember. The defence barrister cross examined the victim in the most heartless way possible. At one point he asked her to lie down on the floor in front of the jury in the position she was raped. I thought the usher was going to punch him until the judge finally intervened and said a description would do. That would not happen these days, but I am worried that the defence will cast doubt over everything Lexi says due to her addiction and health. We have to make things easier for her by corroborating as much as we can."

"So if Lexi is well enough to do a short interview before the strike day, what should I cover?" asked Alison.

"Fawcus and the Doyles to start with, then Noone and Dryden. If she could give some background to the abuse she has suffered, then she would be doing us proud." Advised Albert.

Alison was grateful for some 'one to one' time with Albert.

"How is everything else going? Have you managed to get enough sleep at the hotel? I was hoping I could persuade Jill to do the next couple of nights" enquired Albert.

"It is fine, I get enough sleep as Diane is doing the most work. It is a bit of a break from my boyfriend too. He is a bit over-attentive sometimes, that is the best way I can put it."

"And what does Jody say about him? She has an approach to relationship counselling that 'Atila the Hun' had to diplomatic relations with the countries he invaded."

"The letter 'F' featured a lot, put it that way." Alison had cheered up a little.

Albert arranged to sit down with Alison and Jody to discuss how best to interview with Lexi over a period of time. He also needed Alison to be in the office on Thursday so they could plan the strike day. He explained that Miles had spoken to the Chief and there was no flexibility.

"We'll get there . . . we always do" declared Albert.

Alison and Albert returned to the main office and were introduced to the two TPOs by Susan.

"This is George Davies and Pete Hogarth. They are experienced TPOs and we have them for two days."

Albert welcomed the two detectives and they set about an agreed course of action. It was decided that each TPO would visit two brothels, preferably on separate days. They would use cash and have an exit story at the ready. The two officers from Leeds soon proved to be valuable sources of information.

The older one of the two, George, explained his understanding of what occurs in brothels. "Not all men go to see escorts for sex. Some just go for company, which helps us when we make an excuse and leave once the offer of sex has been made and we establish a few facts. There was only one occasion when I had trouble getting out, when the escort locked the door and would not let me leave until I had done the business. I had to press the panic button on that occasion. Most of the time we are in and out of the premises in less than fifteen minutes."

The younger TPO, called Pete, looked about sixteen to Albert.

"I'm not being funny, but are you allowed out after dark?" asked Albert, still trying to decide if Pete was old enough to have joined the police in the first place.

"Everyone says that, but I am 24. I had an indoor paper round."

Pete went on to say his youthful looks provided a few different exit plans, from not having enough money, to being put up to the visit by his mates.

"Great, lets' get cracking" said Albert "Our lads will be your back-up and do the paperwork and the continuity. Mick Miller knows the most about our local brothels so we'll get him to come and brief you."

Mick Miller had the list of brothels ready and he brought up the Superior Escorts web site on his computer. The escorts working on the day were listed, together with a general area. It was decided to concentrate on north of the Tyne for the time being, with each TPO visiting a brothel before 10pm.

Each escort had her own page within the web site, with a description and some photos. There was also a list of the sex acts they agreed to perform for punters, along with the prices. The basic fee for all of them was £50 per half hour 'incall' and £60 per half hour 'outcall'.

Pete Hogarth rang the main mobile number on the web site to book an escort called 'Jolene' who was in North Shields. He managed to arrange the appointment with a female who described herself as 'Front of House for Superior Escorts' for 7.30pm. He also agreed a cost of £50 and he asked if 'extras' would be available to him.

"That is up to you and Jolene" replied Front of House female. "Whatever happens is between you and her. If you go to George Street in Willington Quay about 10 minutes before your appointment, I will give you the number of the house. Is there anything else I can do for you?"

"No, that is fine. I will ring later" said Pete.

"Thank you for calling Superior Escorts."

George Davies waited about 10 minutes and rang the same number. Front of House female answered almost immediately.

"Hello, I was wondering if you had anyone available in the North Shields or Wallsend area for about half eight tonight please?"

"Let me just look for you . . . is half eight your only time?" asked Front of House. "I only have Sandy free at that time."

"What does she look like?" George asked, trying to get more information from Front of House.

"She is blonde, 36c, five foot three and has a bubbly personality. The fee is £50 per half hour and what happens between you both is your business. Is there anything else you would like to know before booking?"

"Er, yes, does she have any uniforms to dress up in?"

George could hear the tapping of a keyboard as Front of House searched for an answer.

"Yes she does; police, nurse, maid and secretary. Any good?"

George then made the booking for eight thirty and was told to ring back for the house number once he was in Shireside Street, which turned out to be where Fawcus had visited number 18 earlier that day.

The TPOs and their back up team of Dave, Alan, Jimmy and Derek had a bit of time to kill before setting off, so the grabbed a chance to get something to eat and exchange stories about previous operations. George had acted as a TPO for his force and a number of neighbouring forces, for about ten years. In that time there had been some good jobs and one or two disasters. In amongst it all had been a lot of embarrassing moments.

George relayed an incident when another TPO, on his first ever job, had been determined to stay in control of himself. He was asked to go into a massage parlour in Bradford and find out if sex was being offered by the female staff. He paid his money to the receptionist and was shown to a cubicle.

"Everything was going fine" continued George. "He was introduced to his masseuse who he described as wearing a very revealing outfit. He was told to undress and given a towel. She left the cubicle and he had his clothes off in seconds and lay on the bed, face down. She returned and rubbed his shoulders, then his back.

126

They chatted about nothing in particular and no offers of 'extras' were made. She asked him to turn over, which he did as he was still very much in control. That was until she started to rub the top of his legs and pulled the towel to one side. By this time he was saying his times tables backwards to try and take his mind off the inevitable. He told us how he looked down and saw his willy doing circles, as it does before you get an erection. His was like a helicopter and before he knew it, she said it was twenty five quid for a happy ending. He made a swift exit, but at least he got the evidence."

George enjoyed telling his story to a whole new audience and he had clearly relayed it many times since the actual incident occurred. Mick Miller found the story amusing, but he also just wanted to get on with the reason why the TPOs were with them in the first place. His time in FI had been varied and sometimes exciting, but he had often felt frustrated by the lack of interest in the intelligence he collected regarding prostitution. Operation Neon represented the first chance he had to reinforce his argument that criminal gangs made a lot of money from sex work, whilst exploiting the sex workers they controlled.

In four years of collecting the information, Mick had tried to lobby three senior officers who were placed in charge of FI. Two of them had been sympathetic, but had failed to get any response from their managers further up the ranks. The other, a female officer who Mick had hoped would listen to him, was dismissive of every suggestion he made. In the year Miles Ashley had been in charge, Mick had been unable to put the subject on the agenda at all.

Mick confided in Hughie and Brian a conversation he had with Miles after the meeting at FI with CC and FCT. Mick had no idea what the meeting was about, but decided to disclose everything he knew to those who were listening when asked his opinion. Afterwards, Miles had apologised to him for not even knowing about his database and he promised to invest some resources in to the problem as soon as Operation Neon was underway. Mick had appreciated Miles's apology and encouragement and in return had promised himself to see the job through.

Pete Hogarth was taken to George Street and rang Superior Escorts for the number of the house. On this occasion a male answered and was quick to say he had to go to number three and to use the front door.

Derek and Jimmy waited close by and made sure Pete's panic button and his recording device was working. They watched Pete get to the door and enter. Pete was greeted by Jolene, who asked him if would like a drink and for his first name.

"No thanks, I don't want to keep you long. I'm Pete. I have never done this before and my mates have put me up to it. Can I just sit for a while, then leave. I can give you the cash now."

Jolene was completely at ease with his suggestion. She said she was going to have a drink even if he did not want one and produced a blue coloured alcopop. She was wearing a silk night gown and high heels and asked Pete if she could ditch the heels as they were uncomfortable.

"I have one of these after every punter. How old are you anyway?"

"Twenty four" replied Pete, trying his best to look nervous.

"So have you had a shag before? Is that what it is? Have your mates had a whip round?"

"Sort of, here is the fifty quid. Can I just sit for another ten minutes or so? They made me come in and then drove off."

"It is your half hour. Do you not just want a hand job or something? That's all everyone else has had today. We call it 'Tug Tuesday' and tomorrow it will probably be 'Wank Wednesday'." Jolene knew she could embarrass young, inexperienced lads with her straightforward suggestions.

"Look, I might come back another time. I just want it to be on my own terms. When are you here?"

"Most days, just look on the website. My friend Wendy is here every other day. We can do you a special with both of us."

The pair then watched the TV, discussing the news. Pete explained that he was working in the North East for short periods with his employers and he would come back if he could. Jolene told him that she wished she had a normal job, but she could not give up until she had paid a load of debt off, mainly on credit cards. She went on to say she had a few regular clients and she did not mind seeing them. She complained that the agency sent every nutter and lunatic that booked her, so she had no idea who was next at the door. Pete asked if the agency took a lot of money off her, telling her that he had not realised she did not get most of the money. In his mind he knew her answer was likely to be good evidence.

"They take fifteen per cent, plus five pounds per punter for the rent on the flat and for bills. I also have to pay for my own condoms and occasionally they tell me to give one of their friends a blow job for nothing. I reckon they take at least half of my money."

"Their friends?" asked Pete.

"You don't want to know young 'un. Anyway your time is almost up."

Jolene took Pete back to the front door and asked him to tell the agency she was "very good" if they asked.

"Are you nearly finished for today?" asked Pete as he stepped outside.

"Midnight and I'm off, before the drunk arseholes start to ring up. Thanks love, see you soon." Jolene closed the door and went back to her alcopop.

With one brothel evidenced, Jimmy and Derek decided to drop Pete off at his digs so he was ready for the next day. They were interested to know what had been said so they could summarise everything for Albert. Pete explained that she had made the offer of sex, taken the money and confirmed that two sex workers used the premises.

Dave and Alan drove George to his appointment on Shireside Street and he was given the details by a male who advised him it was "number 18, the blue door and not the white door."

George went through the same pre-visit process with his back-up team and knocked on the door at exactly eight thirty.

"Come in, I'm Sandy, nice to see you" as she escorted George to the sitting room. Another girl was sitting on the sofa, with only a towel wrapped around her.

"I'm George, to see just Sandy."

"Oh don't worry about my friend Lizzie. She is going out soon. Would you like a drink George?"

George declined and Sandy then led him through the sitting room and into a rear bedroom. She took off her night gown and asked George if he wanted to shower first."

"No, no, I showered at my mate's house. I visit him twice a year to play golf. He is visiting his Mother in her care home, so I have a bit of time to kill."

"Well it is fifty pounds for sex. I do not do anal and you must wear a condom." Said Sandy

"That's fine, here is the money. Can I just sit here for a minute?"

George sat down and said he felt unwell. Sandy again offered him a drink.

"I get terrible indigestion and I felt it a few minutes ago. I must stop eating pastry."

Sandy sat on the other side of the bed and told him to take his time. She made some small talk about where George lived and asked how much he liked the North East.

"I love it up here . . . the beaches, the golf and the women are lovely. Is this your place?"

"No, this belongs to the landlord the agency deals with. Me and Lizzie pay the rent though."

George winced as if his indigestion was getting the better of him. He asked for another few minutes as he looked around the room. Sandy's uniforms were on a makeshift clothes rail in one corner. A dressing table with a tray of condoms and lube sat beneath the window. The bed took up most of the floor space, bar the chair George sat on. A small lamp on the floor gave the only light.

"Look I'm really sorry but I will have to go. This is not going to pass until I take some medication back at my mate's house. Of all the times . . . I'm sorry Sandy" George was using his exit strategy.

Sandy explained that she had to keep the money as the agency would not believe her and she would have to pay their commission out of her own pocket.

"But it is not your fault" replied George.

"Try telling them that . . . they don't care what happens as long as they get their cut." Sandy went on to say that she would like to work for another agency, but none of them wanted escorts who had been on Superior's books.

130

George made his way through to the front door, saying good bye to Lizzie who was still sitting on the sofa. Sandy followed him and asked if he would be okay to get back to his mate's house. George confirmed he would and went on his way.

Dave and Alan were surprised to see him back so soon, but George told them he did not need to stay any longer as the evidence was obvious from the first minute. With that, they dropped him off at the hotel to join Pete.

### Wednesday 7<sup>th</sup> August

With two brothels evidenced and everything else progressing, Albert was beginning to think he should buy a lottery ticket.

"We are moving things along at a hell of a pace" he told the morning briefing. He asked for more of the same with the TPOs, but south of the Tyne.

Lexi had spent a slightly better night at the hotel and she was due back at the clinic for 10am.

Susan had arranged for the monitoring of Aidan Dryden's computer activity from the moment he commenced duty at 3pm. There was little else they could do with him until the strike day.

Operation Neon was gathering pace and by midday, two more brothels had been evidenced at 5 Deuchar Street and 27 Dock Row by the TPOs.

Fawcus went about his routine, with the technical equipment still doing its job. He visited an estate agents in Wallsend and then called in at Graeme Doyle's house. He was with Doyle for over an hour and then went mobile again.

"He is very close to Lexi's bedsit" announced Brian. "Shall we cover it Albert? The lads should be finished with the TPOs by now."

Albert had expected this to happen sooner or later and he asked Brian to get whoever was closest to start and travel, just in case.

Within a few minutes, Fawcus parked up near to 39 Waterford Way. Dave and Alan were the first to get anywhere near the area and there was little more they could do other than drive along a parallel street and hopefully cover Fawcus as he drove away.

Brian kept up a running commentary, relying on the accuracy of the technical equipment.

"He is still parked up . . . if the map is anywhere near correct, the BMW is about two houses down from 39."

Derek and Jimmy arrived not long after, allowing one of them to walk through the street to see if Fawcus was either in the car or had gone into the bedsit.

Albert phoned Alison to warn her that Fawcus was in Waterford Way. She was with Lexi and explained that they had already discussed a cover story should Fawcus ring.

Derek made his way on to Waterford Way and could see the black BMW parked between several other cars. The street looked a lot busier than when they had been there to rescue Lexi. As Derek approached the car, he saw Fawcus sitting in the driver's seat, making a call on his mobile. Colin Doyle was in the passenger seat, looking down as if he was reading or using his phone. From where the BMW was parked, they had a clear view of the door to Lexi's bedsit. Derek could not hang around very long, so he walked to the other end of the street and took up a position to be able to see if the car moved.

A few minutes passed and Fawcus got out of the car and went to the door of 39. Derek could not see if he gained access, as he lost sight of him for about 20-30 seconds until he re-appeared and went back to the car. Derek could only conclude that he had not been into the house and had given up quite quickly when there was no reply.

Fawcus had been in the car for no more than a minute, when Lexi's phone rang.

"It's him" said Lexi.

"Remember what we said Lexi . . . be calm . . . he cannot get to you now" reassured Alison.

Lexi answered her mobile "Hello Barry, I'm at . . . . " She was in mid-sentence when Fawcus interrupted.

"Where the fuck are you! I have been sitting outside for ages."

"I am at the NHS drop-in. I have been ill." Lexi started to reveal her cover story.

"That is all I hear from you, always fucking ill. You are no real use to me now Lexi; you are a waste of space. No more fucking gear off me until you get your arse back here."

132

"There is a long queue, so I will be a while," Lexi was thinking on her feet.

"I am with Colin and we have some jobs to do. Ring me when you are ready you little slut, I will be back to see you later. Do you understand?"

"Yes, yes, sorry Barry"

"You fucking will be," threatened Fawcus as he rung off abruptly.

Derek observed as the BMW drove away and out of sight. Brian monitored the vehicle as it drove to another potential brothel about two miles away. Albert decided not to risk anyone going too close as he expected there to be another call to Waterford Way. The BMW stayed at the address for over an hour. Dave and Alan were able to drive past and saw that there was no one in the car.

Alison and Albert discussed their next move, in preparation for further calls from Fawcus to Lexi.

"I think we are going to have to let Diane take the next one from him and say that she has been admitted to hospital for tests" suggested Alison.

"Yes, good idea. That is far better than him battering the door down at Waterford Way. It might also provoke him in to using one of his corrupt friends. He might not know that Pat Noone is on holiday so he will have to contact Dryden instead to see where Lexi is. You get Diane prepared and I will sort out the rest of the team."

Albert enlisted the help of Susan's contact in IT to make absolutely sure Dryden could not press a button without Operation Neon knowing about it.

At around 2.45pm the BMW went mobile again, this time through the Tyne Tunnel to the brothels in Deuchar Street and Dock Row, staying for just a few minutes at both flats.

Brian continued to study every move and after Dock Row, the BMW went on a route that was not part of the routine experienced so far.

"He is travelling back towards Gateshead, but on the bottom road which runs past all the industrial estates. There cannot be many brothels there. He must be up to something else" said Brian as he kept up his commentary for the pursuing team.

133

The BMW drove around one industrial estate without stopping, then drove through an access road to another much larger industrial estate. Albert was conscious that this looked like an anti-surveillance manoeuvre, so he made sure everyone kept well back.

Scott and Neil joined the team, in one of the hire cars. Albert asked them to get a bit closer, should the BMW park up.

The BMW continued to cruise around the car parks and the narrow roads of the industrial estate, eventually coming to a stop next to the largest premises on the site. Hughie was quick to confirm that this was a large DIY store, next door to a supermarket and petrol station.

"If the technical is doing its job, the car is at the rear end of the DIY store car park" updated Brian.

Albert had a decision to make; should he send in a car to locate the BMW and see what they were up to, or should they sit tight and not risk a compromise. The team had been very lucky up until now, so was there any real need to push things? He decided to play safe and asked Derek and Jimmy to get into the store, locate security and ask if there was any CCTV covering the car park.

It took Derek and Jimmy about five minutes to phone in with an update, which felt like an eternity for Albert.

"We should have a camera on the BMW in a jiffy. They are moving it around for us now. It normally just keeps an eye on the main entrance" explained Jimmy.

"Okay, it is over to you. Brian will monitor the technical if you keep us updated with any other movement. Can you see who is in the car?" asked Albert.

Jimmy explained that they had a decent view and could see that there were two males in the car. The camera angle was too high to see their faces and could not get any better. The car was parked as far away as possible from the DIY store in the last row of the car park.

Albert rang Alison and asked if Diane was ready with her script. Alison had briefed her to expect a phone call, but Albert wanted to seize the initiative.

"If she feels she can, get her to ring Fawcus now and tell him that Lexi has gone into hospital. If he gets stroppy, ring off. We can evidence the whole lot and see what he does next."

Alison prepared Diane who was ready to make the call. This was another chance for her to outwit the man who had made their lives a misery. Alison phoned Albert and kept him on the line as Diane rang Fawcus.

"Is that Fawcus?" asked Diane in a confident tone.

"You know it is. Who is this, where is Lexi?"

"She is being kept in. She has abdominal pains and they are worried. She wanted you to know and don't even try to find her. She has to stay in this time."

"Ah, so she has her Mother running around after again has she? So fucking what. I will tell you what is going on, not the other way around. I can find out any time I fucking like where she is and you can't keep out of the way either." Fawcus was not best pleased, so he began issuing threats as usual.

"I don't care what you say you big fat twat! Lexi is in hospital so you can do what you want. Goodbye." Diane rang off before Fawcus had a chance to say anything further.

Diane felt empowered; she had stood up to Fawcus and it made her feel good. She knew that he was on his back foot and she had the police to support her.

"Well done. I bet he's having a wobbler as we speak" said Alison as she made sure Albert had heard most of what was said.

Albert confirmed that Fawcus had been on the phone and Jimmy could just about make out that he was now making a further call. It was no surprise when Lexi's phone rang again.

"Ignore it" said Albert. "Switch it off. He can't do anything and for once he is not in complete control. Hopefully his head will explode."

Albert asked for an update from Jimmy, who still had the car on camera, as Fawcus and Colin Doyle remained in it. Fawcus was constantly on his phone; at one point he got out of the car and walked about, looking more and more agitated as he did so.

Scott and Neil were in a position to cover the main car park entrance from some distance away, when a silver Toyota appeared and drove towards the DIY store. They immediately looked at each other, realising they had the same thought.

"That cannot be . . . is that Pat in his car?" said Neil, not really believing what he had seen.

Scott alerted Jimmy, who did not have the Toyota in sight. Derek had been experimenting with the other cameras and he picked it up as it drove around the perimeter fence at the other side of the car park.

"I think it is him, he has the same car but I cannot get the number, hang on" Derek kept everyone in suspense.

The Toyota completed a lap of the car park and then stopped about fifty yards from Fawcus and his BMW. Derek confirmed it was Pat Noone's car.

Albert immediately asked everyone to keep out of the way. He then had a thought – where was Derek and Jimmy's car; if Pat saw it he would recognise it and take flight.

"It is in another group of cars nearer to the building. He cannot see it from where he is and if he goes to see Fawcus he will be about a hundred and fifty metres away." Jimmy put Albert at ease.

The driver's door of the Toyota opened and Pat Noone got out.

"It's him," whispered Jimmy, even though there was no chance of anyone hearing him. "I hope this thing records okay" referring to the camera equipment.

They covered Noone as he sauntered towards the BMW and upon reaching it, shaking hands with Colin Doyle through the open window. Noone got in to the rear of the BMW as Jimmy continued to relay the scene to his team.

"How can he explain this" said Albert to Brian and Hughie, just as Susan came in to the office.

"IT have been trying to ring you Albert. Dryden has booked on and he is going through the logs since his last tour of duty."

"Can you get in touch with them, the next few minutes might be interesting. Noone is with Fawcus now."

"What!" replied Susan "Is he for real?"

Susan quickly caught up with what was happening and she kept the line open with IT. Dryden had so far looked at all of his allocated crimes, past duties and some local intelligence regarding nuisance motor cyclists. He had also looked at the record belonging to a 19 year old female called Rebecca English.

136

"Becky" suggested Hughie.

Pat Noone remained in the car for about fifteen minutes. He then got out and after a few words to Colin Doyle, he walked back to his Toyota.

Susan rang IT again for any update. As she spoke to her contact, her clenched fist went up in the air, as if she had won a trophy.

"Thank you, thank you. Keep all that for me and we will see you later." She ended the call and said "Dryden has just checked Lexi's record. They are all in it together. How stupid can they get? They must think they are untouchable."

"Well that just about sums it up; they have been untouchable and if it was not for Frank and Scott, it could have gone on forever. Roll on strike day when we can get them all in." Albert was pleased with the way things were going, but dismayed at the actions of Pat Noone and Aidan Dryden.

Jimmy tracked Noone on the camera as he left the car park, closely followed by Fawcus who turned in a different direction as he got to the main road. Albert did not want any further surveillance other than the technical for the rest of the day. The evidence continued to mount up and there was no reason to keep taking risks. The operation had now switched to that of containment, instead of being entirely proactive.

Albert and Susan had to decide what they were going to do to keep Fawcus guessing for another 36 hours until the morning of the strike day. They knew that he had managed to find Lexi in hospital the last time she was admitted, but nothing had been found to link Noone or Dryden. There was the option of putting an entry on Lexi's intelligence record to try and put them off looking for her, but that might look too obvious.

Albert consulted Alison, to see if there was anything she and Jody could suggest. After all, they had been with Diane and Lexi long enough to work out how Fawcus might react.

Diane was of the opinion that Fawcus would not rest until he had located Lexi. He did not take kindly to anyone threatening his authority and he would lose face with the Doyles if he was shown up by one of the women he controlled. She thought it was best to switch Lexi's phone back on and pacify him with some texts, perhaps with a promise that Lexi would be back in her bedsit as soon as possible. Fawcus had not specifically told Lexi how he managed to find her in hospital, so he may have found her by luck or had simply rang around himself.

It was eventually decided that a text should be sent, explaining that Lexi would be in for 24-48 hours with a kidney infection, with the hope it was enough for him to leave well alone.

A long two hours passed by until a text was received from Fawcus.

"OK. Ring me tomorrow without fail."

Operation Neon stepped one day closer to the most important phase – arrests and interviews.

**Thursday 8<sup>th</sup> August**

Miles attended the morning briefing and explained to Albert and Susan that the Chief was expecting imminent arrests. Miles had assured her that the main offenders were to be arrested the following day.

"I hope that is the case Albert. Great work yesterday . . . I hope Fawcus continues to believe Diane" commented Miles.

Albert had already made his mind up that they had to move as quickly as possible, now that they had enough evidence to disrupt the Doyle's little empire. He was further encouraged when Alison told him that she thought Lexi was up to a very short video interview that afternoon. Lexi was the person who would provide the evidence of abuse and cruelty at the hands of Fawcus, so Albert asked Alison and Jody to do the interview, as they had a good understanding of what she could tolerate. In the meantime, Jill could obtain a statement from Diane.

Albert discussed the possibility of both Lexi and Diane entering the witness protection scheme with Miles. They were likely to be absolutely crucial to the success of the operation and they deserved to be given special consideration. The content of their interviews would give a better idea of how valuable they would be.

Lexi went to the clinic with Alison and Jody, who both noticed that she was showing signs of withdrawal easing. Dr Newman examined her and noted that her general well-being was still poor, but it was not as bad as a few days previous. Dr Newman pointed out that Lexi was more alert, responsive and looked less exhausted, so she could be spoken to if the interview was a short one.

Alison had booked an interview suite the previous day, in the hope that Lexi would be able to manage. After making sure Lexi ate something and had her medication, the preparations for the interview could begin.

Lexi was shown around the interview suite, made up of a sort of sitting room, with easy chairs and a coffee table. The interview would be video-recorded, with Alison asking some questions whilst Jody looked after the recording equipment. No one else was in the building.

Lexi seemed as relaxed as possible, so Alison went through the formalities of the interview and started with a few questions about Lexi herself, her home and her school. She was unsure of what to say at first until Alison asked her to go through what had happened since her 18$^{th}$ birthday.

"I was pissed off when I did not get a job after my college course and I was sick of my Mam telling me what to do. Becky was with Fawcus in his car one night and I went for a drive and that was it. Heroin, drink, a few tabs . . . you name it they were all on offer and I took the lot. Fawcus gave me twenty quid here and twenty quid there, I drove around some flats where him and Becky got out and after a couple of weeks he asked me to stay with Becky when he went somewhere else. She then told me he wanted his money back and I had to shag a load of men. She said the same had happened to her. I told her to fuck off as she was no friend of mine, but I could not get out as we were locked in. Fawcus came back and he gave me some heroin to calm down, but I was still not happy. He pushed Becky about a bit and said if I did not give him his money she would get a hiding. By then I needed the gear. I was just another junky in the making. So that was it, I began working as a prostitute for Fawcus."

Lexi was able to describe some of the flats she had worked in and how her relationship with her Mam deteriorated.

"Who else did you see with Fawcus?"

"At first, when I still looked pretty, the two fat Doyles would come around, about once a month. They got sex for free as they were the bosses. Fawcus licked their arses all the time, he was just their lacky. Fawcus wanted sex as well, but I refused until the time I was desperate for some gear. I saw him rape Becky a few weeks ago, he pushed her over a chair and did it in front of me. She was screaming for him to stop and there was blood everywhere. I have not seen her since that day."

Lexi confirmed that this had taken place in 39 Waterford Way. She and Becky were together in the bedsit. The punters they were being sent were the ones no one else would see.

"Is there anyone else who got sex for free?"

"Yes. Their mates. One called Pat and another called Aidan. I know they are both coppers. They had that look about them. At first they used to pay but that soon stopped. Fawcus used to tell me they were coming and it was him that told me they were coppers . . . . it was his way of telling me and Becky that there was nothing we could do and if we left they would find us with the help of their bent coppers."

"Do you think that is how they found you in hospital?"

"Unless Fawcus followed my Mam, it must have been them."

"How many other girls have you met who Fawcus and the Doyles had working for them?"

"Susanne, Gayle and some others who I cannot remember."

"Were they with you in the same flat?"

"Sometimes. We had to do double acts together when punters came to watch. I hated doing it with Gayle."

"Why was that?"

"She has got a smelly fanny."

"Right, okay, that is one of those things, erm . . . . where was I . . can I ask about the police officers. When was the last time you saw either of them?"

"Pat was at Holly Gardens I think, months ago and the other one who is a complete dick . . . . must have been well before that."

"Do you think there any other police officers?"

"Not that I know of."

"Lexi, will you let me know if you need a break?"

"Yes. Can we do just a few more questions? I want to go back and see my Mam. There is lots more I could tell you, but I'm just not ready. Some of the punters were bastards, and, they . . . would . . . . . can I leave that for another time"

"Okay. Is Becky's second name English?"

"Yes it is. I think she has used a few surnames . . . she used to go missing a lot like me."

"Just before we break, what does Fawcus's Mother do?"

"She tells him what to do. She is a hard faced old cow. She is in Spain a lot, but when she is here she goes around in the car with him carrying the cash and the gear. She tells him to keep all the lasses in check. She knows he gives out hidings but she does nothing about it. All that matters to her is her holidays and her gold jewellery. She does the phones sometimes at Doyle's house. That is where all the calls are taken. They have a small bedroom with all the books and the lists for when the punters ring up."

"Have you ever been to the Doyle's house to see all of this?"

"You must be joking! Graeme Doyle's wife would go ballistic. She must know what he is up to but she just wants the money. Fawcus says she wears the trousers, but he cannot talk, the Mammy's boy that he is."

Alison terminated the interview as Lexi tired quickly and Jody joined them from the recording room.

"Well done Lexi, you were really strong," encouraged Jody.

There was no real need to try another interview with Lexi, as she had covered enough for the time being. Alison and Jody decided to take her back to the hotel and meet up with Diane and Jill.

Alison was acutely aware that they needed to phone Fawcus and put him off for another day. She asked Diane to make the call, as it would have been unwise to leave it any longer.

Diane was ready with her story. Her confidence was high after the previous encounter with her daughter's tormentor.

"Hello is that Fawcus?"

"Aye" came the abrupt reply.

"Lexi is in until at least tomorrow afternoon. She needs another course of antibiotics and then they think the doctor will let her go."

"Liar" replied Fawcus.

Diane was put off her stride. She had expected a torrent of abuse from Fawcus, but he was calm and to the point. Her worst fears began to re-enter her mind; had his mates in the police helped him again?

"Well that is the way it is" she answered nervously.

"She is not in hospital . . . do you think I am stupid? I know exactly what you are up to."

Alison quickly scribbled 'he's bluffing' on a bit of paper for Diane. She drew a deep breath and went on the offensive.

"Well in that case come and get her. Show your face and I'll get you arrested. You can't pay off all the police in the world. Why don't you ask your Mammy what you should do? You only pick on women you . . . ."

Fawcus interrupted and spoke slowly and menacingly. "I will come and get you both when I want. It will be when you least expect it; could be in five minutes or five hours. She owes me, I want my money and then I will decide what happens next. Do you understand that you skinny fucking bitch? Am I making myself crystal fucking clear?"

Diane looked apprehensive and sought reassurance from Alison and Jody. Alison made a gesture to end the call and Jody mouthed a reply which left no doubt as to what she thought of Fawcus.

Diane stood up from the hotel bed and found some inner courage.

"Well, well, well. I might be a skinny little bitch, but you are a big fat bastard with a tiny knob. The lasses all joke about your little cock and they say it looks like a chipolata on a hippo. Now fuck off and don't expect me to ring you again."

Diane ended the call and Jody started dancing around the room. Alison could hardly stop laughing and Lexi, who had hid in the bathroom during the call, emerged to see all three in a state of joy.

"Have you lot been on the drink or what?" Diane hugged Lexi who stood with a bemused look on her face. Diane knew that with the passing of each day, they were slowly but surely escaping from Fawcus.

Albert had decided to contact Witness Protection for some guidance as to how they could assist the operation. The response had not been as positive as he had hoped. The application for their service would have to go through his supervision, the Command Block and then Finance before a decision could be made. There was one helpful suggestion, which Albert immediately accepted. Witness Protection (WP) had a flat that they used as a stop-gap which was currently empty. Only a handful of officers could be allowed to visit it, so that it remained a relative secret. It would be safer, more comfortable and the risks of being found were greatly reduced.

Arrangements were made for the address to be securely emailed and Albert asked for one of the WP officers to meet either Alison or Jody.

The schedule for the strike day was now foremost in the minds of Albert, Susan and Miles. With limited resources, it would only be possible to arrest and interview the main offenders; the rest would have to await another day unless it was completely unavoidable.

Top of the list were Noone, Dryden, Fawcus, Colin Doyle and Graeme Doyle. Staff from CC would handle the corrupt officers and FCT would deal with the rest with help from FI. As soon as the arrests were made and a search of their homes carried out, resources would then be freed up to visit the brothels.

A policy decision was made to treat the women found in the brothels as potential victims or witnesses. Lexi had already made it plain that she and Becky had suffered at the hands of Fawcus and the Doyles, so there was a distinct possibility there would be more. Albert called a briefing for everyone at 7pm.

Alison and Jody were delighted to hear the news that safe accommodation had been secured, so they helped Diane pack up in readiness for the call from WP. Within an hour they were at the flat in a residential area close to police headquarters. Jody stayed with them whilst Alison attended the briefing.

The briefing was not particularly complicated as the team were all well aware of the alleged offenders with whom they would be dealing. Noone and Dryden would be arrested first, as there was a small chance they would try to alert the others in a last, desperate chance at hiding evidence. Once they were in custody, the rest would have an early morning 'knock' and be taken to a different police station.

Albert asked everyone to be in for 5.30am, with the first arrests scheduled for 6am.

"If we have everyone in by 9am, the bacon sandwiches are on me" encouraged Albert. "We'll allocate interview teams after that and see what they have to say. Hughie has prepared packages for the interviews and Ros the analyst has provided some charts with the connections between the offenders. Tommy has had a look at all the premises we will be visiting. The search warrants are in the folders. The only other thing I need to mention is that I will be going with Alan, Scott and Neil to get Mr Fawcus. I can hardly wait."

**Friday 9<sup>th</sup> August.**
Strike day.

Miles Ashley was one of the first to arrive, explaining that he had hardly slept. Albert had finally dozed off at 1am so he felt as if he had not been to bed at all.

"We'll sleep well tonight Albert and I will probably dream about the Chief ringing me every five minutes," joked Miles, who was again thoroughly enjoying his involvement with the practical side of policing.

With radios tested and teams allocated, Susan left with her colleagues to arrest Noone and Steve led the other CC team to arrest Dryden.

Albert had divided the FCT into three. Tommy, Derek, Jimmy and Jill were to deal with Colin Doyle. Brian, Dave and Alison were entrusted with Graeme Doyle and had Mick Miller to give them a hand.

Albert, Scott, Neil and Alan were tasked with bringing in Fawcus.

Hughie and Miles would stay in the office to coordinate the arrest phase, whilst Jody needed to check in with Lexi and Diane.

Each team drove to a suitable place whilst awaiting confirmation from CC that they had done their job.

Susan and Steve coordinated their warrants and both doors went in at 6.10am.

Noone was in bed in the front bedroom of his house and had hardly woken by the time Susan was in his room, identifying herself and asking him to confirm who he was.

She cautioned him and said "You are under arrest for misconduct in a public office and conspiracy to control prostitution."

Noone just stared at the floor and made no comment as he was detained. He was shown a copy of the warrant and informed a search would be made of the house. He gave no response whatsoever.

Noone was dressed in a t-shirt and boxer shorts, so it was suggested to him he should get dressed. He finally broke his silence and asked if he could use the toilet.

At Dryden's house, the door had been a bit more robust and it took several good hits to gain access. Dryden was out of bed and at the top of the stairs by the time Steve managed to caution and arrest him.

Dryden fell to the floor on his knees and curled up, with his hands over his face. His wife appeared at the bedroom door in a state of shock and was screaming to know what was going on. Several minutes went by until things had calmed down so Steve could confirm that Dryden was in custody.

It was now over to Hughie, in his role as coordinator, to make sure the other three strike teams were in a position to execute their warrants. He called each team and put them on standby.

Albert turned to Scott, as they sat outside Fawcus's address "He loves this bit you know. He has to have everything in order, precise times and instructions. Any second now he will make an announcement."

"Hughie to FCT arrest teams. The time is now 6.26am. STRIKE-STRIKE-STRIKE."

The Doyles lived in almost identical, four bedroomed ex-council houses a few streets away from each other. Access to the front door was relatively easy and within minutes both Colin and Graeme Doyle had been turned out of their beds and were in custody.

Albert and his team had taken a while longer to get to the door of Fawcus's flat, which was on the second floor of the complex. Everything had that brand-new look and smell about it; the flat opposite Fawcus even had a small table and a chair on the landing presumably for visitors or older police officers finding themselves out of breath.

It seemed almost a shame to use the ram on the door as it looked in pristine condition. Alan had a quick push to size it up and then gave it an almighty bash next to the lock. The door flew open and hit something on the other side creating a loud hollow sound. They all rushed in and found Fawcus standing next to his bed, frozen to the spot with his hand hiding his chipolata.

"Police" said Albert. "We have a warrant to search the premises and can I also tell you that you are under arrest for conspiracy to control prostitution and aiding misconduct in a public office. You do not have to say anything but it may harm your defence if you do not mention something which you later rely on in court. Anything you do say may be given in evidence."

"Okay, okay, I've got the message" said Fawcus, resigned to a day in the cells.

Alan asked him to get dressed and sit in the living room during the search.

Albert noticed that the glazed door to the ensuite was closed, but the light was on and the fan was running.

"Anyone in there?" asked Albert.

"See for yourself," replied Fawcus.

Albert knocked on the door and opened it, to find a dark haired female inside. He asked her to come out and get dressed in the spare bedroom. She scurried past them and did as she was told.

Neil took some details from her and she gave her name as Gayle Harrison, from North Shields. It was soon established that she worked for Superior Escorts and she was staying with Fawcus for a few days before his Mother came back from Spain.

"Do you have any belongings in this flat Gayle?" asked Neil.

"No, just my clothes, my bag and some make up" replied a very quiet Gayle.

During the subsequent search, £16,800 in cash was found in the small bedroom, 12 small plastic bags of brown powder were found in the kitchen and a quantity of phones and two lap tops were found in the living room. Documents and financial records were also seized.

The flat was well furnished, with a large flat screen TV adorning every room. The sofa and the other items of furniture all looked brand new. Fawcus had a collection of expensive aftershave and several watches. His wardrobe consisted of almost every style of black coloured shirt and t-shirt on the market.

At the end of the search, Fawcus was additionally arrested for the brown powder which was suspected to be heroin. He had lost the power of speech by that time and his only comment was that he needed legal advice.

The other two searches had progressed equally well. Colin Doyle had £21,000 in cash in a kitchen drawer. Graeme Doyle had £6000 in cash in his garage cupboard and his small bedroom revealed a vast amount of material relating to 'Superior Escorts'. Both houses contained every electrical device possible, luxurious furnishings and accessories. Colin owned a Mercedes and his wife had a MX-5 convertible. Graeme also had a Mercedes and his wife had a brand new Fiat 500 convertible. They were living a well-financed lifestyle.

Colin's wife sat with her son in the living room, hardly uttering a word. She only moved to make herself a cup of tea mid-way through the search.

Graeme's wife was exactly the opposite.

"You will pay for that fucking door and any other damage. This is victimisation. You lot are clueless! We are running a business, it is legit." If she said words to that affect once, she said them twenty times. She paced around the house trying to watch everything that went on all at once. Alison tried to calm her down but with no success, so Dave took Graeme Doyle to one side.

"If she does not calm down she may well have to come with us. Can you have a word and tell her to let us get on with the job and we will get out of here sooner. Does that make sense?"

It must have made sense, as Graeme Doyle turned to his wife and said "Gloria, will you shut your fucking hole for just five minutes so these lot can get finished and out of here? You sound like an old fish wife on speed."

This was not exactly the sort of wording Dave had expected, so he was surprised when Gloria did calm down. However, it did not last long and she turned her attention from the police to her husband once she had processed his insult.

"I'll show what a fish wife is . . . I am going to cut you into fillets the moment you come back through that door you big useless prick! I told you I never wanted the police at my door again and here they are. Everything you touch turns to shite." At that moment she took a swipe at him and connected with the top of his head as he ducked out of the way. Alison grabbed her and took her in to the hallway, where Gloria broke down in tears and sat on the stairs.

"Take the bastard away will you? Lock him up for good, you will be doing me a massive fucking favour." Gloria had just about worn herself out and she remained on the stairs, sobbing, until the search was over.

Graeme Doyle did not give Gloria another look as he was led away to the police car. She took one last opportunity to shout abuse at him as he walked down the driveway. It did not seem to register with him at all. Alison was last to leave and she gave Gloria a copy of the warrant and the search record for her to keep.

"Thank you," said Gloria, her mood and her temper had subsided. "Keep him for as long as you like. I am finished with him this time."

Alison pointed out that her details and her mobile number were on the search record and should Gloria want to know anything, then she could ring her and she would try her best to find out.

Albert and his team were last back to the office at CC, carrying a bagful of bacon sandwiches.

"Did you have to break into your last ten bob note Albert?" asked Hughie, grateful for the free sandwich all the same.

"Ha, Ha. Let's get them eaten and we will work out what to do next." Albert was in his element; progress was being made.

Susan and Steve updated everyone about their searches. Noone had remained calm throughout and gave no indication at all that he was surprised to be arrested, or that he was expecting it. Two phones and a lap top had been found; anything that looked like a financial document was also seized. Dryden had more or less collapsed when he was arrested and had remained in a state of shock. The Custody Officer, back at the police station where Dryden had been lodged, decided to have him continuously monitored in case he tried to do something stupid. Steve's team had also seized phones, lap tops and documentation.

It was quickly decided that Susan and Steve would interview the two corrupt cops, with assistance from another member of CC to

148

monitor the interviews and take notes of any significant developments as Interview Advisor.

Albert and Alison would deal with Fawcus, whilst Scott and Dave were given the Doyles to interview. Tommy was nominated as Interview Advisor, assisting with disclosure for the solicitors and generally keeping things on track whilst the interviews were in progress.

Miles returned from seeing the Chief and explained that she was pleased Operation Neon had been successful. Her next demand was that the offenders should all be charged and remanded in custody for court as soon as possible.

"Blimey, when was the last time she prepared a file of evidence for something like this?" asked Albert.

All Miles could do was shrug his shoulders. "Do you want me to deal with the CPS Albert? I suppose I could give them a run-down of the evidence so far with Hughie's help and it may save time waiting for a charging decision?"

Albert was impressed with Miles offer of help and he agreed immediately. Depending on the availability of Solicitors, it could well be late afternoon before all those in custody had been interviewed and the whole process could possibly extend until the next day.

"I'll put them in the picture and await updates," said Miles, clearly keen to stay involved.

Albert contacted Jody so Diane and Lexi could be told the news. This also made him think about Frank, who had been almost forgotten in the week that Operation Neon had been going at full tilt. He asked Alison if he had been on the phone in the past few days.

"I was just thinking about him too. He sent a text on Wednesday saying he was starting a course of some description on Monday. His doctor had recommended it. I just sent a text back saying 'well done' as we were busy with Lexi. I don't know what he was on about. I'll ring him later today."

Mick Miller had been asked to gather everyone who was not part of the interview teams to start visiting the brothels. The phones seized from Fawcus and the Doyles rang continuously from inside the exhibit bags in which they had been placed. The news of the warrants and arrests must have travelled fast. The most important reason for visiting the brothels was to find Becky and any others who were in the same vulnerable state.

By mid-morning, Solicitors began to arrive at the two police stations and were ready for their disclosure. Noone and Dryden were represented by separate legal firms, neither of which had dealt with a corruption investigation before. Fawcus had asked for Mr Paul Brown and the Doyles were represented by Mr James Short, from the same firm where Nicholas Brannigan was a partner.

Tommy presented the written disclosure to Mr Brown and Mr Short containing details of the arrests and those held in custody, items found and a very simple explanation of the suspicions held by the police.

"I expected to see Mr Brannigan here today . . . he likes our jobs doesn't he?" enquired Tommy to Mr Short.

"He is still in Spain, but due back early on Monday. I'm sure he will make an appearance sooner or later."

Mr Brown asked to see Fawcus for a consultation prior to interview. Mr Short decided to begin with Graeme Doyle and he made himself known to Scott and Dave.

Exactly the same process took place at the police station where Noone and Dryden were being held. Susan had a colleague to assist her and he spoke to both Solicitors at the same time, presenting the written disclosure. DC Trevor Deakin dealt with Mr Robin Wood and Mr Douglas Turner, representing Noone and Dryden respectively. They also consulted with their clients prior to interview.

The first round of interviews in a serious case like Operation Neon, is a time when both sides weigh each other up and look for a reaction or a weakness. The police, on their part, disclose as little as possible, but just enough to cover the main offences. The alleged offender invariably takes legal advice and responds with a 'no reply' to the questions put to him or her. This process can last for at least two interviews in an investigation covering several issues, with a final interview consisting of challenges put to the interviewee.

Most solicitors attending police stations on a regular basis are well aware of the police tactics and they would often sit back and

150

instruct their clients to keep quiet until more detail of the drip-fed evidence is received.

Susan and Steve were the first to commence an interview. Noone sat opposite Susan, with no visible sign of pressure or stress as she went through the formalities before asking the first direct question.

**Q** Are you happy to go ahead with this interview?

**A** Yes

**Q** Do you understand why you have been arrested?

Noone looked at Mr Wood, who nodded in his direction.

**A** No reply

**Q** Do you know Barry Fawcus?

**A** No reply

**Q** Do you know Colin and Graeme Doyle?

**A** No reply

Susan continued to ask him about his friendship with Aidan Dryden, his police career and if he had used an escort agency called Superior Escorts. He made no reply to all her questions.

Steve asked Noone about his whereabouts on the previous day and if he had been to the Gateshead area. He made no reply.

Susan then asked him if he had been to Holly Gardens at any time other than to execute a warrant for drugs. He made no reply.

Steve asked Noone a number of questions about his use of the police computer, his mobile phone, the car he owned, current relationships and his financial arrangements. He also asked if he had ever used a web site called 'punterdate'.

At this point Noone asked for a break in the interview so he could speak to Mr Wood. Susan suggested leaving the tapes in place, so they could re-commence the interview as soon as the consultation was over. This was agreed and the officers left the room.

Within ten minutes, Mr Wood emerged and indicated that they were ready to re-start. Susan repeated all the formalities and explained that there had been a consultation.

Mr Wood promptly produced a hand written document and read it out loud for the benefit of the tape.

*"I, Patrick Noone, wish to offer the following information. I am aware of Barry Fawcus and the Doyle Brothers. In recent months I have been trying to recruit them as intelligence sources for use by*

*the police. I have nothing to do with their escort agency and I accept that I may have cultivated an inappropriate relationship which is not a criminal offence. I have viewed their intelligence screens and records as a matter of course. Aidan Dryden is a colleague who I have known for many years and I want to state that I know very little about his private life. I see no reason why I should answer any questions about my relationships with current or ex-partners or what I do off-duty."*

Susan noted that the document was signed by Noone and dated. Mr Wood stated that this was all his client could say at the present time and they wanted to conclude the interview and await further disclosure, should there be any.

Noone stared at Susan as Mr Wood spoke, watching for her reaction. He was trying to pre-empt the flow of disclosure so he could properly assess the evidence the police had. His own experience of extended interviews must have been telling him that he could not commit to a full explanation until he was challenged and the police had shown all their cards.

Susan carefully wrote out an exhibit label for the hand written note, maintaining a silence in the room as she did so.

"One last question before we break" said Susan. "What is the going rate for thirty minutes with an escort Mr Noone?"

"No reply" was the response. Noone no longer stared at Susan, he knew there were a lot more questions like that to come.

The interview was terminated.

Alison and Albert had commenced an interview with Fawcus just as Susan tried to get in touch. Fawcus was in an equally quiet mood and made no reply to every question. Alison took the lead with the interview and she rattled through a number of questions about his knowledge of prostitution, Superior Escorts, the Doyles, Noone and Dryden. Albert followed up with a number of lifestyle questions, covering everything from personal finances to relationships and his vehicle.

Fawcus was not as controlled and confident as Noone. He shuffled in his chair and constantly looked at Mr Brown for encouragement. Albert then asked Fawcus about the brown powder that had been found in his kitchen.

152

**Q** The brown substance, split in to 12 bags, known as exhibit AT 3 which I am showing you now, has been field tested. We believe it to be heroin. Is it yours?

**A** Personal use only

**Q** By you

**A** Yes. No further comment

**Q** Do you supply heroin Barry

**A** No comment

**Q** Did the young lady we found in your flat use any of your heroin

**A** No comment.

Mr Brown then interrupted. "Officer, my client has given an explanation about the alleged drugs. Unless you have any further evidence so that I can advise my client, then he has no option other than to make no further comment."

Mr Brown had given some breathing space to Fawcus, who was already being defensive. He was ill at ease and everyone in the room knew it.

Alison had a few last questions for this interview.

**Q** Where were you yesterday, Thursday 8th August

**A** No reply

**Q** What is your main source of income Barry

**A** No comment

**Q** Does your Mother know what you do

**A** No comment

**Q** When will she be in the country . . . we may need to speak to her

**A** No comment

Fawcus put his hand on the table in front of Mr Brown's notepad, in a gesture that alerted his Solicitor to his obvious unease.

"Officer, if that question is designed to be provocative, then I must stress that my client's Mother has not been mentioned to me in the disclosure I have been given. There is no point in continuing with this interview if I have to keep interrupting to remind you of the proper procedure."

"No problem Mr Brown. Unless you have anything else to say, this interview is terminated and we will let you know when we are ready to start the next one." Alison was not put off her stride by Mr Brown's rebuke.

Albert was alerted to a message to ring Susan and they compared notes. Scott and Dave had also completed very brief interviews with the Doyles. Mr Short had made it plain that he had advised his clients to make no comment as he considered the disclosure wholly inadequate.

"Fair enough" commented Tommy. "Time to prepare something for them to get their teeth into."

The rest of the team had begun to visit the brothels, where they met a number of sex workers who were either pleased they had an unexpected day off or complained that the police had lost them a load of money. In line with what Mick had said at the initial meeting, the escorts were happy to talk to the police. They had no regard for Fawcus, who was variously described in as many derogatory terms as the dictionary would allow.

A picture began to emerge as to how Superior Escorts ran their operation. Sandy and Lizzie, who had been at 18 Shireside Street when George the TPO paid a visit, were most forthcoming.

Sandy explained what she knew to Mick.

"Fawcus has two sets of escorts, there are ones like us that are not dependent on him for drugs or drink and who don't owe him money other than his daily charge. Then there are the ones who he forces to see punters no one else will touch. You know, the smelly, pervy ones who want you to dress up as their ten year old niece or who want to do anal or water sports. Those escorts are addicts and in a poor way so he can easily put them under pressure. I have not met any of them as they work in the crappy flats. I know one is called Becky and the other is Lexi."

"And Susanne" chipped in Lizzie. "If you want to find them, there will be a list at the Doyles house. All you have to do is ring them and get the address. If not it will be written down somewhere. Fawcus is not as clever as he thinks he is. He is just a plastic gangster."

Mick was aware of the list and 39 Waterford Way was on it, and it certainly ranked as a 'crappy address'. He rang Hughie and

154

explained that they needed to boil the list down to a flat where Becky might be.

Hughie retrieved the list from the exhibits and the only address that shone out was 12 Albion Row, North Shields which was a short distance from the town centre. Beside the address was written 'B' with a number ending 0349.

"That must be Becky. Her name is Rebecca English; she is almost 21 and Ros has identified a number of calls between her and Lexi" reported Hughie. "The phone is dead, we have had no joy with it."

Mick and Jill went straight to the address and it was immediately clear that it was little more than a semi-derelict hovel. It was hard to believe that anyone could live in the property as it had two boarded-up windows on the ground floor, loose guttering hanging and piles of rubbish in the garden. Mick was able to push the door open as the lock was hanging off and barely attached to the door. Inside the small hallway was a child's tricycle and a table covered in coats. Jill opened a door to her right and discovered a bedroom, with a single mattress on the floor surrounded by plates, cups and food wrappers.

She then saw a young woman standing in the corner, holding a knife.

"Becky, are you Becky? We are from the police. Please don't be frightened" Jill moved closer to the young woman and showed her warrant card.

"I'm not Becky! She is not here. What do you want?" The young woman was emaciated; she was wearing a pair of leggings which hardly touched her skin and a tracksuit top covered in stains. The knife shook in tandem with her hand.

The young woman jumped backwards when Mick appeared behind Jill.

"He is with me, don't worry. We have arrested Fawcus and the Doyles, we just want to speak to you and get you out of here. What is your name?"

"I don't believe you! Now fuck off and leave me alone."

"Are you Susanne?" asked Jill. "The other lasses have told us you might be here. Lexi is with us and she is safe. Please put the knife away and we can explain."

"Lexi? Where is she? Becky has been to her bedsit and she is not there."

"She is with us and so is her Mam. You must be Susanne?"

"Okay, okay . . . I want to talk to Lexi."

Mick took out his mobile and told her that he was going to ring his colleague who was with her so she could speak to Lexi and she would confirm everything. Mick quickly spoke to Jody who handed the phone to Lexi. Mick held out his phone so Lexi's voice could be heard.

"Take the phone," said Mick as he placed it on the mattress and stood back.

"Hello Lexi . . . it is Susanne," said the young woman once she had picked up Mick's phone.

"Listen to them; they are not bad for coppers. They have locked up the bent ones."

Susanne Smith was in the same state as Lexi had been. Her young body had endured addiction, beatings and neglect. Heroin had destroyed her ability to exist without its daily curse on her life. Her appearance and her surroundings reflected how painful and forlorn she had become.

After a few words from Lexi, Susanne dropped the knife on to the mattress and handed Mick his phone. She explained that Becky had left to go and look for Lexi at the bedsit on Waterford Way.

Jill then noticed that Susanne's hand was covered in dried blood where she had been holding the knife.

"Are you hurt?"

Susanne rolled up her sleeve as she showed Jill a series of wounds and scratches to her arms. She showed no emotion or discomfort. The slash marks on her arms were a testament to her desperation and anger at what happened. Jill and Mick decided to take her directly to hospital, promising that they would stay with her.

The priority was now to find Becky. Derek and Jimmy were free, whilst Jody started to travel as she was the only female officer available to assist, picking up Alan on route to Waterford Way. All four gathered at the front door of 39 within 20 minutes and the occupant in flat C let them in. He was waiting for them on the landing.

"Can I help you?" he asked Jody.

"No . . . please stand back - we are from the police."

"Ah, well I think I can help you" he repeated.

"Look, just go back inside and let us get on with our job please," came the response from an anxious Jody.

"Suit yourself. At least I tried. Nobody wants to listen these days."

Alan pressed his ear on the door of the bedsit and then knocked. There was no reply, so the decision was made to force an entry to locate Becky but an immediate problem presented itself; neither of the cars they travelled in had a ram in the boot. They had been emptied out with the exhibits that morning.

"Not a problem" said Alan. "That door will go in with one kick, it is rubbish. Watch this."

Alan stood back and sized up the door. All those hours in the gym were about to pay off and he was determined to show his audience that he was not just a poser. He took two steps forward and leapt at the door with his right foot.

His initial thoughts on the door proved to be exactly right; it was rubbish. Alan's entire leg up to his thigh went straight through, leaving him dancing on his left foot. The door was made up of a thin veneer, covering a flimsy structure resembling an egg box. Alan had managed to punch a leg-sized hole in it.

At that moment a young female appeared from Flat C.

"Becky?" asked Jody, to which she nodded.

"I did try and tell you" said the man from Flat C.

Jody then looked at Alan who was still hopping on his left leg. The flimsy door was strong enough to form a tight grip around his thigh. With that image permanently lodged in her memory, she led Becky out of the house.

Derek promptly had his phone out to record the moment for posterity.

"Do something, I'm stuck! Stop messing about!" demanded Alan.

"I'm just doing a quick risk assessment," said Jimmy as he walked around Alan, pretending to survey the scene. "We might have to send for the door extraction specialists for this you know."

Alan eventually managed to pull a section of the broken door to one side and made enough room to get his leg out.

"This is better than watching the telly," commented the man from Flat C.

"It will not be long before this *is* on the telly," joked Derek as he saved his mobile phone recording. "Comedy Hour with Alan Tempest."

In the relative calm of the car, Jody was trying to engage with Becky.

"Are you sure he is a real copper?" she enquired of Alan. "I've never seen anyone get stuck in a door before."

"Don't worry, he has his two carers with him . . . . Becky, all I need to tell you is that Fawcus and the Doyles are locked up. We know what has been going on and I want to hear what has happened to you."

Becky was already wondering why she had not been able to contact Lexi since Sunday, so she recognised that there was an element of truth in what Jody had said.

"All of them locked up? For how long?"

Jody had enough experience to know that vulnerable victims and witnesses take a long time to drop their defences. One of the most effective ways of gaining trust and the essential evidence that generally followed, was to remove any threat. In this case the threat was in the shape of her pimps and their corrupt police officers.

"We have also arrested two coppers we think have been providing information. Does that make sense to you?"

Becky was unsure how to take everything in. She had been under Fawcus's control for over two years and had lost the ability to think for herself. From the moment she woke up, only two things mattered to her; Fawcus and heroin. Whilst the rest of the world walked past her concentrating on their daily lives, choosing where to go and who to be with, Becky was a captive to her pimp and her addiction. She could not easily walk away from the existence she accepted as her life, her normality.

Jody rang Lexi and asked her to speak to Becky. Jody was well aware of the sad irony in her request. The police were now using the same tactics Fawcus had used to recruit young women for his

158

brothels. He had promised money and possessions, using each girl in turn as an example. The police were offering a route out of the suffocating confines he had built around them, but reliant on the words of encouragement from a recent escapee.

Diane also spoke to Becky, urging her to listen to Jody and get help. Becky had not expected to hear from Diane, as previous conversations had always ended badly. Diane often blamed Becky for tricking Lexi into prostitution and when Becky had retaliated with Lexi's recruitment of Susanne, arguments and bad feeling inevitably ensued. Becky found that Diane's attitude towards her sounded different; she seemed to be forgiving her and in doing so, she urged Becky to go with Jody to somewhere safe.

Jody was mindful of what Lexi had told them about Fawcus raping Becky. It was not the best time to approach her with this, so she suggested that Becky accompanied her and Alan to the hospital for a check-up, with the possibility of getting something to eat on the way. Becky decided to go along with it, for now.

The last prisoner to be interviewed was Dryden. He had been in a consultation with Mr Turner for over an hour when they finally indicated that they were ready for interview.

Steve took the lead on this one, quickly going through the formalities before the interview started in earnest. Dryden was struggling to compose himself, his eyes were red as if he had been crying and he looked completely stressed out.

Steve started the interview with a number of questions about Dryden's police career and his personal circumstances. The interview continued with more specific questions.

**Q** What is your knowledge of Superior Escorts

**A** I have paid for sex with some of their escorts.

**Q** When

**A** Ages ago

**Q** How many

**A** Two or three, I can't remember

**Q** Do you know Colin and Graeme Doyle who run the agency

**A** No reply

**Q** Do you know Barry Fawcus

**A** No reply

159

**Q** Have you used the police intelligence data base to look at their records or anyone connected to them

**A** No reply

**Q** What can you tell us about a crime that took place at 12 Hawthorn Place on 30$^{th}$ June this year

**A** I need to speak to Mr Turner.

Dryden was having difficulty holding himself together. He could not look at anyone and covered his face with his hands. Mr Turner intervened and asked for a break, so the interview was terminated.

Dryden was placed back in his supervised cell, whilst Mr Turner asked to speak to Steve and Susan.

"As you can see he is in a bit of a state. I have spoken to him at length and he has agreed that if he is given full disclosure, he will try his best to remember what he can. I think he knows his police career is over and his big worry is being remanded in the short term and receiving a prison sentence after that. I can't properly advise him on the information I have at the moment, so it is now up to you."

Susan told Mr Turner that they were about to move things on and further disclosure was being prepared.

Tommy and Albert were of the opinion that full disclosure should be given to all the solicitors before the next set of interviews, explaining that the cat and mouse style of questioning was not best suited to this investigation. Alison was slightly more cautious as she wanted to see Fawcus squirm for a bit longer. Scott was sure that the Doyles would not give anything away and would remain silent throughout. His reasoning was that they had been through the system many times and knew that cases could collapse without notice. They had nothing to gain or lose by staying quiet. Susan was doubtful that Noone would succumb to pressure, even when challenged.

"So, we have Dryden on the brink, Fawcus very uncomfortable and the rest listening to their briefs who want them to stay silent. Perhaps we should get Tommy and Trevor to prepare full disclosure and get on with Dryden and Fawcus first, then the hard nuts." Albert was clear as to how he wanted to continue.

"Probably best to start with Dryden, as he might shed some light on how they have been working things between them, which might

160

help us with the others," suggested Susan, to which there was general agreement.

Mr Turner was duly given all the information he needed for a further interview with his client. After a brief consultation of ten minutes, they were ready.

Steve repeated the formalities and began the interview.

**Q** You have now been given full disclosure at this stage and consulted with Mr Turner. Is there anything you would like to say at this stage.

**A** Yes. I have a prepared statement.

Dryden then handed Steve a hand written note, dated and timed for the interview. Steve read it out.

*I, Aidan Dryden, wish it be known that I regret my actions and wish to assist with the following. In October of last year I met my friend Pat Noone at a brothel in North Shields by accident. He later contacted me and we both agreed to keep everything quiet. I contact him via punterdate when I need to, but I am no longer a member. I have not met the Doyle Brothers and I have only spoken to Fawcus and texted him once or twice on his mobile. Pat Noone is the go-between and I have checked the police data base for him when he has been unable to do so. I also wrote off the crime at 12 Hawthorn Place by deleting certain information. I have not been to see an escort since January/February and I was trying not to get involved. I realise my career is finished and I wish to resign my post as from now."*

**Q** Can I clear up the crime at 12 Hawthorn first . . . did you delete the circumstances and the offender

**A** Yes

**Q** Why

**A** Pat told me Fawcus was going to tell everyone about our use of escorts if I did not.

**Q** Have you viewed the records of Fawcus, the Doyles and their brothels on the data base

**A** Yes.

**Q** Does anyone else know what you have done, your wife for example, or any other colleague

**A** No. Only Pat.

161

**Q** Can you tell us which escorts you went to see

**A** There have been a few. I don't remember their names.

**Q** Did you pay each time

**A** At first, but then it was free

**Q** How was this arranged

**A** Through Pat. He said he was owed a few favours, so I went along with it.

**Q** Did you access the database for anyone yesterday

**A** Yes. It was a record belonging to Lexi Morrison, who works for Fawcus. Pat rang and said she was missing and Fawcus needed to find her. There was nothing current, so I phoned Pat back and told him.

Susan then asked Dryden about his membership of 'punterdate', his financial situation, his duties and his mobile phone. He was cooperating to an extent, but Susan felt that he was still withholding information. She continued.

**Q** Did you have any idea that the young women working for Superior, such as Lexi, were under duress and were treated to regular beatings

**A** I did not know.

**Q** But you are an experienced Police Officer, your job is to look after people, but that seems to have gone by the wayside in return for free sex

**A** If you say so

**Q** If I say so? I think every right minded person on the planet would say so, did you not see how bad their health was

**A** No

**Q** Bruises, cuts

**A** No

**Q** Neglected appearances, thin, pale, held as virtual prisoners. Do I need to spell it out

**A** No. I am ashamed. What more can I say.

Dryden began to lose his composure again, so Steve asked a few more general questions about his relationship with Pat Noone. It was apparent that Noone had used Dryden when he needed to, spreading the responsibility between them to meet the demands of Fawcus.

**Q** Can you tell us more about 'punterdate'

162

**A** It costs £7.99 per month and you can leave reviews and contact other members. No real names are used, I called myself 'Tonto1' and Pat used 'Virgil'. The only other person who I contacted used a strange title 'SP9005' and him and Pat were on good terms. I have no idea who he is and I only messaged him a couple of times

**Q** Another Police Officer

**A** I honestly do not know, but he went to one of the brothels run by Superior. I don't know how you will find out either, I cancelled my membership, but then found that the registered office in the UK is just a postal address. The website is run from abroad. I deleted everything a few months ago. I have no access now.

**Q** In conclusion, you have entered into an arrangement whereby you get free sex with escorts, in exchange for information taken from the police data base. Is that correct

**A** Yes. It would never have happened if I had not bumped in to Pat at that brothel.

**Q** Did it not occur to you to report what had happened and face far less serious consequences

**A** It did, but I never imagined it would end up like this . . . . I am a fool.

Steve and Susan were more or less happy with what they had heard, so they closed the interview and left Dryden to speak with Mr Turner.

Once a short summary had been passed to the other interview teams, the decision was made to pass on full disclosure to the respective Solicitors and do one more interview with each prisoner.

Albert had also heard from Jody and Jill who were both at the hospital with Becky and Susanne.

"Looks like they will both have to be admitted" explained Jody "They are both in a terrible state . . . dehydrated, suffering withdrawal, numerous injuries and so on. It does mean that they will be better looked after than having to spend the next few days in a hotel room. Becky has made reference to an injury caused by what she called rough sex, so she will be seen by a specialist later. I won't go in to details but she is in a hell of a mess according to the Doctor in A&E. He looked quite shocked so it must be bad."

163

Albert had not pinned any hope on having evidence from Becky and Susanne for this round of interviews with the main suspects, so he asked Jody and Jill to remain with them until they were settled and on a ward. Enquiries could also start to try to locate their families to see if there was any chance they could get involved in some long term support. Jill had tried to approach this with Becky, who was short with details.

"Becky's parents live apart, but it sounds like she has seen them both recently. Susanne has a son who lives with her Mam; he must be about four years old. She has not seen him since Christmas. Jill and I have discussed what to do and we think it may be best to wait until they are both a bit better before we go knocking on doors. It may well open up a few old wounds so we have to be careful Albert. We don't want them to disappear."

Jody was aware of Albert's constant need for progress, so she was trying to get the message across that the care of the most vulnerable witnesses would have to take priority and it would also take time to interview them. On this occasion, Albert took no persuading.

"Yes, I think you are right. I am already thinking of the next set of interviews in a few weeks after we have managed to speak to all of the witnesses. I want as much pressure put on this lot as possible and the best way to do that is to hit them with one charge after another."

Scott and Dave were the first interview team to be notified that they could go ahead. Mr Short who had consulted with his clients in quick succession.

"I don't think either of my clients wishes to say a great deal. It is up to you who you want to start with" said Mr Short, looking at his watch. Perhaps he too wanted to say as little as possible as his weekend was fast approaching.

Scott led the interview with Graeme Doyle, who sat with his arms folded throughout, only moving to occasionally drink some water. He made no reply to every question apart from one.

**Q** You are in partnership with your brother and Barry Fawcus running an escort agency called Superior Escorts. Is that correct

**A** We run a legit business introducing people to one another. What happens between them is their business. We only charge for

164

the introduction and nothing else. I have nothing to do with prostitution and we do not run brothels. There is only ever one person at an address at any one time. I have nothing else to say.

Graeme Doyle went back to making no reply to each question put to him. Colin Doyle was to do exactly the same, providing the same reply to a question about Superior Escorts. It was a defence they had most likely researched and rehearsed.

It was decided to proceed with the interviews with Noone and Fawcus as soon as possible, so that they could provide the CPS with as much information as possible in the hope that a charging decision would be made quickly.

Alison was ready for Fawcus, she wanted to make sure he left the interview room with her questions ringing in his ears.

"Don't punch him whatever you do," advised Albert, who could see that Alison was raring to go.

"I would never dream of it . . . he is a wimp remember," she replied making light of her feelings towards Fawcus.

With the formalities over and a quick re-cap of the first interview, Susan asked Fawcus about Superior Escorts.

**Q** Who runs it

**A** No reply

**Q** You do with the Doyles. And your Mother. Is that right.

**A** No reply

**Q** You make money out of a business selling sex don't you

**A** No reply. . . . . erm no I do not, it is up to the clients what they do, not me.

**Q** So why do you list sex acts on the web site

**A** No reply

**Q** You make a lot of money don't you, all that cash in your flat and the rent is expensive is it not

**A** That is savings and the rent is okay

**Q** You also drive a big BMW worth £20,000

**A** No reply

**Q** The people who really pay for your lifestyle are Lexi, Becky, Susanne and all the other women, is that right

**A** No reply

**Q** And if they step out of line you give them a hiding

**A** No reply

**Q** Or threaten them with your corrupt relationship with Noone and Dryden

**A** No reply

**Q** Do you enjoy threatening women half your size

**A** No reply

**Q** You make it worse by making sure they are addicted to heroin don't you

**A** Not all

**Q** Oh, not all, just some. That is okay then . . . are they the ones that you have to control the most or are those the ones you have no regard for whatsoever

**A** No reply

**Q** I heard you telling Lexi she was a slut and no use to you anymore. Do you deny that

**A** No reply

**Q** What is the worst thing you have done to the girls

**A** No reply

**Q** Do you force yourself on them

Mr Brown interrupted "There is nothing in the disclosure about an assault of a sexual nature. My client cannot possibly answer that question."

**Q** Have you had sex with any of the escorts under your control

**A** No reply

**Q** Is Gayle, who we found in your flat today, an escort

**A** No reply

Albert then asked some questions about Noone and Dryden.

**Q** You met Pat Noone, a serving Police Officer yesterday. Why

**A** No reply

**Q** We have footage of that meeting, I refer to exhibit JR 1 and some stills taken from it. Is that your car

**A** No reply

**Q** Is that you, with Colin Doyle and Pat Noone on this image

**A** No reply

**Q** Aidan Dryden, another serving Police Officer, was contacted whilst you met with Pat Noone and he provided information about Lexi Morrison. How do explain that

166

**A** No reply

**Q** It is because you have a corrupt relationship with them. They get free sex for providing you with what you and the Doyles want from the police data base

**A** No reply

**Q** And they even covered up for you when you smashed Diane Morrison's windows

**A** No reply

**Q** Do you take pleasure in terrorising people

**A** No reply

**Q** Especially women

**A** No reply

**Q** You rang Diane Morrison yesterday and threatened her. Is that correct

**A** No reply

**Q** Your Mother accompanies you to brothels and hides the cash and the drugs

**A** My Mother has nothing to do with this

**Q** Really. Our enquiries will continue.

Susan summarised the interview and gave Fawcus one last chance to explain his role and to provide his version of events to the police. He declined and asked for the interview to be concluded.

Mr Brown was clearly keen to leave and explained that unless any further interviews were planned, he would appreciate a phone call when the charging decision had been made.

Susan and Steve started their interview with Noone when the others had finished. Susan was also ready to challenge him on a number of issues.

Steve covered the formalities and asked Noone about his membership of 'punterdate'.

**A** No reply

**Q** Was your contact name 'Virgil'

**A** No reply

**Q** Who is 'Tonto1'

**A** No reply

**Q** Do you pay your subscription by direct debit

**A** No reply

**Q** Are you still a member

**A** No reply

**Q** Have you been given free sex with Lexi Morrison

**A** No reply

**Q** This is the escort who you asked Aidan Dryden to check on the data base yesterday. Is that right

**A** No reply

**Q** Can I show you some stills taken from exhibit JR1. Is that you with Barry Fawcus and Colin Doyle

**A** No reply.

**Q** Did you phone Dryden when you were with them and obtain intelligence about Lexi

**A** No reply

**Q** How many brothels did you visit run by Superior Escorts

**A** No reply

**Q** You have checked quite a few and we know you have been to Holly Gardens

**A** No reply

Noone began to shuffle in his seat. He sat further back from the table as if he was trying to distance himself from the difficult questions he was facing.

Susan continued.

**Q** Fawcus is your paymaster, is that right

**A** No reply

**Q** He arranges free sex whilst you provide all the information he wants

**A** No reply

**Q** You even covered for him when he smashed the windows at Diane Morrison's flat

**A** No reply.

The verbal sparring of the first interview had given way to some solid jabs in this interview and Noone started to feel under pressure. He 'no replied' to further questions about the criminal damage at Diane Morrison's flat.

**Q** I want to know why you allowed Fawcus to threaten and bully a number of defenceless women whilst you stood by and let him

168

**A** No reply. Look I am not going to answer any questions so you are wasting your time.

**Q** You saw the state they were in, how could they escape with you and Dryden protecting him

**A** No reply

**Q** But you still had sex with them

**A** No reply

**Q** Were they just a sort of convenience for your own sexual requirements

**A** No reply

**Q** Is this why your recent relationships broke down

**A** No reply

**Q** You claimed that you were trying to recruit the Doyles and Fawcus as informants. This is a complete lie.

**A** No reply

**Q** You just make things up to suit your circumstances don't you

**A** No reply

**Q** What other corrupt relationships do you have

**A** No reply. I don't see the point of going on any further. I want to speak to Mr Wood.

**Q** In a minute. I just want you to tell us why you have stooped so low? You are a serving Police Officer who is expected to safeguard the vulnerable from the cruel. You have done exactly the opposite. You have ensured that a number of frightened, isolated and exploited young women have been subjected to one horrendous experience after another, in the knowledge that a bent copper thinks more of their pimp than he does of their well-being. What have you got to say for yourself

**A** No reply. This interview is over. Mr Wood . . . . .

Mr Wood had buried himself in his notes. He would never be able to admit it, but he was unlikely to feel comfortable with what he was hearing.

"I think my client has expressed his thoughts. Have you any further questions?"

Susan continued

**Q** Just a couple to finish with and then that will be it. Apart from free sex have you been given anything else

**A** No reply

**Q** Is there anything else you want to say

**A** Nothing

**Q** Not even the word sorry, or perhaps something like - I have behaved in such a bad way I am ashamed of myself

**A** No reply. That is it. No more questions.

**Q** You are completely and utterly corrupt. But I suppose you have known that for quite a while. Or are you so arrogant that you think you can talk your way out of it.

**A** Whatever.

Susan ended the interview. Noone could not look at her and Steve as they left the room with the tapes and the exhibits.

"I will be out in one minute" said Mr Wood.

Susan and Steve went out in to the corridor and spoke briefly about the interview.

"He just does not seem to appreciate what he has done" reflected Susan.

"That might have been the case when we started, but by the time you had finished with him he looked worried. I was watching what Wood was scribbling as you were doing the talking and at one point he wrote the word 'sunk'. I think the meeting they had in the car park has them by the balls. I have no idea how they can get out of that one. Noone was squirming at the end; he could not get any further away from you unless he tunnelled through the wall. It was great to watch, he deserves it."

With all the interviews completed, it was up to the CPS to make a decision on the appropriate charges. Miles Ashley had already provided the background information covering the surveillance, the brothels and the TPO evidence. The interviews were summarised and emailed, along with Ros's charts which showed the connections between the accused. Diane's initial statement and Lexi's interview were also added to the evidence, providing a compelling version of how they had suffered at the hands of Fawcus, the Doyles and the corrupt officers.

Mr Brown had already left and Mr Short did not wait very long either. He explained that it was unlikely he would be with the case long term. Mr Wood and Mr Turner hung around for a while, but as they knew the CPS had a lot of evidence to consider, they too left after making a request to know what the decision was before charge.

In the meantime there was a window of opportunity to head back to the office and take stock. Albert decided to ring Polly and tell her that he may get home before 9pm.

"Should I send you directions?" asked Polly "And Audrey has been on the phone, she and Bill are coming over tomorrow night to see us before the jet off to Cyprus on Monday. Bill has bought a new car he wants to show you."

"Oh, what kind of car has he bought?" enquired Albert.

"Audrey said it was a red one," replied Polly.

"I meant make . . . . never mind I will be home as soon as I can." Albert knew there was no point in asking Polly any more questions about cars.

It took about two hours to get a reply from the CPS. The allocated lawyer, Peter Chandler, authorised that all the accused should be charged with conspiracy to control prostitution. Fawcus and the Doyles should be charged with aid and abet misconduct in a public office and the two police officers with misconduct in a public office and paying for the sexual services of a prostitute subjected to force. Fawcus was to be bailed for the drugs offence until a laboratory report was available.

Miles had already made representations about remanding all five in custody for court the next day. Mr Chandler agreed as there was sufficient evidence to suspect that they would interfere with witnesses and the evidence in general. The charges were serious enough to be referred straight to the Crown Court by the City Magistrates.

Solicitors for the accused were informed of the decision and made no representations regarding their clients being kept for court.

Susan took great delight in charging Noone, who stood emotionless throughout. Dryden crumbled at the thought of staying in the cell block for another minute and the custody officer decided to call a doctor to examine him and perhaps give him something to help him sleep.

Fawcus and the Doyles put on a brave face when charged. They had expected little else.

Albert asked Alison, Scott and Susan to prepare the file and sent everyone else home. Jody and Jill were to keep in contact with the hospital and Lexi.

**Saturday 10<sup>th</sup> August**

A special court was convened at the City Magistrates for 10am. Mr Chandler presented the facts to the Magistrates and there were no applications for bail from Fawcus, the Doyles and Noone.

Mr Turner, acting for Dryden, made an application for bail on the basis of his client's previous good character and his 'minor' role in the offences previously described by Mr Chandler. Dryden sat apart from the other four in the dock, trying his best to look as if he did not belong with them.

It did not work, as the Magistrates remanded them all in custody and the case was passed directly to the Crown Court. Peter Chandler explained to Albert that he thought that the defence would make applications for bail as soon as they could to the Crown Court, as they always thought they had a better chance with Judges than Magistrates.

The police had done what they set out to do and now the real hard work was about to begin. Gathering evidence from the witnesses was going to be difficult for all parties but it had to be done. With everyone updated, Albert went home to cut his grass and look forward to seeing Bill in his new red car.

As the afternoon progressed, Albert could not wind down from the previous seven days and he decided to ring Jody for any witness updates.

"They are as well as can be expected Albert. You are like a mother hen, stop clucking about . . . and I said clucking so don't go on about ten pence."

"As long as they are safe, I'm happy. Thanks Jody and I am so grateful for all your hard work I have decided to give you a whole pound as credit for the swear box."

"Fan-fucking-tastic. I'm going to spend the lot if you don't bugger off. Give my regards to the other old git when you see him and tell him to enjoy Cyprus."

172

Albert did as she said and before long Bill and Audrey arrived in a 1975 Triumph Stag. It was red as Polly had described and she was quick to point that out to Albert.

Polly and Audrey retreated indoors whilst Bill and Albert looked around the Stag. It turned out that Bill had always wanted one after admiring the car as a teenager, but he could not have afforded one at the time.

Bill was keen to find out how Operation Neon had progressed, so Albert gave a summary of the events so far. As he did so, the car became a bit of an attraction to Albert's neighbours and they were soon joined by three of them.

Polly and Audrey surveyed the scene from the kitchen window, having opened a bottle of wine.

"Look at them . . . they don't really grow up do they? Five men gathered around a car pretending they know how it works. Bill could not start it this morning and he had to ring the bloke he bought it off. Still, it keeps them occupied and they love being in a little gang with their mates, talking cars and football. I don't know if it makes me happy or sad watching them," reflected Audrey.

"That's where man-caves come in handy. Set them a task and before you know it they are hiding away in the shed. Albert goes in there to brood about things as he is hopeless at talking things through. He has to retreat and have a think." Polly was not moaning about Albert, but she would certainly prefer him to communicate a bit more.

Audrey could see what Polly meant "The younger generation are far better. They seem to be less embarrassed about things."

"Yes, and they put it all over the internet, clothed or unclothed!" joked Polly.

All four then sat down for a meal prepared by Polly. Bill looked relaxed and he explained how he was looking forward to his retirement, but would miss his colleagues, the mickey taking and the general atmosphere of the office. After Cyprus, Audrey wanted a new kitchen and perhaps some work done in the garden. Bill rolled his eyes and commented that he did not retire to take up hard labour.

After a few hours of friendly company, it was time for Bill and Audrey to leave.

"Do you need a hand to put the roof up on the car?" asked Albert.

"Ah, well, that is not as easy as it sounds. I have not got a clue how you do it. It is nice and warm so we'll be okay," admitted Bill.

Audrey and Polly exchanged a knowing look and they both began to giggle.

"If it rains on the way home, I'm going to Cyprus on my own," declared Audrey as she hugged Albert and Polly goodbye.

As they disappeared in to the distance, Albert asked Polly if she wanted a nightcap.

"Can I put Mama Mia on? I've bought the DVD!"

Albert was in no position to argue.

**Sunday 11<sup>th</sup> August**

Everyone needed a day off, but there had to be someone available should any of the vulnerable witnesses need help. Alison and Hughie had volunteered to be on standby, checking with the hospital and keeping in touch with Denise and Lexi.

At 6.30pm Alison rang Hughie as she had been called out by Diane. Lexi was suffering from stomach cramps and felt unwell. They soon discovered that Lexi had begun a period, her first for some time.

"Hughie can you go to the shops and get some feminine products please? Lexi has just come on and I cannot leave them."

"What do you mean? What is it you want?" It had not registered with Hughie as to what Alison meant exactly.

"Come on Hughie, you have been married for twenty odd years. Ask Karen."

"She is out . . . . do you mean the . . .once a month. . .doo dahs or whatever they are?"

"If that is how you want to describe it, then yes."

With that Hughie drove to the supermarket and found the appropriate aisle. On surveying the display, he found several products which confused him. Which were the right ones?

With wings or without wings - day wear or night wear - with a string or without – towel or tampon. Hughie's logical mind could not make sense of it all. He thought about ringing Alison but she would never let him hear the last of it if he did.

In the end he did what many men would do and he bought a selection. Proud of his decision, he made his way to the check out, hoping to use one of the automatic tills. To his dismay, they were closed and the only till available was staffed by a young woman in her early twenties.

Hughie took the products he selected from his basket and watched them drift along the conveyer belt towards the young cashier. With every beep of the bar code, she looked at Hughie. He tried to look everywhere but at her.

"That will be £18.65 please."

"What? That is a lot" said Hughie. "I don't usually buy these things you know. It is an emergency."

"It must be," said the cashier.

Without another word, he paid for the items with what cash he had in his wallet.

"Do you need a bag?" asked the cashier.

"Erm, I think that would be a good idea," replied Hughie, as his embarrassment increased.

"Yes, it looks like you need some good ideas. Have a nice day."

Hughie left the supermarket as quickly as he could and delivered the items to Alison at the secret flat. Alison and Diane could not help laughing at the contents of the bag, but were grateful for Hughie's efforts.

# Chapter Five

# The Road to Crown Court

**Monday 12ᵗʰ August**

The natural thing to do following the arrest stage is to sit down with everyone concerned and plot the route to Crown Court. The evidence must pass the one simple test that is applied in all cases – it has to be beyond reasonable doubt. Albert and Miles knew they would be able to depend on the surveillance evidence gathered the previous week, the analytical work that Ros would produce and the statements from the TPOs, FCT and CC. They were less confident about the evidence from the young women that had suffered at the hands of Fawcus and the Doyles. Alison had already considered the difficulties and approached Dr Val Newman who had agreed to meet with the police to offer some guidance.

The press had also shown a great deal of interest and the Chief had decided to release a holding statement to them, briefly outlining the circumstances and the fact that an investigation was ongoing.

With the team following up enquiries and updating records, Albert, Susan and Alison met with Peter Chandler at the CPS offices to go through the detail of the case. Peter Chandler outlined the potential timetable.

"As you all know, if the main offenders stay on remand, the case should be heard a lot earlier than if they were released on bail. That means we could possibly be at Court before Christmas, if everything progresses well and there is space at court. I need to know how far you are down the line with your enquiries and when I can expect the full file."

Albert and Susan summarised the work completed and the enquiries that remained unfinished or untouched. Alison explained the difficulties with the most vulnerable victims and witnesses.

"The three victims we rescued are in a terrible state, but the medical staff are sure they can help them through the next few weeks which will be the most difficult period for their physical health. It is their mental health that is the most concern, due to the things they have experienced and the suffering they have endured. I think we have just scratched the surface so far. There is at least one serious sexual assault that took place recently and I have no doubt there will be more. They have all been kept under duress, with little contact from their families and anyone else that could help them."

"So the interviews are likely to be crucial and could take time?" asked Peter Chandler.

"Absolutely. It is hard to know where to start. Some of the escorts who have not experienced the worst conditions have already indicated that they were aware of how badly others were treated."

"And with the help of two corrupt police officers" added Peter Chandler.

Susan was keen to point out that this would be a 'warts and all' investigation and whatever the failings of the police, there would be no disguising them.

"As an organisation, the force has failed to pick up on how Noone and Dryden were behaving and we have been part of the problem. Had things been different, then the victims would not have suffered as much as they have. We think it is important for you to know this."

"I think you are right and the public should be reassured once all the facts come out. Do you think there are any others within the organisation, as yet unidentified?"

Albert was unsure. "There may be, but we have no positive leads at the moment. I am hoping that the phone billing, the examination of the lap tops we found and whatever we get from our IT department will give us a far better idea. I think there could be others, but whether or not they have been operating at the same level as Noone and Dryden is yet to be confirmed."

The meeting then progressed to how to deal with any future bail applications, as Dryden's legal team had already made their position clear.

"I might be wrong" continued Albert, "but Dryden is the one who is the weakest. He has had 48 hours on remand and I am not sure he

177

will cope at all. He might see sense and come across at some stage once he has further disclosure."

"Okay, he might do but we'll have to be prepared for all eventualities. Are you planning to arrest them for any further offences?"

"We will know better once we have interviewed the victims and all the other witnesses. There will no doubt be others arrested, probably the ones who have been involved in running Superior Escorts."

"Perhaps relatives and spouses?" asked Peter Chandler, knowing full well that the police would apply pressure from all sides.

"You took the words right out of my mouth," said Albert.

The next meeting was scheduled for the end of the week, unless a bail application was requested by the defence.

Back at the office, Hughie and Brian were busy with the documents and exhibits from the searches. Brian estimated that he would have the phones examined and billing requested within a couple of days, whilst Hughie had about one day's work to enter all the material he had on to his data base.

"Were there any books on gynaecology seized Hughie?" enquired Albert who had heard of his shopping trip the night before.

"No, but there is a one on diplomacy." Hughie was quick as a flash.

Albert found a computer to catch up with his emails and was surprised to see some good news from HR. Miles had asked for Tommy and Jill to remain on Operation Neon for a further four weeks and they had agreed. Unfortunately they would not allow Sam and John to remain, as they were direct replacements for vacancies that had already existed for too long.

Albert rang Sam and then John, mainly out of courtesy but also to ask if they had noticed anything about Pat Noone's recent behaviour. John was oblivious to the whole saga and told Albert that he thought Pat was a good colleague who kept himself to himself. He could not really remember a conversation he had had with him about anything other than work. Sam was more or less the same, although he knew that Tommy did not rate him, calling Pat 'lazy and a bit of a perv'.

Albert explained that they would no doubt need a statement at some stage and looked forward to seeing them at Bill's retirement.

Alison received a phone call from Dr Newman saying that she was on her way. Albert, Jody, Jill and Susan made themselves available to meet with her.

Dr Newman had a number of years' experience working with men and women who were addicted to alcohol and drugs. She had also listened to her clients as they explained their problems and how they had been treated by others. Many of them had been victims of serious wrong doing and many had committed crimes themselves. Her advice to Alison the previous week had struck a chord with her, so Alison was keen to learn more.

Alison had already provided Dr Newman with an update on the three young women who the police had found, so she was aware of the current state of Lexi, Becky and Susanne in relation to Operation Neon. Dr Newman gave a short appraisal.

"Lexi is progressing well and she is very close to being through the worst of her withdrawal. I think the fact that she is relatively young has helped her. She has a better power of recovery than someone who is older, for example someone over 25. Becky and Susanne are at a very similar stage and will be in hospital for at least another 3-4 days. I have been able to speak to the staff on the ward and there is concern for Becky's physical health, specifically due to injuries to her anus. I think they want her to be examined by a consultant and that will take place later today, if there are no emergencies. Susanne's self-harm injuries are mainly superficial, but more importantly, they give us a clear indication of how bad her mental health is."

Alison confirmed to Dr Newman that Lexi had witnessed a sexual assault on Becky and her injuries may be a direct result.

"Probably, but all we can do is await confirmation and she may well decide to tell us in her own time. I take it you will need to interview all three as soon as possible, so can I give you an insight as to what could be going on in their minds at this moment?"

Dr Newman had already told Alison about the power and control Fawcus had over Lexi and there was no reason why it would not be the same with the other two women.

"What you have to avoid is taking his place in their lives. You have rescued them and given them another chance, so within a short space of time, you will become the most important person they know. He has tortured and persecuted them over a long period, but they have a loyalty to him which most people cannot comprehend. I often get asked why addicts and victims don't just walk away from their dealers and abusers, but we know that is virtually impossible due to their complete reliance on the person who supplies drugs, shelter, money and so on. I also support a lot of women who have suffered domestic abuse and the circumstances are largely the same."

Jody was keen to know how they should interact with the three young women.

"You must give them a chance to make their own decisions and allow them to regain some of the emotions they have lost over the past two years or so. They will probably think everything is their fault. Lexi, for example, has grown up in a single parent family and she has told me that she feels responsible for her parent's marriage breaking down, even though she was only two and has no idea how it happened. There could be similar things in the lives of Becky and Susanne. This is what you could find yourself confronted with and they will be looking to you for solutions, so you must position yourself carefully and not allow them to think you will be their rescuer forever."

"So Fawcus knew exactly the type of girl he could exploit" asked Susan.

"Absolutely. He would have canvassed the others first, then made a move. It is the same with drug dealers. They give a few bags of heroin away to someone whom they have identified with a view to getting them addicted, then extract every penny they can for as long as they can. Fawcus has probably told each of them that they are worthless and only he has time for them. In return they have to do what he says and if they disobey, he most likely punished them by withdrawing attention, drugs or whatever he chose to. There is little doubt that he has also assaulted them, so fear will be very prominent in their minds when they talk about him."

Albert wanted to know more about how Fawcus could be so cruel and domineering.

"It is his state of mind. He has to have someone to pick on, or to blame. There are lots of reasons why he could be like that; perhaps he has learnt it from an abusive parent or he has an axe to grind with the whole world. He will try to shift everything away from himself and will try not to look like an under-achiever or a loser. He clearly sees Lexi, Becky and Susanne as completely worthless and there to be used as and when he decides. He appears to have been completely detached from how much pain he has inflicted, or how ill and neglected they all looked. This is all to do with the complete unopposed power he has had over them for a long time. This mind set makes him worse and the only person he will feel sorry for is himself."

"So what we have are the three victims who are entirely reliant and have had no choice but to survive in the circumstances in which they find themselves in, whilst Fawcus will use whatever means he can to make sure his demands are met?" asked Jody.

"More or less. Once you have interviewed them, all of you will get a better idea of the true extent of his control over them. He had them trapped to say the least. It will be a long and difficult process, but by showing them there is an alternative and encouraging them to make their own decisions, you will cease to be their rescuer and they will see themselves as stronger individuals in the future. They will also have the skills to recognise people like Fawcus and steer clear. Of course this is all in an ideal world and there is a long way to go. They will need a lot of counselling and encouragement."

"How will they ever get over being victims of Fawcus?" asked Jill.

"They will always have terrible memories, but the long term aim must be to give them the strength and the emotional resilience to deal with those memories. The police can help by starting the process with their support and understanding, but the real progress will take place much later. I expect to be seeing them for a while yet and there is one other thing you should all be aware of."

Dr Newman continued as the team listened to every word.

"Depending on how well each of them has coped, they will feel as if they do not belong in mainstream society. They will see themselves as alone or set adrift. In simple terms they do not have a family to depend on or feel part of, they do not have a wide circle of friends who they can confide in and, in this case, they obviously have no dependable work colleagues. It will take some careful exploration of their feelings and relationships with others for this to improve."

"Will this be the case for some of the other escorts too?" asked Alison.

"Well, it depends on their circumstances. But I don't think I would like to be working on my own in a house or a flat and it cannot be classed as a safe environment when you consider what they do. There must be a high level of stress for many of the women. They have no one to talk to, it is not like they have regular meetings with other escorts or social events when they can get together outside work. Some of them are quite possibly leading secret lives and do not want anyone to know what they are doing. This will inevitably lead to feelings of separation or exclusion."

As learning curves go, this was one of the steepest that the FCT had ever encountered. Dr Newman's advice was illuminating and invaluable and it gave the team confidence.

## Tuesday 13th August

As enquiries were moving at a decent pace, Albert decided to call a de-brief in the office for 5pm. Everyone except Jill was able to attend, as she was at the hospital speaking to Becky's medical team.

Some of the team had been tracking down the women who had worked for Superior Escorts, using the list found in Graeme Doyle's house. Of the 38 on the list, 29 had been spoken to over the phone or in person. Scott had collected all the details.

"None of them has anything good to say about Fawcus and the Doyles. Most describe them as either bully boys or tell us that they have no interest in what happens to them once they have sent a punter. They also complain about the money that is deducted and the website is not popular. The vast majority of the women do not want to do anal sex, but their profiles on the website say they do. This causes more arguments than anything else with punters. Many of the escorts who have had abusive clients told us that they get no help and have to deal with them alone. Four of them have seen Noone and possibly the same for Dryden. They were told to give them sex for free so that is how they remembered. There are two others who get free sex, one is an estate agent called Oliver and the other is a bloke who they call 'the suit' . . . . he only goes to one escort who we have yet to trace, but a couple of others have heard of him. The estate agent has made a nuisance of himself, he turns up unannounced and he likes to spank the women. He makes sure they are alone in the house as he gets quite rough. One day he went to a flat and one of the escorts was visiting her friend, so he did not expect to see two in the same place. One hid and when he had his clothes off and started to get rough, she jumped out and they both set about him. They lashed him over the arse with his own belt and chucked his clothes out on the street. He rang the agency to complain, but thankfully Gloria Doyle thought it was funny and told him to sod off."

"So what does he do for his free sex?" asked Albert.

"He arranges short term lets for the agency on favourable terms. We think we might get his full details from the billing and the phones."

"Good. He will be coming in pretty soon to explain himself. Does Gloria do much for the agency Scott?"

"Sounds like it; she takes bookings, the rota and the money from punters who pay by card. So does Mrs Fawcus when she is not in Spain. She is due back on Thursday from Alicante."

"They can come in too - Barry Fawcus won't like it when his Mother is locked up."

"We have no idea who the bloke they call 'the suit' is and there is a chance that he is no longer about. The rumours are from about a year ago," explained Scott.

"It is not another police officer is it?" sighed Susan.

"Not sure, but who knows? The two women who mentioned it only know what they have heard from the escort he has seen in the past. She uses the name 'Luscious Loryn' at the moment, but was known as 'Juicy Joanne' up to a few months ago. We have a number for her, but there has been no reply as yet and she has not turned up at the flat she supposedly works from."

Albert wanted to know if any of the escorts was willing to make statements, but Scott and the others had encountered the same response.

"They are waiting to see if they stay on remand and how good the police case is. They are a bit nervous about putting pen to paper, but they are generally happy to tell us what is going on."

## Wednesday 14th August

In the ten days since Lexi had been found at Waterford Way, her health had improved enough to try some further interviews. Alison and Jody had spent a great deal of time with both Lexi and Diane, keeping them safe and up-to-date with the police enquiry. Lexi had found her initial interview very difficult, for obvious reasons, and she discussed her thoughts with Alison.

"There is so much I want to tell you, but the words just don't come out. Some of the days I spent with Becky at the last flat are a bit of a blur . . . I can only remember bits and pieces. I don't think anyone will believe me anyway, Fawcus and his coppers will make much better witnesses."

Alison wanted Lexi to know that she should not worry about what people thought, but from what Dr Newman had said, this was unlikely to be understood by Lexi for quite some time. Alison's job was to guide Lexi through the process as best as she could, allowing Lexi to gain confidence and at the same time provide the police with the evidence they needed.

"One step at a time Lexi. We have come a long way in a short time and we will only do an interview if you feel up to it. How about we do things in short bursts, say thirty or forty minutes at a time? What do you think of that?"

Alison was carefully inviting Lexi to make choices, giving her some control over what she did.

"So I can decide when to stop and start?" asked Lexi, unsure as to how far she was being allowed to go.

"Sounds like a plan to me. I can ask some questions and if you want to answer them that would be great, if not we can leave it to another time."

Lexi's fragility was still obvious to everyone who met her, but there were signs that she was beginning to realise that Fawcus was not in charge anymore. She told Alison that she was ready to do a couple of short interviews and to take it from there.

The interview suite at HQ had been block-booked for Operation Neon, ensuring that there would be nobody else hanging around the building. Alison and Jody gave Lexi a tour of the interview room and the tape recording room, giving her a period of time to relax and get used to the thought of being interviewed on camera.

They were soon ready to start and Alison asked Lexi some very general questions about Superior Escorts and how it was run.

"The bosses are the Doyles. Fawcus runs about after them. His Mother does the phones and helps him on his rounds, Gloria Doyle does the phones and takes the money. They do everything and we just have to put up with the punters."

Alison then spent about ten minutes asking Lexi for as much detail as possible about the way Superior Escorts operated on a daily basis, before moving on to clients.

"Do they ever ask you if you would prefer not to see a punter?"

"Never," said Lexi.

"What happens if there is a punter who arrives and gets aggressive or asks you do something you do not want to do?"

"Fawcus is supposed to come and deal with that, but he never does. They do not care who they send. I have had men turn up who are complete deviants and then there are the big fat smelly ones. There have been men who can hardly speak English; I think they are asylum seekers. Lots of Asian men, Chinese, posh blokes, businessmen . . . . you name it and they have all been."

"Have you been assaulted by a punter?"

"Loads of times. Some are really rough. I remember one man saying he could do what he liked because he had paid for me and that was that. I belonged to him for half an hour. He kept slapping my face when he was on top of me. Another bloke bit me all over. Fawcus just said it was part of the job and took no notice when I told him."

"So he had no regard for you or the other escorts, he just told you to get on with it."

"Yes . . . . . I am struggling to tell you about some other things that happened. I keep trying to block it out but they just keep coming back into my head."

Alison could tell Lexi was dealing with some strong emotions as she recalled her worst experiences. Lexi sat forward on the sofa and began to clutch a cushion she had placed on her knees.

"Take your time Lexi, we have all day."

"I got a call one day from Fawcus to say that two brothers were on their way over and they had already paid Gloria by card. When they arrived there was three of them."

Lexi paused, pulling the cushion up in front of her. Alison asked if they had been abusive.

"No, they were not rough or anything, it was just that the third one was . . . I can hardly say it . . . " Lexi began to cry and buried her face in the cushion.

Alison gave her a tissue and a drink of water and asked Lexi if she wanted to continue or have a break.

"No, no, lets carry on . . . the third one was down's syndrome . . . the other two were his brothers and they wanted me to have sex with him . . . . . I mean everyone has feelings but I don't even think he knew what he was there for. He just smiled at me and then looked around as if he was wondering what was going on. He looked lost."

Alison was almost stuck for words. She had not expected anything like this to emerge from the interview. Jody sat motionless in the recording room watching the screen as Lexi's painful memories were committed to tape.

"Can you tell me what happened Lexi? Don't worry if you don't want to," asked Alison.

"One of his brothers left as he lost his bottle, but the other wanted me to carry on . . . . . I could not, so it ended up with him ringing Fawcus. They had a few words and he passed his phone to me. Fawcus went off it and said they would lose £250 if I did not try. He was going berserk as usual."

Alison asked Lexi if she knew who the men were.

"No, we don't get their names, but the down's syndrome lad had an old fashioned name. He had very thick glasses and hardly any hair. That's all I can remember. His brother told him to lie on the bed and do as 'the lady' said. He told me to give him a hand job and make it quick while he waited outside the door . . . the other brother then came in and grabbed the lad and took him out. He kept saying sorry and that it would not happen again. I was so relieved, but then there was an almighty argument between the brothers and the lad began to cry. It was terrible . . . . . I can still see his face, all upset and crying and not knowing what was going on."

"I'm sorry we have had to bring this out Lexi. I had no idea this had happened."

Lexi took her time and dried her eyes. "It's okay. It had to come out sooner or later. I feel so sorry for the lad who they brought to see me . . . . . I just hope they did not take him anywhere else."

"Can I just ask where this happened?"

"Holly Gardens, about February or March."

Alison had many more questions about Lexi's experiences, but she felt that they were relatively insignificant after what she had just heard.

"I think we will break soon. Can I just ask about the two police officers who Fawcus told you to give free sex. Did they ever tell you they were in the police?"

"Sort of. Pat was only interested in getting a blow job as fast as he could. He did not speak a lot, but he always implied that Fawcus was his mate and that I knew why he did not pay. He was full of himself, a right poser. The other one, Aidan, was a bit of a wimp. He tried talking about gardening and shit like that . . . . when would I go to a garden centre for fuck sake? Anyway, his warrant card dropped on the floor once and I saw the police badge. I know what one looks like after all the times I was arrested. He just wanted a hand job . . . . what a boring wanker he was. He did ask me not to tell anyone he was a policeman, so I told him I would not. Not until today anyway . . . they deserve everything they get."

"Is there anyone else who got free sex?"

"Not from me, but there is a pervy landlord who has been to see some of the others. I don't know who he is. I just hear stories about him."

"Is there anything else before we break Lexi?"

Lexi sat back and looked towards the window of the interview room. She had been able to reveal one of her most upsetting memories and she now had the chance to get another out in to the open.

"It is about Becky. I told you Fawcus raped her a couple of weeks ago."

"Do you want to tell me about it now?" asked Alison, aware that Lexi had been in the interview room for forty minutes.

"Yes . . . yes I do . . . he came to the flat full of hell because a couple of punters had refused to see us because of the state we were in. He said he was moving Becky out to another flat as we were no good together. Becky was having none of it and I did not want to be alone either. Becky refused to collect her things and he began to push her about the flat. She scratched his arm somehow and he lost it completely. He slapped her and kneed her in the stomach. She was on the floor and he came at me so I ended up in the corner of the room trying not to get hit. Becky stood up and told him he was a fat bastard and the next thing I know he had her doubled over the arm chair and began to have sex with her . . . . . . she was trying to get him off, but she had no chance. Both of us tried yelling at him to stop, but he did not until Becky began to bleed. He jumped back and shouted at her that she was a dirty slut, pushed her away and went to the toilet. I got a towel for Becky who was in agony and then Fawcus came out and dragged her to his car. The bloke from Flat C was on the landing as he had heard the noise, so Fawcus told him that he had seen nothing and, if he reported it, his legs would be broken . . . . or something like that."

"Did you see Becky again after that?"

"No. She rang a couple of times, but I have no idea where she was. She said she was ill and could not see punters. Fawcus had more or less abandoned her."

Alison was satisfied that Lexi had worked hard and spoken about things that most people could never imagine, so she brought the interview to a close.

Jody sealed the tapes and all three gathered in the interview room. The conversation did not flow as easily as it usually did. Alison and Jody were experiencing one of those moments that all police officers have when they hear something that was so incomprehensible, so cruel and so shocking that it takes a while to be able to react.

Lexi was unsure if she had been right to talk about her experiences, although she did feel relieved at how she had found the

188

words to describe what had happened. She felt exhausted and emotionally drained. A few minutes went by until all three had a cup of coffee in front of them and they began to open up to each other.

"I should not say this, but I am beginning to despise Fawcus and everyone around him. I can't tell you how important your interview will be when we get to court Lexi, you have told us exactly how bad he is and that will help everyone," explained Jody.

"But what if they do not believe me?" asked Lexi, still doubting that her word was worth as much as her abuser's.

"They will Lexi, they will" responded Alison.


### Thursday 15th August

Alison, Jody and Jill needed to speak to Albert. They decided to corner him in his office before he got tied up with other jobs.

"Blimey, it's the Sisterhood! What have I done?" asked Albert as the three of them purposefully descended into his office.

"We just want to discuss how to progress with Lexi, Becky and Susanne. There is a lot going on and we have to put things in place now so they can get the best possible help later on" explained Alison.

"Yes, I see what you mean. What were you thinking?" asked Albert as he opened up the discussion. Jill began with an update on Becky.

"Her withdrawal has been awful, but she is bearing up. It is her injuries that are most concerning. The consultant has managed to examine her and she explained that Becky has a number of injuries to her anal region, including tears to the tissue that lines the rectum. This was most likely caused by penetration. The consultant will provide a statement in a couple of days. She is run off her feet. Becky has made an initial disclosure about the injuries and she said it was Fawcus."

"This corroborates what Lexi told us in interview yesterday. She has described how Fawcus raped Becky following an argument over punters" added Alison.

Jill had also been to see Susanne.

"Her withdrawal has been pretty bad too. Her self-harm injuries have been treated and there is no sign of infection which is brilliant when you think about where she was. She has told me that she would love to be able to see her Mam again and try to make amends with her. She also has a four year old son, who lives with his Granny. There is obviously a story behind it all and I will have to get in touch with Social Services as they have been involved at some stage. I don't think Susanne has seen her son since last Christmas and you can tell she feels terrible about it."

"What about Becky's family?" enquired Albert.

"Her Mam might be the best place to start. She says her Dad just loses his temper every time she sees him. The parents live apart. As far as interviews with Becky and Susanne are concerned, we think next week at the earliest."

"Thanks Jody." Albert paused for a few moments. "I will chase up WP to see when they can take Lexi and Diane to their new address and start to look after them full time. After speaking with Dr Newman yesterday, I'm not sure we can do the same for Becky and Susanne. They will be on their own and that cannot be good. Perhaps we should try to make contact with their families and see if they can help? We also need Social Services to either take part or give us some guidance. And last but not least we need to get Fawcus in for rape. I will email Peter Chandler at the CPS to pre-warn him and generally update him."

Albert then looked at the three policewomen, waiting for a response.

"Is there anything else? Is that a plan?"

"Yes Albert it is," replied Jody "And it is exactly what we thought you would say."

"Here we go again . . . female intuition . . . I don't know why we men exist."

"To lift heavy things," came the reply from Alison.

Albert knew better than to counter with any witty repartee as taking on all three at once would have meant certain defeat. They left his office as quickly as they had arrived, sure in the knowledge that they were on the right lines and doing their best for the victims.

**Friday 16<sup>th</sup> August**

190

Peter Chandler replied to Albert's email regarding the further offences and the plans to arrest the minor players. He also mentioned that Dryden's legal team had made an application for a bail hearing, which was likely to take place at Crown Court at around 10am.

Albert rang Miles to put him in the picture and forwarded the email to Susan.

"I don't think it is a disaster for us if Dryden gets bail. He is not the main man and I doubt if he will interfere with the witnesses or the evidence. The word is that his wife has left him and took off somewhere. She is a teacher so she is on holiday at the moment, but she must also be in a bit of a state. I am also hoping that he sees sense and comes across, so if he does get released on bail, we will be able to get a hold of him far easier."

"It sounds like he has been Noone's puppet all along. What an idiot. If he gets out it is no real problem. I hope he gets strict bail conditions though" said Miles.

"I'll reply to Peter Chandler and ask for all the usual conditions and perhaps a curfew if they can argue the case for one."

Albert considered Dryden to be little more than an also-ran, someone who had got involved through his own careless approach and who was too weak to deal with his predicament. He had allowed Noone to manipulate him, dragging him down the same corrupt route.

Scott and Dave were trying their best to trace the escort who may have known the man nicknamed 'the suit'. The phone number they had for her kept going through to answer machine, so they had tried asking a few others if they could get in touch. A suggestion was to look on the various internet forums used by escorts and punters. One of the forums covering the North East had lots of gossip about the closure of Superior Escorts on their news page.

The comments were mostly anonymous and they were all revelling in the possible demise of the agency. Scott had managed to accumulate a great deal of information about the agencies operating in the North East and had concluded that Superior Escorts was by far the worst when it came to a lack interest in the women on their books.

"Listen to this comment," said Scott to Dave, "Don't go to this agency. They will rip you off. The so-called brothel in North Shields is a doss house full of junkies. Keep clear."

Scott continued to scroll down the page.

"And another. Worst agency ever. Old bag on the phone told me to go to the wrong place and when I rang up she said it was my fault. Never again, amateur outfit. . . . . ah, here is an interesting one, a punter has been sent to a brothel in Gosforth and was told to look for a  estate agent's sign. He says he found two, one belonging to Chappell's and another for Smart Homes. I wonder if they have an agent called Oliver working for them?"

Dave quickly looked up the estate agencies and found that Chappell and Company were local and the other was internet-based. He rang the number for the local company and asked if they had someone called Oliver working for them.

"Can I ask the reason for your call," enquired the receptionist.

"A pal of mine has just rented a house through Oliver and he has recommended him. I just wanted to see if he had anything similar," replied Dave with his fingers crossed as he told a little fib.

"Mr Wise is only at this office on Monday and Tuesday. Would you like to leave me a contact telephone number and he will call you back?"

"That's okay," said Dave, "I will ring him once I have had a good look at the area where I want to live over the weekend. Thanks very much for your help."

Oliver Wise was found to be a 64 year old male, with no previous convictions other than a couple of speeding fines, who lived in the prosperous suburb of Jesmond near Newcastle. His photo on the website belonging to Chappell and Company described him as their Senior Letting Agent and he compared favourably with the description given to the police by the escorts.

"Another one for an early morning knock next week." Suggested Scott.

Just after lunchtime Albert received a phone call from Peter Chandler to inform him that Dryden had been granted conditional bail. He had to reside at his home address, surrender his passport and remain indoors between 8pm and 6am. He was also warned not to directly, or indirectly, contact any of the witnesses.

"Will this encourage the others to try to get bail?" asked Albert.

"Possibly, but I also think they know there will be further offences put to them, so they may hold off for a few days yet. Are you anywhere near further arrests?"

"I was thinking next Tuesday or Wednesday, if we can get interviews done with the victims. How did Dryden look?"

"Like a ghost. He must have lost about 10 pounds and not slept a wink in the week since you arrested him. The Judge was not very impressed with him, but he got the benefit of the doubt. Can you let me know what you plan for next week?"

Albert confirmed he would and immediately got in touch with Alison.

"Dryden has managed to get conditional bail, so I would like to speed up the second wave of arrests. What is the chance of getting interviews done with Becky and Susanne?"

"They are doing okay, but we just have not had the time to get to know them like we did with Lexi. We have been to see both sets of family and they are very wary of having them back in the house. It is the usual scenario of desperate addicts stealing from them and not showing up for ages. Susanne's Mam has the little boy settled and she does not want any dramas, her word not mine, so it is a bit delicate."

Albert and Alison continued to discuss the various options. The risks of putting both women in a place on their own was too great. Lexi had Diane to support her and this arrangement almost guaranteed that she stayed on the straight and narrow. Both Becky and Susanne were likely to be discharged from hospital very soon, so Albert asked Alison to try her best with the families.

"Can you go back and tell them everything they need to know. We can offer support and I suppose Social Services might chip in. Try your best we need to get the interviews done and get as much as possible for the next arrest day."

Just as Albert was making plans with Alison on how to support Becky and Susanne, external pressures forced an immediate change. Jill received a phone call to inform her that both women were ready to be discharged from hospital, preferably by that evening. With little chance to arrange accommodation with their parents, or anyone else for that matter, the prospect of lodging them in a B&B seemed to be the only viable alternative.

Jill and Alan travelled to the hospital to make arrangements at that end, whilst Alison and Jody went to visit the parents of the women in a desperate attempt to persuade them to help. They went straight to see Carol English, mother of Becky.

"Back again so soon?" declared Carol as she answered the door.

"Sorry to be a nuisance Carol, but we need your help." Alison decided to be as direct as she possibly could.

"Becky is about to be discharged from hospital and we need somewhere for her to stay. We have nowhere we can use other than a B&B and we don't want her left alone. Is there any way at all she can have her room here, even if it is for a short while?"

Carol had not expected things to have moved so quickly and she was wary of the fact that her daughter had been betrayed by the corrupt officers conspiring with Fawcus and the Doyles. She was aware that Becky had been rescued barely a week before and her health was poor. She had decided not to visit her in hospital because her relationship with her daughter had broken down.

"Hang on, hang on. I'm a bit confused here. She is a heroin addict with lots of problems and I cannot cope alone. I have asked for help before from everyone I know and all I got was one appointment after another that I could not keep. How was I supposed to get Becky to her Doctor when I did not know where she was or who with? All that happened was that I kept getting pushed to the back of the queue. I'm only five foot and a rizla paper, what did they want me to do – drag her there?"

"I'm sorry Carol, but all I can say is that we will be on-call all weekend. She has gone through the worst of withdrawal and has stabilised, so we are desperate to find her somewhere safe to stay. She has medication and I also think the district nurse will be calling to deal with her injuries, so you will not be on your own completely."

Carol took a few moments to think things over.

"I have been down this road so many times . . . she used to come home for a day or two then disappear with that arse hole Fawcus for another couple of months. Every time she got worse and worse. I even told the local community police about Fawcus and they said they would pass the information on to the right people, but that is in doubt now after what you have told me and what I've seen in the paper. I don't know, I don't know." Carol shook her head and sat down, her despair was obvious.

"Fawcus and the others are on remand and we hope to arrest him for further offences next week. To make sure of that we have to interview Becky as soon as possible, but we need her somewhere safe. I know you have been let down before and all I can say is we are trying our best. Is there any . . . . . "

Carol interrupted Alison and she agreed to let Becky come home.

"On one condition" she continued "I have your numbers and if I need help you provide it. Is that clear?"

"It is. Crystal clear. Thank you Carol. We will give you a ring once we know she is on her way."

Alison and Jody went directly to see Susanne's Mother, in the hope of repeating their success in finding a place to stay for Becky.

"Impossible" explained Joyce . . . . "After your last visit I rang the social services and they said that Susanne cannot be in the same home as the little one, due to her previous behaviour and the order that was placed on his care when she left him."

"Left him?" asked Jody.

"You had better ask her that. It is a long story and I'm sorry but I cannot help this time."

"Is there anyone else we can ask? We are desperate for her not to be left alone" pleaded Jody, sensing that there was no point in trying to persuade Joyce to change her mind.

"The only other person is my sister, who lives a few minutes away. She gets on better with her than I do. I can ring and ask, but don't build your hopes up."

Jody urged Joyce to ring her sister and explain things as best she could. Joyce rang and got an answer immediately.

"Aye, it is me. Cathy, can you speak to this policewoman about Susanne? They need some help." Joyce promptly handed the phone to Jody, who was momentarily taken aback.

"Hello Cathy, my name is Jody Gallagher and I need a favour."

Jody began to explain things to Cathy whilst Alison went into the kitchen with Joyce. Alison could see that Joyce was managing to hold things together, but the experiences of the past were beginning to show.

"We're sorry to upset you Joyce. I cannot imagine what you have been through but at least we are trying to do something about it."

"I am almost past being upset . . . . . Susanne was a lovely bairn, always happy and full of mischief. She could be a proper little sod when she wanted to, but she was never in trouble. It was when her Dad died that it all went wrong. She was his little princess . . . he doted on her and they went everywhere together, he used to take her to the pictures, the park, even fishing when she said she wanted to go with him. He got cancer and died when she was just short of her fifteenth birthday. We have never had a lot of money, but we did okay when Larry was alive. Once his insurance money had gone and we were down to one wage, things got harder and harder."

"I'm sorry Joyce. I had no idea. We have hardly had a chance to speak with Susanne properly," explained Alison.

"That's okay. I just want her to be back to the way she was, but I have given up. I just do my best for Laurence, her little boy. If Cathy agrees to have her I'll be pleased, but she must try to get better, for all our sakes."

Alison could hear Jody finalising the call to Cathy and she felt a sudden wave of anxiety as she waited to hear if Cathy had agreed to help.

"Cathy can look after her for a few days and then we'll have to review it. We can drop her off straight from the hospital," declared a relieved Jody.

Alison turned to Joyce and thanked her. She could have easily hidden behind the child protection order and washed her hands of Susanne, but she had provided a solution instead.

"That's families for you. What would we do without them?" concluded Joyce.

Jody and Alison drove straight to the hospital to assist with transport. As Jody parked the car, she shared her thoughts with Alison.

"You know when Dr Newman said that they would feel as if they did not belong anywhere, I can see how they end up thinking like that. It is as if they have been put in a box labelled 'too difficult to deal with' and then left. What would you do without your family, your mates and your colleagues? There is always someone to ask a favour of, or give you a bit of help with one thing or another. They have just had Fawcus making their lives a misery. They must feel angry towards the world and everyone in it."

"What is the history with Susanne's little lad? Did Joyce say?" asked Jody.

"No, she wanted us to ask her. I think we will have to approach that subject carefully, Jody. Let's hope we can get them settled and interviewed soon."

As the normal working day drew to a close, Albert had cleared the office of those who did not need to work another long shift. He stayed in the office with Susan and Scott in case there was a need to go to assist with the transport detail from the hospital.

Susan still had a nagging thought in her mind about the suspicion of other corrupt officers linked to Operation Neon. She asked Scott about the phone calls he had overheard Noone making which he thought sounded odd.

"They were definitely with someone who knew police terminology and systems. He did not have to explain anything . . . the conversation flowed as if they knew what each other was on about. I have checked the surveillance logs and I was out with him the day after the incident at Diane's flat when she had her windows put out. So that suggests it was Dryden and the phone billing should prove it once and for all. The other calls were before that, but I feel sure it was to a different person. He was not as familiar, sort of a bit formal as if this person was a superior or perhaps someone he did not know very well. I wish I had had the sense to record him on my phone."

The conversation continued as Albert summarised a few emails he had received.

"Ros will have her preliminary analysis done by the middle of next week. She says there are a lot of links between the main players as a result of the work Brian has done with the phones. The billing is expected soon. Unfortunately we are getting nowhere with 'punterdate' as it looks like it is based abroad and that will take ages to sort out, so forget that for the time being. If we can get the financial enquiries under way and the victims interviewed, we will be doing well. How are we getting on with the escorts Scott?"

"Derek has proposed to fourteen of them so far, but they all said he was too old to marry! Seriously, only three have given us a statement, confirming they work as escorts for Superior and not much else. It is obvious they are very nervous and it is early days. I have spoken to two other agency owners who cannot stand the Doyles and Fawcus. They are happy to speak to us, but there is no chance they will give a statement, even though they have lost a lot of business to Superior and get nothing but hassle if they take on an escort that used to be on Superior's books."

"What have the escorts said off the record?" Susan wanted to hear if there was anything else she could follow up.

"They have all been told to say the same thing. If the police ever asked them how they got clients, they had to say that Superior was just an introduction service and the sex that took place was nothing to do with them. It was between the escort and the punter. They also had to say that they worked alone in the house, but we know that was not true from the TPO visits. None of the escorts spoken to have said they know the prostitution laws and most of them get confused when you try and to explain . . . . the vast majority think they are in trouble no matter what they do."

Within a short time Becky and Susanne were discharged and on their way to their respective homes, with strict instructions from the medical staff to keep away from any sort of drug other than the ones prescribed to them. Alison contacted Albert with an update.

"They are looking a lot better than this time last week, but they are still fragile to say the least. I was thinking that Jill and Alan could work tomorrow, perhaps calling to see them both, then Jody and I could do Sunday. We may even get a short interview done with both of them if things go well. We'll just have to see how it goes."

In reality, there was little else that anyone could do as both women had suffered a great deal of abuse over a long period and one or two interviews were not going to cover everything. Albert was well aware of the task facing the interviewing officers.

"Do what you can. I think the guidance we have had from Dr Newman is the best way ahead. It will take time to get the full picture, but if you do manage an interview and we have more to put to the offenders, then great, go for it."

### Saturday 17<sup>th</sup> August

Jill and Alan visited both Becky and Susanne, spending enough time with both to answer questions about the police enquiry and to reassure everyone that the police were on hand to deal with eventualities as they occurred.

### Sunday 18<sup>th</sup> August

Alison and Jody decided to visit Becky first to see how she felt about being interviewed. Carol was there to greet them and she had ideas of her own.

"I had a long chat with the other coppers yesterday about Becky being interviewed and I have told her to try her best and get it done as soon as possible. I want her to get it all out of her head so she can get well. If she can get Fawcus locked up for a long time, then all the better."

Alison went to see Becky in her bedroom. Becky explained that she felt tired, but had slept reasonably well and had tried to eat some breakfast. Alison looked around the room, noticing that all Becky's childhood belongings were neatly displayed; posters on the wall from her teenage crushes, a row of small soft toys and a bookcase with her school files and assignments at the foot of the bed.

"Good to be home Becky?" asked Alison.

"Sort of. My Mam has kept everything the same. She said she wished we could turn the clock back and start again. I don't know why this has happened to me, I look at all my old stuff and it seems like another world, from ages ago."

Alison was not sure if this was the time to ask about a trip out to begin an interview.

"My Mam said that you want to interview me, so you can get Fawcus for more crimes?"

"That's the plan Becky, but it has to be when you are ready; don't think you have to rush into anything."

Becky had already made her mind up and she told Alison that she would prefer to be doing something rather than be in the house all day. Within the hour, they were set to begin an interview at HQ.

Alison began the interview with a few general questions, designed to make Becky feel at ease and forget the fact that she was being recorded. Becky recalled how she had fallen into the same trap as all the others of her age, initially enjoying the attention that Fawcus gave them until she was addicted to heroin and forced into prostitution.

"He was really nice to start with . . . he bought me some clothes and we went to nightclubs where he bought loads of drinks. I was not happy at home so I just stayed in different flats. Occasionally I would go back and see my Mam, but we kept falling out. She knew straight away I was on the gear and she hated Fawcus from then."

"What did Fawcus say to you when he made you have sex with various men?"

"He said I owed him and I had to do it unless I could pay him back. He never said how much, he just said I was part of his business and I had to do whatever him and the Doyles said. I was just 18 and knew nothing."

"So you met the Doyles?"

"Yes. They used to come around for a couple of months at the start and I had to suck them off as they were the bosses. They could hardly be bothered to speak to me never mind anything else. Fawcus was always with them when they arrived and he tried to have sex whenever he wanted."

"What was the daily routine when you were in one of the flats they provided?"

"We started work at around ten in the morning. Sometimes it was four or five the next day before we got some sleep. The most punters I have seen in one day is fifteen, the average about eight. That is until we got so bad no one wanted to touch us."

"Because of heroin?"

"Aye. If I had not needed the gear I would have done a shoot and told Fawcus to fuck off."

"Who sent the punters?"

"Sometimes Fawcus, but mostly Gloria or old bag Mrs Fawcus would text to say they were on their way. They even started giving taxi drivers a ten pound bonus if they dropped off a car load. On a weekend we could get four or five drunks turning up from the nightclub all at once . . . . thanks to a twat of a taxi driver who wanted his tenner. Some of them were useless though; they could not even raise an eyebrow never mind anything else and some fell asleep. We still got fifty quid off them, as they were clueless when they woke up."

"Who was with you in the flats?"

"I have only worked with Lexi and Susanne. Gayle has done some out calls with us, but not very often. We were the lowest of the low, the ones that would have to see the punters the others would not. You know . . . the dirty smelly ones or the creepy ones. Fawcus would not let them turn anyone away, all he wanted was money."

"Did you get paid for what you had to do?"

"Paid? You must be joking. We got a couple of tenner bags if we were lucky and a few quid for food now and again. He must have been making four or five hundred quid a day out of each of us before things got bad and we saw nothing like that."

"Did you not get a chance to keep some of the money?"

"Now and again, but not much. We had to hide it elsewhere, but I can't go in to that."

"Can I ask you about Fawcus? You said he wanted sex from you when he wanted. Did he give you any choice?"

"Obviously not. If I wanted heroin, he had to have a shag. That is the way it was."

"And if you said no?"

"He took no notice. He is much bigger than me. I think you must know why I have internal injuries. The doctor explained everything to me. He came to the shit hole flat at Waterford Way after a punter complained about me and Lexi being off our heads. Fawcus went mad and was hitting both of us, so I scratched him. He chucked me over the chair and did what he did. The injuries are there to prove it.

201

Lexi saw it all and there was a man on the landing as I left. The pain was terrible, I did not eat for days as I was scared to go to the toilet. The doctor says I will have trouble for quite a while yet."

"Have there been any other times this has happened?"

"Well, not as rough as that, but I never wanted to have sex with Fawcus, or the Doyles, or anyone else other than a proper boyfriend. I have no chance now have I? Who is going to want to be with me, a prostitute, a slag and a junkie?"

"You are not any of those things Becky. Please don't think like that. We have covered a lot, but all I need to ask you about is the two policemen who were working with Fawcus and the Doyles. What do you remember about them?"

"I'm sure they were already punters before we knew they were coppers and I'm sure they both came to Holly Gardens. The one called Aidan was a bit boring and the other called Pat treated us like shit, just like the Doyles. He just wanted his blow job and left without hardly a word. Fawcus told us they were coppers and if we said anything they would find us so we had to behave."

"Thanks Becky. I think we should have a break now."

Alison brought the interview to an end and Jody sealed the tapes. She then joined Alison and Becky and they chatted for a while, praising Becky for the interview she had just given.

"What happens after all this is done?" Becky asked "I mean who I talk to when you are away on another job?"

"We are going to try to speak to Social Services, to see what they can suggest. There are some good Social Workers who want to help."

"Come off it Alison, what are they going to do? I saw a social worker last year and when I told her what I was doing she went red and pulled a funny face, twisted about in her seat and started talking about a college course. She made appointments with the doctor about detox, but I was all over the place."

"There is also Dr Newman and her team. They have helped us a lot," suggested Jody.

"We need someone there when it matters, not just an appointment." Becky summed up her situation in one sentence and the policewomen knew it. How did anyone think that two years of abuse could be discussed and worked through within the confines of a thirty minute session once a week?

Becky was then taken back home, via a drive-through for some lunch. She picked at her burger and ate a few chips, but at least she managed to get through most of her milk shake. Food was still not a high priority as her injuries were weighing on her mind. Carol looked pleased when she was told that Becky had been interviewed. Perhaps this marked a significant milestone for her. Becky was not under Fawcus's complete control anymore and the tide was at last turning the other way.

Alison and Jody decided to call in to see Susanne as it was less than five minutes away. They rang ahead and were greeted at the door by Cathy, who mentioned that Susanne was still feeling a bit unwell, but otherwise much better than she had been for a long time. The conversation turned to Becky and Jody explained that she was also feeling better and had managed an interview with them. This seemed to motivate Susanne, who indicated that she would like to speak to the police sooner, rather than later.

There was no reason why the interview could not be done straight away, so they gathered a few belongings together and returned to the interview suite at HQ. Jody took the lead this time and showed Susanne around the room and made sure she was comfortable.

Jody began with a few general questions, as with all the other interviews to date. Susanne was much quieter than both Lexi and Becky. She sat forward on the sofa, holding a tissue in her hands. She explained how she had been recruited by Fawcus, using Lexi as an example of how to make money and get what he had called 'nice things'. Within two weeks of meeting him, she was addicted to heroin and was drinking far too much.

In a depressing repeat of the interviews with Becky and Lexi, Susanne recalled how she was forced to have sex with countless men for very little money, driven around from flat to flat and had to endure sex with Fawcus and the Doyle Brothers. Before long she had fallen out with her family and there were constant arguments about the care of her son, who was then not quite three years old.

"Where were you living Susanne?"

"I had a flat of my own in the next street from my Aunt Cathy. Just me and Laurence. I had him just before I was 17 and the social services let me keep him as long as my Mam and Cathy supported me. The thing is I had no money and there were no jobs I could take . . . . I would have lost my benefits. His Dad is in prison for robbery and we don't hear anything from him. When I saw Lexi in the take-away with Fawcus, he made a fuss and he must have found out where I lived because he came around a couple of days later. Lexi was with him and she said she was doing okay and had money . . . I ended up going out to a couple of parties and then the heroin got passed around. That was my biggest mistake. Fawcus then started picking me up and taking me to flats to have sex with punters."

"So he gave you heroin as payment?"

"Yes and the odd £20."

"Did you keep your flat?"

"No. That is the worst thing that happened. Fawcus began picking me up more and more, but I could not find a babysitter every time. My Mam and Cathy work, so they were not always around and the neighbour helped me a couple of times but that was it . . . . I . . . I . . ."

"Take your time Susanne . . . we can have a break if you need it, just say."

". . . . I had to leave Laurence on his own a few times . . . . . Fawcus would ring and say he was coming so I had to get ready. He would pull up outside, rev his engine and beep the horn so I had to hurry and rush out . . . Laurence got to know what was happening . . . every time the mobile rang he would look frightened, then he would see me put on my make-up and by the time Fawcus arrived and revved his car, Laurence was crying and saying *mammy please, mammy please* and standing in front of the door."

Susanne sobbed at the memory of the forced neglect and her part in it.

"It was not your fault, Susanne. Did Fawcus know about Laurence?"

"Yes he did. I used to plead with him to take me back, but he would just say that I had to do as he said. He was not bothered at all. I had to go and have sex with a load of men just to make him some money and to get a tenner bag. The one time I refused to go he came around the next day and punched me in the stomach. He said it was a lesson."

"How long would you be away?"

"About three hours. All I could think about was Laurence . . . . I felt so guilty, his voice was always in my head, begging me not to go . . . he was alone with just the telly and some sweets. One time Fawcus did not even take me all the way home, he told me to get out of the car and I had to run as fast as I could. Laurence was curled up on the settee and when I cuddled him he said *mammy not love me*."

"He is fine now Susanne. The main thing nothing happened to him and he is safe with your Mam."

"I know, I know, but it should never have happened. My Mam went around one day and saw that Laurence was on his own and he was in a state. She soon realised what was happening and she took him to her house. The social services found out and she got custody of him. I did not see either of them for months . . . . I am so ashamed of what I have done."

"Please don't be. Your Mam and Cathy want things to work and I'm sure they will. What happened was not your fault."

Jody could see no reason to continue the interview after hearing what Susanne had endured at the hands of Fawcus. There was a limit to the painful memories she had to re-live at any one time and Jody felt that the limit had been reached for now.

Susanne asked to go to the toilet, which meant that Jody had a few moments with Alison.

"I want to rip that fat bastard's head off. What a fucking disgrace he is, leaving a young bairn like that." Jody had remained calm with Susanne, but was raging inside.

"I think there is going to be a queue. Wait until this becomes common knowledge. He will be a marked man in the prisons, never mind anywhere else."

Alison, Jody and Susanne stayed in the interview suite for a while, chatting and consoling Susanne when she became upset. Eventually they went back to Cathy's house.

"Before we go in, do you want me to tell Cathy about what we have talked about in interview? It might help," asked Jody.

Susanne nodded her permission. Jody took Cathy to one side as Susanne went in to the kitchen with Alison.

"She has told us everything about how she lost custody of Laurence and from what we know about Fawcus, she had very little choice. He is as bad as it gets."

"We were all disgusted with her when it happened, but it then dawned on me that she would never do anything like that without there being something else going on. I have come to terms with it and so has Joyce. We just need some time to get Susanne back to where she was a couple of years ago. Laurence asks about his Mam, but he is doing well otherwise."

## Monday 19th August

Alison and Jody decided to check with Lexi and Diane before going to the office, so they left a message for Albert to ensure he was around at 10 o'clock for an update. This arrangement would also allow Miles Ashley to get back from 'morning prayers' with the Chief Constable. Albert had enjoyed a couple of days away from work, apart from a few phone calls, and he was looking forward to another week of good progress. He had already processed the applications to have the defendants produced from prison on Wednesday 21st.

As Albert sat in his office scrolling through his emails, Miles Ashley arrived. He had not been to morning prayers as usual. Albert could see that he looked concerned, if not worried. The expression on his face indicated that he had some urgent news.

"Albert, have you been in since eight this morning?"

"Yes, I was in about quarter to eight," replied Albert, mirroring the worried look in Mile's face.

"I have just heard some devastating news. I don't know how to put it, but the British Embassy in Cyprus has been in touch with the Command Block and there has been an accident over there, it is the worst news possible . . . . "

Albert rose to his feet, listening to every word.

"Is it about Bill? And Audrey?" he asked, not at all sure he wanted to know the answer.

206

"They were in an accident last night on the way back to their hotel. A drunk crashed into their taxi. Bill was killed and Audrey died on the way to hospital. I'm sorry Albert. This is the last thing I expected, I can hardly believe it."

Albert was unable to comprehend the news and sunk back into his chair. He wanted to phone Polly, but she would be on her way to work.

"Are they sure?" asked Albert after a short pause.

"Bill still had his warrant card on him and their passports were at the hotel, so unless they have made a terrible mistake . . . ." Miles was unable to provide any hope. "The media have already got hold of it and it was on the news at 8am. I'll get everyone to come back here."

Albert remained in his office for a few minutes, until the initial shock subsided and he felt ready to venture out. He was met by Hughie, Brian, Jimmy and Derek. It was obvious they had heard the news. Derek explained that everyone was on their way back. Alan was the only one missing as he had a day off so Jody was going to ring him before he heard from elsewhere.

Further details started to filter through, describing how the taxi driver had tried to avoid the collision with the drunk, but he had stood little chance. He was seriously hurt, but stable, in hospital. So was the drunk driver, who had been seen minutes earlier driving on the wrong side of the road.

The FCT ran on automatic for the rest of the day. It was too difficult to think or to speak.

### Tuesday 20<sup>th</sup> August

The team gathered at 8am, some still struggling with the events of the previous day. Miles had been the first to arrive for work and he decided to speak openly about Bill and what they could expect to happen over the next few weeks.

"Bill was one of the best detectives the FCT has ever had. He made sure this team had everything it needed and his knowledge was second to none. I spent last night thinking about nothing else, but today I want us all to think about how he would want us to continue. He knew Operation Neon was one of the most difficult jobs we have ever taken on and when he said so, I was not too sure. How right he was. That is what I will miss the most; his leadership and his wise advice. The British Embassy have been keeping us informed, but it is unlikely that Bill and Audrey will be brought home this week. The local police are still dealing with the accident and they are waiting to speak to the taxi driver and the drunk driver."

Miles looked at Albert inviting him to say something.

"Bill and I had a conversation just before he left. He asked me to make sure that Pat Noone and the others got what was coming to them. I promised I would make sure. I think you all would have said the same. If anyone has a message for Bill and Audrey's family, Polly and I are going to drop a card off tonight and I'm sure they will be comforted to know we are all thinking about them."

The overwhelming feeling of sadness was evident in every member of the team, but they also knew that they had several offenders to interview the next day and two more to arrest. Alison and Jody summarised the work they had done over the weekend, outlining the content of the interviews with Becky and Susanne.

Jody found it difficult to relay the part of Susanne's interview where she described how her son was left on his own whilst she was forced to go with Fawcus to various brothels. The extent of the offending had gone up another level whilst Fawcus had stooped to the lowest level possible. As Jody described what had happened, the others glanced at each other, making eye contact as they did so. Subconsciously they were looking to see the determination they were feeling in their colleagues. Words were not necessary; they all knew what they had to do.

That evening Albert and Polly left a bundle of cards and letters for Bill and Audrey's family.

### Wednesday 21st August

The morning began with the arrests of Gloria Doyle and Brenda Fawcus. Gloria was not surprised at all. She had been on the verge of contacting the police to come and hear what she had to say. Jimmy and Derek duly obliged, but it had to be done formally and with her solicitor. Brenda Fawcus was not as amenable, trying to tell Neil and Jill that she was not available to be arrested on a Wednesday as she had a regular hairdressing appointment. Both were taken to a police station for interview.

Alan and Neil tracked down Oliver Wise at a branch of Chappell and Partners in Newcastle. He was arrested and taken to the same police station as Gloria and Brenda.

At a separate police station, Fawcus and the Doyles were produced by the security company in charge of prisoner transport. Alison wasted no time in arresting Fawcus for the rape of Becky, trafficking Lexi, Becky and Susanne for the purposes of sexual exploitation and a number of assaults on all three victims. Fawcus looked dazed and he asked if his solicitor was on his way.

Scott and Dave arrested the Doyles for trafficking. They made no comment and gave no indication as to what they were thinking. Colin Doyle asked if he could have a breakfast meal as he had not been given anything at the prison; his casual demeanour was clear.

Mr Brown was the first solicitor to arrive and he was given full disclosure so he could advise Fawcus accordingly.

"That is everything we have so far Mr Brown," explained Tommy who was again helping the interview teams. "We can't hang about too long as they have to be back at the prison by 4pm. It is up to him now."

Mr Brown was shown to an interview room to have his consultation with Fawcus, just as Mr Brannigan arrived to represent the Doyles. He was met by Tommy, who was about to present him with disclosure, when Mr Brannigan offered his condolences.

"I heard about DI Reynolds on the news. It has been a while since he dealt with any of my clients but I was sorry to hear what happened. He always did things the right way, although we still had a few disagreements. I had a lot of time for him."

Tommy thanked Mr Brannigan and gave him all the information he needed.

"Over to you. In their previous interviews they said very little, but I suppose you have Mr Short's notes to assist. We have to get them back to prison this afternoon, so we don't want to hang about." Tommy made sure everyone knew where they stood.

Thank you Officer. I don't think my clients will have much to say this time either, but let's see how it goes."

With consultations underway, Tommy left the custody area to meet up with the interview teams in a side room. Alison and Albert had already decided to dispense with the cat-and-mouse interview strategy and go straight to the 'challenge' stage with Fawcus.

"He needs to feel as much pressure as possible. I want him to know his world is about to cave in and we have all the victims on board. He probably thinks he still controls them but he is about to get a shock." Alison was in no mood to give Fawcus an inch.

"Brannigan is here for the Doyles and he has indicated that they will say very little. That is what they always do," explained Tommy.

Within a few minutes Scott and Dave were called through by the Custody Officer to start their interviews. The consultations had been brief, so the interviews were not going to be long. The Doyles and Mr Brannigan made their intentions clear before a tape was even put into the recording machine.

Fawcus, on the other hand, was still in consultation with Mr Brown. He remained in consultation as Graeme Doyle was interviewed over a twenty minute period and placed back in his cell after refusing to make any comment to the questions put to him.

The same thing happened as Colin Doyle was interviewed over a slightly longer period of twenty five minutes. Scott and Dave emerged with the words 'no reply' ringing in their ears.

After a consultation of almost an hour and a half, Mr Brown declared that his client was ready for interview. Alison was ready to go and Albert could sense her determination.

Albert presided over the formalities and handed over to Alison to cover the further offences for which Fawcus had been arrested.

**Q** You have been arrested for the rape of Becky English. Do you understand.

**A** No reply.

**Q** You raped her at 39 Waterford Way after you took exception to a complaint by one of her clients.

**A** No reply

**Q** Lexi Morrison saw it all and she has corroborated Becky's evidence.

**A** No reply.

**Q** You raped her and caused injuries to her anus and her rectum. You have had the medical evidence outlined to you. What have you to say about it.

**A** No reply.

**Q** Is this how you deal with your escorts, by using rape as a punishment

**A** No reply

**Q** How many others have you raped

**A** No reply.

**Q** You dragged her out of the flat and took her away. It was obvious she was bleeding and needed medical help. Did you try to help her.

**A** No reply.

**Q** You just abandoned her

**A** No reply

**Q** Let me ask about Susanne. She has told us that you punished her one day by punching her in her stomach. Is that right.

**A** No reply

**Q** That was because she refused to leave her little boy on his own when you wanted her to go out and see clients. Is she telling the truth.

**A** No reply.

**Q** He was just three years old. You made her leave him on other occasions, is that right.

**A** No reply. I want to speak to Mr Brown.

**Q** In a minute. We have some questions to put to you about trafficking Susanne, Becky and Lexi. Perhaps they will not make you feel so uncomfortable.

**A** Okay, then I want to speak to Mr Brown.

Albert took over.

**Q** Okay Barry, is it fair to say that you ran the operations for Superior Escorts, running the women from one address to another as part of your job.

**A** No reply.

**Q** You picked them up and dropped them off at brothels so men could have sex with them.

**A** No reply.

211

**Q** Lexi, Becky and Susanne were made to go with you and they had to have sex with anyone you decided. They had no choice, they were under duress.

**A** No reply.

**Q** Tell us about the down's syndrome lad and his brothers.

**A** No reply.

**Q** Lexi has told us about it, why can't you.

**A** No reply. I want to speak to Mr Brown. Interview over.

Fawcus was increasingly agitated and insisted that Mr Brown intervened on his behalf.

"My client has asked for a break on two occasions. It is obvious he wants to consult with me."

**Q** One last question and then we will finish the interview. Who takes the calls to the agency and allocates the punters to the escorts, is it Gloria Doyle or your Mother. Or is it all three of you.

**A** No reply. I have nothing else to say.

Albert finalised the interview and they left the room.

Alison turned to Albert as they made their way out to see Tommy.

"Makes me wonder how solicitors can sit in the same room as some of the people we deal with. I could not do it."

Albert and Alison were keen to hear how the other interviews were going, so they contacted Brian who was assisting his colleagues with disclosure.

"Gloria has been well prepared and she has stuck to the story about being an introduction agency and whatever happens after that is between the escort and the punter. Brenda Fawcus has played the innocent throughout and claims to know nothing about Superior Escorts or what her son does and she says she has never met the Doyles. She did say that she went out occasionally with Barry, but just to go shopping or to have lunch."

"And what about their friendly estate agent?" asked Albert.

"His world has caved in. He clearly thought nothing would come back to him so he got a surprise when he was locked up. His office are digging out all his rental files and they are as shocked as he was. He was obviously giving the Doyles a huge discount on rents. He has not said much in interview, but admits dealing with the Doyles and Fawcus. He said he had no idea they were pimps and he has never visited any of the flats he looks after when operating as a brothel. As soon as he was challenged he reverted to 'no replies'. His solicitor, Miss Alvarez struggled to keep a straight face when the story of him being lashed with his own belt was put to him. Mr Wise is apparently a pillar of the community. He is on the parish council and his wife is a trustee of various organisations, so he has some explaining to do when he gets home. He won't be on the dinner party circuit for much longer . . . . unless there is anything from your end to put to them, we are going to bail them shortly and prepare the paperwork for the CPS."

Albert rang Peter Chandler at the CPS in relation to the Doyles and Fawcus. He was already aware of the evidence and simply wanted to know if the interviews had revealed anything of interest.

"Very little I'm afraid" explained Albert "The Doyles never comment on anything and Fawcus went to pieces a bit, he is still in consultation with Mr Brown."

Peter Chandler had already made up his mind to authorise the further charging of Fawcus with rape, various assaults and trafficking. The Doyles would also face a charge of trafficking.

"Thanks Albert. I will send an email through now authorising the charges. I also think this will put off any bail applications for a while."

The further charges were promptly prepared and put to the Doyles, their casual indifference continuing throughout. Fawcus was charged by Alison, her delight was in complete contrast to his increasing anxiety.

### Thursday 22<sup>nd</sup> August

The news from Cyprus did not get much better. The taxi driver's condition had worsened due to his injuries. The drunk driver was out of intensive care and was technically under arrest at the hospital. Arrangements to bring Bill and Audrey back home were still not finalised and it was likely to be several more days before the transport problem was resolved.

Miles Ashley forwarded an email to Albert from the Chief Constable offering her sympathy. He added a line informing him that she was to visit FCT the following day and meet everyone engaged on Operation Neon.

## Friday 23rd August

There was not a great deal of enthusiasm surrounding the imminent visit by the Chief. Jody was succinct, as always.

"If she had not decided to get rid of all the old-timers, Bill would still be here today. I don't know if I want to meet her."

There were nods of agreement amongst the team, as Jody was simply stating a fact. Jimmy agreed, but stated that it was impossible to predict what had happened.

"She must feel as bad as us . . . . she could not have known what was going to happen. We'll just have to sit and listen to what she says and move on. Bill would have done the same."

Miles Ashley accompanied the Chief Constable and her Staff Officer to the main office and he introduced the entire Operation Neon enquiry team to her. Chief Constable Angela Redmond placed herself at one end of the room and expressed her sadness at Bill's death. She was unable to say much about him as they had never met in the year she had been with the force. She did say that she had instructed the welfare department to assist Bill's family in any way they could, before and after the funerals had taken place.

She then turned to Operation Neon and congratulated the enquiry team for their efforts. She spoke slowly and carefully, switching her attention from one person to another as they listened. Her voice had no sign of an accent and she could easily have found a job with the BBC World Service, so good was her diction.

"I will be speaking to Supt Ashley, DI Fenwick and T/DI Bennison immediately after this meeting about the practical demands of Operation Neon, but I just want you all to know I am very grateful for the work you have done so far. . . . . I have been led to believe that it is very difficult dealing with an ex-colleague who has turned out to be corrupt . . . . . but I feel sure that the public would not expect anything other than a thorough investigation. Now unless you have any questions, I must speak with the operational leads."

There were no questions, so Miles led the Chief Constable to his office. She immediately took his chair and asked Albert to close the door behind him. Her Staff Officer, a very young looking Inspector called Bruce Carter sat in the corner taking notes.

"Superintendent Ashley has kept me up to date with the investigation . . . . is there anything else I should know?"

Miles, Susan and Albert looked at each other before shaking their heads.

"Good. I want this operation tied up by the end of the month . . . . there are other priorities coming along and we need to get officers freed up . . . . any questions?"

"Several Ma'am," said Albert "How do we support three vulnerable witnesses after the end of the month, how do we interview them about two years of abuse in the next seven days; how do we trace any other corrupt officers; how do we do all the mobile phone and computer log traces in time and not to mention all the other routine enquiries?"

"Those are operational decisions you must take . . . . there are other demands on your team and also CC. Mr Ashley will have to give you guidance if you have difficulty prioritising."

Miles Ashley had been listening carefully and as she looked at him for his agreement, he spoke up.

"We cannot do the operation justice by the end of the month. We will run the risk of leaving gaping holes in the prosecution case and I do not see how this enquiry will be finalised by the end of September at the earliest."

"I can only agree Ma'am. We have promised the CPS a warts-and-all enquiry and we must make every effort to try to trace the male known as 'The Suit', as I still think he may be another corrupt officer. He has covered his tracks well," said Susan.

The Chief Constable was not used to such direct challenges to her authority, but she had underestimated the enquiry and the officers leading it. This was not some sort of initiative designed to grab headlines and reassure the public. Operation Neon was much more than that. The suffering and the level of criminality uncovered by the victims and the operational team were beyond her comprehension and she had proved it by setting an impossible deadline.

"I will speak with Mr Ashley . . . . the rest of you probably have other things to do. You can go too Bruce. Wait for me downstairs." Albert, Susan and Bruce Carter left the room.

"Shall we grab a cup of tea?" suggested Albert. "Not for me," said Bruce as he made his way to the stairs, smiling broadly, "but thanks for the offer and thanks for the last few minutes, it has been enlightening."

Miles Ashley sat quietly waiting for the Chief Constable to express her thoughts.

"I have a list of priorities handed down from the Home Office and prostitution is not one of them. I understand that we have a corruption element, so I expect you and your team to concentrate on that and get the convictions we need to reference the entire job as detected . . . . that is all I expect to hear from now on. I am not going to allow a further allocation of overtime for this operation . . . . . hand over the victims to social services and there is no further need to go on looking for other offenders . . . . . from what I hear there is no tangible evidence . . . . . is that clear?"

"I will assess the entire operation and I will submit a report promptly Ma'am. I can only repeat that the amount of work is substantial," said Miles, trying to be as diplomatic as possible.

The Chief did not respond. She got up and walked a few steps to the window, keeping her back towards Miles.

"The promotion boards are soon, are they not? . . . . . you will be seen in a very good light should this operation prove successful and on budget . . . . have you thought of that Mr Ashley?"

Miles looked at the Chief's silhouette in the bright light of the window. She did not even have the decency to face him whilst she made thinly disguised threats to his future career. She may have been in the bright light of the window, but she had put herself in the shade as far as he was concerned.

"I will be taking all things in to consideration Ma'am," said Miles, still keeping his options open.

"I'm sure you will and so will I . . . . and one last thing. I need to know about DI Reynolds funeral arrangements as soon as they are known. I will be attending and I would like to know where I will be sitting in the church before I arrive. Is that clear?"

"Yes Ma'am." Miles was in no mood for any further conversation and he left the room. He continued along the corridor, passing Susan and Albert as he did so.

"Show her out will you Albert? I'll be in the kitchen."

Albert could sense that Miles was not his usual calm and collected self and he immediately found the Chief Constable, thanked her for attending and made sure she found the way to her car. Together with Susan they ventured to the kitchen, looking for Miles with a feeling of trepidation as they did so.

"Everything okay?" said Susan, knowing that it was probably not.

"Well, that was a meeting and a half," said Miles "We are going to have to get our act together and make sure we can convince her to give us more time. I will compile a report with all the enquiries, I need Hughie to give me all the information he has and Ros will no doubt have as much again. One thing I might not be able to change is her decision to withdraw any further overtime. She has the final say and the Finance Officer will not do a thing without her signature."

"I would not worry too much about that. Bill and I have a reserve account with about 150 hours overtime in it. We can use that," said Albert.

"Pardon . . . . you have what? . . . . Albert is there any situation where you don't have a back-up plan?"

"It is simple, any underspend is put in our 'Court Appearances and Miscellaneous Overtime Fund'. Finance know all about it. Bill argued that we had to keep the money as we always had long trials and rather than give it back and then re-apply for the same job, it would save time and resources."

"And they fell for that?" asked Miles.

"Bill was great with figures and he was very persuasive . . . . even now, when he is not here his decisions and influence are not far away."

**Saturday and Sunday 24<sup>th</sup>/25<sup>th</sup> August. Bank Holiday Monday 26<sup>th</sup> August**

This proved to be the first long weekend that Becky and Susanne felt well enough to do some of the simple things; shopping, meeting family, friends and generally acquainting themselves with a world free from Fawcus.

### Tuesday 27<sup>th</sup> August

Miles, Albert and Susan met at 8am to go through the progress report prepared by Miles for the Chief. It consisted of all the unfinished enquiries coupled with a projection of the time needed to provide the CPS with a full file of evidence. As they worked through the text, Albert received an email from Peter Chandler asking him to contact him at his earliest convenience. He rang him straight away.

"Morning Peter, did you have a good weekend?"

"I did Albert. And it may have just got better. I have received an email from Mr Brown who is representing Fawcus. He indicates that his client wants to assist the police with their enquiries. I replied asking him exactly what he meant and the long and short of it is that he wants to give Queen's Evidence. Fawcus has gone to pieces . . . . Mr Brown says his client does not want to spend a long time in jail and he has read up about so called 'super grasses' who get discounted sentences for cooperating. I don't know what you think? It could possibly save a lot of work. The other thing I should mention is that we cannot deny him this opportunity . . . . if someone wants to tell the truth at court as part of the prosecution, then they should be allowed to do so unless we can prove that their evidence is tainted, wholly unreliable or does not assist the prosecution case. It may be that we need to have an initial interview with him to hear what he has to say."

"Blimey, that is a turn up for the books. I have only dealt with a couple of offenders who gave QE. They can also create a lot of work. Fawcus is a coward . . . . I'm sure the victims will take it badly if he gets a short sentence."

"I don't blame them. I will email you the current Home Office Guidance on QE and let Mr Brown know we will be in touch. Give me a ring later and we can decide how to proceed. Thanks Albert."

Albert relayed the conversation to Miles and Susan. It did not take long for them to conclude that there would be nothing lost by listening to what Fawcus had to say. Foremost in their minds was the potential for him to identify 'The Suit' and any others who may be involved. Miles decided to delay sending his report to the Chief until they had been able to consider everything carefully.

The guidance Peter Chandler emailed was extensive and Albert had always struggled with long winded official documents. All he wanted was a summary and an idea of how to proceed. Susan and Miles had more patience and they went through the guidance, section by section. In the end, the choice was straightforward; before Fawcus could become an 'Assisting Offender', he had to let the prosecution know what he wanted to say; he had to fully admit his part in all the crimes he had committed as part of Operation Neon and any others; he could not be granted immunity and he would be dealt with by the trial judge who was the only person allowed to give him discount on his sentence.

"So if there is general agreement to hear what he has to say, we have not got a great deal to lose," concluded Albert.

Albert duly contacted Peter Chandler and he suggested contacting Mr Brown to provide an account of what Fawcus was prepared to divulge. Mr Brown was not representing anyone else and his firm of solicitors was independent of any connection to the other offenders, so it was safe to use him as a go-between.

"Mr Brown obviously knows what he wants to say, his first email was just an opening to the dialogue. If he gives enough detail then it may be beneficial to have Fawcus produced so that he can be interviewed about his criminality and at the same time get a better perspective of his value to our case. I'll get in touch with him and suggest he lets us know as a matter of urgency," said Peter.

Albert was keen to find out how Alison and Jody felt about this development and he summoned them to a brief meeting. He explained the basics to them and their reaction was mixed.

"He should not get any favours at all," said Alison "He is a cruel bastard and I think he will tell a pack of lies to save himself."

"I think he is not worth bothering with either, unless he comes up with something we don't know. Do we still think there are any other bent coppers out there?" said Jody.

"Look, this could be a lot of work for nothing and I also think the victims will take it badly if we are seen to do a favour for Fawcus. It is natural for them, and their families, to expect him to go to jail for a long time. But I also think he could be useful and I agree with Alison, he will tell lies and lose part, if not all, of his discount when sentencing comes around. He will shift the blame and try to be a victim, he will try anything to save himself," said Albert.

"And his Mother," added Alison.

"Exactly. We don't have to proceed if Fawcus does not come up to scratch and I think he will end up regretting his decision to grass his mates up. He has a lot to answer for and his charge sheet is going to be a long one. Get as much as you can from the victims and we will put everything to him. If he wants to cooperate he will have to admit the lot . . . . and that could be a big mistake on his part," said Albert.

Alison gave Albert a short update of where they were with the victims.

"Witness protection are due to move Lexi and Diane later this week, so we are interviewing her before she goes. Becky and Susanne are more or less settled, but their health is still a concern. Susanne is sleeping a lot during the day and then gets up during the night . . . . her Auntie Cathy is coping for the time being but it must be difficult for all of them. Becky's Mam is on the phone about four times a day, mostly for advice but I think she wants us to be at her house when Becky gets emotional or upset. There does not seem to be the same bond between her and Becky that there is between Lexi and Diane."

"If there is one thing to come out of this enquiry, it is the need for specialists to look after these victims. It is way more complex than anything we have dealt with before and we are not equipped to deal with it. Dr Newman has been brilliant, but we need more than a bit of guidance" said Jody.

"What about Social services? The Chief thinks we should just hand the victims over," asked Albert.

"All three have given us permission to view their files and we have seen Susanne's. She is described as chaotic and out of control, but they allowed her to keep her bairn. They must have known all about Fawcus when Susanne lost custody of him. There is a report on the file from her social worker describing what happened and how she began working as a prostitute just after her 18<sup>th</sup> birthday. There is nothing on the file to suggest that the information was passed to the police and if it was we have not recorded it on our system. It is embarrassing and annoying; all of this could have been avoided if just one professional had raised the alarm," said Alison.

"And if they had listened to Mick Miller at some stage," added Albert.

Albert retreated to his office to study the QE guidelines and to read his emails, but it was not long before Miles joined him.

"I've just had a call from the Command Block. The British Embassy are saying that Bill and Audrey will be flown home on Thursday as the RAF have a flight returning to base in North Yorkshire so they have kindly stepped in . . . . at least the family can start to make some arrangements. Have you heard how they are doing?"

"I have not heard much since we dropped the cards off. Audrey's sister rang and spoke to Polly the day after . . . I think their son and daughter are still in a state of shock. I think we all are to an extent, one minute Bill is here and the next . . . "

"It is on your mind all the time . . . . the Chief has confirmed she will be at the funeral and she wants to know where she is sitting," said Miles.

"That's a strange thing to ask. How do you think she will react to your report?"

"Who knows Albert . . . as I told you a while back she changes her mind constantly, depending on who she last spoke to. If Fawcus comes across with something valuable, that might allow her some flexibility to give us more time. I cannot understand why she makes snap decisions and then has to back track all the time."

Albert recalled how Miles looked out of sorts when he came out of his private meeting with the Chief and decided to ask Miles what happened.

"Was she prepared to listen at all when you spoke after we left the room?"

"In a word, no. She even tried the oldest arm twisting trick in the book . . . "

"Promotion . . . . career?" said Albert.

221

"You guessed it. She suggested that I should make sure the operation comes in on time and on budget. In other words do as you are told . . . . keep that to yourself Albert I don't want any unpleasant side shows in the office. Will you let me know the minute something comes through from Mr Brown?"

Albert returned to his emails and caught up with the material he had been sent by Ros and Hughie. It confirmed that the enquiry was far too big to close down by the end of the month. Fawcus had suddenly gained a degree of importance; his decision to roll over had given the team a bit of breathing space – or so Albert hoped.

### Wednesday 28th August

The day began early for Miles Ashley, as he wanted to have his report ready for the Chief before his meeting with her at 3pm. His hope was that a reply had been received from Mr Brown, but there was another issue to take in before anyone could even turn their attentions to Fawcus.

Aidan Dryden had been released on conditional bail following an application by his legal team after he had spent a week on remand. One of his conditions was to live at his home address and stay indoors between 8pm and 6am. Every night a local officer had checked that Dryden was at home and there had been no concerns. Until last night – Dryden was not in when a check had been done at 9.30pm, his car was not on the drive and his neighbours had not seen him since the previous day. Miles began to check the data base for all the enquiries the night shift had made, when Albert and Scott arrived in the office. Miles quickly told them about Dryden's apparent disappearance.

"I can't say I am entirely surprised to be honest," said Albert "He must be under a lot of strain. His wife has left him, he has resigned so his money will run out sooner rather than later . . . . and he must be dreading the trial and going back to prison."

"And he is now in breach of bail. I hope they find him before he does anything stupid," said Scott.

Miles Ashley read out the log relating to Dryden.

"They have searched his house and garden, completed house-to-house enquiries and circulated his vehicle. Dryden will know that all

222

this will be getting done. They have also asked for his wife to be seen . . . . not sure where she is from this log . . . . ah, she is in Derby with her parents. No response as yet."

As there was little FCT could do about Dryden's breach of bail, work continued on Operation Neon and the anticipation of an email from Mr Brown.

At 9.30am, the email arrived in Albert's queue. He quickly forwarded it to Miles and went the short distance to his office so they could consider the content at the same time. Miles printed out the email and it was encouraging, but to the point.

*Dear T/DI Bennison,*

*I represent Barry Fawcus and he has instructed me to contact the police in relation to his recent arrest and charging with various offences of a serious nature. He has had time to consider his position and has consulted with me for relevant advice.*

*He would like to offer his considerable knowledge and evidence for the benefit of the prosecution. He informs me that he can shed light on the criminal activities of all of his co-accused and that of others related to the case. He wishes to cooperate by providing details of how 'Superior Escorts' operated, who benefitted and how the two police officers became involved. He has also assured me that there are other issues he wants to disclose.*

*I will look forward to your response. Douglas Brown.*

Miles and Albert were in agreement to go ahead and get Fawcus produced from prison so he could be interviewed.

"Who is best placed to interview him, Albert?"

"It cannot be Alison or Jody. They are too important to the victims. I think Dave and Scott should have a go at him. They know as much as anyone and the experience will be good for them."

"Right, let's get on with it. I'll add a bit to my report . . . . I am seeing Her Majesty at 3pm, so hopefully she will give us the go-ahead. In the mean time we could start a prisoner production order to get Fawcus on tape as soon as possible?" said Miles.

Albert rang Peter Chandler to let him know that things were moving along. Scott and Dave were told to keep Friday free so that they could interview Fawcus once the Chief had been seen.

Albert then looked at the log covering Dryden's disappearance. An update had been received from Mrs Dryden, who had not seen her husband since the day of his arrest and she had not spoken to him in over a week. She had told him she wanted a divorce and had made arrangements for her belongings to be collected from the house. She also wanted the house sold as soon as possible. Her only suggestion for where he could be was one of his favourite walking spots near Kielder Reservoir in North Northumberland. She stated that he would go there at least once a month and sometimes camp overnight when the weather was good.

Scott reappeared in Albert's office and asked him if he had read the log about Dryden.

"Yes, I think it is all going one way Scott. He is not as resilient as Noone. Don't be surprised if his car is found up at Kielder."

The day continued at a fast pace and Miles soon found himself in the Chief's office, waiting for her to give a verdict on his report. She sat behind her large desk, glancing over the top of her reading glasses at Miles as she went through his report, point by point. Inspector Bruce Carter sat behind Miles, taking notes.

"I see there has been a considerable amount of work put into this operation. There is a lot of good evidence already . . . . do you agree Superintendent Ashley?"

"There is Ma'am."

"And you are now making an application for one of the main offenders to be treated as an 'Assisting Offender'?"

"Yes Ma'am . . . . it may well strengthen our case and lead us to other offenders who have not been identified by routine means," said Miles, emphasising his point.

Chief Constable Angela Redmond was well aware of the value of Assisting Offenders. In her role as an Assistant Chief Constable in her previous force, she had sat on the Association of Chief Police Officers (ACPO) sub-committee tasked with reviewing the Home Office guidance relating to their use. Miles was aware of her prior knowledge and she was on record stating that the use of Assisting Offenders should be considered whenever the opportunity arose and their effective use should be encouraged. Miles felt confident, but he did not want her to know it. He was also acutely aware of the Chief's ability to change her mind at any moment.

"The problem I have is that we are going to tie-up resources when there are several initiatives in the pipeline. What is the minimum you can continue with Mr Ashley?"

"I think the entire team should stay with the operation for another month, together with the support we have had from CC and FI" said Miles, starting his negotiations at the current staffing level.

"Impossible," snapped Angela Redmond. "You will reduce the team to four officers, with assistance from other departments only when absolutely necessary . . . . and there is no overtime left. Use the Assisting Offender as best you can, but do not waste any time on him if he does not cooperate fully from day one . . . . . that is all. Bruce, can you liaise with Mr Ashley and ensure all the correct authorisations are in place?"

Bruce Carter nodded and said "I will Ma'am and can I remind you we have to be in Sunderland by 4pm for a meeting with the Council?"

Miles left the room without exchanging pleasantries and went straight back to the office to see Albert, who confirmed the production order was arranged for Fawcus.

"We'll see what he has to say on Friday, Scott and Dave will deal with him. Peter Chandler is happy and we will have Mr Brown present throughout. We can't take the risk of any future accusations that we did a deal with Fawcus and he was promised the earth."

"Sounds good Albert. All we can tell him is that he may be granted a reduction in sentence and that is down to the Judge. He will probably end up in the Witness Protection Scheme, but we will cross that bridge when we come to it. Has there been an update on Aidan Dryden while I've been away?"

"No, nothing. No sightings and his car has not been found. I think the next stage is to check to see if he has used his bank account, but that will be tomorrow at the earliest. His mobile phone is switched off. How was the Chief when you saw her?"

"She was straight to the point as usual, which is not a bad thing I suppose. She just does not know how to negotiate . . . everything is on her terms. I think she has surrounded herself with people who do not question or suggest anything other than what she decides and that is not good for her or them. I remember the first station I worked at there was a sergeant who looked after his favourites . . . they got the overtime, the better jobs and so on. Everything he did went unchallenged as his sycophants agreed without question and the rest of us ignored him. In the end they got themselves into a fight and there was no rush to go to their assistance . . . . there was a few words exchanged and the sergeant was transferred a while later."

"Always best to have debate and an exchange of views," said Albert.

"In the end the sergeant became a figure of fun. He was a RSPB member in his spare time and he would obsess about rare species. He won a chicken in the monthly meat draw and the prize list was put on the wall . . . . someone crossed out the word 'chicken' and put 'dead bird'. He went berserk . . . . he did not see the humour, just a challenge to his authority and the image he had of himself. We still laugh about it when I see lads off the shift."

"Personalities and egos. They spoil a good job," said Albert.

**Thursday 29ᵗʰ August**
Diane and Lexi had been told to pack their belongings as they were being moved to their new home. Jody, Alison and Jill went to see them before they left.

"I want to thank you for everything" said Diane "I have Lexi back and we have a new start. I never thought this would happen in a hundred years."

In a few short weeks Lexi's life had turned around completely. She was coping well with her methadone and it was preventing her from taking heroin. She was reconciled with Diane and she was at last feeling better and eating regularly. Diane had told Jody that Lexi still talked about Fawcus more than any other person, as if she expected him to turn up at any moment. In Diane's opinion the move to another area, with a new identity and a place to call home, was the best thing they could do.

"We will keep in touch via WP. By all accounts your new flat is has just been refurbished, so you can soon have it the way you want" said Alison.

"Thank you for everything" said Lexi as she climbed aboard WP's people carrier. Alison, Jody and Jill waved them off as they were driven away by WP staff.

"I'll miss them, even though it was hard work looking after them," said Jody, "I hope they make a go of it."

Albert and Miles had checked the log to see if there was any news about Dryden, but there was no further update. He was still classed as missing and in breach of bail.

"Audrey's sister rang last night," said Albert, "The RAF flight should be in by about 1pm and then the undertakers are bringing Bill and Audrey back to the Chapel of Rest. She does not know when the funeral is as yet; they are in the hands of the coroner as the deaths happened abroad. I'll send an email out for everyone."

"Thanks Albert. It will be some sort of comfort when we get a date for the arrangements," said Miles.

Susan, Miles and Albert had arranged for a meeting with Ros the analyst to go through all her findings. Albert had invited Hughie, as his brain was as good as a computer. He was good at spotting links in the evidence.

Ros brought a number of large charts with her and she started with the management of 'Superior Escorts'. She explained her findings.

"Graeme and Colin Doyle are at the head of the empire, with Fawcus doing their running about. As you can see we have gone back six months and there are literally hundreds of phone calls and texts between them. Then there is Gloria Doyle and Brenda Fawcus, who take most of the calls to the agency. This is obvious by the texts they send confirming a punter, as they add either 'G' or 'B' after the message. There are constant calls to the escorts when they are working and I have cross referenced with the duty rotas we found. This shows how often the women work and gives an indication of how many punters they see on a daily basis. The average is six, the most on one day is fifteen and the least was one."

Ros had clearly done a good job and she had further charts concentrating on individuals.

"I have looked closely at the Doyles as we suspect there could be others involved. There is one number that is only contacted by them

227

and it ends in 7620. This is a pay-as-you-go with no subscriber. There are a few texts sent to it by both Doyles and they are interesting, especially at the end of June and through July. They are obviously meeting someone that they do not want anyone to know about. At the same time as they send texts to 7620, they send texts to Fawcus telling him they are busy or otherwise engaged. They clearly don't want him around."

"So do you think this is the person we refer to as 'The Suit'?" asked Susan.

"Could be, but I have not found anyone referred to by that name in any of the texts," said Ros as she turned to the next chart.

"This one shows how Fawcus operates. He gets all the calls to the brothels which we think housed Lexi, Becky and Susanne, possibly because they were getting the punters no one else would see and Fawcus had to enforce the rules. His texts are often threatening or abusive. He is obviously dealing as there are lots of texts from the women asking for gear and he will often reply telling them to wait or that they do not deserve any. His Mother texts him constantly, even when she is in Spain . . . . in one text she says that he better be keeping those girls under control and don't let them take the piss. That is the sort of language she uses all the time."

"Can we link him with Noone and Dryden?" asked Albert.

"Yes we can. Both their numbers appear on a regular basis, Dryden's less so after about Easter. Noone must be in touch once or twice a week with either Fawcus, Graeme or Colin. There is a pattern on Noone's calls showing how he uses Dryden to check the computer, then calls Fawcus or the Doyles soon after. He is getting Dryden to take the risks."

Hughie's work backed up Ros's findings and he explained the links.

"I have checked the computer data base with Steve and IT. Both Dryden and Noone check the same logs and intelligence, basically covering everything we know about Superior Escorts. They even check the escorts and sometimes they have carried out extensive searches to find out everything about them. They have acted like a verification service."

228

"Thanks Ros, thanks Hughie," said Miles "I'm concerned that we do not really have any idea who else may be on their books. If the Doyles have someone they are keeping to themselves, how are we going to find him? And the worry is he might be another corrupt officer."

"Perhaps Fawcus can help us with that tomorrow," concluded Albert.

By 5pm the news came through that Bill and Audrey were at the Chapel of Rest.

Dryden was still missing. With no further immediate lines of enquiry left to be made, he had quietly and efficiently disappeared.

### Friday 30th August

Scott and Dave were well prepared for their interview with Fawcus. Mr Brown was aware of the procedure and he was given a copy of the Home Office guidance detailing how the police intended to proceed with Fawcus.

The interviews took place at a police station which was kept in reserve, it was not manned but still functioned as a custody suite, as and when it was required. This eliminated the chance of interruptions, and more importantly, prying eyes and loose lips. Albert and Susan also attended, so they could monitor the interview in a separate room.

The first interview consisted of Scott reading out the Home Office guidance and asking Fawcus if he agreed to go ahead with his plans to admit his criminality and to provide evidence of the crimes committed by others. Fawcus was keen to ask Mr Brown for his opinion at every stage, but he gently and consistently told Fawcus that it had to be his decision. Fawcus eventually signed all the necessary documents, which gave Scott and Dave a chance to terminate the interview.

After a short break and a conversation with Mr Brown outlining the material the police wanted Fawcus to tell them about, another interview was commenced.

Scott took the lead with the formalities and then set the scene "Barry we are going to start with the offences you have been charged with so far and you are free to tell us anything you like. Is that clear?"

**A** Aye

**Q** You have been accused of raping Becky English. Is there anything you want to say

**A** Yes. I want to admit that I did force myself on her when I lost my temper. I do not think I caused all her injuries though, but I should not have done it.

**Q** Is losing your temper a reason to rape

**A** I am making no excuses . . . . . I did it and that is that

Scott continued to ask Fawcus several questions about the circumstances leading up to the rape and what happened immediately after. Fawcus answered every question, but was clearly trying to minimise his offending.

**Q** You transport the women from one place to another, trafficking them to meet men for sex. They are often forced to do this.

**A** Well that's their job, I just take them where they have to go. Sometimes they did not want to go and I had to make them. If that is trafficking then I am guilty.

**Q** They were under duress, they were sometimes ill, sometimes tired and hungry but you took no notice Barry, you just shoved them in your car and took them to see punters.

**A** I did, okay I see what you mean, I did do it against their will sometimes.

**Q** And you even took Susanne away from her three year old child

**A** Yes

**Q** Is there any explanation for that

**A** I have admitted it, I did it and I can't turn the clock back.

**Q** You supply heroin to the women under your control

**A** Yes. I have been a dealer for years. That is how I met the Doyles. They have made a fortune but wanted to be out of the business when competition arrived in the shape of Gordon Napier and his team so they buy off him now.

Fawcus went on to describe how he began dealing for the Doyles when in his mid-20s, making a decent amount of money. He had not touched any drugs himself and gave details of the suppliers the

230

Doyles prefer to use, buying a kilo at a time. He was more inclined to speak about his drug dealing, as if it was not particularly serious.

Q Heroin ruins people's lives Barry, you must know that

A It's their life. I don't smoke it or inject it for them, I just sell it.

Q You have assaulted the women by punching them and slapping them.

A So they do as they are told. I admit I was heavy handed but they used to take the piss sometimes. How was I supposed to let a punter go to the flat when it was like a shit hole . . . they did not take care of it . . . or themselves for that matter.

Scott asked several more questions relating to the assaults inflicted on Lexi, Becky and Susanne. Fawcus reluctantly admitted each one.

Dave then took over and asked about the organisation behind Superior Escorts.

A I get £10 per punter, more if there are extras or they book for longer. I get paid by either Graeme or Colin as they keep a close eye on the money. Gloria does the books and she accounts for every penny.

Q How much do you make a week

A Eight hundred . . . . about a thousand, plus whatever I get from a bag of heroin. The Doyles make much more than that.

Q So the Doyles also supply you with the heroin

A Yes. Or they send me to collect it, they have all the contacts

Dave asked about the detail behind the drug dealing and the day-to-day running of Superior Escorts. Fawcus fully admitted his role and that of others, providing explanations of how the agency attracted punters, administered the website and recruited escorts. He also outlined how escorts were put in brothels depending on how well they behaved. Dave asked him to explain.

A If they just did as they were told and saw plenty of punters, they would get the best flats. Anyone who complained was sent to the crappy areas and had to put up with arsehole punters. One escort at Willington Quay does nothing but whinge and I had to bollock her a few weeks ago.

Q What do you mean

**A** Well, you know, a bit of a threat . . . . maybes hold their money back a week . . . . or take away the pixelation from their face on the website . . . . stuff like that.

**Q** So you threatened to expose them for all to see on the website

**A** Sometimes . . . . a few are not bothered and their faces are on the pictures, others don't want their family to know what they do

**Q** What happens when an escort does not want you to put that she does anal, or sex without a condom on the website

**A** Ignore it basically . . . . they can go and work for someone else for all I care. They know what they are letting themselves in for. Anyway it is Gloria who updates the web pages, ask her.

**Q** What happens when a punter assaults or mistreats an escort

**A** Well . . . . erm . . . . if I was about I would have clipped him, but I can't be everywhere can I

**Q** Do you have sex with the escorts under your control

**A** I have had sex with some of them, either Colin or Graeme does first. If they are no good they don't get a job

**Q** So having sex with Colin and Graeme is like having an interview for a job

**A** Yes. That is one way of putting it.

Dave continued with further questions regarding the treatment of escorts and the various financial arrangements surrounding Superior Escorts until the first tape came to an end. A break followed and it gave Albert and Susan a chance to speak to the interview team.

"It is going well. He has admitted his role so far . . . . I thought he was a bit reluctant now and again" said Albert.

"It is the bits where he has no one else to blame. He was happier dropping the Doyles in it than talking about what he has done to the lasses" replied Dave.

"Okay, get him to tell you all about Noone, Dryden and 'The Suit' in the next interview, leave his Mother out of it unless he mentions her. Time is marching on" said Albert, reminding everyone that the job was only half done.

Scott and Dave commenced the next interview and quickly reminded Fawcus of the formalities. Both Fawcus and Mr Brown were happy to continue. Dave took the lead.

232

**Q** Barry you have been charged with an offence relating to the misconduct of two serving Police Officers. What can you tell us

**A** You mean Pat Noone and Aidan Dryden.

**Q** Yes. Tell us about Pat Noone first

**A** He was a punter, simple as that . . . . then Colin Doyle recognised him from somewhere and did a bit of homework . . . . he found out that he was a copper somehow.

**Q** How

**A** I have no idea . . . . they have a lot of contacts and they keep things close to their chest. They are always looking to recruit people who are of use to them.

**Q** When did you first meet him

**A** At least a year ago, if not more. He used our agency at least twice a month . . . he was a good customer. I saw him at a couple of brothels when I was doing my rounds but he kept out of my way. That is until Colin said he had to have free sex about this time last year.

**Q** And you eventually met him properly

**A** Yes . . . . I was given his number to check up on one of the lasses who was giving us grief. She was unreliable. I rang him and he told me she was always getting locked up for shoplifting so we dropped her.

**Q** So he got free sex for information provided to you and the Doyles.

**A** Spot on.

**Q** What about Aidan Dryden

**A** Not exactly the same. He dropped his warrant card in a brothel and he also bumped into Pat at another flat so he was a bit stupid to be honest . . . . a few weeks later he got free sex because Colin and Graeme said so. I don't know for sure but I think Pat was behind it all, he must have told the Doyles and they made sure Aidan did as he was told.

**Q** How was that done

**A** I'm not sure, but I overheard a conversation between Colin and Pat saying Aidan was worried his wife would find out . . . . they probably blackmailed him and he was such a soft shite he let them.

Dave explored the relationship between the corrupt officers and Superior Escorts by asking the details about how they communicated, passed information and arranged for their free sex. Fawcus grew in confidence as he spoke about the wrong-doing of others and his answers were straight to the point.

**Q** You met Pat Noone in a car park on an industrial estate. What was that all about

**A** Lexi going missing and Colin wanted to meet him as he had not seen him for a while . . . . he turned up and rang Aidan who said there was nothing on Lexi.

**Q** What else did you talk about

**A** Just general stuff . . . . . new escorts . . . . Pat said the police were not interested in prostitution. I was more interested in finding Lexi to be honest.

Scott continued with some further questions

**Q** You said the Doyles have a lot of contacts that are of use to them, do you think there are other corrupt police officers involved

**A** I have not met one but that does not mean to say there are not any . . . . they seem to know a lot though . . . I think they have got someone else . . . he might be one of the bosses in the police . . . they are always one step ahead

**Q** Until we caught up with them

**A** That's true . . . . they were not best pleased with Pat I can tell you. He is under their protection in prison so he has been left alone so far. One word from them and he is a gonner . . . . why is he not in a different prison

**Q** Not up to us Barry. Do they think Pat got careless or what, are they blaming him for getting caught

**A** Partly, they think there was always a chance they would get caught eventually but he always said the police had no interest and there was no intelligence on them . . . . there must be something else though . . . . Colin has it in his head that there is a grass and he wants to find out who it is as soon as possible . . . . this is why I think they have someone else as they have told me that as soon as they get disclosure from the police they will know who it is and he will be sorted . . . they are sure that is not any of the escorts and they know it

234

was not me as I am in more trouble than them . . . . so they are just waiting

**Q** Will they pass on all the material they get from the police to their other contact, is that what you are saying

**A** What else could they do? Whoever the other contact is he must be good and they want to keep him to themselves . . . . as I said they are always one step ahead

**Q** Okay, can we move on . . . what about 'punterdate', do you use that

**A** It is pathetic . . . . a load of stupid fantasists who think they are great lovers and put reviews on the internet telling people how much the escort enjoyed being shagged by them . . . . half-wits the whole lot. If they are that good why are they paying

**Q** Do you know how they communicate with each other

**A** There is some sort of messaging service on it. Colin and Graeme know how to access it, I think Pat and Aidan used it but I only went on it to look at some of the reviews.

**Q** What names did they use

**A** I am not sure, but I think I heard them use cartoon characters names, or kid's TV programmes . .

**Q** Virgil . . . Tonto . . . . do they ring a bell

**A** Virgil does – he drove a Thunderbird . . . that could be Pat . . . but Tonto . . . . . not sure . . . . possibly . . . they only used nicknames and I know that is how the Doyles preferred to contact their informants as it was easier to disguise. They could not have got all their information from just Pat and Aidan. That is why they must have had someone else

**Q** You seem sure

**A** They knew when people had been locked up before it became common knowledge . . . . they would always drop a dealer if they were arrested and they knew what was going to happen to them at court . . they could just be good operators but someone must have been tipping them off as they knew all the detail

**Q** Is there anything else you want to tell us about Pat Noone or Aidan Dryden

**A** Nothing about Dryden, he was Pat's run around. Pat once asked me if I knew anyone who could slash some tyres for him, it was while ago . . . . I said that a lad I knew would do it for a few quid so he gave me the details of a green Toyota and a couple of days later it got done.

**Q** Do you know why he wanted this done

**A** No idea, he just said someone was getting above themselves and he wanted to teach them a lesson . . . . I thought it might be someone who he had arrested and got off at court . . . . a bit of revenge maybes

Scott asked a number of questions about the damage to the Toyota, but Fawcus was not able to recall exactly what happened. He also failed to remember the name of the person he paid to do it on behalf of Noone.

**Q** Has Noone ever mentioned his girlfriends to you

**A** No, I thought he was single

**Q** Where else have you met him

**A** Twice at the DIY store that you have the pictures of . . . . once at Sunderland near the docks and a few times around Wallsend where the park is . . . . he suggests places out of the way

**Q** Before we finish this interview is there anything else you want to tell us about

**A** Not much . . . just a few minor things really. I smashed the windows at Diane's house when she was hiding Lexi and I asked Pat Noone to cover it up . . . . he said he had and Dryden had written off the crime . . . . I went back and kicked her door in a couple of days later to frighten her . . . Colin and Graeme did not want anyone reporting us to the police so I made it plain to her to shut up or else

**Q** Did they say how they had written the crime off

**A** No . . . just that I was lucky and not to do it again as it would not be as easy

**Q** Is this when Lexi was in hospital

**A** Yes it was come to think of it . . . I asked both of them to find her but they said there was nothing on her intelligence so I rang around and found her myself.

**Q** Then what did you do

**A** I visited her but got thrown out when Diane started to kick off . . . . so I waited a day or two and got a message to Lexi to meet me downstairs and I took her away . . . . she said something about being discharged but I was not interested. I took her to Waterford Way and left her there with a couple of bags of heroin

Q She had just gone through withdrawal you could have killed her

A She said she wanted it, so I gave her some to keep her happy . . . . anyway Becky was there so she would have got some gear off her

Scott brought the interview to an end and left Fawcus with Mr Brown. The decision was made to leave any further interviews to another day and provide Fawcus with a cover story as to why he had been produced. He was given a charge sheet with fictitious offences on it to use in prison if he was challenged.

By providing the police with an interview covering all his criminality and that of his closest associates, Fawcus had sold his soul. There was now no going back for him and the prosecution could use him to good effect, but only if they could corroborate what he had said. The only disappointment was the lack of a name attached to the Doyle's other contact, who they clearly kept to themselves.

"It has to be another cop" said Scott "If it was the same bloke I heard Pat talk to I would put some money on it."

Susan was not so sure "I just cannot make my mind up . . . we have checked every log to do with all the victims, witnesses and incidents without finding anything suspicious. The phone billing and subscriber checks give us any amount of evidence on the main players but there is no obvious link to another cop."

"Recently retired?" suggested Albert "There has been a lot go in the last eighteen months or so."

"It is possible I suppose, but all we have is SP9005 to go on and we have no chance of accessing 'punterdate' to find out. It is frustrating," said Susan.

Fawcus was assured that he would be interviewed again and was sent back to prison with his cover story. Albert began to think of the next step and he decided to call a de-brief for everyone at 8am, Monday 2nd September. He then spoke to Scott and Dave before they left.

"Good work today, the interviews went well . . . . lots of detail for us to go on. It is not pleasant having to be civil to such an individual like Fawcus, but you coaxed a lot out of him. Go and have a few pints tonight and we'll get cracking on Monday."

"The first one won't touch the sides Albert" said Dave "And by the way, did Alison tell you about Frank? He has given up the drink and he is on a twelve week addiction recovery course. He is a new man."

"When was this?" asked Albert.

"We spoke to him a few days ago. His doctor sent him to see an alcohol advisor or counsellor in North Shields and he now goes five days a week, nine 'til five. He loves it . . . he does group work and he seems to be making a big effort . . . he says the warrant on his house was the best thing that has happened to him in years."

"Good for him," said Albert, "And he must be pleased we have found Lexi and Becky?"

"He is . . . I think he is proud of himself."

As Albert prepared to finish his working day, he rang Miles to let him know how the interviews had gone. In a short time the conversation turned to another subject.

"This would have been Bill's last official day . . . I hope we get some word soon about the arrangements," said Albert.

"Yes, I thought about him earlier on . . . he was going to call at the office and hand his warrant card over . . . but it was not to be. As far as I know the Coroner will open and close an inquest and there will not be any further delays. Have a good weekend Albert. See you first thing on Monday" said Miles.

## Saturday 31st August and Sunday 1st September

With Lexi and Diane now with WP and out of the area, the FCT could concentrate on Becky and Susanne. Alison and Dave visited them both during the course of Saturday and took them out separately so the family could have a break. It became apparent that whilst both of them showed signs that their physical health was improving, they continued to struggle with the aftermath of their two years under the control of Fawcus and the Doyles.

Dave and Alison had a chance to reflect on the whole operation in between visits. Weekend working was more relaxed than an ordinary working day, unless there was a panic.

238

"We can't go on reassuring them that things will turn out okay once we have been to court and the bad lads have all been put away, can we? There must be something else we can do, these lasses need more than comforting words and encouragement from us," said Dave.

"They do, they do . . . Dr Newman cannot do it on her own either. She has any amount of work to do . . . and to be fair so have social services," said Alison, despairing at the lack of available support for women like Becky and Susanne.

"I'm beginning to feel like Mick Miller. He has bashed his head against a brick wall for years and it has taken a corruption case to highlight what has been going on. When all this is over we need to sit down and list all the things we need to do . . . a proper de-brief," said Dave.

"Too right," agreed Alison.

The following day Jody and Scott were on call and they repeated the visits of the day before. Becky had remained up late and decided to stay at home and sleep, but at least she knew there was someone to speak to if she wanted to. Susanne was pleased to see Jody and wanted some time with her. Susanne wanted Jody's opinion on how she could mend fences with her Mam and eventually regain custody of little Laurence. Jody had to be very careful with her advice and choice of words. She could not tell Susanne that everything would work out the way she hoped, but she did not want to spoil her dreams either. In the end Jody had to stay in middle ground, just like some politicians do; talking a lot but not actually answering the question.

After spending a few hours with Susanne, Jody was keen to hear how Scott had got on with Fawcus.

"He has admitted everything. He has given us Noone and Dryden on a plate and the same goes for the Doyles. No mention of his Mother mind . . . surprise-surprise. There are a couple of things I was not sure about, but we can do some digging next week. We'll have to interview him again and then do a long statement."

"So, will the twat end up with WP," asked Jody.

"If he continues to cooperate he will, yes."

"Arse hole, I hope he gets found out and they give him a good hiding. I hate the bastard."

239

## Monday 2<sup>nd</sup> September

The entire team assembled at 8am. Miles took the lead as he had limited time before he had to dash over to HQ for morning prayers with the Chief.

"Okay everyone, there has been some great work over the past month or so, but the Chief now wants to use the resources we have elsewhere . . . there will be four detectives left to run Operation Neon . . . the rest of us will have to deal with all the other jobs waiting in the queue. This is not ideal and I'm sure there will be times when we have to re-group and help out. I have to go over to HQ but before I go I would like to thank Tommy and Jill who will be leaving us on Friday, we could not have got this far without you both."

Miles made his excuses and left the briefing to Albert and Susan to continue. It had been decided that Alison, Jody, Scott and Dave would remain on Neon full time, with Hughie and Brian continuing to provide support with disclosure and technical tasks.

"If we need to support the Neon team we will use some of our overtime," said Albert, "And that includes Mick and Steve who have been with us all along."

Susan ran through the interviews Dave and Scott had done with Fawcus.

"He has admitted a lot and provided good evidence of his former mates' activities but it is fair to say we are not entirely happy with him. There is still a suspicion that there is another bent cop and we have to make that a priority for now."

Albert then asked Hughie for a brief summary of the evidential material accumulated so far.

"We now have eighteen statements from escorts outlining how they work for Superior. There are seven statements from punters believe it or not, describing how they book escorts and visit them. The phone billing and other checks have all been analysed by Ros and her charts will explain everything to the jury. The interviews with the victims have been transcribed and a lot of what they have said has been corroborated one way or another. In total we have over eight hundred documents, including one hundred and seventy nine statements . . . at the last count we have two hundred and thirty four exhibits."

"That compares with most murder enquiries" said Derek.

"So what is happening to the rest of us, Albert?" asked Neil.

"I don't know what they have in store for us, we'll just have to see."

# Chapter Six

# Waiting is the Worst Part

There is a general pattern to most large scale police enquiries. They begin with an incident or a significant piece of information that soon expands into a number of urgent leads, including a 'golden hour' when vital evidence is either lost or found. There follows a period of consolidation, when offenders are arrested and charged; victims, witnesses and experts are interviewed and brought together to form the basis of a viable prosecution. Then there is a lull; a long period when the court date seems to be in the distance, but work has to continue tying up any loose ends and generally reviewing the material to see if anything could be added which may be of use.

Operation Neon had entered an enforced lull. With only four detectives full time, their duties were dominated by the need to maintain contact with the victims and witnesses, assist with disclosure and ensure every piece of evidence was properly presented and accounted for. Dave and Scott interviewed Fawcus several more times, mainly adding detail to his initial admissions. He reluctantly mentioned his Mother, who he said had a minimal role to play, and only answered the phones when Gloria Doyle was ill. He was eventually taken in to the Assisting Offender scheme and spirited away to another establishment with a false identity. This alerted the Doyles to his treachery and they promptly put a price on his head, through their prison network. Honour amongst thieves does not exist, but revenge amongst offenders most certainly does.

Albert and the rest of the team were involved in force-wide initiatives, executing warrants on those suspected of handling stolen goods and a number of street dealers. They were little more than PR exercises, grabbing the headlines but not solving the underlying problems. Teams of officers in riot gear were shown regularly on local TV smashing their way through one uPVC door after another, then dragging suspects out of the same broken door in their pyjamas looking pale and fed up. Very few convictions resulted from the days of action by the police and there were no headlines to be found when the odd case made its way to court.

The Chief, however, was delighted at how things were going. Miles continued to suffer morning prayers, listening to the latest facts and figures from her experts in initiatives. The FCT had more or less ceased to operate as a team countering serious organised crime and had become a back-up to command units who needed assistance with the never ending list of quick and easy Home Office inspired hits.

The only time the entire team was together for a day was Bill and Audrey's funeral. It took place two weeks after they had been flown home and there was an immense feeling of sadness amongst all who attended. Albert had been to quite a few funerals over the years in remembrance of old colleagues and more often than not they ended up in a pub or a club. That was not the case this time; Polly and Albert accompanied Miles back to Bill's house so they could speak privately with his family and they gathered in the dining room with a cup of tea. Polly had broken her heart at the church, but was able to mix with the other mourners at the house, whilst Albert and Miles had maintained their manly composure throughout. Albert and Miles circulated within the company and found themselves chatting to Audrey's sister in the kitchen. She asked them to help her bring some more chairs from the garage and she opened the door to show them through. Albert immediately recognised the shape of Bill's classic car, shrouded under a grey dust sheet. It stopped him in his tracks. If only he had been able to enjoy it more, thought Albert, as he fought with the lump in his throat.

By the end of September, Peter Chandler had been able to review the evidence and he recommended further charges of money laundering, by Fawcus and the Doyles. He also recommended a further charge of conspiracy to commit criminal damage for Noone and Fawcus, as a result of what happened to PC Sissons' car. Gloria Doyle and Brenda Fawcus were charged with conspiracy to control prostitution and Oliver Wise was charged with aid and abet the control of prostitution. Peter Chandler had also appointed a barrister to run the prosecution case with a junior counsel, so he invited everyone to a case conference at his office.

"Welcome everyone. Can I introduce Sarah Jane Walker QC and Junior Counsel, Lee Hunter. They will be leading the prosecution. I have also been offered a court date; it is cutting it a bit fine but, as most of the defendants are still on remand and we have a timescale to meet . . . the suggested court period is the first three weeks in December. Is this possible?"

Miles and Albert both knew that the police rarely had any say in court dates, so they accepted they were in the hands of others.

"Mr Hunter and I have trials up to the end of November, so if they do not overrun and there are no problems with the case file, we are probably okay with that," said Sarah Jane Walker. She was direct and to the point and had already acquainted herself with the case.

"Could I just run through a few points with the Officers please?" said Miss Walker. Peter Chandler invited her to continue.

"Are the victims and witnesses still on board, especially the young women who Fawcus has abused so badly?"

"Yes they are, Lexi is settled with her new home, Becky has had a one or two bad days and Susanne has had various problems with her health lately, but they are determined to give evidence" said Alison.

"Good, good . . . and has Fawcus cooperated fully?"

"To a large extent, but we will not rely on anything we cannot corroborate. He has been minimal with the truth about the role played by his Mother and we are not sure about his version of events concerning the damage to PC Sisson's car," said Albert.

"Good. My impression, so far, is that there is a good case if the victims and Fawcus stand up to scrutiny. The documentary evidence will stand alone and I have no concerns in that department. I understand that Mr Kinnear will be defending the Doyles, Mr Unsworth is representing Noone and I am yet to hear about counsel for Mr Wise, Mrs Doyle and Mrs Fawcus. I take it the two ladies are likely bargaining chips?"

"That is a possibility," said Miles as Peter Chandler nodded in agreement.

"Good, good . . . it is always a welcome test for a criminal to see how fast he falls on his sword when his wife or his mother is in the dock with him," said Sarah Jane Walker.

Miles, Albert and Alison liked what they were hearing. Miss Walker had grasped the basics of the case and was already scheming in an attempt to gain the upper hand over the defence.

"When can we expect the full file so that we can start bombarding the defence with evidence of their client's wrongdoing? Asked Miss Walker.

"It is ready now. All we are waiting for is a couple of mobile billing requests to arrive and all the paperwork is done," said Alison.

"Good, good . . . . and the possibility of one other corrupt officer?"

"No progress there I'm afraid," said Susan.

"And can I ask about Aidan Dryden?"

"There has been no sign of him since he disappeared four weeks ago. His car has not been found, his mobile has not been used and he has not accessed his bank account. He has vanished," said Miles.

"Gosh . . . I had no idea that could be done these days, not with all the CCTV we have. It will be interesting to see how the defence approach his role in all of this if his disappearance is unexplained. There is no foul play suspected I take it?"

"No, nothing. He is officially missing from home and in breach of bail," said Miles.

Towards the end of the meeting Miss Walker explained that she had not prosecuted a corruption case before and was relishing the challenge. Lee Hunter asked about the opinions of other serving officers to the case and Miles explained that those who knew the full extent of the evidence were hoping that long sentences were dished out.

"There are other officers who have given us the cold shoulder . . . there was bound to be a few who did not want one of their own prosecuted . . . but once they hear the details I'm sure they will change their minds," said Miles.

As the police team left the building, Albert was optimistic.

"I like her. She is a little pocket dynamo . . . it is always a comfort when you have good barrister on your side. I hope she takes no nonsense from Kinnear and Unsworth. They can be aggravating so and so's. "

The FCT were often at court and involved in long-term trials, so they relied on prosecuting counsel for guidance and a good result. Barristers tend to live in a world of hindsight and anyone can make themselves look clever armed with all the information, but the best barristers take command of the court and present the evidence efficiently and succinctly. Their confidence in the evidence is more often than not transferred to the Jury, who soon work out to who they should listen.

As the weeks passed by, the case file was served on the defence and letters from the CPS, requesting clarification, were received and answered. The defence started probing for further information as to how the police had obtained their evidence and how the enquiry had started. Most barristers prosecute and defend, allowing themselves the opportunity to gain vital experience and knowledge from both sides. This means that when defending they actively fish for withheld information, such as the identity of informants, or the use of technical equipment used by the police. The defence will automatically know that FCT will have used all sorts of lawful means to build a case against their clients, but with the judge's permission, following a precise procedure, sensitive information can be withheld.

In many of FCT's cases, the defence steered clear of the strong evidence and concentrated on exposing a police informant. It is a game of brinkmanship, with the result that the police have no choice but to drop the case, as opposed to surrendering the informant. Both Mr Kinnear and Mr Unsworth were exponents of this tactic and had been successful in the past, much to the annoyance of Albert and Bill.

By mid-November, the team had successfully defeated all the attempts by the defence to prise open the chest of sensitive information. Various visits had been made by counsel for both the prosecution and the defence to inspect unused material and the exhibits. Peter Chandler arranged another case conference at his office to discuss last minute issues and the order in which witnesses would give evidence.

"Thanks for attending everyone. We are just about ready for next month. I think the defence have everything they have asked for apart from a witness running order . . . Miss Walker?"

"I want the following in first – Miss Morrison, Miss English and Miss Smith. Then Mrs Morrison. If any of the escorts is prepared to give evidence I would be grateful, but if not we will simply read out their statements . . . I don't want the jury getting bored so if we can have some attend, all the better. I then want Fawcus and I'm sure he will get a hard time . . . . not that I sympathise but he should be ready. Following that I will invite the medical evidence and then the police evidence; we can decide who we want later."

Alison then gave a brief update.

"Lexi, Becky and Susanne are bearing up, but as the date for the trial gets closer they are more and more anxious. This is causing problems with their families. We have spent a great deal of time with Becky and Susanne lately and they will be visiting the court to look around soon. All the other potential witnesses are warned."

"Good, good . . . any news on Mr Dryden?"

"Nothing at all," said Miles.

They all then concentrated on Ros's charts which Miss Walker said she wanted to use extensively for the benefit of the jury. Hughie's list of disclosure was scrutinised and found to be present and correct.

"We are all set then," said Peter Chandler, "And the next time we meet will be when Fawcus admits all his crimes at a hearing a couple of weeks before the main event."

A few days later it became apparent that one defendant would not be at court. Aidan Dryden's car was found in a remote area near Loch Tay, in Perthshire. The Scottish police had been alerted to its location by a walking group who had seen it several weeks previous, only to realise it was still there on a return to the same forest path. The car was hidden from the nearest track. The first officer on the scene confirmed that the car was empty and that a few belongings had been found, but most notably a letter had been left on the dashboard. It was in a sealed envelope with no addressee.

"The Scottish police have removed as much as they can and the car is being towed out as we speak," said Miles, "it is in the middle of nowhere and looks like it has been there for a while . . . he has disguised the number plates by making the F into and E and the P into an R with black tape. He obviously did not want to be traced on his way up there."

"So we can assume the worst. Is there any sign of him?" said Albert.

"Not yet. They are doing a search with the help of the local mountain rescue team, but the area is massive. His family is being informed and we will wait to see what the letter says once they have opened it back at the local station in Aberfeldy," said Miles.

It was not long before an image was emailed of the letter.

*To Whom it may Concern.*

*I wish to leave all my worldly possessions to my wife. I know that I have betrayed her in many ways and I hope that she goes on to find happiness in her life. Her future will be better without me.*

*When I was interviewed I admitted my part in the circumstances surrounding the investigation. I am deeply sorry for the part I played in the misery that the women involved endured. I cannot forgive myself for what has happened.*

*I told the interviewing officers that I was not aware of any other corrupt officers apart from my ex-friend Pat Noone. I do not believe that to be the case and I am sure there is one other. I do not know who it is and I ask that this letter is passed to the officer in charge of the investigation so he or she can extend their enquiries. I am convinced the answer lies in the messages and communication held by punterdate.*

*I have written a separate letter for my family, which you will find next to me. If you follow the track in a northerly direction for one mile, there is a gap in the trees overlooking the loch. You will find me in a bivouac below the crag. There is a red marker on a tree close by.*

*Aidan Dryden 31ˢᵗ August*

A note attached to the email suggested that it would not be long before the search team located the place Dryden had indicated and true to their word, confirmation that a body had been found was received within thirty minutes.

248

"I feel sorry that this has happened, but I still don't like what he did," said Albert.

"I see what you mean . . . perhaps we should have one last go at punterdate . . . . it is the one enquiry we have not been able to finalise that keeps coming up," said Miles.

The FCT had joined punterdate and gained access to the reviews and the forums. A search had been made of the entries and the nicknames Dryden had disclosed were found. Tonto1 and Virgil were attached to three reviews and SP9005 appeared on one review submitted by Virgil. The only way anyone could communicate directly with another member was to send a contact request and for it to be accepted. The FCT had been unsuccessful with a request sent to SP9005. The administrators of the website were believed to be based in the Philippines, following extensive research by Interpol.

"I think we have gone as far as we can with punternet. There is absolutely no chance of getting any cooperation from them, we don't even have a proper address. They even ignored requests we sent through their own system. Only the Doyles and Noone know who SP9005 is," said Albert.

"It is frustrating Albert. The thought that there is someone else providing information and covering the backs of those lot is a thorn in our side. The defence will make an issue of it."

# Chapter Seven

# Men in Wigs

**Monday 3<sup>rd</sup> December**

It is very rare for a case as large as Operation Neon to start hearing evidence on the first day. Background manoeuvrings are the main order of play; the defence continues to probe for weaknesses and the prosecution tries to hold fast in the face of last minute arguments and applications for the delivery of further sensitive information.

Mr Kinnear and Mr Unsworth made it plain that they would be running the defence, whilst those representing Gloria Doyle, Brenda Fawcus and Oliver Wise were of little consequence. Miss Walker was convinced that guilty pleas were inevitable from the minor offenders and they were just waiting for the go-head from the more senior offenders and their barristers. As was the custom, the solicitors who had attended the interviews also made an appearance.

His Honour Judge Irwin QC called everyone into court at noon as he wanted to hear from both sides what they had planned.

"Your Honour, the prosecution is ready. My learned friends have been supplied with all the disclosure, a running order and we are prepared for a trial. There is a defendant who wishes to give Queen's Evidence and he has already pleaded guilty to his indictments," said Miss Stafford.

Mr Kinnear responded "Your Honour, this trial has been complicated by the death of one of the defendants and the wish of another defendant to give Queen's Evidence . . . . this is not likely to be a straightforward trial. My clients are also wary of the fact that one of their co-defendants is related to Mr Fawcus who will be giving evidence against them. This has been mentioned in previous administrative hearings."

"So what are your suggestions Mr Kinnear?" said Judge Irwin.

Mr Kinnear rose to his feet again. He struggled to create enough space between his bench, his files and his belly as he did so. He was a large man to say the least.

"Mrs Fawcus should be removed from this trial as it is a clear disadvantage to my client and the others, your Honour."

"And what is the opinion of Mrs Fawcus?" asked Judge Irwin.

"Your Honour, my client is ready to progress with a plea. She has little desire to remain in the dock" said Mr Field who had no interest in prolonging the discussion. "I wish to discuss this with Miss Walker at the earliest opportunity."

Mr Kinnear and Mr Unsworth could not hide their annoyance at being trumped by a 'bit part' player so early in the trial. Miss Walker smiled in appreciation of the development.

"I suggest you discuss things further and we will gather again at 2pm," said Judge Irwin.

With an order from the Usher for everyone to rise, the Judge departed for his chambers behind the court room and left the barristers to sort themselves out.

Albert had remained outside the court whilst this first round of judicial tactics had taken place. He greeted Miss Walker as she came out and then noticed Mr Brannigan as he followed her through the large oak-panelled doors.

"Ah Mr Brannigan. You look a lot paler than when I last saw you, the Spanish suntan has worn off," said Albert.

"It has . . . it seems a long time ago on a grey day like this," said Mr Brannigan as he hurried past Albert and went down the stairs.

Miss Walker asked the team to join her in a side office and she relayed what had happened in the court.

"What is the bottom line on the minor offenders? Could we accept lesser charges and effectively get them out of our hair. Mrs Fawcus obviously does not want to be anywhere near her co-defendants. What are your thoughts?"

"If Mr Chandler agrees, then the police would have no problem," said Albert.

"Good, good" said Miss Walker, using her regular phraseology.

At 2pm the court convened for the second time and Mrs Fawcus entered a plea to a lesser charge of aid and abet the control of prostitution. Mr Kinnear and Mr Unsworth then successfully argued that they needed more time with their clients to discuss the development and seek their opinions. The court was adjourned for the day.

"One down, one dead and five to go" said Jody "Keep this up and we'll be finished by the weekend."

## Tuesday 4th December

For every one hour the court hears evidence in a large case, a further two can often be taken up with legal argument and representations. Defence Barristers swing from smug indifference when faced with good quality evidence, to complete outrage when they suspect a fault in procedure. The court becomes a stage on which the best advocates use all their Shakespearian skills, phrases and sense of drama to influence the jury or the judge. Mr Kinnear had been at the fore front of many performances and he was ready to star in another.

"Your Honour. My clients are ready to defend themselves. I will lead them in their quest."

Judge Irwin was either eating a sweet or trying not to smile when he thanked Mr Kinnear and asked the opinions of the other barristers. Mr Stewart and Miss Thurman, acting for Gloria Doyle and Oliver Wise respectively, indicated they were ready to proceed. Mr Unsworth was also ready to go ahead, but seemed less inclined to make it look like a crusade. Judge Irwin instructed the Ushers to organise the jury and have them sworn in, with opening speeches to begin as soon as possible.

Lexi and Diane had been brought back to Newcastle the night before by WP so that they were ready to give evidence. Jody and Alison had been to meet them at the secret flat and they were pleasantly surprised to see how Lexi had continued to recover. She had put on weight, had her teeth fixed and generally had a healthy glow about her. Diane was happier than ever; she had found a part-time job and they had made a good start to their new lives.

Lexi was naturally nervous about giving evidence and she wanted to know if there was a chance they would all plead guilty and save the ordeal of standing up in front of her tormentors. Diane had rang

Jody some weeks before when they heard about Fawcus giving Queen's Evidence and she had become upset at the thought he would walk away unpunished. She felt better when she realised that he would not be in the dock with the rest and would still face a prison sentence.

Becky and Susanne were not as well prepared as Lexi. They had not enjoyed the same level of support; Alison and Jody had been on hand when there was an emergency, but with all their other duties it had been difficult to respond every time. Susanne had argued with her Mam on several occasions and she had stayed out all night after one particularly bad episode. There was a suspicion that she had relapsed, but her blood tests were negative for opiates, although she was obviously having the odd spliff. Dr Newman had emphasised to the police that there would be many difficulties experienced by the victims and the imminent court proceedings were bound to be testing.

With a jury in place, the court was prepared and ready to start hearing the evidence. The jury was made up of six men and six women; their ages spanned from 23 to 64 and their professions varied; a teacher, retired accountant, shop workers, office workers and a housewife. Ordinary people brought into unfamiliar surroundings, to be bombarded with information, procedure and points of law. They had to take in and understand the evidence at the first attempt. There would be little chance of being allowed to press the rewind button and listen to the evidence again. Neither would they be prepared for the graphic nature of the evidence; the photos of injuries and the brutal way those injuries were inflicted. All they would get as a warning as to what was in store were a few advisory words from Judge Irwin.

Miss Walker began her opening speech concisely and with confidence. She outlined to the jury how the Doyles and Fawcus headed a business selling sex and they maintained that business with threats, violence and a corrupt relationship with two police officers.

One by one the defence barristers played down the role of their clients, choosing to blame Fawcus and the unreliable witnesses the jury was about to hear from.

Lexi was the first witness to take the stand. The court Usher led her through the oath and Lexi looked around the court, taking her time to get her bearings and to stare at the Doyles who sat at one end of the dock, with Noone at the other. Gloria Doyle and Oliver Wise filled in the gaps with two prison officers. In front of them sat several rows of solicitors and legal assistants, with Hughie parked on the end of the rear bench with his numerous boxes of disclosure and exhibits.

Miss Walker led Lexi through her evidence, outlining how she had been tricked in to sex work and an addiction to heroin. She occasionally pointed at the defendants as she answered Miss Walker's prompts. The jury listened intently; they were getting first hand evidence of a world they probably did not know existed.

Mr Kinnear was the first to cross-examine Lexi. He predictably undermined her memory for facts, dates, places and incidents implying that she was under the influence of controlled drugs and could not be relied upon.

"Miss Morrison, you told the police that the events that took place in the period before they found you were a blur, that is right is it not?"

"Sometimes, but I did not imagine the punters, the texts, the phone calls and the beatings did I? The records are there to see," responded Lexi.

"But you have not seen or heard from my clients for a long time have you?"

"Only because they were of getting sex from their latest recruits. They soon got bored with the likes of me and went on to someone else."

Mr Kinnear paused for a moment and stared down at his papers. Lexi was indeed corroborated by other witnesses and all the other evidence the police had accumulated.

"The police have provided you with a new flat and a new life have they not Miss Morrison?"

"Yes they have," said Lexi.

"In exchange for giving evidence for them?"

"Yes .... but I want to anyway," said Lexi.

"It must have cost a lot. Have you been asked to contribute anything apart from your appearance today?"

Miss Walker rose to her feet at that point and Judge Irwin intervened.

"Mr Kinnear, if you have any concerns about the witness and her relationship with the police, please be more specific. Miss Walker have you any comment to make?"

"Very briefly your Honour, the witness has been treated within the Home Office rules and all the material surrounding her arrangements have been disclosed to the defence. There are no irregularities at all."

Mr Kinnear continued to question Lexi about her earnings from Superior Escorts, suggesting that she only paid them to act as an introductory service and the money she earned from the sex acts she kept for herself.

"Get away, what planet are you lot on? I was in rags when the police found me, all I had was a packet of crisps and some pot noodles to my name. Not flash cars, swanky houses and holidays every other week. I had nothing," said Lexi.

Mr Kinnear passed the cross examination over to Mr Unsworth who looked small in comparison to the larger man. He spent a great deal of time covering the actions of Fawcus and how his behaviour eclipsed that of his client who was a respected police officer. Lexi stood her ground and refused to back down, with the result that Mr Unsworth ran out of steam. None of the other barristers had any questions for her, leaving about an hour of court time to fill. After some careful consideration, Miss Walker knew she did not have time to go through Becky's evidence in full and suggested to the court that the next witness should be Diane Morrison.

Diane was duly sworn in and she gave her evidence confidently and, at times, was filled with emotion as she re-told the story of how Lexi had deteriorated over the two years she was controlled by the defendants. She was particularly scathing towards Fawcus, perhaps assisting Mr Kinnear as she did so. He made great play of her hatred towards him and she helped him describe his cruelty towards the escorts.

Miss Walker was able to balance matters at the end of her evidence by asking Diane about the others and Diane redeemed herself.

"He could not have operated without the Doyles and his bent coppers could he? He is not the brains, he is just the bastard who goes around beating up young girls," said Diane, who immediately apologised for swearing.

Miss Walker was pleased with the first day. She told Albert that the witnesses had been far better than she had expected and that the jury would have a firm idea what the case was all about. Alison spoke to Becky and Susanne, telling them that it was more than likely they would be in court the next day. The waiting was proving unbearable and as they were not allowed to talk to Lexi to see how things had gone, there was no way they could obtain any encouragement from her.

### Wednesday 5th December

Becky was a bundle of nerves. She was unable to eat breakfast and she could not sit still. Her eyes darted from one corner of the waiting room to another, anticipating every movement to be her call to enter the court and give her evidence. After a short delay, the call came and she accompanied the Usher through the oak-panelled doors into the court. Becky was no stranger to the judicial system, but all of her experiences had been at Magistrates as a youngster. This time the court looked bigger, there were lots of people staring at her, some in ordinary clothes and others in wigs and cloaks.

She took the oath and Judge Irwin spoke kindly to her, reminding her to speak slowly so that everyone could hear what she was saying. It was his way of making her feel comfortable. Miss Walker led Becky through her evidence and she answered well, but nervously. Her tiny frame looked lost in the witness box. If at any time she had felt the need to sit down she was likely to disappear from view, apart from the top of her head.

Mr Kinnear did not preamble with background questions as he had with Lexi. He pressed Becky on how much money she had made and who had paid for her drugs. Becky remained resilient until Mr Kinnear produced her record of interview.

"When you were asked about how much money you made you implied that you kept some elsewhere, but you would not tell the police anything more. Why was that?"

"Because . . . I am not a grass and I'm not telling you where we kept our money," said Becky.

"So you had your own money and someone kept it for you?"

"Sort of," said Becky, looking increasingly nervous.

"So who had your money Miss English . . . a boyfriend . . . your Mother . . . who?"

"A friend . . . . and it was only a hundred quid or so. It was for food and clothes, we had nothing and we had to live . . . . would you like to shag a load of smelly men for nothing?" Becky had been cornered and she used her fighting spirit to claw her way back out.

"Miss English, I am only trying to find out the truth. My clients did not take all your money did they? You kept the money you made for yourself and you have tried to conceal the fact. They just introduced you to clients did they not?"

"They did everything. Got the clients, got the money, supplied the drugs you name it they did it apart from the sex . . . ." said Becky.

Mr Unsworth, acting for Noone, carried on from where he left off with Lexi, trying to put doubt in the minds of the jury as to how reliable the prosecution witnesses were due to their addictions and how it was mainly the fault of Fawcus that his client had been charged.

"The last time I saw him was at Holly Gardens, for his usual free blow job. Some copper he is," said Becky, growing in confidence as her time in court was coming to an end.

Noone sat forward and looked to the floor. Things were not going well for him or the other defendants. The Doyles had been confident that the witnesses would not turn up at court and even if they did, they would be nothing more than useless junkies. Their assumptions were proving to be completely wrong.

Miss Thurman was the only other Barrister to ask a question, confirming that Becky had never met her client in his capacity as a rental agent, or as a punter. Miss Walker covered a few points with Becky and after over an hour of giving evidence, she was allowed to stand down from the witness box. As Becky left the court, Mr Kinnear was passed a note from his clients via Mr Brannigan. There was clearly something of interest as he digested the content and gave a thumbs up sign towards the dock. He murmured something to Mr

257

Brannigan who then left the court. Hughie tried his best to get an indication as to what they were up to, but he was not close enough.

Miss Walker suggested that with the remaining time before lunch, Mr Hunter would read out a number of statements for the benefit of the jury. The statements were from witnesses that the defence had agreed did not need to attend court and give evidence. With that in place, she left the court to speak with Albert, Susan and Alison.

"It is going well. We have had a few blips but the witnesses have been excellent so far. If we can get Susanne in this afternoon, the jury are going to be wondering where the defence is coming from. Did you see where that little weasel Brannigan went to?"

"No idea" said Albert, "he came out and went down the stairs, I think he was on his phone."

"Ummm . . . . they must have something, Mr Kinnear looked a bit smug when he was passed a note. He gave Becky a hard time about some money she held back, but she came out fighting," said Miss Walker.

An alarm rang in Albert's head. He wanted to know more about what had been said. As Miss Walker relayed the cross examination from her notes, Alison knew exactly why Albert had asked for more detail. The defence had stumbled on to Frank by accident and Brannigan was his brief. Albert thanked Miss Walker for her help and he took Alison to one side.

"If they have put two and two together and come up with Frank, they will make a big thing of it. I hope Brannigan has not betrayed a confidence. When was the last time you heard from Frank?" said Albert.

"Last week I think . . . he is on his recovery course. He just wants the drugs warrant cleared up as it is holding him back, but the lab have still have not finished their bit," said Alison.

"You will have to go and see him tonight, we need to make sure he has not told Brannigan anything. We should know as soon as they will start asking for things."

The court stood down for lunch and it was not long before Miss Walker had been asked for all the documents the police had in their unused material for the brothel in Holly Gardens. Albert had been right to think the defence had discovered an opportunity to dig deeper.

Albert asked Hughie to retrieve everything they had on the brothel and he copied it for the defence. It contained no reference to Frank and his warrant, but then again it had no reason to. It was not part of the prosecution case and it did not undermine the evidence. It was now a matter of waiting to see what the next move was to be.

When the court reconvened at 2pm, Mr Kinnear asked if he could address the bench in closed court. He went on to ask Judge Irwin if they could have a short time to study the new disclosure and decide if there was anything else they needed. The Judge agreed, but he warned Mr Kinnear that the trial could not be held up for too long.

Alison and Albert found a quiet place to discuss the worst-case scenario.

"Brannigan knows all about the warrant at Frank's house and he must realise that it was done just as Operation Neon got going. Noone knows he has been to Holly Gardens and got free sex . . . . if he thinks for one minute Frank recognised him somehow, they will keep digging and digging. If Frank has opened up to anyone and they have found out, we have a serious problem," said Albert.

"And then we end up having to expose Frank to save the case?" said Alison.

"I hope not, that will be a decision for Miles and the HQ hierarchy. I thought it was going too well . . . that old toad Kinnear, he does it every time," said Albert.

Miss Walker then appeared back from meeting with Mr Kinnear and asked Albert if there was anything at all about Holly Gardens that she should know.

"Not about the brothel, no. We executed a warrant across the road and the person arrested has given us information about Pat Noone, he recognised him as a punter when he saw him in the flat. It has all been documented in the policy book and the forms have been classed as sensitive, Judge Irwin reviewed everything at the pre-trial hearing."

"So why are they making a fuss, how do they know to start asking difficult questions. They now want details of the closure of the brothel and the officers involved," said Miss Walker.

"Well the brothel had closed by the time the police got there, so that will not help them. This raises the question again about who else is pulling the strings," said Albert.

"And we have no idea who that is," asked Miss Walker.

"Not a clue," said Albert.

"Their next move will be to imply that there is another corrupt officer and that will delay the case. Unfortunately we cannot say this has not been discussed and investigated . . . . and that does undermine the case as they will make an application to say that it does . . . and they would be right." Miss Walker was not optimistic.

"We can still prove Noone was corrupt, whatever they say," said Albert.

"We can, but it will make the whole case messy and the jury will not like it. The defence have a golden opportunity and we will have to face up to it," said Miss Walker, who returned to Chambers to see if the defence were making any further demands.

"Crumbs" said Albert "This case is going from good-good to bad-bad in a few short minutes."

The delay was not helping Susanne who had expected to be in court at 2pm. She had no understanding of the games being played and the waiting was taking its toll on her. Her Aunt Cathy had accompanied her to the court and knew her well enough to see when she had reached a certain limit before she imploded. Alison came to the waiting room and explained that everything had been supplied to the defence and the court had no reason not to resume. Susanne came back from the edge of her anxiety for the time being.

Soon after, Judge Irwin recalled the barristers to a closed court and asked for an update. Mr Kinnear was upbeat and sprung to his feet, suddenly finding the extra strength to lift his substantial frame far more quickly than normal.

"Your Honour, we were just about to ask for further disclosure of all the material leading the police to the identity of the offenders and especially the alleged corruption."

"With a view to what exactly, Mr Kinnear?"

"That there is another source of information coming from the police and this undermines the evidence we have been presented with."

260

"Miss Walker, any comment?"

"I will need to review the disclosure with the officers Your Honour, but can I assure the court that all the details are there in the file."

"So be it. I will expect an update in thirty minutes," said Judge Irwin.

Miss Walker called the entire team and went through the options. There was a real chance that Frank would have to be exposed to save the case and the problem of the further corrupt source would have to be openly discussed in the hope that it would not affect the case against Noone.

"But it is likely that the Doyles know exactly who the source is. They have known about SP9005 all along and it is in the disclosure," said Alison.

"They must do, but they have played a good game. They have known all along that they could cause a huge black cloud to develop over the prosecution case and they have nothing to lose. I don't suppose for one minute they care about their corrupt source being found out if it saves their skins. I don't think Mr Kinnear or Mr Brannigan knew anything about it either. The both looked a bit surprised when the note was passed around. The rest of them are just waiting to see what happens," said Miss Walker.

Susanne was now ready to walk away from the court and not give evidence. The constant delays were too much for her. When the news of a further long wait reached her she broke down in tears and ran from the waiting room. Jody and Cathy went after her, but she got into a lift before they could stop her. By the time they reached the ground floor, Susanne was gone.

"Shit! I knew this would happen," said an out-of-breath Jody. "Where will she go Cathy?"

"Home I hope. I will go there and ring you, let me know if she comes back here."

Judge Irwin recalled everyone to closed court and asked Miss Walker for her update.

"We will have to disclose some further information to the defence immediately, Your Honour. I have no doubt they will need time to digest it."

"In that case we will adjourn until 10.30am tomorrow. Can the Ushers send the jury home for today please?"

Hughie copied all the information he had about the suspicion of a third corrupt officer and gave it to Miss Walker to review.

"Ummm . . . . so we cannot say it is definitely a police officer from the enquiries, but equally we cannot say for sure he or she is not. This is going to be interesting. The Doyles have a decision to make soon . . . are they going to tell us who SP9005 is or what?"

"Noone must know who it is too, so this is turning in to a three way game of chess," said Albert.

"We will see soon enough. I will consider everything tonight. It may be helpful to have your informant warned and ready, it is up to you but I don't think we can let these victims down without a fight. Mr Kinnear and Mr Unsworth are in for a long night working this lot out," said Miss Walker.

Jody caught up with Albert and Alison and relayed the news about Susanne's melt down. Neither were surprised and their immediate reaction was to task the team with finding her.

"Go to all her old haunts, find her friends, keep trying her phone," instructed Albert.

He then asked Dave and Scott to make contact with Frank, meet up with him and tell him what was going on at court. Albert could only hope that Frank understood the predicament they faced. He emailed Miles with the developments and received an instant reply to say that he would see him at court the next day.

By 9pm there was no sign of Susanne. Alison rang all the local hospitals, but there was no news. Cathy and her Mam had exhausted the list of people and places they thought she could have ended up with or arrived at.

Scott and Dave had managed to meet up with Frank and they had been able to explain everything to him. A long discussion had followed and Dave relayed it to Albert.

"Frank is not bothered if he has to give evidence. He says he is not frightened of the Doyles and the last thing he wants is for the case to fail. I think he still feels guilty that he did not report what was happening to Lexi and Becky before he did . . . he is some bloke, nothing like the person we met when we did the warrant . . . he is off

262

the drink, his house is tidy, Mrs Baker makes his sandwiches every day before he goes on his recovery course . . . I think he will be okay. We have taken a brief statement from him that should be enough for now. He is ready to come to court if he is required."

Albert was somewhere between ecstatic and bewildered when he heard what Dave had to say. He was also very grateful.

At 11pm Hughie checked the incident logs for the city centre and he found out where Susanne was.

"Believe it or not she was locked up for being drunk and disorderly. She is in custody. They have just put her name on the log from 7pm, she will be given a fixed penalty ticket. I will ring them now."

Jody and Alison made their way to the custody suite and spoke to the detention staff. Susanne had been drunk and abusive to members of the public near to the Quayside and had been locked up. She had continued to behave badly when the police arrived. No one had checked her intelligence, which would have given them an idea of what Susanne was involved in and who to contact.

Jody was not in the mood for excuses and made plain her thoughts. A hard pressed custody officer realised there had been a misunderstanding and he explained.

"Look, I know you are annoyed, but we have forty seven prisoners in custody and I have four jailers. This is a production line and we have never stopped. This place is chaos and there is no end to it, we have two more coming in right now. I'm sorry if there has been a bollock dropped, but it won't be the only one tonight." The point he made was reinforced by the constant shouts from those locked in the cells and the banging of doors by the most agitated. The cell complex was a tank of captivity and chaos.

Alison and Jody took Susanne home with her fixed penalty ticket and her hangover. She went straight to bed after apologising to Cathy.

"We will see you in the morning Cathy, at least Susanne is going to get some sleep" said Jody as the day came to a close.

## Thursday 6<sup>th</sup> December

Miss Walker and Mr Hunter were waiting for Albert and his team at the court, keen to hear what had happened the night before. They also had some news concerning the defence.

"Mr Kinnear is not a happy man. Brannigan has flown to Spain early this morning, with the excuse that his mother has fallen seriously ill and he needs to see her. He has all of Kinnear's notes with him and he needs them for this morning," said Miss Walker.

"Why would Brannigan have his notes?" asked Miles.

"Because he is too lazy to make notes himself . . . he always uses the client solicitor to do them for him. He also has the note sent by the Doyles to Mr Kinnear in court yesterday."

Miles outlined how Frank had made a brief statement and if necessary he would give evidence. The police would support him in whatever he decided to do and it was deemed good news for the case. Miss Walker was encouraged, but she pointed out that the further disclosure was still problematic.

"Is Susanne okay? Has she recovered?" asked Miss Walker.

"She is, but slightly subdued," said Jody.

"Right. We will be back in court at 10.30am to see what the defence come up with this time."

About twenty minutes before the court began the morning session, Mr Kinnear asked Miss Walker for assistance with his urgent need to contact Mr Brannigan. He gave her a number and the name of the holiday complex, supplied by his practice. Miss Walker passed the details to Albert who in turn asked Hughie to do the necessary.

"He needs a favour, perhaps the police could help him out this time?" asked Miss Walker.

Hughie tried the number, but had no joy. He knew that to go through the usual international protocols would take too long so he looked up the address he was given on the internet. It turned out to be a large complex called San Polensa, near Marbella. He then tried to find a contact number for the caretaker, or perhaps a sales office - in other words anyone who could help.

Hughie scanned the website for the complex, almost feeling jealous of Brannigan and his good fortune. It was when he looked at the contact page that he realised that there was a good reason why Brannigan had left so suddenly. The last few digits in the complex phone number were 9005. Hughie looked twice as his heart began to thump in his chest. He immediately called Albert over and he pointed at the screen.

"There it is Albert. SP – San Polensa – 9005. It is Brannigan. He is the one supplying the information to the Doyles, not a bent cop."

"Well, I'll go to the foot of our stairs. He has been covering for Noone and vice-versa. The Doyles have spoiled that arrangement . . . so Scott was right, it was someone who knew all about police tactics and language and when he spoke to him it was all a bit formal. The Doyles must have had Brannigan over a barrel too. I bet he has been giving them all sorts of information. Well, well, well. No wonder he looked after Frank. Hughie I owe you a thousand favours."

"But why blow him out? Surely they have just convicted themselves?" said Hughie.

"Yes, but little did they know he would do off to Spain with Kinnear's notes. Brannigan must have known it was game over yesterday. The Doyles have blown it. Print that page off and highlight the details, I can't wait to see Kinnear's face," said Albert.

Armed with the print out, Albert and Hughie gathered the team and asked them to come with them into the court. Hughie gave the document to Miss Walker and she was lost for words when she saw the highlighted SP and 9005. She immediately told Mr Kinnear that the identity of SP9005 was known. Miles, Susan and the others all looked at each other in bemused anticipation.

"Ah, so you have found out who the culprit is for me?" said Mr Kinnear.

"No Mr Kinnear. You have for me." Miss Walker gave the print out to him and after a few seconds he began to turn alternate shades of red and pink.

"No wonder Mr Brannigan has fled the country. Good grief." Mr Kinnear could only stare at the ceiling in response to the news.

"Shall I ask the Usher to inform the Judge we are ready?"

He gave no answer and soon all the other barristers realised the gravity of Hughie's discovery. They sank into their seats, knowing that the case was about to end suddenly.

Judge Irwin was presented with the print out and his response was a mixture of admiration for Hughie's initiative and anger towards Mr Brannigan.

"I expect that there will be some consultations in the very near future Mr Kinnear?"

"Yes Your Honour."

"Once you have recovered from your shock, I want to hear exactly how you and your learned friends plan to proceed. You have one hour."

The team left the court, congratulating Hughie as they did so. Jody rushed to tell Susanne, who could not understand the complexities, but was relieved to hear that she would not be giving evidence.

Albert asked Alison to ring the airport and make sure Brannigan had been on a flight to Spain. "Special Branch will have the passenger lists and they will confirm where he went."

Miss Walker then gave her thoughts. "There are a couple of options, we could end up having a re-trial with Mr Brannigan lining up with the rest, or they could all enter pleas in the hope that the Judge gives them some sort of credit . . . I would advise them to enter a plea and hope for the best."

A general discussion followed about the role Brannigan had played. There was a consensus that his career was finished, no matter what explanation he managed to concoct. Peter Chandler arrived at the court and his opinion was in line with Miss Walker's.

"I think guilty pleas are the order of the day, we can deal with Brannigan when he is found . . . what a surprise he has turned out to be . . . just when you think you have heard it all," said Peter Chandler.

Albert was beginning to feel that he should have realised much earlier that Brannigan was involved.

"If only we had got somewhere with punterdate," said Albert, "Brannigan would be downstairs in the cells with the rest of them, not in Spain. I wonder what he is doing? Did we miss a trick?"

"He will be waiting for a loud knock on the door in his hideaway" said Susan.

"Not yet he is not," interrupted Alison. "He is still at the airport, he is on a flight to Paris in 50 minutes. Special Branch (SB) only have one officer available and they need our help. If we go now we should make it before he boards."

There was no time to consider any other option so Alison, Dave and Scott left immediately. Albert shouted instructions as they headed for the stairs.

"Stay on the phone to me and Hughie will stay in touch with SB. Drag him off the plane if you have to! Don't let him get away."

Albert knew that the journey would take at least 15 minutes, driving as fast as the traffic would allow. "Brian, get on to the control room and let them know one of our cars will be tanking it to the airport. I don't want motor patrols messing this up by chasing them and causing a delay."

SB informed Hughie that check-in for the Paris flight was well under way and passengers were to make their way to gate 21.

Dave took the wheel of the FCT car and was soon on the central motorway heading to the airport. They had to cover six miles as fast as they could. The car was unmarked and it began to draw attention from other drivers who were alarmed at its speed. Albert remained on the phone to Alison.

"SB will meet you there, they are monitoring gate 21. He will know if Brannigan has tried to board by the time you get there. Where are you?"

"Just going over the A1. We have jumped a couple of lights but we are getting held up by drivers who don't use their mirrors."

Albert could hear Dave in the background shouting at other vehicles to get out of the way.

The remaining members of the team gathered around Hughie and Albert as they kept in contact with SB and the arrest team. The tension soon extended to the prosecution team, who rarely witnessed the urgency of practical police work.

"We are in sight of the airport," said Alison, "We will have to abandon the car and go straight in, where is gate 21?"

267

Hughie had asked the SB officer to meet the team at the main entrance, so they wasted no time in going to the right place. Albert relayed the instructions to Alison who was almost ready to jump out of the car.

"You have about 25 minutes before the plane is due to depart," said Albert. "Boarding has started."

Alison, Dave and Scott ran to the main entrance and identified themselves to the SB Officer, Grant Arkle.

"Quick as you like. We can go through the security door over here and we should be at gate 21 within five minutes," said Grant. He led his colleagues to a large door near the check-in desks and used his security pass to open it. They were soon running along a corridor used exclusively by airport staff. There were no windows, just white plastic walls and green plastic floors.

They all arrived at another security door and Grant swiped his card to open it. The light flashed red and not green. This was not good news. He tried again, but the red light denied access.

"Come on, come on," urged Grant as he tried his card for a third time. It still did not work. He immediately radioed airport security control asking for assistance. The operator could not find a problem with the system, so Grant tried again, this time with great care as he swiped his card. Panic began to spread through the team as the system refused to cooperate. The team were now stuck between two security doors in a sterile corridor. The radio operator circulated a message over the radio for anyone to assist from the other side, and after a few agonising seconds a voice confirmed they could.

Albert remained in contact with Alison. "You still have about 20 minutes, don't worry, Brannigan will think he is home and dry in the Departure Lounge."

Alison was not entirely convinced, but she was relieved when the door finally opened. A startled security officer stood to one side as the four police officers thanked him all at once and ran to the stairs leading to gate 21.

"Gate 21 is just up here, third door on the left," said Grant, leading the way.

As they approached the Departure Lounge attached to gate 21, they could see that boarding had begun. Alison, Scott and Dave

268

scoured the waiting queue for Brannigan, but he was not to be seen. Grant spoke to the staff on the boarding gate and they confirmed that Brannigan had checked in, but had not boarded.

"Where the hell is he?" asked Scott.

"We are here Albert, but there is no sign of him," said Alison over her mobile.

"He must be there," said Albert, "cover the gate and the exits in case he has had a tip-off."

Dave walked back to the entrance to the Departure Lounge and caught sight of a male in a blue baseball cap entering the toilets. Something made him follow. He was just a few seconds behind as he went through the first door to the toilets, then a secondary door to the main room. He immediately recognised Brannigan, who was at the mirror, taking off his cap.

"Mr Brannigan. Can I have word?"

Daniel Brannigan's shoulders slumped as Dave approached him. He was ten minutes away from escaping justice for a few more months at least, whilst the extradition process took its course. Unfortunately for him, his luck had finally ran out and he realised it.

Dave cautioned and arrested a despondent Brannigan and led him back to the departure lounge where Alison, Scott and Grant were delighted and relieved to see them.

Alison was still on her mobile. "Dave has got him Albert, he was waiting to board at the last minute."

Albert conveyed the news to the rest of the team and Alison heard the words of appreciation over her phone.

"Get him lodged and we will deal with him later. I will update the court. Well done Alison," said Albert.

Judge Irwin was impatient to hear what had happened with Brannigan and what the defence had in mind. The court was silent when Mr Kinnear rose slowly to his feet.

"Your Honour my clients wish to enter guilty pleas and I have advised them to consult with my learned friend and the CPS. I will no longer represent them in these proceedings and they will instruct new counsel in due course. I think you aware that Mr Brannigan has been apprehended by the police at the airport and he will be interviewed later today. Can I assure his Honour that no one from my chambers will represent him. May I place on record that I will supply a statement for the police in due course."

"Entirely understandable Mr Kinnear and I respect your intentions. I suggest we stand down until a week on Friday, by which time all parties will have considered their position. Miss Walker, have you any further comments or suggestions?"

"No Your Honour, we will look forward to hearing from the defence."

With the court adjourned for a week, there was time for the FCT to deal with Brannigan, visit all the witnesses, explain what had happened and thank them for their efforts. Most of the escorts had by that time found new agencies to work for and were pleased to see the back of Superior Escorts. Lexi, Becky and Susanne were relieved, and for the first time in several years, they also felt a sense of achievement. News and rumours began to filter through about the note passed to Mr Kinnear that proved to be so crucial; the Doyles and Noone had fallen out over Brannigan and the Doyles thought they could stop the trial in its tracks by implying there was another corrupt source within the Police. They gambled that the prosecution could not identify SP9005. Brannigan was tipped off by Noone and he panicked when they sent the note in full view of everyone. If he had held his nerve there was a likelihood the trial would have collapsed.

Brannigan was interviewed by Dave and Scott. As he knew all about the evidence in the case, he could hardly hide behind a lack of disclosure. He was represented by a firm from Manchester, as no local practice wanted to be involved. Brannigan admitted as much as he felt he needed to. He explained that he used escorts for sex as he did not want to be in a permanent relationship. The Doyles had discovered who he was and had checked him out with Pat Noone, who made himself known through 'punterdate'. Brannigan was adamant that he had not betrayed Frank, stating that Noone had guessed all along that the warrant at Frank's house was the beginning of the end for all of them.

Brannigan revealed himself to be a solitary figure, he had never married or been engaged. His Mother was fit and well living in Spain and she appeared to be the only constant in his life. He did show a

270

degree of remorse concerning the abuse suffered by the women under the control of the Doyles and Fawcus. It transpired that he had been given the exclusive services of one particular escort, so he had not witnessed the exploitation of the others. He refused to say who she was.

With his career in the legal profession well and truly over, Brannigan made it clear that he would be pleading guilty at the earliest opportunity.

The following week Albert and Miles met to discuss the outcome and the future of FCT.

"There have been more twists and turns in Neon than any other operation I have worked on," said Albert "At one point I thought we were going to lose the case, but we have ridden our luck throughout."

"You make your own luck Albert, I am convinced of that. Everyone rolled up their sleeves and got stuck in," said Miles.

"How is the Chief? Has she mentioned anything?" asked Albert.

"She most certainly has and she is looking forward to the press conference after the guilty pleas and sentencing. She took me to one side after morning prayers and she told me that any career development I had in mind would be more or less granted. I asked her if that included a move of my choice and she said yes, I had her word."

"So what are you going to do?"

"Absolutely nothing. I am staying here. There are more important things than career development. I have learned a lot Albert and I want to stay and continue to be part of the team."

Albert was surprised at what Miles said, but he was also full of admiration.

"That is good to hear and I'm sure the team will be over the moon. It is half the battle when you know you have the backing of everyone, stress levels just fade away."

Albert received a phone call from Alison a few moments later. "The lab have just sent a result from the warrant at Frank's House. They found one set of prints on the packaging and they have been identified as belonging to a lad called Jordan Lawson. I thought you would like to know straightaway Albert."

271

"Great news" said Albert "Who is he? It is not a name I am familiar with."

"Well that is the surprise Albert. He is a minor player, but more significantly he is Mrs Baker's nephew according to his intelligence. He lived with her a few years ago. Frank obviously did not want to expose him and upset her. At least we can progress that enquiry; who knows what will crop up next."

"I have given up predicting things now, Alison. It just goes to show how you need to keep an open mind and follow the evidence. These last few months have had me round the twist."

272

# Chapter Eight

# Judgement

Peter Chandler and Sarah Jane Walker had been busy liaising with the Doyle's new Counsel during the days before sentencing. Various indictments had been laid, agreed and finalised. The FCT had given all of the witnesses the opportunity to attend the hearing and watch as the Judge dealt with the defendants. Lexi, Diane, Becky, Joyce, Susanne, Carol and Cathy were allocated reserved seats in the public gallery. The press battled with the Operation Neon team for the remaining seats. Susan and Miles sat next to Mr Hunter, directly behind Miss Walker and Mr Chandler. Albert found a space next to Hughie and his pile of boxes. The jury had been brought back just in case there had been a sudden change of plan. They were given an explanation of what was about to happen and they nodded enthusiastically when invited to stay by Judge Irwin.

The Court was packed and in complete silence as the Court Clerk rose to her feet with a list of indictments. One by one each defendant offered guilty pleas to the charges read out to them.

Judge Irwin dealt with Oliver Wise first. His Barrister provided mitigation on his behalf. The Judge wasted no more time.

"I accept you played a minor role in this criminal organisation, but you did it for your own selfish reasons. I take into account your previous good character and the fact that you are no longer a respected member of your community. Your sentence will be six months suspended for two years and you will also pay a fine of £1200. The Usher will give you details of how to pay. You may leave the court."

Oliver Wise left the dock and had to walk past those who had prosecuted him. He was unable to look anywhere but the floor immediately in front of his next step. His shame and embarrassment complete.

The Judge then turned to Gloria Doyle. Her barrister, Mr Stewart, gave a good account of himself in his mitigating remarks on her behalf. Judge Irwin paused to look at his notes and then asked Mrs Doyle to stand up.

"Your role was not minor, you filled a job best described as Middle Management. You enjoyed all the financial benefits paid for by the women you actively controlled from your office in your comfortable home. I take into account your two children and I am loathed to deprive them of their Mother. I can tell you that it was my intention to sentence you to a custodial term, but I see that has little benefit to your family. I sentence you to twelve months imprisonment, suspended for two years. I also take into account the forthcoming hearing where the Crown will be considering your assets and the fact that you did not visit the brothels. I suggest you regard yourself as very lucky Mrs Doyle. You can leave the court."

Gloria Doyle, by then red in the face and crying, walked out of the court as fast as she could. She did not look at her husband who had sat to her left throughout.

Mr Field, representing Mrs Fawcus outlined her early guilty plea and tried to minimise her part in the proceedings, repeatedly mentioning her advanced years. He tried his best in the face of some damning evidence.

"Brenda Fawcus, I take into account your age, your early guilty plea and the fact that there were periods when you were not in this country when the events of this case took place. However, your callous disregard for the victims troubles me and that fact will no doubt trouble the public too. You saw first-hand the suffering and the misery, yet you chose to do nothing about it. All you were concerned with was assisting your son to make as much money as possible. The only credit I can give you is that you seem to have been unaware of his corrupt relationships. You will serve a sentence of six months in custody. Take her away."

Brenda Fawcus looked dazed as she was taken by the female prison officer to the secure door which led directly to the cell complex.

Albert whispered to Hughie "Blumming heck Hughie, I did not expect that." They both looked over to where the victims were sitting and noticed how their surprise soon turned to smiles as the secure door closed on Brenda Fawcus.

Mr Unsworth stood up to mitigate for Pat Noone. He made mention of a previous good character and the commendations for good police work Noone had been awarded. He knew he had little else to offer and Judge Irwin was ready to deal with his client.

"Patrick Noone stand up. You are a disgrace to your profession. Your selfish behaviour has driven you to become corrupt in the worst possible way. You were trusted by the public to protect them and you have lied, conspired and cheated in a way that is entirely unacceptable. The police should take credit for their role in ensuring you were dealt with as soon as they knew about your corrupt practices. I take note of Mr Unsworth's comments, but there is very little I can give you credit for. You are therefore sentenced to eight years imprisonment."

Noone did not look across to his ex-colleagues. He turned and walked to the secure door, with his back to the court. As he was led away, Miss Walker turned to Miles and Susan and said she thought that was a fair sentence, she had expected seven years, so eight was a good result.

Judge Irwin then invited Miss Cartwright to begin her representations on behalf of Colin and Graeme Doyle. He thanked her for standing in at short notice, but because of their previous bad character and the attempt to sabotage the trial, she struggled to make an impact.

"Colin Doyle and Graeme Doyle stand up . . . . . and take your hands out of your pockets. You are both equally to blame for the circumstances which you now face. Your criminal outlook on life has done nothing but bring misfortune to all those around you. You supply drugs, you cause prostitution by threatening those much weaker than yourselves and you have taken every opportunity to protect your business by corrupting public officials and obstructing the course of justice. Society must be protected from people as cruel as you. I sentence you both to ten years imprisonment. Remove them to the cells."

Arrogant as ever, The Doyles ambled towards the secure door.

275

Judge Irwin then suggested a break for ten minutes whilst Barry Fawcus could be produced without seeing any of the other defendants. He had pleaded guilty before the trial and had not been required to give evidence, much to his relief.

Fawcus eventually appeared through the secure door and took a centre seat in the dock. He had been made aware of the sentences handed out to the Doyles and his demeanour was that of a man who had gambled and was about to get his winnings. Lexi, Becky and Susanne sat together, staring at the man who had almost destroyed their lives.

"I think he is about to get a shock," said Albert "That self-satisfied smirk will soon disappear."

Miss Walker reminded the court about Fawcus's indictments and his earlier guilty plea. The Judge had received written mitigation and he ran through it for the benefit of those present.

"Stand up Barry Fawcus and listen carefully. You elected to give Queen's Evidence for one reason only . . . . to save yourself from a substantial custodial sentence. Your list of indictments contain some of the most serious offences in this entire case. You have entered guilty pleas to rape, numerous assaults, damage, trafficking, dealing in controlled drugs and last but not least you had a corrupt relationship with two police officers. Your criminality exceeds every other defendant in this case. You are a viscous bully who has no place in society. Your greed and arrogance led you to make the young women under your control lose touch with their families and their friends. You even made them endure appointments with men who assaulted and abused them. The incident with the young man who was described as having down's syndrome is shameful . . . I have read your statements given to the police after you elected to give Queen's Evidence and I find large parts wholly unreliable. You have played down the role of your Mother; you unconvincingly told the police of an incident of criminal damage to a green Toyota and at every opportunity you blamed the Doyle Brothers for your criminality. The police could not rely on your evidence unless it was corroborated and I am mindful of that. In arriving at a sentence I have taken account of your apparent cooperation . . . and my conclusion is that you cannot be given the full discount. In total, your sentence amounts to twenty four years and because of the obvious shortcomings in your evidence, I am going to allow a discount of eight years. You will therefore go to prison for sixteen years and remain on the sex offenders register for life. Take him away."

Fawcus held up his hands in horror. "So I got the biggest sentence . . . come off it . . . this is justice?" he continued to argue as he was led through the secure door.

Judge Irwin thanked the court and the jury for their attendance and their efforts. He then turned to Lexi, Becky and Susanne.

"Miss Morrison, Miss English, Miss Smith . . . . all three of you have my utmost admiration. Without your evidence this case would not have proceeded as it has. On behalf of everyone present in this room can I thank you for your patience and your determination. I wish all of you . . . and your families . . . the best of luck in everything you do from now on."

None of them really knew how to respond as they had no idea if they were allowed to speak to the Judge. They nodded as he spoke and in a completely spontaneous moment, Becky gave him a 'thumbs up' sign. The court rippled with gentle laughter as they witnessed her innocent gesture.

"Thank you Miss English" said Judge Irwin "I take it you are happy with what has happened today?"

Becky nodded enthusiastically and decided that her show of approval was enough to let the Judge know she was entirely grateful.

Miss Walker then rose to her feet and thanked the Judge for his comments. She then asked if he would like to commend the investigative team for their work.

"Yes, I would. The officers in this case should be proud of themselves. Please supply me with a list and I will ensure they are properly recognised."

Within an hour the FCT had retreated to the nearest public house, which was almost attached to the court. Albert, Miles and Susan emptied their pockets in appreciation of their team. Phone calls were made and received; the press were particularly persistent with Miles who repeated himself over and over again, advising them to speak to the press office at HQ. After several more calls, Miles switched off his phone and then took a moment to thank the entire team. He also proposed a toast to Bill, who would have been delighted at the outcome of the trial.

Through the pub window they saw the Chief Constable arrive and, within seconds, she was surrounded by members of the press on the court steps. Suddenly, she became the face of Operation Neon.

"You have to admire her timing" said Miles, as he finished his drink and headed to the bar.

Albert and Alison reflected on the events of the previous few weeks and Alison summarised her thoughts on the prostitution laws and all of the research she had found on the internet.

"It goes on and on Albert. The laws are confusing and the debates are never ending. No wonder they call it the oldest profession. They can't agree on anything and there are people who need protecting."

"Yes, I know what you mean. It is about time decisions were made and all the talk ended. The oldest profession has turned into the oldest debate" said Albert.

Alison continued. "Lexi, Becky and Susanne had their lives taken away, first by the Doyles and Fawcus. Then by Noone and Dryden. The men they had sex with thought they owned them for fifty quid and their heroin addiction acted as a ball and chain from which they could not escape . . . and how do we know this is not going on elsewhere?"

"We don't" said Miles as he re-joined his colleagues. "And that is our biggest problem".

The following week, Jordan Lawson was arrested and interviewed about the drugs found in Frank's house. To the surprise of the FCT, he admitted his part and explained that Frank had no idea what was in the packages. True or not, the CPS allowed Frank the benefit of the doubt. Frank deserved the break; he had protected Lexi and Becky as best he could, whilst many others had looked the other way.

Five weeks later, a disgraced Daniel Brannigan was sentenced to six years imprisonment by His Honour Judge Irwin.

The escort Brannigan had been provided with was not identified. She was known only to him and the Doyles. The FCT had to accept that, for the time being, she remained in the ownership of her pimps.

#0040 - 230818 - C0 - 210/148/15 - PB - DID2284404